UNDER MY SKIN

Other books by Charles de Lint

UNDER MY SKIN

Wildlings Book 1

Charles de Lint

TRISKELL
PRESS

Triskell Press
P.O. Box 9480
Ottawa, ON
Canada K1G 3V2
www.triskellpress.com

This one's for my wife, MaryAnn,
whose intelligence, love and support
help me in all things.

The ancients were people, yet also animals. In form, some looked human, while some walked on all fours like animals. Some could fly like birds; others could swim like fishes. All had the gift of speech, as well as greater powers and cunning than either animals or people.

- Okanogan folklore

JOSH

My mom's got a lot of good qualities, but picking boyfriends isn't one of them. More often than not, she's trying to save some loser from himself. Steve—the latest—is actually a step up from the usual lot because at least he has a job. He even owns a suit. But he has that same mean streak as the rest.

Whenever I try to point this out to Mom, I get shut down for having a smart mouth. It's not until the relationship is over that it's all, why didn't I listen to you at the beginning?

I don't get it. I mean, Mom's smart—she basically runs Dr. Esposito's office—and she's really together about pretty much everything in her life, except for these guys. Even my dad treated her badly, which is why, hello, he doesn't live with us.

I've learned the hard way that this isn't anything I can fix. So mostly I just try to keep my head down and wait it out. Sooner or later, it all falls apart and then it's smooth sailing when it's only Mom and me. Until the next loser comes along.

Today is a perfect example of trying to fly under the radar. It's a Tuesday afternoon and I've just come home from school. I see Steve's at the dining room table, frowning at his laptop, so I slip down the hall and go into my room. If I'd known he was here, I'd have taken Marina up on her offer to go to the skate park. But I have an essay due, so I quietly close my door and surf the Net before doing any actual homework.

When Steve comes into my room, I'm streaming a demo cut from The Wild Surf's website while clicking through the photo gallery of their lead singer, Joanie Jones, who I've got a mad crush on. I mean, who wouldn't?

I drop my headphones around my neck and turn to face him.

"Have you been using my laptop?" he asks.

Steve's got his macho on and my heart sinks. He doesn't have as much

1

muscle as the last couple of boyfriends, but I'm not kidding myself. I could never take him. I'm seventeen, but small for my age—five-foot-five last time I measured and I measure often. When you're my size, people get a kick out of pushing you around.

"I've got my own computer," I tell him.

I point to the screen where Joanie Jones is wearing a perky top hat and a jean jacket over a black bikini. She's sitting on the shoulders of Chuy Martinez, the band's drummer.

"You didn't answer the question," he says in a tight voice.

"Actually, I pretty much did. Why would I use your machine, when I've got one of my own?"

The corner of Steve's mouth twitches and his eyes narrow. Here we go.

"That's what *I* want to know," he says.

"Well, I didn't."

"Then why does it have some freaking virus on it that shuts down the Internet every time I try to go online?"

I shrug. "I don't know. Maybe you should stop hanging around in porn sites."

I was anticipating something, but he moves so fast it still catches me off guard. It's only the flat of his hand, but it whacks me on the back of the head with enough force to knock me out of my chair. My head fills with white noise. I land on the floor and the headphones rip out of the computer. My chair goes wheeling off to hit my bed. He takes a step toward me, yelling something I can't hear because my ears are still ringing and something just snaps in me.

I am so pissed off. This is *my* house. He has no right, *no right* to hit me.

He aims a kick at me and I come up off the floor. I know he's going to beat the crap out of me, but I don't care.

And that's when it gets weird.

It's me wanting to take a swing at him, but by the time I'm off the floor, I'm something else. Some kind of huge animal. My hand's a paw that slashes the side of his head and sends him reeling back into the hall. Blood sprays from the wound. Onto the walls. Seeps through his fingers as he puts his hand to his head and tries to keep his balance. His eyes are huge. His mouth is open, but he's not threatening me anymore. I think he's screaming.

He trips over his own feet, falling to the ground, and the whatever-I-am pounces on top of him. My paws hold him in place. I want to rip out his throat. The whatever-I-am could do it, no problem. I've got a serious mouthful of teeth.

But in my peripheral vision I catch a glance at myself. Down the hall, Mom's bedroom door is open. In her mirror I can see a reflection of Steve lying on the carpet with this huge, pissed-off mountain lion standing over him.

I realize it's me. The whatever-I-am is a mountain lion. A huge badass wildcat that's about to tear apart my mom's boyfriend.

I freak.

I jump off him and race down the hall, away from the mirror. The front door's closed, so I bolt for the kitchen. I skid on the tile, claws trying to find purchase, and bang up against the cabinet under the sink. The back door's closed, too, but it's just a screen. I leap through it like it's made of paper and land in the backyard.

I stand there for a long moment. A thousand smells hit me. Then I bound over the backyard fence and flee down the alley as hard and fast as I can make this strange body go.

I wanted so much for it to have been a bad dream. But when I wake up at dawn the next morning, I'm lying dirty and naked behind a dumpster. I remember running from home and Steve's bleeding body. I remember hiding between a hedge and a garage, crouching there until it finally gets dark. Then it was more running running running with the sound of barking dogs following me from yard to yard to yard.

I don't know when I got to this alleyway.

I don't know what happened to my clothes.

I don't know what's happening to me.

I sit there holding my head in my hands—a human head, thankfully, held with human hands—when I realize I'm not alone. I look up to see a boy sitting on his haunches a few yards away. He's around my age with dark skin and darker hair, dressed in jeans, a T-shirt, runners and a hoodie. When he sees I'm awake, he throws a bundle of something at me. I catch it without thinking.

"First thing you learn," he says, "is to bring your clothes with you. It's not hard. You just have to remember what you're wearing and make sure you're still wearing it when you change back."

"What?"

"Get dressed. I don't get any thrill looking at your skinny black ass."

I hold the bundle of clothes against my chest.

"Who are you?" I ask.

The boy grins.

"You can call me Cory," he says.

For a moment, there's a coyote head on his shoulders.

I back up until I'm pressed tight against the dumpster, but then there's just the boy once more.

"You—it looked like you had—it was like there was this coyote head ..."

"Yeah, get used to it, 'cause you're one of us now."

He sighs at my blank look.

"What they're all calling Wildlings," Cory says. "Who came up with that name, anyway? Some smart-ass headline writer, I'll bet."

So now I've got a word for what he is, pulled from a hundred news reports over the past six months. Wildlings.

I shake my head. "No, I'm not like you."

"That's right." Cory agrees. "I'm old school, kid. Been around forever."

He sniffs at the air like a dog. "And I'm canid, not feline. Full-blooded coyote, but not *Coyote*—if you know what I mean. There's only one of him. I'm like his little cousin."

He studies me for a long moment. "You're cat clan. Big one, too. Mountain lion?"

I have a flash of Steve, of what I did to him, of what I became. But I shake my head again.

"I'm not a Wildling."

Cory shrugs and shakes his head.

"You look like you need to eat," he says. "We can talk about what you are or aren't over breakfast."

"I need to go home."

"Sure, whatever. But first you need to hear a few things. Get dressed, kid. I went Dumpster-diving especially for you to get those thrift store specials."

When I refuse to put the clothes on, he tells me he got them from the donations box for the thrift store up at the mall. That's not as grotty as somebody's throwaways pulled out of the garbage. I get dressed without a lot of enthusiasm. The T-shirt's tight and the hoodie and sweatpants are too big, but the runners are actually my size. I roll up the pants until I'm not tripping over the hems. And I zip up the hoodie to hide the Hannah Montana logo on the T-shirt.

I know I look like crap, but it beats being naked.

Cory tosses me a black knit skullcap.

"Here, put this on, too," he says. "It'll help hide those little dreads of yours and make you harder to recognize."

"Why would that matter?" I ask.

Except I have a flash of slashing Steve with a mountain lion's paw.

"First things first," Cory says. "There's a diner around the corner. We can talk after we've ordered."

I pull the skullcap over my dreads. And they're not that little. They come down to my shoulders now. My friend Marina says they're pretty cool and Marina would never lie to me. I wish Rachel Armstrong thought they were cool, too, but she's a senior and I'm a sophomore, so why would she even look at me? But a guy can hope.

"Are you still with me?" Cory asks.

"Yeah. I was just thinking."

"How's that usually work out for you?"

I figure he's only generalizing, but I know what he means. Think too much and you tend to worry about life instead of living it. Mom's got all kinds of good advice like that when she's single.

I let him lead the way out of the alley and around the block to Pete's Diner. We're on the east end of 12th Street, up around the baseball field. Santa Feliz isn't big—the population's what? Twenty thousand?—but it's big enough that I don't go to this part of town much. Usually, I hang out in my own neighbourhood, closer to the ocean where Marina and Desmond also live. We hang at the beach a lot because Marina's a surfer and we all skate. After hours, when the tourists have gone home and the restaurant at the end of the pier is closed, we work on tricks in the parking lots. At least until the cops chase us off. Other than that, we go to school, the skate park, maybe hit the mall from time to time for a movie or just to goof around.

We don't have much reason to go anywhere else, unless it's to the wildlife refuge near the old naval base, hunting frogs and that kind of thing. But we don't do that so much since we got into high school.

Pete's Diner is filled with people who look like they're on their way to work and it smells better than any restaurant I can remember. Actually, everything smells more intense than normal.

"I don't have any money," I tell Cory as we slide into a window booth at the far end of the diner.

This section is pretty much empty and I guess that's why Cory led us here.

"No kidding. And if you did, I wouldn't want to touch it, considering where it would've had to have been."

"Gross."

He laughs. "Order whatever you want. I'll cover it."

"How come you're being so nice to me?"

He opens his menu. "Order, then we'll talk."

I realize how hungry I am as I start to read the menu. I can't remember the last time I ate, except then I get another one of my flashes. This time, I'm crouched in the branches of a black walnut, leaping down on a whitetail rabbit that goes down my throat in a few quick bites, blood and guts juicing out of my mouth and dribbling down my chin ...

I shake the image away. It leaves me feeling uncomfortable, but also hungrier than ever.

When the waitress comes, Cory orders the Hungry Man's Breakfast deal: bacon and eggs, pancakes, sausages, home fries, coffee, O.J. and toast. When she turns to me, I tell her I'll have the same. Cory smiles.

"You sure that'll be enough?" he asks.

To be honest, I'm so ravenous that I'm not at all sure, but we're on his dime, so I nod.

"How did you find me?" I ask. "How'd you know I'd need these clothes? Why are you buying me breakfast?"

Instead of answering any of my questions, he says, "None of this is new, you know. Wildlings have been around since forever. What's new is all these kids in this one small town being changed."

"I don't understand."

"Me neither," he says. "Why here, why these kids, why one at a time instead of all at once? Why you?"

"That's not what I meant. And I'm not a Wildling."

"Pretending it's all some big mistake isn't an option. Or what do you call running around in the shape of a mountain lion all night?"

"I—I ..."

A cop comes in and Cory breaks off. His shoulders go stiff. The cop takes off his hat and stands in the doorway, giving the room a once-over before he takes a seat at the counter and orders a coffee. It's weird that I can hear him so clearly from way over here.

"Are you in trouble with the cops?" I ask.

He shakes his head. "If he's looking for one of us, it isn't me."

"What's that supposed to mean?"

He points to the TV. They're running that same old surveillance camera footage that they always do when anything involving Wildlings hits the news. I've seen it so many times that I have that stuff memorized by now—like everybody in town does.

The first confirmed case was last November. Caught on a video surveillance camera, the grainy footage seems to run endlessly on CNN. A teenage boy crossing a parking lot is about to be swarmed by a half-dozen other kids. Halfway across the lot, he changes into a hawk—snap! Just like that. The footage ends with him flying out of camera range. All that's left on the ground is a heap of clothes and a pair of running shoes.

It's been a little over six months now and still no one has any idea why some kids change, while most don't, or why it's only happening to kids in Santa Feliz. All anybody living here really knows is that every other week or so, some poor kid or another turns into a shape-changing freak. At least, that's what my buddy Dillon calls them.

Then I see my high school picture on the TV and I realize this story's about *me*. About what happened yesterday after Steve hit me. I have to face the facts.

I'm one of those shape-changing freaks now.

I cast a quick glance in the cop's direction, then duck my head.

"I am so screwed."

It's not until Cory answers that I realize I spoke aloud.

"It doesn't have to be the end of the world," he says.

I look at him.

"Name one good thing."

"I can do better than that," he says and starts to count off on his fingers. "You're stronger and faster. You're going to live longer and you won't get sick as easily. All your senses are heightened—smell, hearing, vision. And that's just in your human form. You can also turn into a mountain lion—I mean, how cool is that?"

"Very cool—if you want to live your life like a freak."

He raises his eyebrows.

"Uh—no offence."

Humour tugs up a corner of his mouth. "None taken."

I think about what he's just told me. I've already noticed how everything smells stronger, which is both good and bad because not only does the food in here smell like it's to die for, I also get a powerful reek of B.O. from the guy three booths down that makes me want to gag. And now I realize that it's not unusually loud in the restaurant. It's just that I can hear better.

I glance over to the counter, where the cop's looking at a paper someone left behind. I can read not only the headlines of the page he has open, but also the tiny print that makes up the stories.

"Can I turn it down?" I ask.

"Turn what down?"

"The volume. All these intense smells and sounds."

"You'll adjust. Quicker than you think, actually."

I sigh.

"So, why me?" I say.

"Like I said, I don't know any more than anybody else. My guess is that kids like you—the ones that change—carry traces of the old animal blood. It's not something scientists can measure because it's not purely a physical thing. It's in your spirit. The real question is, how and why did someone or something jumpstart that old blood?"

My head is spinning. I don't want to be having this conversation. I want to go back to my old life. But that option seems to drift farther and farther out of reach with each passing moment.

Cory shrugs when I tell him I just want to go home.

"I get that you want to go back to your old life, but this is permanent. You can stop yourself from shifting into your animal form, but you can't change the fact that you can do it."

"A Wildling."

He shrugs. "If that's the name you want to give it."

"Well, what do you call yourselves?"

"Cousins."

"That doesn't make any sense."

"It does when you consider how we're all connected by our animal blood." He laughs. "We're just one big dysfunctional family."

We break off when the waitress approaches with our order. The food smells delicious and I'm so hungry I can actually feel myself salivating. It's all I can do not to just grab it off the plate and shove it in my mouth with my hands. I force myself to wait until she sets it down in front of me, and I use a fork and knife, but I'll tell you, I never tasted anything so good.

The cop gets up while we're still eating. He glances in our direction and I feel myself go tense. I know I've got guilt written all over my face. But his gaze slides right by me. He puts on his hat and heads out the door.

"Well, at least he didn't arrest me," I say.

"Why would he?" Cory asks.

"Because I killed Steve."

"Who's Steve?"

"My mom's latest loser boyfriend." I nod toward the TV. "That's why I'm on the TV, right? They're looking for me."

"Yeah, but not for the reason you think. I caught the story earlier this morning. The first thing you need to know is this Steve guy isn't dead."

"But there was all this blood ..."

Cory waves it off. "Head wounds always bleed like crazy. According to the news reports, he had to get a pile of stitches, a rabies test and a tetanus shot, but he doesn't even have a concussion."

"But he must have told them it was me?"

"I don't know," Cory says. "Maybe he didn't. Maybe he did, but they didn't believe him. You're only on the news because you're missing. They think maybe the mountain lion that attacked him dragged you off. Or you ran off because you were scared."

"I did run because I was scared."

"That's good. Hold on to that when you're talking to the cops. The best way to lie is to have your story be mostly true."

I feel a bit sick. I've never been that good a liar. Inside, I'm freaking out. But the part of me that's doing it feels like it's a long way away, deep inside me. Mostly, I'm feeling this weird über-confidence. I mean, I can turn into a mountain lion. Who's going to mess with a kid who can turn into a mountain lion?

"I've seen that look before," Cory says. "The one that comes after the shock wears off and you start to feel cocky."

"I'm not feeling cocky."

Except that's exactly how I feel.

"Fine," he says. "But just remember. A Taser's going to take you down, whether you're a mountain lion or a kid. A bullet in the head is still going to kill you. When you're in your animal shape, they don't have to rationalize whether or not to shoot you."

I swallow hard. Shoot me?

"Who would want to shoot me?" I ask.

"Cops don't exactly take kindly to mountain lions roaming the streets. And the government is getting real handy with the tranquilizer guns."

"I thought the government was trying to help the kids who've turned into Wildlings."

"Sure," Cory says, "They're running those public service announcements about how they should all come in for orientation and training in their new abilities. But not one Wildling that's gone to the government holding facility out on the old naval base has been seen again."

"You think they're *killing* them?"

He shakes his head. "More like studying them. And keeping them locked up so that they're under control. Word is, they're even snatching kids off the streets, or right out of their homes. I've even heard that some of the movers and shakers in big industry are looking to get themselves their own Wildlings."

"What would some big company want with ... us?"

The longer I sit here with him, the easier it is to accept that I'm one of them, a Wildling, but I stumble over owning the word. I keep thinking about how Dillon and I have been calling them freaks. And now I'm one of them. A freak.

"Think about it," Cory says. "People with our abilities would make excellent spies—political or industrial. If you were in charge of national security, or ran some big company, wouldn't you want us working for you?"

"I guess."

I pull at the ends of my dreads where they hang out from under the skullcap. This is getting weirder by the minute.

"Why would a kid want to get involved with stuff like that?" I say.

"Are you kidding me? For some kids, feeling important and powerful is a rush. And then there are the perks. Grow up in the projects or the barrio, you're going to turn up your nose at a nice apartment, a fancy car, all the money you can spend?"

"That's not really happening, is it?"

"Hard to say what's happened so far. This has gone down real fast. We don't know how many kids have changed. It's not like anybody ever got a head count. But it seems like quite a few and, like I said, everyone has an agenda. Take that bible-thumping congressman Clayton Householder. He keeps trying to push a bill through Congress that will put all of Santa Feliz under quarantine, to supposedly contain this so-called disease. Who knows what his real agenda is, but I'm betting it's way off the nut-bar chart."

"Yeah, some of the kids at school were talking about him like he's really out in la-la land." I give him a careful look before I add, "So what about you? Do you have an agenda, too?"

Cory laughs. "Of course I do. Mine's to make sure that virgins like you keep yourselves safe from whoever wants to use you."

"That's it?"

"I don't have time for anything else. The more kids I can convince to keep a low profile, the less fallout there's going to be about all of this. The cousins aren't exactly happy about having been outed the way we have."

"You've been around longer than six months," I say.

It's just beginning to dawn on me what he's been saying.

Cory grins. "We've been around forever, kid. Dig up the oldest fossil you can find and the bones of a cousin will be lying deep underneath it."

He falls silent, gazing at the TV, where they're still rehashing the whole Wildlings business. Now they're talking about the Federal holding facility out on the old naval base.

"I wonder what's really going on in that place," he says.

"Why should I trust you?" I ask.

"I don't care if you do or don't. I just want you to think before you start making alliances. And to watch out that you don't get grabbed off the street."

"This is a lot to process," I say.

He nods. "Yeah. I get that." He pulls some money from his pocket and tosses it onto the table, then stands up. "I need to jet. Think about what I've said. The best thing you can do right now is convince everybody you never changed."

"How am I supposed to do that?"

He shrugs. "Like I said, lie."

"Wait," I say as he turns to leave.

He stops and looks at me, but I realize I've got nothing to say. Or rather, I've got a million things to say, but he's obviously got more important things to do than baby-sit me.

"Thanks," I say. "You know, for everything."

He smiles. "Be careful," he says. "Keep your head way down. That's all the thanks I need."

And then he's walking away.

I watch until the door closes behind him, then I look around the diner, trying to figure out if anybody's paying attention to me. They're not. Or if they are, they're doing a really good job of hiding it.

Thanks, Cory, I think. Now you've got me completely paranoid.

That's probably not a bad thing. Not if what he's been telling me is true.

Finally I leave as well and head for home to face the music.

MARINA

The swells have been running high all week—not quite overhead, but still sweet—and I'm pumped when I get home from catching a few waves on the early tide. But my mood comes crashing down when I step into the kitchen. Mamá tells me that Josh is missing—she says it's been all over the news this morning. Yesterday evening, some wild animal dragged him right out of his mother's house. His mom's boyfriend was clawed bad and had to be stitched up at the hospital. The cops are still trying to find Josh.

My Josh.

I'm so scared I want to throw up.

I jump in the shower and rinse off quick. Throwing on some clothes, I race out the door, my hair dripping. Mamá calls after me, but I just wave to her and drop my skateboard on the pavement. I head for Josh's house, going so fast I could almost be flying. If anything's happened to him, I swear I'll die. He's everything to me, even though I've never told him so. There's never been the right time and now it may be too late.

Josh's mom gives me a big hug as soon as I show up. She's trying to hold herself together, but I can see that she's as worried as I am, probably more, if that's even possible. Her usually flawless chocolate skin has a grey cast and there are dark circles under her big brown eyes.

"Detective Foley," she says to the man in the living room with her. "This is Marina Lopez. She's one of my son's best friends."

He's a big guy in a good suit who went a little heavy on the aftershave this morning. He probably does it every morning to cover up the fact that he doesn't use soap when he showers. *If* he even showers. I wrinkle my nose and turn back to Josh's mom.

"What happened, Naomi? Mamá told me that Josh is missing and that he might even be hurt."

"When was the last time you saw Joshua?" the cop breaks in, ignoring my question and not giving Josh's mom a chance to talk.

"Yesterday," I tell him. "We left school together, but he said he was going home. He had to work on an essay that's due Friday."

"And he hasn't contacted you since?"

I look from the cop to Josh's mom and shake my head.

"No," I say, answering him but looking at her. "Please, Naomi. Tell me what happened to him."

"We don't know yet, honey," she tells me. "Some kind of big cat like a mountain lion broke into the house. It attacked Steve and chased Josh out the door. No one's seen him since and I'm worried sick." She shoots the cop a look. "The police think it must have been one of those Wildlings, but really. What would one of those creatures want with us?"

It seems that people blame Wildlings for everything that goes wrong these days in Santa Feliz.

"Ma'am," the detective says, "We've got every spare officer in town looking for your son, but let's not jump to conclusions. You know how teenagers are. Could be he decided to do a little partying after school and never even came home in the first place. Your friend Steve's story wasn't exactly consistent when we interviewed him at the hospital. It's obvious that he's hiding something, so we don't consider him a reliable witness. But we'll find your boy. We'll get to the bottom of this. I promise you that."

"No way Josh just took off," I say. "He isn't a partier. He doesn't even like crowds. He hangs out with a few people from school and that's it."

Detective Foley takes out a notebook. "Such as?"

"Me, our friend Desmond and sometimes Barry or Dillon. If he had other plans, I'd know. He'd never lie to me."

The cop gives Naomi a wry smile, then tilts his head and looks back at me, a smirk on his face.

"I hate to break it to you, sweetheart," he says, "but *all* boys lie to their girlfriends."

Patronizing bastard, I want to tell him, but I swallow the words and just shake my head.

"It's not like that. He's not my boyfriend."

Before the cop can come out with some other snarky comment, the door opens and in walks Josh, wearing a black skullcap over his beautiful dreads and the goofiest outfit I've ever seen him in. He looks like a Walmart special, but at least he seems perfectly okay. I want to throw my arms around him and never let go, but his mother beats me to it and I manage to keep my cool.

I just smile and lift my eyebrows.

"Good to see you, Saunders," I say. "Nice duds."

JOSH

By the time I finish telling my edited version of the facts to the cop, I half believe the story myself. I'm glad that Marina headed off to school. I wouldn't be a very good liar around her. We're so tight, she'd see right through me.

But I do turn out to be pretty good at it when it counts—or maybe that's something else being a Wildling has given me. There's a bad moment when the detective takes me down the hall to my room for some private questioning. He points to my jeans and T-shirt lying on the carpet and asks me why I wasn't wearing them. Turns out the best way to be believable is to embarrass yourself. Good thing Mom is waiting in the living room.

"I was just, you know, looking at some pictures on my computer," I say.

He gets a smirk. I guess he saw the photos of Joanie Jones on my screen when he was first called in to investigate the attack and thinks I was sitting there jacking off when Steve came in my room.

I go on, feeling a flush darken my already brown skin. "Steve comes in yelling about how I broke his laptop—which I never touched—and he hits me across the back of the head and then all of a sudden this giant cat is all over him and I just took off."

"Naked."

"Well, I was still wearing my boxers."

He nods and writes something in his notebook. Good thing he doesn't check because right now I'm going commando. Cory didn't provide me with underwear and I wouldn't have put on somebody else's old skivvies even if he had.

"And these clothes you came home in?"

"They're from a donation box out near the mall."

Cory said to tell the truth as much as possible and it seems to work. I didn't take the clothes from the box, but that's where they came from.

18

The detective nods again.

"And why did you wait until the morning to come home?"

"I was scared. I knew Steve was already mad at me. I thought he'd find a way to blame me for everything."

"But you finally came back because ...?"

I shrug. "Where else am I going to go? I'm just a kid. And then when I was in this diner, I saw my picture on the news and I thought I'd better come home ..."

"Tell me about this giant cat. What do you mean? Was it a house cat or something bigger?"

Somehow I wasn't expecting this question and I'm sure I probably have guilt written all over my face. What do I tell this cop? Again, I think about Cory's advice.

"It was bigger," I say. "A ... mountain lion, I think."

"And did you see it come in the house?" the detective asks.

"No. It just showed up all of a sudden. There was no warning."

The cop looks at me thoughtfully. He makes some more notes, then closes his notebook.

"I think we're done here," he says.

I walk with him back out to the living room. Mom jumps up from the couch and I let her give me a hug. She turns to the cop, her arm still around my shoulders.

"You okay with your boyfriend disciplining your son?" he asks her.

He says it like she shouldn't be and goes up a point or two in my estimation.

"What do you mean?" Mom asks, eyes open wide.

"Well, if you want to press charges for him hitting your boy ..."

Mom presses her lips together and her gaze hardens. She moves back in front of me, grabs both shoulders and holds me at arm's length. She's obviously waiting for me to tell her what happened. I shake my head.

"I just want this all to be over," I say.

"Steve's not going to be a problem," she tells the detective. "Not anymore."

The detective shrugs. "If your son had any obvious injuries, we would be pressing charges, Mrs. Saunders. It's the law."

"So would I, officer, but he seems to be all right. For the moment, anyway."

Mom walks the detective to the door. When she comes back, she gives me another hug.

"Tell me everything," she says. "God, the things I was imagining ..."

I feel guilty about lying to my mom, but I've had some practice with the detective, so the story rolls off my tongue pretty easily, even though I'm squirming inside. Mom's always trusted me and I've tried to live up to that trust. But I'm just not ready to tell her I'm a Wildling. Up until yesterday, I thought they were freaks. But now I'm one of them. What does that say about me?

"Josh, I'm so sorry about Steve. I can't understand what would have gotten into him that he would actually hit you."

Like I said, she's got this blind spot. I can tell she's feeling kind of mad and depressed at the same time.

"I swear, Mom. I really didn't touch Steve's computer."

"I know you wouldn't do anything like that. He's been under a lot of pressure at work, but what he did was completely unacceptable. That's the end of it. He doesn't get a do-over."

"Thanks. I'm going to go take a shower if that's okay."

"That would probably be a very good idea," she says, smiling sadly and wrinkling her nose. That's what I get for sleeping behind a Dumpster in an alleyway.

I grab some fresh clothes from my room.

❧

When I'm inside the bathroom, I strip down and look at myself in the mirror. I don't look any different. I guess I thought maybe I'd be a little more buff or something, but I'm still the skinny kid I've always been. Or, as I like to say when Desmond rags me, I'm wiry.

I lean on the sink and give my reflection a closer look. Okay. Cory said that you just have to think about it to change. I've been wanting to do this ever since he started filling my head with all this stuff. Is it really true, or just some weird-ass delusion?

I figure it's safe in here. The window's too small for me to squeeze through, never mind a mountain lion, and the door's locked. Nobody can get hurt.

So ...

As I will the change, I keep studying my reflection, looking for whatever telltale sign is going to show it starting to happen. I never get the chance to see it. As soon as I make the decision to change, the mountain lion's face is glaring at me from the reflection.

I panic, pushing on the sink to get away because, for one long second, I don't realize that's me in the mirror. Me, in my Wildling shape.

The mountain lion's powerful muscles shove down hard on the sink and the plumbing breaks away from the wall. Water spews out of the broken pipes, drenching me.

I think the water spraying me in the face is all that saves me from completely losing it. It kicks me out of the mountain lion's point of view and, just like that, I shift back to myself. I scrabble in the debris of the sink, which is half hanging from the wall. Water's gushing everywhere until I finally find the shut-off valves and twist them closed.

I sit back on the floor, water pooling all around me, my heart drumming in my chest. Then comes the banging on the door that almost shifts me back into the mountain lion.

"Josh! Joshua! Are you all right in there?"

It's Mom.

I look at the mess I've created.

"Joshua!"

"I'm okay," I call back. "I was just leaning a little too hard on the sink and it kind of broke away."

I get up and wrap a towel around myself before I unlock the door.

"Oh, God," Mom says, taking in the mess. "What were you *doing* in here?"

"Nothing. I was just leaning in close and it came away under me. Honest. I'll clean this all up."

"But the sink ..."

"I can fix it."

"When did you become a plumber?" she asks.

"I'm not. But I'll look it up on the Internet. How hard can it be to fix?"

She looks like she's going to say something else, but then she shakes her head and turns away.

"Just finish your shower," she says in the same tone of voice that she had when I hit a baseball through the front window a couple of years ago. "At least you weren't hurt."

I close the door slowly and look in the mirror again. I can't see any trace of the mountain lion. It's like it was before, just me, except this time I'm soaking wet. Finally, I turn away. I drop the towel and get into the shower.

MARINA

I really don't want to leave Josh's place, but the detective won't let me stay. I think about hanging around until after he's gone, but who knows how long that'll be? From where I stand on the sidewalk, I can look in through the living room window and see them talking. I'm dying to hear what they're saying, but then the detective glances in my direction. He's got that smirk on his face again, so I turn my back to him. I drop my skateboard on the pavement and push off, heading for school. I'll just be a little early for my first class.

I'm not sure whether Josh will even show up for school today. I know he'll tell me everything that happened when we do see each other and that's bound to be soon—after school at the latest—but the idea of having to wait is hard. We're never far apart for long, even though I'd like to be close in a different way. I'm just not sure that he feels the same toward me.

Desmond rolls up on the sidewalk outside school at the same time as me.

"Dude!" he yells, even though I'm right in front of him. "Did you check the newsfeeds this morning? Josh got himself kidnapped by some big-ass tiger or something! We've got to put a posse together and find him."

"Jeez, chill, would you?" I say. "He's okay. I just came from his house. He walked in the door ten minutes ago, all on his own."

"What? Crap, I hate being the last to know. How is he? Is he all scratched up? What happened?"

"Who knows? Other than wearing a ridiculous pair of sweats and a Hannah Montana T-shirt, he looks fine. There's not a mark on him. But there was a cop at the house and he made me leave before I could find out what happened."

"You should have texted me."

"It all happened so fast I didn't think of it."

Desmond nods, then he grins. "Oh, man. Hannah Montana. That's pure gold. He's never going to live it down."

Seeing the look of anticipation on his face, I wish I'd never mentioned it. He's going to rag Josh mercilessly.

"Dial it down, Wilson. We don't know what he's been through. We shouldn't assume that everything's fine until he tells us so himself."

He grins. "Overprotective much?"

I know he's teasing, but I bristle all the same. Des is a sweet goof, but sometimes he makes me want to smack him. Like right now.

He catches my look and pretends to cringe.

"Sorry," he says. "I get it. Let me buy you a slushie at lunch to make up for it."

"That's more like it, gringo."

We head up the walk and through the main doors, our boards under our arms. The school lobby is buzzing with gossip about Josh. Kids are standing around in little groups trading stories, trying to figure out what happened. Josh would hate this. He can't stand being the center of attention.

As soon as the other kids notice Des and me in the lobby, we get a few stares because they all know we're best friends with Josh. The volume goes down some, but it doesn't matter. Every second word is still cougar, tiger, lion.

I know, because my Wildling hearing is so acute.

JOSH

I'm sitting in front of my computer looking at a list of plumbing sites that I Googled. So far, I haven't found anything useful to my real problem. Getting the sink fastened back to the wall and the pipes reconnected—that doesn't look too hard. It's the plaster that broke away from the wall that I need to figure out how to replace.

I'm about to click on another link when my cell rings out the theme to that old TV show *The Twilight Zone*, played by The Ventures. Considering how things have been going for the past twenty-four hours, it seems all too appropriate.

When I check the display, I see there's another text from Desmond: *Dude yr back? Call me.*

It's the latest of a bunch from him. There's also a couple from Marina. I send them both a message to meet at the parking lot by the pier after they get out of school, then I turn off the phone, close down my computer and go out to the garage.

Mom's parents own our house, which is why we can afford to live here, just a couple of blocks east of the boardwalk and the beach. Gramps was in on the whole Silicon Valley dot-com thing, but he got out before the bust, so he didn't lose his shirt like so many others. He bought this place because he always loved Santa Feliz—I think he used to vacation here when he was a kid—but he and Gramma live in Costa Rica now, which I guess they love even more. When Dad walked out on Mom and me, they insisted that we move in.

I wasn't even in kindergarten yet, so living here is all I know. But even though we don't own the house, Mom insists we look after it like it's our own. I've learned how to do all kinds of things—from rebuilding a stone wall to replacing window panes.

In the garage, I check under the workbench and sure enough, there's some screening left over from when we redid the windows last summer. I may not know how to fix big holes in plaster—yet!—but I know how to fix the damage I did to the screen door yesterday. I grab the roll of screening and some tools and step out of the garage on my way to the backyard.

A prickle starts up at the nape of my neck and my gaze goes down the street to where a white man in a dark suit is standing in front of the Evoras' house, looking at a map. He's got one of those little Bluetooth headsets in his ear—the kind I always assume just drug dealers and people trying to look important wear—and it occurs to me that it could just as easily be some Secret Service communications device. I know. Paranoia. But he shoots me a look and hurries off as soon as he sees I've noticed him.

I watch him turn the corner and Cory's words come back to me.

Word is they're even snatching kids off the streets, or right out of their homes.

The prickle at the nape of my neck intensifies, then slowly fades away.

I stand there looking out of the garage for a few minutes, but he doesn't come back. I try to tell myself that it was nothing, but I can't remember the last time I saw somebody in a suit and tie on this street who wasn't a cop, like the detective who took my statement earlier today. The adults around here all wear golf shirts and chinos or shorts.

Finally, I head to the backyard to fix the screen door. Mom comes out and actually smiles when she sees me at work.

"I have to get back to the office for a few more hours," she says. "Will you be all right until I get back?"

"Will Steve be coming around?"

She shakes her head and gets that look in her eye that I know too well.

"I told you," she says. "Steve won't be coming around at all anymore."

"I'm sorry, Mom."

I'm not, but it's the right thing to say.

"Don't be," she says.

I walk her to the car.

"I was going to meet Desmond and Marina down by the pier when they get out of school," I say. "Is that okay?"

"Of course it is. Tell them I said hi."

I lean in her window after she gets into the car. She puts a hand on my arm before I can speak.

"Stop looking so guilty," she says. "I should have seen it coming."

I agree, but I keep my mouth shut.

"Pizza tonight?" she says. "You can invite Desmond and Marina if you want. I'll pick up an extra large."

"Sounds great."

I watch her drive off, feeling the way I always do. Sad for her. Happy for me. Guilty because I feel happy.

Why does everything have to be so complicated?

Then I think of what else is going on in my life. Complicated doesn't begin to cover it.

ఞఞ

I'm sitting on a bench at the end of the pier watching the gulls when Desmond and Marina come rolling up on their skateboards. Desmond does a fancy dismount, steps on his board so that it flies up into his hand, then plonks himself down on the bench beside me. Marina does a circle around the bench before she drops down between us. I always get a kick out of how neither of them fits their image.

Desmond looks like a surfer: tall, tanned, long blond hair tied back in a ponytail, wearing sneakers, baggy shorts and a loose T-shirt. But although he's got the surfer look, Des can't swim very well and doesn't even like the water. He's a skater, through and through.

Girls love him. Marina says he's got a glow—a shine that draws like honey. I wouldn't know. I'm sure not the player he is. I've never even had a steady girlfriend.

Marina, on the other hand, always gets mistaken for a skater. Brown-skinned and trim, her wild dark hair tamed under a skullcap, she's wearing baggy pants and a tight sleeveless T under her hoodie. But she only skates because it's what Desmond and I do. Her family may have come from Mexico, but she's an American surfer girl through and through. Her heart's out there with the waves, big or small. I paddle out with her sometimes, but I'm crap at it and I'm always falling off one of her spare boards.

The place where we really come together is our music. We're all crazy about surf and spy instrumentals and have been playing in Desmond's garage for a couple of years. Marina on drums, Desmond on bass and keys, me on lead guitar. We've yet to play out anywhere—we haven't even agreed on a name—but we practice whenever we can.

"What the hell *happened* to you?" Desmond asks.

Marina nods and bangs her knee against mine. "Yeah, you really had us worried, Saunders."

I'm still trying to decide what to tell them. They're my best friends, so I don't want to hide anything from them. But what if telling them puts them in danger? And what—I hate to think this—but what if this thing I've become turns them against me? Some people obviously have a lot of negative feelings toward Wildlings. When you think about it, it's pretty much the same as racism, which makes me feel kind of ashamed that I've never called my friend Dillon on it. What makes me feel worse is that I've called them freaks myself.

I've thought about Marina and Des a lot since talking to Cory in the diner, how it would go if the roles were reversed and it was one of them instead of me. I'm pretty sure I wouldn't let it make a difference. Sitting here with them, feeling their concern, all I can do is give them the benefit of the doubt.

"Don't look right now," I say, "but did you notice that black SUV parked at the far end of the lot?"

Desmond starts to turn around but Marina elbows him in the side.

"Jeez, Des," she tells him. "He said don't look right away." Then she turns to me. "What about it?"

"I'm pretty sure whoever's in it has been watching me. It showed up just after I got here and nobody's gotten out of it in the ten minutes since."

Desmond laughs. "Paranoid much?"

But Marina gives me a considering look.

"Why would anybody be watching you?" she asks.

I take a breath and let it out.

"That thing that's going around," I say. "It's happening to me. I've become a Wildling."

Desmond grins. "Shut up."

But I'm facing Marina as I speak. I see the flicker of something in her eyes—I don't know quite what—before she drops her gaze. When she looks up again, whatever it was is gone.

"Oh, Josh," she says. She puts a world of empathy into the words.

"Yeah," I say. "I know."

Desmond jumps to his feet. "What's with the 'Oh, Josh'? This is *awesome*." He punches the air, once, twice. "So it was really you who laid out Steve?"

I nod.

"I never liked that guy," he says.

"Who did?" I say.

"Well, your mom, for one."

Marina grabs his arm and pulls him back onto the bench. "This is serious, Des."

"I know that. But come on. He can turn into a freaking tiger. How cool is that? I've always been afraid if it happened to me I'd end up like that kid who's some kind of South American tree frog. I mean, how useless would that be?"

"Mountain lion. Not tiger." I say.

"Whoa! Cooler still, dude." Desmond is practically bouncing, he's so excited.

Marina shakes her head and turns back to me.

"How do you feel?" she asks.

"Scared. Confused. A little bit excited."

Desmond grins. "Sounds like a good name for a tune."

"Don't you ever stop joking?" Marina says.

"I'm not. I think it would rock."

"You know what I mean."

Desmond nods. "Yeah, I do. But I think it's cool. Seriously. Do you know how often I lie in bed at night trying to decide what I'd want to be if I was a Wildling?"

"Lay off, Wilson," Marina says.

"It's okay," I tell her. "I'd rather get a response like that than the two of you screaming and running off."

"We'd never do that."

"I know. That's why I told you. But you can't tell anybody else." I look from one to the other. "*Seriously*. You can't. Swear to me you won't."

Marina looks at me strangely. Maybe this isn't so okay with her. She seems uncomfortable, but I guess I can't blame her. It's not as though it's just some little quirk I have.

"Sure," she says. "Of course. How did your mom take it?"

"I haven't told her."

Her eyebrow goes up and I know what she's thinking. I pretty much tell my mom everything.

"Wait a minute," Desmond says. "Why can't we tell anyone? The cops know, Steve knows—unless you whacked him in the head when he was sleeping, which I'd totally get. The guy's buff. But keeping any of this secret? The cat's out of the bag, man, pun intended."

"Actually, it's not," I say.

I tell them the whole story, only leaving out the bit about the Joanie

Jones pictures. I just say I was listening to demos The Wild Surf has posted on their site when Steve came into my room and hit me.

Desmond laughs when I tell them about how I wrecked the sink, but they both get sober looks as I finish up with the guy in the suit I saw standing on my street.

"Intense," Desmond says.

Marina nods. "So you think whoever's in the SUV is connected to the man you saw?"

"Or they're two separate groups with the same interest in me. Whichever, after what Cory told me, I just want to keep my head down."

"So the change is permanent," Desmond says.

"Yeah. But it doesn't mean I *have* to go running around in my Wildling shape. I just want things to get back to normal as soon as they can."

"But Steve knows," Marina says.

I nod. "There's that. But apparently he tripped up in telling his story to the cops. Maybe he's afraid he'll get charged for hitting me, or maybe he thinks I'll come after him and finish the job. Anyway, the cops seemed to believe me."

"Unless they're just letting the Feds handle it," Desmond says.

"Or Steve's talked to someone else," Marina adds.

"I know. I'm so screwed."

She gives me a sympathetic look and asks, "What are you going to do?"

"Long term, I have no idea. Right now—Mom said I could invite you over for pizza. Tomorrow I'm going to school and get that gawk-fest over with."

"Going to school," Desmond says. "With what you can do, that's like somebody winning the lottery and then just going back to their crappy job."

"What am I supposed to do? Join the circus?"

He shakes his head. "No. I'm just saying. Wildlings should be amazing. We should treat them like rock stars. But instead, it's like everything else— just another opportunity for people to make it all scary and weird."

"The mountain lion that's inside you," Marina says. "That's a big animal. Is it hard to control?"

"It's not a different creature inside me," I try to explain. "It's like I can be one or the other, but when I'm in my Wildling shape, I'm still supposed to be myself. I haven't quite got the hang of that yet. But the good thing is, I have to actually will it to happen."

"But the two times you changed before ... it sounds like it took over."

"I know. But the first time, it caught me by surprise, and the second time, I was stupid enough to will it to happen and then got freaked out that it did."

"I think it would freak me out, too," she says.

"What would you be if it happened to you?" Desmond asks her. "I mean, if it was going to happen anyway, what animal would you choose?"

She crosses and uncrosses her legs, then deflects the question to Des. "What would you choose?"

"I'm kind of torn between a wolf and an eagle."

"An eagle would be cool," I say. "You could just float up there away from everything."

Desmond nods. "I know. But wolves. You've got to dig them."

"I might want to be a dolphin," Marina says.

Desmond and I both smile.

"Yeah," Desmond says. "No big surprise there."

We fall silent. I look out at the beach. Some kids are playing volleyball. There are surfers out past the end of the pier, but there aren't any waves, so they're just hanging there, sitting on their boards. People are fishing off the pier or just ambling along. A couple of kids we know are practicing tricks in the parking lot, their skateboards rattling on the pavement.

I've already learned how to tune down the sharpness of my senses. But if I let myself, I could count the freckles on the red-haired surfer's face. I could hear the conversation that the man and woman are having where they lean on the railing and look out over the sea. I could smell the fish in the bucket of the old man with his rod hanging over the water. But I leave it all be. If I want to be seen as normal, the best thing I can do is act as normal as possible.

I turn to my friends.

"So what do you think?" I say.

Desmond shrugs. "I don't know. I could go for pizza."

Marina elbows him again. She does that lot.

"Head down, lips sealed," she says. "And we'll have your back." Then she smiles. "Pizza would be good."

"Hey," Desmond says, "maybe we should invite your friends in the SUV to come along."

But when I turn to look, the big black vehicle is gone. I never even saw it leave.

MARINA

The three of us are on our boards, skating toward Josh's place for pizza. I'm glad that his mom will be there, because we won't be talking about Wildlings.

I am so screwed. Here I've been hiding this huge secret of mine from Josh and Des for months and as soon as it happens to Josh, he tells us right away. He'll never forgive me for not doing the same.

But the way Dillon and Josh are always talking about Wildlings being such freaks, I was sure that Josh would hate me if he ever found out. He's never been judgmental about other fringe groups, but he seemed to really buy Dillon's negative viewpoint on this one. Maybe Josh was just humouring Dillon. Friendship can make people go along with some pretty bad stuff.

And then there's Desmond. Just look at how he's bursting to blather the news about Josh being a Wildling. I only pray that for once in his life, he'll be able to contain himself.

I know I've really messed up. Damned if you do and damned if you don't. For sure, Josh will see my withholding this secret as a major betrayal. It's beyond ironic how some things can come back and bite you on the butt.

We wheel around the corner onto Josh's street and see a van from CSFA TV outside his house. We all make a quick stop. Josh looks furious, but Desmond is delighted.

"Dude, you're already famous," he says, grinning ear to ear.

"They'd better not be hassling my mom," says Josh, face glowering. "Let's cut through behind the condo over on 9th. Des, maybe you can give us a leg up over the fence."

Des looks disappointed about not meeting the news team, but heads over to 9th with us. It turns out to be pretty easy to jump the fence. We leave our boards by the back door and head inside.

Josh's mom meets us out in the back hall.

"I've been trying to reach you to warn you, honey," she says.

"Sorry, Mom. I've had my phone turned off. Have they been bugging you?"

"Not as much as the reporters who've been phoning. I told the first couple to call the police instead of us, but after that, I just stopped answering. Then CSFA showed up. I said 'no comment' and asked them to please leave and contact police for information, but they're still out there. That was smart of you kids to come in through the back. I hope this doesn't last."

Thankfully, it doesn't. The phone only rings a few more times and the CSFA van pulls away about fifteen minutes later.

Josh's mom takes the pizza out of the oven, where she'd been keeping it warm, and we all eat a relatively subdued dinner. Even Des is uncharacteristically quiet. Naomi looks exhausted and Josh is not a whole lot better. I guess he had a long night, running around scared and confused in his Wildling shape. I know from personal experience that this is a huge thing to deal with. I only wish I could help him, but I can't take the chance of exposing myself and losing his trust forever.

After supper I give Des a little kick under the table and shoot him a look. For once, he seems to get it and follows my lead. I tell Josh and his mom that we can't stick around, that I haven't been home since this morning and Mamá will be anxious to hear that Josh is okay. This is all true and I'm glad of the excuse to leave.

Josh walks us out.

"Listen guys," he says. "Can we meet at Des's place before school tomorrow? I'm kind of nervous about being alone if some government agent is trying to disappear me or something."

"We're in, dude," says Desmond, his face brightening. "Any creep tries to take you, I want to personally be there to watch you rip his throat out. I am so dying to see you in action."

Josh just sighs and pushes Des and me away on our boards. The two of us go rolling down the street.

JOSH

The next morning, I take my skateboard one street over to pick up Desmond and Marina. Along the way, I check for news vans, black SUVs or skulkers, but I don't see any. The people I do see don't seem out of place. Mrs. Evora is checking her mailbox like she does every morning at this time, even though we all know the mailman doesn't come until just before noon. There's Mr. Steininger walking Judy, his little Boston terrier. A couple of middle school kids are sneaking a smoke at the far end of block.

When I get to 11th Street, I see Desmond sitting alone on the low wall in front of his house. His backpack is on the pavement by his feet.

"Where's Marina?" I ask.

"She sent me a text around five this morning that just said 'surf's up.' I'm sure she copied you."

"I left my phone off. I don't know if they can find out my cell number, but I don't want to get calls from reporters. The phone at the house started ringing again first thing this morning."

"The price of fame."

"Ha ha. So why were you awake at five?"

"I wasn't. I got that from the date-stamp, dude. Anyway, she was leaving to catch a few waves and you know what that means."

I nod. "She could blow off the whole morning."

"Yeah. Or ..." His voice drops lower. "Maybe that's just a cover-up. Maybe your men in black have grabbed her and right now she's in some little room being grilled about you."

"Not funny, Des."

"Come on. It's not like it's ever going to happen."

"We don't know that."

"Man, you have *got* to lighten up," he says. When I give him a sour look,

34

he adds, "So have you seen any of them around this morning?"

I shake my head.

He gets up and swings his backpack to his shoulder.

"You know," he says, "they're not always going to be wearing black suits and driving SUVs. They could be anybody. We totally need to check for new kids at school today—you know, like on TV, where they're dressed like us but you know they're really like thirty-something."

"Thanks for adding to my paranoia."

He laughs. "When did you get so easy to rag on? And I haven't even started on your new taste in music. Hannah Montana? Really?"

I don't bother to answer. I know he's right. Since all of this started, it *is* easy to get a rise out of me. But I'm pretty sure my fears are justified.

❧

I'm not the most popular guy at school, but I'm not a complete misfit, either. Like most kids, I just blend in, and part of that is knowing your limits. Like, I don't try to hang out with the jocks because that would put me on their radar and not in a good way. We're talking head-down-the-toilet-bowl, a slushie in the face and other crap like that. I don't hang with the stoners because I don't do drugs and I don't need them deciding I'm a narc. And I really don't mess with any of the gangs—Mexican or black. The gangs don't show their colours at school, but everybody knows who they are. Get on *their* radar and your problems will most likely be solved with a knife or a gun.

I'm expecting a little notoriety from having been on the news and all. In school, gossip runs as fast as wildfires in the hills when the Santa Ana winds are blowing. People who know me are going to want details. Those who don't are going to stare, pretending they don't care but eager for whatever information they can pick up all the same.

Bobby White doesn't fit into either category, but he still pushes off the railing he's leaning against and approaches us as Desmond and I head for the front door. He's a tall black kid with a quarter-inch of fuzz covering his skull and reflective shades that hide his eyes as they show our own reflections. He doesn't say anything, just points at me and then jerks a thumb toward some picnic tables under the palm and eucalyptus trees.

I know who's sitting there, butt on the table, feet on the seat. He's there every day. It says Theodore Washington on his school records, but everybody knows him as Chaingang. He's the biggest guy in school—maybe two hundred and fifty pounds on a six-foot-two frame—and maybe the oldest, since a couple of the years that the rest of us spent learning calculus and Shakespeare and cutting up frogs in bio, he spent in jail. Juvie, but it's still jail.

His brother heads up the Ocean Avenue Crips. The story is, he took the rap on a drug bust so that his brother wouldn't do adult time at the penitentiary. Nobody knows why he came back to school after serving his time. Not that he actually attends classes. He spends most of the day sitting where he is now, doing I don't know what, and I don't want to know. Except now he wants to talk to me.

Reluctantly, I head over to where he's sitting. Desmond starts to fall in step beside me, except Bobby lays the flat of his hand against Desmond's chest, stopping him.

"Just the brother," Bobby says.

I'd laugh if I wasn't so scared.

The thing is, I may be half black but I'm not from the 'hood. I'm less gangster than any of those white kids from the Valley with hip hop and rap booming from their cars, throwing down signs and swagger. I'm the one with some colour to my skin that runs deeper than a light suntan and they're trying to live the ghetto life.

I don't want to do this. What if Chaingang's decided he wants to jump me into the Ocean Avers? How do I say no? Do I even *get* to say no?

The loose control I've had over my heightened senses starts to unravel. I can hear too much—all the kids hanging around in front of the school, laughing and talking. Music from portable MP3 docks and car stereos. The traffic going by. I smell the sour stink of my own fear. I feel a spark of that weird nervous energy that went through me before I changed, but I rein it in. The last thing I need is to have the mountain lion running wild here at school.

But then I'm standing in front of Chaingang and I think having access to something like the mountain lion's not such a bad thing. Chaingang hasn't said word one, but he doesn't need to. Never mind his reputation. This close up, he seems huge—thick with muscles, head shaved, shades hiding his eyes. I find myself staring at his hands. They're so big I'm sure he could pop my head like a pimple.

I try to shake off a zingy feeling in my head that I attribute to nerves and an overload of sensory input, but I can't seem to tone it down.

He takes off his shades and studies me for a moment.

"I hear you've got a surf band going," he finally says.

All I can do is stare at him, trying to process this weird moment. Chaingang Washington wants to talk to me about surf music?

"Um—yeah," I manage to get out.

"You guys any good?"

I shrug. "We just play in the garage."

He nods. "Gotta start somewhere."

What alternate universe have I stumbled into? I know how odd this sounds, but standing around shooting the breeze with Chaingang is light-years stranger than finding out I've got a mountain lion sitting inside me, just waiting to jump out of my skin.

"I didn't know you were into surf," I say.

"Not so much. I like to feel the bass thumping in my chest with homeboys throwing down their rhymes."

"So why ...?"

"I just wanted to tell you I've got your back. I expect you plan to play it cool. Keep a low profile. And that's good. That's smart. But the shit goes down. I'll do what I can."

This makes even less sense than making small talk about music.

"You—I mean ..."

He grins, but it doesn't feel very comforting.

"Look, I know how you're letting it ride. Mountain lion? Never happened. But you can't play a playa. You understand what I'm saying?"

"Not really."

"I'm saying I know what you are. Once you settle into your skin and get used to your new world, you'll see. You won't be able to *not* tell who's got an animal under his skin. It's the smell mostly, but there's also a little something that goes *ping* in here." He taps a big finger against his temple.

I give a slow nod. "So, you're a—" *Wildling, too*, I'm about to finish, but he cuts me off.

"One more kid doing his time in this shit-ass school. Just like you."

I nod again. He doesn't want to talk about it.

"Can I ask you a question?" I say.

"Shoot."

"Why?"

"Why what?"

"Why do you have my back?"

"This thing we have," he says. "Nobody knows what it is yet, you follow me?"

I nod.

"The solo profile plays just fine, so long as there aren't any problems. But I think there's going to come times when we need something that the people in our lives can't give us. They don't know what it's like—not the way we do. Say the Feds come down on you or me, what are we going to do? Call in our gang? Your friends—are they going to be able to do anything?" He shakes his head. "So if we don't have a Wildling gang, we at least need some alliances, right?"

"I guess ..."

"It's all new to you," he says. "I get it. Don't worry. We're not going to have meetings or hang or anything. But you need a helping hand, you got it. That's all I'm saying."

"And if you need ..."

I let the sentence trail off because what's he ever going to need my help for? But he nods.

"Works both ways, bro. If you want it."

I'm about to ask, do I really have a choice here? Except, while he's hard to read and I totally don't see what I could ever do for him, I get that it is my choice. If I want to, I can just walk away. But this really *is* a new world I'm in and who knows what lies ahead. Having a guy like Chaingang in my corner could make all the difference and it's not like he's asking me to push dope for him.

"I—thanks," I say.

The hint of a smile touches the corner of his mouth.

"Don't worry so much," he says. "Keep your head down and you'll be fine. I changed a week before that kid who turned into the hawk on the video and nobody's the wiser."

"I won't tell anyone."

"Oh, I know you won't."

The words are mild. His eyes are the same. But I realize we've just made a pact that I'd better never screw up.

"So if Wildlings can sense each other," I say, "what stops them from outing each other?"

"Nothing except for the blowback—knowing they'll be outed, too. But I hear the Feds are looking to get themselves some tame Wildlings and then we'll all be in trouble."

I find myself wanting to ask him what kind of animal he can change into, but he's already made it clear this conversation's not going there. But

38

that's not the only thing I'm curious about.

"Can I ask you something else?" I say.

"Go for it."

"Why'd you come back to school?"

He chuckles. "To get my paper, just like everybody else."

"But you don't attend classes."

"Don't need to. I had a lot of free time in juvie. Some I spent seeing to business, but I got studying done, too. People think I'm on a fast track to nowhere and maybe I am, when you look at the big picture. But you know what? I'm still going to ace my finals and, at the end of the year, I'll be walking onstage with the rest of them. They're going to see that a brother can stay on top of their game as well as his own."

"Sweet."

"Yeah, but that's me. You've still got to put in the time."

He holds out his fist. I hesitate a moment, then bump mine against his. The difference in size looks absurd, but he doesn't seem to notice.

"Hang loose, Josh," he says.

The shades go back on and I realize I've been dismissed.

ൟ

"What the hell was that all about?" Desmond says in a low voice as we head for our lockers to put away our boards.

I can't really tell him, not without also telling him that Chaingang's a Wildling just like me, but I'm not going to be the one to out him.

I settle for, "He wanted to know how our band's doing."

"Seriously?"

I shrug. "I guess there's a part of him that digs surf music."

"That so doesn't scan."

"What can I say?"

He nods. "You know everybody's watching you, right?"

I do. But I figure it won't last. By lunchtime, some new drama will have come along and I'll be old news.

Except it does last. The morning drags on and no one treats me the same. It's not just the other kids. Even the teachers seem ... I don't want to say wary, but they treat me differently. Maybe they're just concerned because of what I went through—and by that I mean the news reports that said I was chased out of the house by a mountain lion—but they don't seem comfortable having me in their class.

Dillon catches me in the hall. He's not much taller than me but he's got the longest fingers I've ever seen. He can do a seven-fret stretch like nobody I know.

"Josh, is it true?" he says under his breath, looking around as if we're about to be jumped. "Did one of those goddamn freaks really come right into your house?"

"I'll tell you about it later. Got to get to history."

"Yeah, but—"

"It's cool," I tell him. "Really."

I clap him lightly on the back as we part.

I don't know how I'm going to handle things with Dillon from now on. This is such a drag. I love jamming in the music room with the guy, but he's so down on Wildlings that I don't think I'm going to want to spend much time in his company.

Just before last period in the morning, Ms. Chandra, the guidance counsellor, stops me in the hall to assure me that she's here for me if I need to talk about my "ordeal." Instead of telling her that all this attention is the real ordeal, I nod and say thanks before I move on to my class. I know I just need to get through this, but I'm starting to wish I'd waited another day before coming back to school.

I spend a lot of time staring out windows, looking for black SUVs and men in suits. All I see is a lone CSFA van. I was surprised there wasn't one outside the house again this morning, but they probably realized it might be easier to get hold of me here.

Or maybe I'm just being paranoid and it has nothing to do with me. Could be they finally have some real news to cover around here.

⚜

"Now I know what animals in the zoo feel like," I say to Desmond at lunch.

"Why's that?" Marina slides into a seat beside me as she asks the question.

"I feel like I'm on display," I tell her. "Everybody's watching me and wondering."

"You can't blame them," she says. "You're the new celebrity buzz."

I have to smile when I see her. Her hair's still damp from the ocean and she's got that glow she always gets when she's been out on her board. She looks so relaxed I wish I'd gone to the beach with her this morning.

"Yeah?" I say. "I don't think so. I'm more like an accident they're

40

slowing down to stare at to see the damage."

"How were the sets?" Desmond asks Marina.

She grins. "Bitchin'."

We all laugh. Doesn't matter what they were like, that's always her answer.

Then Desmond leans forward. "Guess who was asking about the band?"

"Which so needs a name."

"You're not guessing."

She scrunches her face as she pretends to think hard, then says, "I give up. Who?"

"Come on. You're not even trying."

"Okay," she says. "Principal Hayden, because he wants to hire us for a pep rally."

"*Bzzzt*. Wrong answer. It was Chaingang Washington."

Marina turns to me for confirmation and I give a reluctant nod.

"*Seriously?*" she says.

"No, we're making it up," Desmond tells her. "Of course, seriously."

"Are we're talking about the same—"

"Big black dude who sits out at the picnic tables all day?"

"But—*why?*"

She turns to me again and I see the concern in her eyes.

"It was cool," I tell her. "I don't know why he decided to quiz me about us. Maybe he just wanted a little dose of that celebrity buzz you were talking about."

"Ha ha."

I'm still freaked about the whole mountain lion business—come on, who wouldn't be?—and I hate all the attention I'm getting, but the thing that bugs me the most right now is how I have to lie to my friends. Nobody can stop me from sharing my own secrets, but I can't, in good conscience, share someone else's.

Something stirs in my gut and it takes a moment before I realize it's the part of me that's a mountain lion. I resent Chaingang for putting me in this position and the mountain lion wants to take it out on him.

Marina puts a hand on my arm. "Are you okay?"

And that's enough to ground me.

"Yeah. I'm fine."

"Because you had this intense look in your eyes ..."

I shrug. "It's been a really stressful morning."

She holds my gaze for a long moment, then finally nods.

"No surprise there," she says. "You should have come out with me this morning."

"It wouldn't have helped," Desmond says. "He'd just have spent the whole time looking out for guys in black bathing suits."

I go to punch him in the shoulder but he pulls back out of range.

"Seriously, dude," he says. "You ought to blow off the rest of the day."

I shake my head. "The last thing I am today is anonymous. They'd know I was skipping and I don't need detention on top of everything else."

"You could go to the office," Marina says. "I bet they'll understand if you need more time to deal with this."

"No, I just need to get through the day. I want things to go back to normal and that's not going to happen if the school decides to start treating me with kid gloves."

"Yeah, they'd probably make him go see Ms. Chandra," Desmond says, "and she'll want him to talk about his *feelings*."

"Probably. She already stopped me in the hall on my way to calculus."

The bell rings for us to go back to class. Marina and I have study period, so we head off to the library while Desmond goes to English. We get our usual table at the far end of the room, except I take the chair Marina normally does so that I can look out the window. I don't like having my back to doors or windows anymore.

"Desmond doesn't get it yet," Marina says.

She leans forward over the table, pitching her voice low so that the librarian won't come over to shush us. The mountain lion lets me smell the salt in her hair.

"He hasn't really thought it through," she adds. "You know, how huge a change this is and how you have to work through a few things."

"I know."

I glance down the row of tables along the window and see Rachel Armstrong sitting with some of her friends. She looks away quickly and I realize she's been staring at me. I've had a huge crush on her since the school year started and didn't think she even knew who I was. But I guess everybody does now. The trouble is, it's for all the wrong reasons.

Marina rolls her eyes when she notices.

"Forget Ms. Chandra," she says. "Maybe you should talk to Rachel about your *feelings*."

"Shut up."

But that only makes her smile and shake her head.

"Desmond's right," she says. "You're way too easy to tease these days."

"It's just—I feel like my life's falling to pieces around me. Like I don't have any control over anything anymore."

That stops the teasing.

"I know," she says. "But he's partly right, too. You can't change what's happened. So maybe it's time you embraced it."

"What? Like change into a mountain lion and go racing through the halls?"

"Don't be an idiot. I just mean that all we seem to hear about with the Wildlings is the negative stuff."

"Because that's all there is."

She goes on like I didn't interrupt. "But maybe there are some good things, too."

"Like what?"

But I remember Cory answering that for me.

You're stronger and faster than you were before. You're going to live longer and you won't get sick as easily. All your senses are heightened—smell, hearing, vision. And that's just in your human form.

"I don't know," Marina says. "But this is your life now. If you don't look for the silver lining, then all you're stuck with is the crap."

"Is that what you'd do?"

She looks down at the table, but she nods. "But then, I'm a cup-half-full girl."

"Where would you start?"

"Have you heard of this thing called the Internet?"

"Very funny."

"But I wouldn't go looking up news reports. I'd be looking for blogs. For all we know, some Wildling is out there on WordPress or whatever, talking about the very same stuff you're going through."

"That's a good idea."

She smiles. "It sure beats playing Animal Planet in the halls and spending the rest of the school year in detention."

"If the government doesn't come along and take me away first."

"Yeah," she says, a worried look in her eyes. "There's always that. So promise me you won't do anything stupid."

Not unless it's stupid to just try to be normal again.

"I promise," I tell her.

༺⚬༻

Speaking of detention, that's where Desmond is when school's over. He was goofing around with some guys out in the hall between classes and Principal Hayden himself busted them, so there was no chance they'd get off easy. And since Marina's mom picked her up to go to the mall, I'm on my own, skateboarding home. I don't mind. Last night after Desmond and Marina left, I was bouncing off the walls of my bedroom, wishing I had someone to talk to. But with the day I've just had, I'm relieved to be by myself, pushing along on my board, hoodie pulled over my head.

Anonymous.

I make the trip across town in record time and I'm not even winded. I guess there's something to say for the stronger and faster part of me. When I get to the pier, I snap my board up into my hand and carry it under my arm as I step from the pavement onto its wooden slats. There's a good wind coming in from the sea and waves are crashing against the support beams below, spraying water. I smell the salt and listen to the conversations around me, the cries of the gulls. Leaning on the north side balustrade, I watch the surfers for a while, then sit down on a nearby bench. I drop my skateboard to the ground. Putting my feet on it, I lean my head back and close my eyes.

I'm really enjoying my solitude, so of course someone has to sit down beside me. I don't bother to open my eyes. Maybe they'll go away.

"Saunders?"

It's a girl's voice. One I don't recognize. But there's something else—a faint animal musk and a little *ping* inside my head. I remember what Chaingang said—*Once you settle into your skin and get used to your new world, you'll see. You won't be able to* not *tell who's got an animal under his skin*—and I figure this must be what he's talking about. It's so slight that I doubt it would be noticed by anybody—. I hesitate over the word, but there isn't another one I can use.

Anybody *human.*

I turn to look at her. She's a white girl, my age, maybe a little older, with a dark tan and reddish-brown hair in long dreads that put the little ones I have to shame. A tribal pattern is tattooed like a necklace on her chest bone and she has a dozen silver rings piercing the curve of her right ear. Her left ear just has a stud in the shape of a feather. Her feet are bare under khaki capris and a tight white tank top. She's got the greenest eyes I've ever seen and she's so cute that I know this is as implausible as Chaingang wanting to talk to me. How do I know? Because I can tell you exactly the last time a girl this cute

44

struck up a conversation with me: never.

"Sorry," I tell her. "You've got me confused with someone else."

She shakes her head. "Nice try, but your face was plastered all over the news. You're definitely Joshua Saunders. I'm Elzie."

I sigh and look away.

"I'm not a reporter," she says.

"I kind of figured that out. Look, no offence, but I just want some down time. I don't know who put me on the Wildling Welcome Wagon list—or maybe you're from some Wildling outreach program—but I'm calling time-out."

"You should be a little more careful talking about that stuff with a stranger."

"Yeah, except I know you're a Wildling, too, though I don't know exactly what kind."

"That's good," she says. "It takes most of us more than a few days to be able to start recognizing others."

I don't say anything.

"I take it you've already been approached by someone?" she says.

I nod, but I don't start handing out names. Maybe Wildlings can smell each other out or something, but if I have to lie to my friends about Chaingang, I'm sure not going to give him up to a stranger.

"Let me guess," she says. "One of them was a guy named Cory and he warned you to watch out for me."

I shake my head. "I've met Cory, but he didn't say anything about you. Why would he?"

She shrugs. "Let's just say he doesn't like my politics."

I study her for a moment.

"You don't go to Sunny Hill, do you?" I say.

Because a girl as cute as she is, I'd remember.

"I'm from Long Beach," she says.

"So you didn't get changed like the rest of us. You're like Cory."

"No, I changed."

"I didn't think it happened anywhere outside of Santa Feliz."

"So far as I know, it hasn't," she says. "I changed when I was here visiting a friend. I tried to go back home, but my parents wouldn't let me. They were afraid of me."

"That's harsh."

I can't imagine Mom turning her back on me like that. But I haven't told her yet, have I, so what does that say?

She shrugs again. "I don't blame them. They were afraid something would happen to my little brother if I stayed. So I dropped out of school and I live here now."

"Something like what? What did they think you were going to do?"

"Come on, don't play dumb. You heard about that kid who turned into a rattler and bit his old man, right?"

"Yeah, but your own *brother*? You wouldn't do anything like that."

She shakes her head. "Except they couldn't know for *sure* for sure."

"That totally sucks."

"Anyway," she says. She waves her hand like none of it matters, but you'd have to be pretty dim not to see the pain in her eyes before she pushes it away. "I guess I am kind of like a Welcome Wagon. I just wanted to talk to you—let you know some of your options."

"I know my options," I tell her.

I'm not interested in talking about all that again. Cory already did and I don't need a bigger dose of paranoia than I already have.

"Where do you live?" I ask, to change the subject. "How do you get by?"

And do you have a boyfriend? I add to myself. Not like it'll make any difference, but I'd still like to know.

My questions get me yet another shrug.

"I live wherever," she says, "and I get by. Did Cory tell you how some of us are working to make this a better world?"

"I'm not sure what you mean. He talked about how we're all connected by our animal blood and how some Wildlings have been around forever. I guess the old ones don't really like that the new Wildlings have kind of screwed up the secret existence that they had."

"Yeah," she says, "but they need to look at the bigger picture."

I look past her. There's a guy who's been standing with his back to the balustrade a little way down the pier, elbows on the railing. He's looking everywhere except at us and I find myself remembering what Desmond said about the Federal agents.

They're not always going to be wearing black suits and driving SUVs. They could be anybody.

This guy doesn't seem much older than me, but it's obvious he's been living hard. He's got the dark tan of a beach bum and he's wearing a dirty white T-shirt, baggy shorts, sandals, a small olive-green backpack hanging from one shoulder. His hair looks like he slept on it badly and didn't bother to comb it when he got up. I've seen his type on the beach before, but there's something off about him. I can't quite put my finger on it.

"Don't look," I say quietly, "but I think we're being spied on."

Of course, she looks.

"Oh, don't worry," she says. "That's just Danny. He's with me."

So she does have a boyfriend. I mean, I know why she's really talking to me—she's on some sort of a recruitment drive, just like Cory warned me about—but until she said that, I could pretend otherwise.

"He doesn't have to stand way over there," I say.

She smiles. "He kind of does. The Feds have ID'd him, so I don't want him close. But he kept insisting that I shouldn't meet you by myself. I guess he followed me here."

"Why? Do I look dangerous?"

Her smile fades. "You should know by now that our bodies can hide any kind of Wildling."

"Sure," I say.

I haven't been thinking any such thing. Mostly, I've been trying to figure out how to get my life back. I know it's not going to happen, but it's kind of like when I hit that ball through our front window. There's that moment when you know it's happening, but you still have this impossible hope that it's only going to bounce off the glass. Of course, it just smashes right through.

I want to believe that I'm in that moment where things aren't completely screwed up yet. I know they are, but that doesn't stop me from wishing I could still wake up from all of this.

"So you and Danny," I start.

But then I don't know where I'm going with this—or rather, I do, but I think better of it and end up just letting the words hang there.

She looks at me, the smile is back. "Are you asking if he's my boyfriend?"

"I guess."

"I don't have time for boyfriends."

"Right. Of course not. You're too busy trying to round up Wildlings for some cause or other."

"Why would you think that? Wait, why do I even ask? That coyote sticks his nose into everybody's business. What did he tell you about us?"

"That depends on who 'us' is," I tell her. "But you in particular? Nothing."

"I'm surprised."

"I take it you don't much like Cory."

"Nah, he's a good guy in his own way. He just doesn't see the big picture."

"I don't think I do, either."

"He didn't mention the ferals?"

My stomach does a little flip. Ferals? I don't like the sound of that. I shake my head.

"Do I really want to know this?" I ask.

"Sure," she replies. "It's one of the good things about the change. We—the ferals that is—think this is happening so that the world can revert back to what it was like before people came along. We're working toward helping that process. There aren't a lot of us yet, but I hope we can get more Wildlings involved. It's important."

"The environment *is* pretty messed up," I say. "But tearing everything down and starting at scratch isn't really a solution. Unless you don't care about a lot of people getting hurt."

"Oh, it's not going to happen all at once, of course. But really, you have to admit that people have messed up this planet pretty bad and it's only going to get worse if we let things go on this way."

"Well, sure. We need to do something—all of us, not just Wildlings. But I love my mom and my friends too much to let them die just to make it happen."

"Who says anybody has to die?"

"Kind of goes hand in hand with the whole getting rid of all the people part of your plan."

"I ..."

"Tell me you thought about that."

"It's people who are the problem."

"Maybe they can be the solution, too," I say.

"Don't be so naive."

"Yeah? And what about your family and friends? Are you willing to sacrifice them as well?"

"They all turned their backs on me."

"Even your brother?"

Her eyes flash. "Screw you, Saunders."

She gets up, her back stiff with anger.

"Wait," I say before she can go.

She shakes her head. "I don't think we have anything more to—"

I cut her off. "No, it's your friend."

She turns and sees what I see. Danny has wandered down to the end of the pier. But as soon as he gets there, the doors pop open on a white van that's been parked in one of the disabled parking spots. Men in SWAT gear fan out from the van. Behind them are a couple of guys in dark suits.

I want to shout a warning but I don't have to. Danny sees the men and he bolts toward the boardwalk.

And then it happens.

I've never seen it for real before—except for that thing Cory did with his head, switching from human to coyote and back again. This is different. Surreal. One moment there's a kid trying to escape, the next he's changed into—I'm not sure what. Something like a deer, but with small, spiral horns.

The SWAT guys shoot him—*bam, bam*! It sounds like a car backfiring. Almost before he hits the ground, they're throwing some kind of net over him. They roll him up in it and toss him into the back of the van.

Elzie leans against the railing as though her knees have gone weak.

"Oh, Danny," she says. "Why couldn't you just have stayed away?"

I look back at the van, feeling sick.

"They killed him," I say. "They just up and killed him."

Elzie shakes her head. "No, those were tranq guns. They just want him down for the count so they can take him away. Not as harsh as using Tasers, but damn!"

She smacks the railing with her palm.

Everything has happened so fast that it's over before most people even have the chance to notice. Some kid on the boardwalk has his phone out, shooting a video, but one of the agents runs over and grabs it away from him. The kid protests until the agent opens his suit coat and shows the kid something. I don't know what it is. His badge, maybe? His gun? Whatever it is, the kid shuts right up.

The other men are talking, then they look down the pier. The one who took the phone from the kid starts toward us.

Elzie gets up and starts to walk away from me. "Got to go," she says. "What's your cell number?"

The argument we were having appears to be forgotten.

I tell her the number.

"I'll call you," she says and heads briskly toward the restaurant at the end of the pier.

I turn to watch her go. Though she doesn't appear to be exerting herself, she's really motoring along. But it's not going to do her any good. There's nothing on the other side of the restaurant except for the Pacific Ocean and it's a ten- maybe fifteen-foot drop to the water.

When I look back, the man in the suit has almost reached me. I brace myself for whatever he's going to do to me, but he goes right by my bench, talking into his Bluetooth. He's chasing after Elzie, not me.

I realize that's my cue to leave.

I stand up, pop my skateboard into my hand and go the other way, toward the parking lot. As I walk by the van, an itchy nervous tension has me feeling like I've had too much caffeine. I drop my skateboard to the pavement, but before I can push off, a hand falls on my shoulder.

I almost growl at the touch, stopping myself before the sound actually comes out of my mouth. I turn to find the other guy in a suit has stopped me. The guy back on the pier was white, this one's Hispanic. He drops his hand and flashes me a picture ID billfold with the letters "FBI" prominently displayed on it.

"That girl you were talking to," he says.

I give him a puzzled look. "You mean the one with the dreads?"

He nods. "How do you know her?"

"Am I in trouble?"

I let some of my nervousness spill into my voice. I hope it sounds like anybody would when a Federal agent stops them, not that I'm guilty of anything.

"I want to know what your relationship is."

I use Cory's advice again. *The best way to lie is to have your story be mostly true.*

"I just met her," I say. "She's some kind of eco-freak, but she was pretty cute so I let her go into her spiel."

I can't tell what he's thinking behind those dark sunglasses. I don't let myself look at the van where they've got Danny tranquilized and wrapped up in a net.

"What kind of spiel?" the agent asks.

I shrug. "You know, the usual. Save the whales. We're destroying the planet. Don't eat meat."

"So you've never met her before?"

"No, sir."

He starts to say something, then puts a hand to the headset in his ear, obviously listening to something.

"I'll be right there," he says.

I pretend I don't know what he's talking about.

"Excuse me?"

"Not you," he says to me. He takes a business card out of his pocket. "If she should approach you again, please call the number on the card."

I look down the length of the pier.

"What's going on?" I ask. "Is she in trouble?"

"Just call the number if you see her again."

Then he motions to a couple of the SWAT team guys and the three of them set off at a jog down the pier. I watch them for a moment, then I put a foot on my board and get the hell out of there before someone changes their mind.

❧

We have band practice that evening in Desmond's garage. While Desmond and I are tuning up, I tell them what happened.

"I've seen that girl around," Marina says from behind her drum kit, "with her dreads and that tattooed necklace. She's a total skank."

"What makes you say that?"

"You know the kind. She's just always mooching for stuff. Like she's trying to get guys to buy her a coffee or lunch, panhandling along the boardwalk, or she's trying to borrow stuff. One time she actually asked Stu if she could use his board."

"Not cool," Desmond says.

"She's homeless," I tell them.

Desmond shrugs. "So how's that our problem?"

"Her parents kicked her out of the house because she changed," I say. "What happened to me happened to her, except her parents just threw her out to fend for herself."

"Dude," Desmond says, "I hate to rain on your parade, but your mother doesn't even *know* you're a Wildling."

"Yeah, but if she did, she wouldn't do that to me."

"Probably not," Marina says. "Yours should give good-mom courses."

Desmond nods in agreement. "Except for the jerk boyfriends thing."

That hurts, but it's true, so I let it slide.

"And while I can see why you sympathize with that girl," Marina goes on.

"Elzie. Her name's Elzie."

"Okay. Elzie. I just think you should be careful if she comes around again. Some people are takers and she seems like one of them."

"I don't know," I say. "She seems to care a lot about the environment and stuff. So that doesn't seem like a taker to me. I don't really agree with everything she says, but you can't pretend things aren't pretty messed up."

"Things are totally messed up," Marina agrees.

I nod. "And at least she seems committed to do something about it."

"I just don't trust her."

"You don't know her."

"And neither do you," Marina says. "I get it. You're both Wildlings. But that doesn't mean you have to automatically get involved in whatever she's doing."

I'm a little surprised. Marina usually sees the best in people, so I can't figure out why she's so down on this girl she really doesn't know anything about.

"Guys, guys," Desmond says.

We both turn to him.

"You know Marina's just looking out for you," he says to me. "It's not like she's jealous or anything. And Marina. Come on. Cut the dude some slack. He's just had his world turned on its ass. So let him enjoy a bit of attention from some cute little Rasta girl. It sure beats him mooning over Rachel Armstrong."

I look at Marina. Jealous? That'd be the day.

"You're right," she tells Des. She gives me a peace sign. "We're cool, right?"

"Of course we're cool."

"So let's play some music."

MARINA

Every beat on my drum kit lets me blow off some of the steam I feel about Josh hooking up with that girl Elzie. I hate the fact that it's her and Josh making Wildling alliances instead of him and me. I know. It's my own fault. But still.

I am so not a fan of jealousy, but it's one of those emotions that worms its way under your skin. I've never been all that bugged by his mooning over that stupid jock-magnet Rachel Armstrong. She never gave Josh a second look before he was on the news.

But this is different. He only just met Elzie and it's already like he's all connected with her, standing up for her and everything.

I feel a bit guilty for not having more sympathy that her parents threw her out. That does suck big-time, but why does it have to be Josh that she turns to? Elzie's gorgeous. She could have her pick of any guy she wanted.

And then there's Chaingang getting all friendly with Josh. I didn't expect them to get buddy-buddy. I know they weren't really talking about the band. Josh only said that for our sake. Chaingang gave me the same pep talk on being a Wildling after I changed.

He wasn't the first to give me advice, though. A guy named Jez showed up the first time I changed and told me the basics. I'm glad it wasn't Chaingang who did that, because I was buck naked. I've learned to change back wearing my clothes since then.

But when Chaingang did approach me, he was really sweet. Before I actually met him, I was scared to death of the guy. When he called me over at the beach that day, I thought I may as well drown myself right then and there. Instead, he told me that he knew what I was and warned me to be careful and all. He said he'd protect me if I got into trouble.

I kind of enjoyed the fact that he was, I don't know, softer around me than he'd ever acted before. I guess I felt as though he'd specifically chosen me to be close to. Now I realize I misread him. I know he won't out me to Josh, but somehow it hurts that they're all pals now.

Josh is free to like whoever he wants and so is Chaingang, but it's just hard to feel less and less special to either one of them.

Tomorrow morning I'm going to catch the biggest swells I can find and ride them like there's nothing on the planet except for me and a few tons of crazy water.

JOSH

My phone vibrates under my pillow that night at around two in the morning. I'd turned it on with the ringer off. Let's face it, I was curious if Elzie would call. I look at the call display and my pulse does a little jump.

"Josh?" her voice says in my ear as soon as I press talk.

"Hi," I say. "Are you okay?"

"Oh sure."

"How'd you get away?"

"I'm good at that kind of thing."

"I guess you are."

"Did they stop you at all?" she asks.

"Just to ask a couple of questions."

"What did they want to know?"

"Mostly how I knew you."

"What did you say?"

"That I didn't. I told them that you just came up to me and started trying to sell me on getting proactive about the environment and I was only listening because you're cute."

I want to call the word back as soon as it comes out of my mouth, but it's too late.

"You think I'm cute?"

"Well ... um ..."

She responds with a throaty laugh and I feel something stirring under the sheets. I never really got the concept of phone sex before, but I think I do now.

"That's sweet," she says. "Living like I do, I kind of forget that there are nice guys like you out there."

Nice. Man. Do I want to be the nice guy? The nice guy never gets the

55

girl.

"So where are you now?" I ask.

"Safe. But maybe not for long."

"Why not? Are they still after you?"

"I don't know if they're exactly *after* me. I think I'm just a 'person of interest' because they've seen me hanging around with Danny."

"So why aren't you safe?"

"I'm going after Danny."

"Really? But the FBI has him."

"And that's so not right. I've tried to get some of the others to help me, but everybody thinks Danny's a flake and that we should just cut him loose."

"But you can't."

"I know he's a flake," she says, "but he's still one of us. They shouldn't be allowed to take him away like that. He never did anything to anyone. And he helped me sometimes."

"So what are you going to do?"

She doesn't answer right away, but then she says, "I was hoping you might help me."

I remember what Marina said about her being a taker, but I think of how I'd feel if I was the one that the FBI shot full of tranqs and then locked away in some secret place. I'd sure want someone to help me.

"What do you want me to do?" I ask.

๛

Fifteen minutes later, I'm standing in the shadows by the Evoras' garage. I've done what Elzie asked. I'm waiting for her here, dressed in black jeans and runners with a dark hoodie over my T-shirt. I shift my weight from foot to foot, trying to use the mountain lion to sense what's out there in the night. I guess I'm not very good at it yet, because suddenly Elzie's standing right beside me. I never saw or heard her approach.

She puts a hand on my upper arm and gives it a squeeze as we start walking.

"Thanks for coming," she says. "It means a lot."

"If it was me instead of him, I'd like to think people were trying to get me out, so it was hard to say no."

"Yeah, but you still could have."

I shrug, trying to be cool.

"Do you know where he is?" I ask.

"It has to be the old naval base. That's where everyone says the government's keeping the Wildlings they take off the street."

"Won't they have guards all over that place? We used to goof around in the wildlife refuge near there, but you can't get in at all anymore. I'm not so sure anyone can get by their security."

"I've got to try," she says.

Oh boy. What have I gotten myself into?

A couple of blocks from my street, she stops at a car and goes around to the driver's side.

"Is this your car?" I say. "I thought you were homeless."

It's not fancy, just a 2001 Ford Taurus wagon, but a car costs money— not only for the initial outlay, but for gas and upkeep, too. You don't see homeless people driving around. You see them on traffic islands, trying to cadge change from the drivers stopped at the lights.

"It's borrowed," she says.

"Borrowed?"

"Relax. It's Danny's. I don't think he's going to mind if we use it to rescue him."

A sour smell hits me when I open the door. I see that the back seats are down and there's a rough bed taking up the length of the rear compartment, along with piles of clothing and a collection of fast food wrappers and empty pop cans.

"Yeah," Elzie says as she slides in behind the wheel. "He's not exactly the world's best housekeeper."

"This is where he *lives*?"

"Beats couch surfing or sleeping on the beach. At least he's got a place."

"I guess."

There's a bunch of junk on the passenger's seat and on the floor. A damp towel that I wish I hadn't touched, old newspapers, a pizza box, a screwdriver, some paperbacks with the covers torn off. I toss it all into the back and get in.

❧

She takes us out the Pacific Coast Highway heading south. With the windows all open, front and back, the stench isn't as pervasive. Eventually it pretty much goes away. It's that or I'm just getting used to it.

I expect her to be a reckless driver—everything about her seems a little wild and reckless—but she sticks to just a few miles over the speed limit. Fifteen minutes later, she pulls into a parking lot overlooking the ocean.

There are over a dozen cars and vans in the lot and I can see a fire down on the beach. Surfer party. It makes me think of Marina. I should go out with her tomorrow morning if the waves are good. I'll make a fool of myself—I don't know why I can ride my wheels like they're a pair of shoes, yet I keep falling off a surfboard—but we always have a good time.

Elzie pulls the Taurus into a spot between a classic Woody, oak panels gleaming in our headlights, and a powder-blue T-Bird convertible with the top down. Killing the engine, she reaches under the seat and pulls out a pair of *luchador* head masks and hands me one. Mine's shiny gold with red flames around the eye and mouth holes. Hers is a deep blue with yellow highlights.

"You've got to be kidding me," I say. "What's going out like Mexican wrestlers going to prove?"

"It'll keep your secret identity secret."

"Come on, seriously?"

She puts hers on. All I can see is her green eyes, nose and lips. The long dreads are bunched at the back of her neck and make a weird bump under the mask.

"There are cameras everywhere now," she says. "Weather cameras, traffic cameras and at the base, there are sure to be security cameras."

I sigh and put on the mask she gave me. I feel like an idiot.

"Stick some of these in your pockets," she says, passing me a handful of energy bars. "It's in case we have to change," she adds. "You know how to focus on keeping your clothes when you change so that you've got them when you've come back out of your animal shape?"

I nod. "That's what Cory told me, but I haven't tried it. How does that even work, anyway?"

"Don't know, don't care," she says. "Just so long as it works. The food's for if we have to take our animal shapes. Whatever makes it work uses up a lot of energy. You'll be starving."

I remember how hungry I was the morning Cory found me in the alley. It didn't happen the second time in my bathroom, but I'd only been in the mountain lion shape for a moment before switching back.

"You ready?" she asks.

"Yeah."

I join her on the pavement. We wait for a car to go by, then cross the highway and duck into the scrub along the verge. Moments later we come to the chain-link fence that protects the wild bird sanctuary from intruders. I can smell the salt marsh, rich and heady.

"We need to keep low," she says. "They've got cameras in there for monthly night surveys of mammals passing through. I don't know what night they do the survey, but I'm guessing they actually leave them running all the time."

"How do you know that?"

"I Googled the refuge. It's got its own website."

"Of course it does."

We follow the fence along the highway, turning when it leads us inland. Elzie starts out at a fast walk, but as soon as we make the turn, she breaks into a jog. I want to tell her that I'm not really in shape for a long run, but I don't think she's going to listen, so I just try to keep up for as long as I can. Five minutes into our run, when I should be calling for a time-out, I'm not even out of breath.

Stronger and faster. No kidding.

"I feel like I could run like this forever," I say.

Elzie laughs. "You could make even better time in your animal shape, but even as humans we've got serious chops. Why do you think everybody wants a piece of what we are?"

"I thought they couldn't figure out what causes the whole Wildlings thing."

"Maybe not yet. Which is why they're after us. They can't duplicate what we are, so they want us to work for them."

It isn't fair. This should be like Desmond thinks it is—totally cool. We shouldn't have to live in the shadows, hiding from our own government.

It makes me think a little more about Elzie's agenda. Getting rid of everybody human isn't the answer, but there must be something we can do. Not just to save the natural world the way she wants to, but to save all of us.

ॐ

It should have taken us around forty-five minutes to get to the old naval base. We make it in twenty. Elzie stops us at an embankment shored up with boulders. When we peer over it, we see a long stretch of flat land on the other side of the chain-link fence, acres of pavement beyond it, flat warehouse-type buildings past that.

"It's a big place," I say.

She nods.

"Do you have any idea where they keep their prisoners?"

"No. I'm going to scout around a bit. You wait here for me."

59

"I don't think that's such a good idea."

"You should listen to him, cousin," a new voice says.

We turn to find Cory sitting on his haunches looking at us. He's in human form but he still gives off a doggish vibe.

How did he get so close without either of us noticing?

Well, with me it's not such a big surprise, I guess, but Elzie's been at this a lot longer than I have. You'd think she would have twigged to his presence.

"And why the hell are you wearing those goofy masks?" he asks.

I want to tell him that the surf band Los Straitjackets wears them for gigs and they're a pretty cool band, but Elzie's already talking.

"You know they've got cameras in the wildlife refuge?" she says. "Without these, they'd have our pictures on file. Maybe they could use them to track us down."

"So go in your real shapes."

"Yeah, like a mountain lion trotting through their property's not going to send up any warning flares."

"Point taken. But you look like a couple of kids playing Halloween."

"If you're not here to help," Elzie tells him, "you should just go away."

He shrugs and turns his attention to me. "Do you remember what I told you about keeping a low profile? And alliances? Are you sure this is the choice you want to make?"

"This isn't about politics," I say. "It's about stepping up when someone's in a jam."

He looks from her to me. "So which one of you's in a jam?"

Elzie mutters, "Loser," and turns her attention back to our target.

"I'm serious," he says, "because Danny Reed doesn't need rescuing."

"What the hell is that supposed to mean?" Elzie says.

I can hear an angry growl in her voice.

"Well," Cory drawls. "Right now he's sitting in his brand new apartment waiting to start his brand new government job in the morning."

"Bullshit."

"I have it on good authority."

"Yeah? And whose would that be?"

"Auntie Min's."

"You know I can check that out."

"Be my guest. She says the whole charade of him getting taken down was so that nobody would start sniffing around asking questions. I guess they didn't figure on you going all hero to bust him out."

"Who's Auntie Min?" I ask.

"Queen of the street cousins," Cory says. "She's over in the cardboard city under the Santa Feliz Boulevard overpass."

"How does she know?" Elzie asks.

"She said she's seen it coming for awhile."

"Why wouldn't she have told me?"

Cory shrugs. "You know how it is. That's a pretty serious accusation. Nobody's going to come right out and say it, based only on a feeling."

"Except she's Auntie Min. Everybody knows she's a mojo woman."

"I know," Cory says. "All the more reason for her to be sure first."

Elzie seems to shrink inside herself for a moment. I wonder what her face looks like behind the mask.

"Crap," she finally says.

"I'm sorry to have to be the one to tell you," Cory tells her.

"And that's why you came all the way out here?"

Cory shakes his head. "This *is* a holding facility for those of us who don't want to play the Feds' game. I'm here for the same reason you are, scouting a way in. The difference is, the cousins I'm looking for are actually in there."

"And you're going to break them out. Some low profile *you're* keeping."

"Oh *I'm* going to remain invisible," he tells her. "Like you, I'm just doing some recon for them. It's only natural that they'd break themselves out, but they need to know the lay of the land. Speaking of which ...."

He tips a finger against his brow and points it at me. Then he's up and over the fence so fast I can hardly register the movement.

"Top wire's got juice," he says when he lands on the other side.

Then, just like that, there's a coyote in his place. It turns away from us, loping toward the buildings.

"Aren't we going with him?" I ask.

"He doesn't need our help."

She turns and starts to walk fast, back the way we came. I look across the big empty space, trying to spot Cory, but even my night vision can't penetrate that far into the darkness.

"I'm sorry about how things worked out," I say when I catch up to Elzie.

She looks at me, but keeps on walking. I don't have to see her features to know she's upset.

"No biggie," she says. "I'm getting used to it. Wasn't your fault anyway."

"I know that. But it must be hard to find out that somebody you thought you knew really well turns out to be somebody you didn't know at all."

"Yeah, that pretty much sucks. I'd never have thought it of him. He always seemed so committed to the cause."

That makes me think of something else.

"I guess he'll have told his new bosses all about us," I say. "You, me, the rest of your group."

"I thought about that, but I don't think anything's changed. I was already on their radar. And I doubt you have to worry. Danny never got close enough to you to know for sure if you're a Wildling or not. And even if he did finger you, there's nothing they can do unless you screw up and change in front of them or something."

"Is that why they're following me around?"

"Probably."

"What are you going to do?" I ask.

"Lay low for awhile, just until I can figure something out."

"Well, I'm still not joining your cause or anything, but if you need a hand with something ..."

She stops and looks at me again. There's something in her eyes, but I can't quite read what it is.

"I've ... you know ..." I say, falling back on what Chaingang said to me. "I've got your back."

"Why?" she says.

"Why not?"

She grins. "Good answer."

"Plus there's, um, you know. The cuteness factor."

"An even better answer."

She turns around so that she's walking backwards, which she still manages to do with a swagger.

"Race you?" she says.

She takes off before I can answer, running full out. I take off after her, but I can't catch her. I end up trailing behind all the way back to the highway. We tear off the *luchador* masks when we get back to the car, sweat streaming down our faces. She tosses hers inside the car and I follow suit. We can hear music coming from the campfire below. It sounds like somebody doing a pretty good version of a Dave Matthews song.

"Do you want to check out the party?" Elzie asks.

It's late, but I'm not tired. And while there's a bit of a burn in my muscles from our run, I'm not at all sore. Truth is, I feel really alive.

"Sure," I tell her. "Wish I'd brought my guitar. I love jamming."

She gives me an admiring look. "You play? Cool."

Nobody takes any real notice of us when we approach the campfire, except for a few nods of hello. I like hanging with the surf crowd. They're all so laid-back and easygoing, and this bunch is no exception. They have a nice, relaxed vibe and the music's good. The Dave Matthews song segues into a Beach Boys medley and we all sing along. Everybody breaks up at the end, laughing and clapping. Somebody hands me a beer, but I shake my head.

"I'll have it," Elzie says. "Thanks."

She toasts the guy who gave it to her, then takes a long swallow.

"Anybody else know any more of those old corny songs?" a girl close to the fire asks.

"I bet Josh here does," Elzie says.

"I just know instrumentals," I protest.

I get a guitar put in my hands all the same. This little Yamaha acoustic's way different from my Les Paul, but I give it a go, starting out with "Walk, Don't Run," sliding into the theme from the old Batman TV show with everybody shouting "Batman!" at the appropriate place and ending with "Wipe Out." I have to laugh as everybody plays on the drum solo, using their thighs, the backs of other guitars, the logs they're sitting on.

When I'm done, I pass the guitar on to a girl who does a low, husky-voiced version of a Jewel song.

Later, when things are winding down, Elzie and I go walking along the tide line. She's still in her bare feet. I've taken off my runners, tied the laces and let the shoes dangle over my shoulder. The water's cold, but it feels good on my feet. Out in the distance, we can see the lights of a freighter going by.

"I'm curious about something," she says.

I turn to look at her.

"Were you listening to The Wild Surf when you changed?"

"How would you know that?"

"The paper said that when you disappeared your computer was on their site and the police thought you might've taken off to go to one of their shows."

"I was just listening to demos of their new album," I tell her.

"Did you know that they're all Wildlings?"

"That can't be true."

"Totally is. I heard they were going to change their name to The Wildlings, but I guess they smartened up in time."

"But they've been around since long before people started changing."

"Maybe what happened to me happened to them when they had a gig here. Or maybe they're old school like Cory. Born that way."

"How do you know they're Wildlings?"

"From time to time we have these ... they're kind of like raves. Sometimes back in the hills. Sometimes in an empty warehouse. I don't know who puts them on, but the word gets out and people show up. A few weeks ago, I found a very drunk La Bamba staggering around the parking area after one of them."

"He is *such* a great guitarist."

"Well, he was a real pukemeister that night. God, he was drunk. I found his car and drove him home, and he told me his whole life story on the way." She laughs. "He probably still doesn't remember how he got home."

I think about her telling me all this. Is she telling other Wildlings about me?

"I thought Wildlings weren't supposed to out each other."

"Just not to humans. And even if I didn't tell you, you'd have known as soon as you met any of them. When you get up close, how can you not know? The only thing that might throw you off is if you knew the person before you changed. They'd still smell the same—nothing would be different. They'd probably have to tell you before you could figure it out on your own."

"I told my friends Marina and Desmond about you," I admit. "I wasn't thinking and I didn't expect to see you again."

"Do you trust them?"

I nod.

"Then it's cool."

"Just like that?"

A little smirk plays at the corners of her mouth. "Well," she drawls, "I know where you live ..."

We drive back to where Elzie first brought me to the car, a couple of blocks away from my house.

"So that was an interesting night," she says as she shuts off the engine.

She rests her forehead against the steering wheel.. "I still can't believe Danny went over to the dark side."

"I put my hand on her shoulder. Are you going to be okay?"

She turns her face toward me and smiles. "I liked Danny and I'm disappointed that he abandoned us the way he did, but it's not the end of my world. And except for that part of the night, I really enjoyed myself."

"Me, too."

I don't want to take my hand away.

She studies me for a moment. "Are you going to school tomorrow?"

I nod, thinking vaguely about that history essay that I never finished.

"Well, that's still hours away," she says.

She leans over and kisses me, long and hard. When she breaks off, I have to catch my breath. Remember that whole heightened senses thing? Mine just went into overdrive and I feel like I'm vibrating all over.

"Wow," I say.

"You want to make out?" she asks.

She pulls her shirt over her head before I can answer and squeezes between the seats to get into the back area of the Taurus.

I think, this car's parked here on the street where anybody can just walk by and see us. But it's four in the morning and right at this moment I don't care who might come walking by. I also no longer care about my essay. I wriggle my own way between the seats. As soon as I get back there, she puts her arms around my neck and pulls me down for another long kiss. She grins when we stop to get some air and looks down at the bulge in my pants.

"I think someone's happy to see me," she says, reaching down.

It just gets better from there.

෨ඐ

"Don't worry," she says later when we're lying side by side, her hand casually draped over my stomach. "This isn't going to tie you down into some kind of monogamous relationship."

"How do you know I don't want that?"

"I don't. I just know that I—"

"Don't have time for boyfriends," I finish for her.

"Exactly. Especially right now."

"What are you going to do?"

She shrugs. "I don't know. Go underground for a while, I guess. But right now you need to scoot. I have to get this car off the street in case the police are looking for it."

"I thought you said Danny wouldn't mind your using it."

"That was when I still thought we were rescuing him. Now all bets are off."

I want to say, will I see you again? But it'll probably sound dorky to her.

I wriggle into my pants and pull my shirt on over my head.

"Be careful," I say.

"Always." She grabs my chin and kisses me. "Just because I'm not looking for a boyfriend doesn't mean I don't really like you. You know that, right?"

"I do now."

She kisses me again, then gives me a little push.

"Now you really have to go," she says.

I only sleep for a couple of hours after I get home, but I don't feel at all tired when I get up in the morning. Mom gives me a look when I come into the kitchen after my shower, humming a Ventures tune.

"Somebody's in a good mood," she says.

"I'm just happy to get my life back, I guess."

She nods. "Or could it have something to do with you getting in at five this morning?"

Uh-oh. Busted. But she goes on before I can figure out how to explain.

"I know you've had a rough couple of days," she says, "so I'm not going to call you on this. I trust you enough to know that you must have felt it was important. But this is a one-time reprieve—understand? Pull something like this again, buster—especially on a school night—and you'll be grounded until you forget what it was ever like to be allowed out of the house."

"You're really not going to grill me?"

"Did you do anything for which you should feel ashamed?"

"I didn't do anything that you haven't done yourself."

"Well, then, let's just leave it at this. The next time you feel the need to leave the house in the middle of the night, you come see me first. Deal?"

"Deal," I say.

The next day at school goes much better than my first day back did. I haven't completely reclaimed my usual anonymity, but people are moving on to other things and I don't feel quite so much like the zoo monkey in his cage. At lunch I tell Marina and Desmond about my night—though I don't go so far as talking about what happened in the back seat of Danny's car.

Marina shakes her head. "I told you she was trouble."

"What's that supposed to mean?"

"Hello? Breaking into a government facility?"

"We didn't."

"But you would have if that Cory guy hadn't come along."

"If those agents had grabbed me," I say, "I'd sure appreciate somebody making the effort to get me out."

Desmond nods. "Dude, you have such an awesome life now. You're like freaking James Bond."

"It's not like that," I tell him.

"No," Marina says. "It's really really dangerous."

"I know," I say. "Trust me. I know just how dangerous it is."

She shakes her head. "I don't think you do. I only hope you don't ever find out."

"Listen, I was warned about stuff by Cory right after I changed. So I found out then."

"Well, if I were all wired up for a big rescue last night," Desmond says, "I'd be feeling let down after."

I shake my head. "No, in real life you'd feel relieved—just like I did. But the night wasn't a total washout. When we got back to the car, we went down to the beach where a bunch of surfers were having a campfire. We sat around with them for awhile, singing songs and stuff."

Marina perks up some. "Anybody we know?"

"No, but they were a nice bunch. Now here comes the cruncher. I didn't know it, but my mom heard me coming in. When I saw her this morning, she totally busted me for sneaking out."

Desmond shakes his head. "Dude, are you telling me that you've got this awesome mountain lion thing going for you, but now you're grounded for like forever?"

"That's the thing. She said she knows I've had a rough couple of days, so she gave me a one-time-only free pass."

Desmond puts his hand up for a high-five.

"You are golden," he says as I slap his hand.

"Unless I pull the same thing again. Then my ass is grass."

"Are we practicing tonight?" Marina asks.

"Why don't we go to the skate park first?" Desmond says. "Everybody cool with that?"

❧

My phone vibrates in my pocket as Marina, Desmond and I walk out the front door of Sunny Hill at the end of the day. It's a text from Elzie: *Wanna hang?*

"You guys mind if Elzie tags along?" I ask.

I catch Marina's frown, but all she says is, "Has she got a board?"

"I can lend her my spare."

She rolls her eyes at that.

"Come on," I say. "Give her a chance."

When she puts her hands up in surrender and nods, I turn to Desmond.

"This isn't going to be a boyfriend-girlfriend thing, is it?" he asks. "Because that leaves Marina and me as the other couple."

Marina makes gagging sounds.

"Nice," he says.

"No, we'll just hang," I assure them.

"What the hell," Desmond says. "I'd like to check out the hot Rasta Wildling."

Marina and I both shush him at the same time.

"What?" he says. "Oh yeah." He looks around. "It's cool. Nobody's listening."

"You have to be more careful," Marina says. "If you out somebody, it won't be a joke. You could be screwing up their whole life."

"I know, I know. But why can't this be a cool thing? If it was me and I had to keep it a secret, I think I'd explode."

"I know what you mean," I say as I text Elzie back. "It shouldn't have to be a secret."

My phone vibrates almost as soon as I've sent the text. I smile when I read her reply. *Kiss kiss. c u @ your place.*

I know I shouldn't read too much into it, but I can't help but get a little buzz.

"What's with the goofy grin?" Desmond asks. Then he shakes his head. "Aw, man. Did she just sext you? Tell me she didn't just send you a naked picture of herself."

"Mind out of the gutter," I tell him.

Marina just shakes her head. I hope my being a Wildling isn't what's distancing her. She's hard to read these days.

MARINA

I'm glad to grab an hour at home before we meet up at the skate park. I need a distraction from the Josh-and-Elzie thing anyway.

I haven't had time in the past couple of days to work on my blog and with so many kids following me, I sort of feel like I've been abandoning them. Not that all of them are Wildlings, but even so, it's better to give some genuine perspective on what it's like to have changed than what the media's been putting out. That's been getting worse every day.

It's pretty amazing how alone being a Wildling can make you feel. Maybe I'm nuts to post on the Net about it, but I've been careful to cover my tracks, and what I'm writing is obviously helping some kids who've been having a rough time.

It became pretty clear when I started that a lot of them didn't have the benefit of someone like Jez or Chaingang to give them advice. I'm kind of trying to fill that gap.

What worries me is that I think some of the kids who've posted comments regularly have since disappeared. At least, they're not posting comments on my page anymore. Those government ads give me the creeps. And now, hearing about how this guy Danny turned out to be a traitor, I figure it won't hurt to give kids another warning about not necessarily trusting other Wildlings.

So I dash off a quick couple of paragraphs—not naming any names, of course— and take another ten minutes to respond to some of the latest comments.

Then it's time to head for the skate park.

I tilt my head from side to side trying to get the tightness out of my shoulders. I knew this was coming—that sooner or later I'd have to witness Josh and Elzie up close and personal. But I didn't think it would happen this fast. I roll down the street, my wheels skimming along on the smooth pavement. As they say, know your enemy.

That's not really fair, but it feels like it's true all the same.

JOSH

I see a girl with a short buzz cut waiting out in front of my house when I turn the corner onto my street. She's wearing a Big Daddy Roth T-shirt, a jean miniskirt and short pink cowboy boots. It takes me a moment to realize it's Elzie.

"What happened to your hair?"

She shrugs. "I needed a new look. What do you think?"

"You look great. But what happened to lying low? Isn't the FBI still looking for you?"

"Hence the disguise," she says.

"But those dreads. They were so serious."

"It's just hair. I can grow them back." She hugs me and gives me a quick peck on the cheek. "Did you miss me?" Before I can answer, she adds, "Because I missed you."

I blink in surprise and she raises an eyebrow.

"I'm confused," I tell her. "I mean, yeah, of course I missed you. But I thought—where are we going with this?"

"I don't know. Let's just see where it takes us. Are you okay with that?"

The whole day I've been up and down. Buzzed because of the amazing night we had, bummed because I thought I was maybe never going to see her again. And now here she is, acting like my girlfriend. I don't know what to think. But I'm not about to walk away from her.

"Of course I'm okay with it." I clear my throat. "So do you want to use my spare board?"

She nods. "But my moves are going to be a bit rusty."

"Nobody's going to care," I tell her. "We just skate to have fun."

With the way Marina's been acting lately, I'm nervous when we get to the park. Normally, I'd never worry about how she'll be around people, but she's got such a bee in her bonnet about Elzie that I'm half-expecting fireworks when I introduce the two of them. But something funny happens. They say hello and shake hands, then they just stand there, still holding hands, looking like they're trying to read each other's mind. Finally, a little smile tugs up the corner of Elzie's mouth and they step apart.

"Nice boots," Marina says. "Where'd you get them?"

"The thrift shop."

"No way. Those are Fluevogs. They're worth a fortune."

"You can get all kinds of deals there," Elzie says. "You just have to go in on a regular basis. Let me know if there's anything you're looking for and I'll keep an eye out for it."

I sigh with relief. If they're talking shoes, it's going to be okay.

Desmond wheels up and pops his board.

"This is Desmond," I say. "And this is Elzie."

Desmond gets a puzzled look. "What happened to the dreads? I thought you were a Rasta girl."

Elzie shoots me an amused look. "I was never a Rasta girl."

"Don't mind him," Marina says. "He always has to reduce everything to its most basic element. Since your dreads are gone and you've got a board, he's probably going to start calling you skater chick."

Desmond sticks his nose in the air in an exaggerated pose. "Would not."

Marina looks at him. "So you don't call me drummer girl when you're hanging with your skater buddies at school?"

"Are we going to talk," Desmond says, "or are we going to skateboard?"

We skateboard.

There's always someone with an iPod dock blasting out music here. Right now it's cranked to an old Jay-Z song. We couldn't be farther from

New York City than we are at this moment, but everybody sings along with Alicia Keys on the chorus.

I ask Elzie at one point what happened there when she and Marina were first saying hello.

"Girl stuff," she says and that's all I can get out of her.

But later on I see the two of them, heads together, having what looks like a serious conversation. This time I don't ask.

MARINA

As much as I don't want to like Elzie, I can't help but feel her charisma as soon as she grasps my hand. Worse, as soon as she looks at me, I just know that she can see the otter sitting under my skin. My pulse goes into double time, like my big bass drum is pounding right inside my chest. I'm so sure she's going to out me to Josh and Desmond, but she's cool enough to not blow my cover and never says a word. Her eyes just flicker with recognition, but the expression's gone so quickly that I doubt Josh has noticed anything unusual. Unless, that is, two girls holding hands for this long makes him wonder if we've got the hots for each other.

I smile to myself. Now wouldn't *that* be ironic?

But of course, it's not that at all.

Later on, we take a breather on one of the benches while the boys are showing off.

"How did you know about ... you know?" I ask.

"That you're a Wildling?"

I nod.

"I just did. It's like I get a little *ping* in my head whenever I meet someone who's got an animal skin under their human one."

"It just happens?"

She shrugs. "You have to learn to pay attention and work at it a bit, but it'll come quick. Any Wildling can do it."

"I don't know ..."

"Trust me," she says. When I still look dubious, she adds, "Have you never gotten a little twinge at the back of your neck when you first met someone, or even just saw someone?"

"I guess that happened earlier, when we met. I didn't realize it was because you're a Wildling."

"Well, that's your animal self sending you a message. And now you know what it means."

"Can Josh do it?"

"Sure. To some degree."

"Then how come he doesn't know about me?"

"He's too close to you. Your smell is familiar to him. If he concentrated, he might figure it out, but he doesn't try because he knows you so well. Maybe if you'd changed after him, he'd notice, but you've been a Wildling for a while. He'll pick up on it a lot quicker with strangers than with anyone he knows."

Okay, I think. So I'm safe for now.

"But now I've got a question," Elzie says. "I got the impression from Josh that you guys are all really tight. So why haven't you told him?"

"It's complicated," I say. "I don't know. All the negative crap on the news and stuff about Wildlings had me scared, I guess. Especially about Desmond. You can see that he's a doll, but he's not exactly the most inhibited person on the planet. He's hot-wired for excitement. Fun as hell to hang out with, but a bit unpredictable when it comes to keeping secrets."

"Okay, but why not tell Josh? He's so cool. You must know that he'd be totally down with it."

Elzie's persistence forces me to think fast. I don't want to reveal my true feelings toward Josh, so I do my best to brush her off.

"Yeah, but we're like The Gang of Three, you know? It wouldn't be fair to tell Josh and not Des. I was going to get around to it sooner or later, but the time just never seemed right and now that Josh has changed ... well, I'm kind of screwed. He told Des and me right away, so I know he'll be pissed as hell that I didn't do the same."

"You've probably got that right, girlfriend," she says, giving me a quick one-armed hug. "Hey, don't worry. Your secret's safe with me. I wouldn't want to get in the middle of this one anyway. Way too messy for me."

Then she tosses her head back as if she's still got a mass of dreads and gives a little laugh. "Let's not give the boys any more suspicions about our girlish love than they already have."

She flips the board back on the ground and zooms back over to Josh, giving him a swaggery little hip action on her dismount followed by a playful smooch. Her tongue darts into his mouth and I see him almost shudder with pleasure.

This is going to be hard.

JOSH

It just seems natural that we all grab a bite together after and that Elzie comes along to our band practice.

I take Marina aside before we go in the garage.

"She's not going to Yoko Ono the band," I say.

"Relax, Josh. I like her."

"You do?"

"What's not to like? She's smart and funny and I'll bet she doesn't take crap from anybody. And besides, if she's part of your life now, then she's part of mine, too."

I feel my whole body relax. This is more the Marina I know.

"She's probably not even going to stick around that long," I say. "She told me she doesn't want a relationship right now."

Marina just gives me a look. "Are you kidding? Do you see the way she looks at you? The girl's smitten."

"Smitten?" I laugh. "I don't think I've ever heard that word said aloud."

She punches me in the arm.

Elzie turns around from where she's walking with Desmond.

"What are you guys talking about?" she asks.

"How I need to smite him," Marina says.

Elzie laughs. "Oh yeah. We do have to keep 'em in line, don't we?"

We hang out together all weekend. Mom likes Elzie right off the bat. Marina manages to hold any remaining reservations she has at bay. And Desmond ... well, he's just Desmond. So long as there's no drama, everybody's his friend.

It's a bit strange. I'm not complaining, but for a girl who didn't want any commitment, Elzie's pretty steadfast. Every day at the end of school, she's waiting for us outside. Sometimes the four of us go do something as a group, sometimes Elzie and I go off on our own. It's all good. Better than good. I'm even starting to relax about the whole Wildling thing. At least I am until we all go to the skate park the next Friday—the four of us, along with Cindy Hudson, a blonde surfer girl that Desmond met in Pages Café & Used Books over on Main Street.

We're laughing and joking as we make our way to the skate park, but when we get there, nobody's on their boards. The place is silent. Everybody's standing around like they're in shock—the way it must have been when John Lennon or Kurt Cobain died.

"What's going on?" Desmond asks Kevin Blain, who's just sitting on his board, staring at nothing.

Kevin doesn't answer, but his older brother David does.

"You know your buddy Mike Castle?" he says.

Desmond frowns. "Castle the Asshole's no buddy of mine."

Last summer we were hanging around at the end of the pier when we saw Castle hassling Clarence Dooley—this old guy who likes to walk his cat along the boardwalk in a baby carriage. He might not be all there, but he's harmless. Castle had taken the carriage from Dooley and kept pushing him away from it. Dooley looked like he was about to cry by the time we got over there.

"That's enough," Desmond told Castle. "Leave him alone."

"Why? What are you going to—"

He never got to finish. Desmond just hauled off and punched him in the face. Before you knew it, he had Castle on the ground and was pounding away on him until me and a couple of guys pulled him off. I'd never seen Des lose it like that before. When I asked him what happened, he could only shake his head.

"Dude, I have no idea," he'd said. "I just saw Castle pushing Dooley around and I saw red. I mean, everything really just went red."

"So what did he do?" Desmond asks David now.

"He took his dad's .22 up under the freeway with Brian Canfield and they killed Laura Connor with it."

"*What?*"

"The cops showed up because somebody'd complained about hearing shooting. When they got there, they found the two of them standing over

Laura and she's lying on the ground with a bullet in her head. And get this. She was naked."

A couple comes up while he's telling us this. Todd Copley and Juanita Herrera. I know them from school.

"What I heard," Todd says, "is that they were fooling around trying to shoot birds, then he shot a rat up on the embankment, but when it fell back to where they were standing, it was Laura."

Juanita's got a tight grip on his arm.

"Jesus," Desmond says.

Marina and Elzie are white with shock. Marina's trembling. I put my arms around both of them. I want to say something comforting, but I feel sick myself. Desmond holds Cindy, who's starting to cry.

"Man, I *knew* her," Kevin says from where he's sitting on his board. "I used to think about asking her out ..."

We all knew her. Everyone kind of knows everyone around here—in a town of twenty thousand people, that just happens. Not that we knew her really well, but she was on the girls' volleyball team and she often came down to the pier when we were all hanging around. A tall lanky girl with a bright smile and a big laugh.

David shakes his head. "I can't believe Laura was a Wildling."

"If she even was," Desmond says. When everybody looks at him, he adds, "Come on. This is Mike Castle we're talking about. I wouldn't put anything past him. And Canfield's not much better."

People start talking about stuff Castle and Canfield have done in the past, and how well they did or didn't know Laura, and how if you're going to be a Wildling, it's pretty lame being stuck as a rat. I feel Elzie's shoulders stiffen under my arm.

"I'm out of here," she says.

"Yeah, can we just go?" Marina adds.

I nod. "Des?" I say.

"On it," he says.

He takes Cindy by the hand and we leave. The others are so busy with what they're talking about I don't think they even notice us going.

"I didn't mean to set that off," Desmond says when we're walking away.

"You didn't," Elzie tells him. "It's just the way people are."

He looks at his feet. "Guys like Castle really push my buttons."

Elzie nudges Des with the tip of my spare board.

"We're cool," she says.

∽❧

"I can't stop thinking about Laura," I say later that night.

We gave up on band practice and we're all hanging around in Desmond's back yard. Our hearts just weren't in it and we were playing like crap.

"Do you think she was happy being a rat?" Desmond asks.

He's stretched out on a patio couch, his head in Cindy's lap. Marina's sitting cross-legged on one of the patio chairs. Elzie and I are slouched on two more, holding hands in the space between our chairs.

"Do you mean having a rat as her Wildling shape?" Marina asks.

"Yeah. If it happened to me, I'd be majorly disappointed. Like when you consider all the cool animals you could be ..." He shrugs. "I don't know. I'd just feel cheated."

"I think rats are cute," Cindy says. "Not the scuzzy ones that live in storm drains and stuff, but the kind you get from a pet store. I had pet rat when I was a kid and I just loved him."

We all look at her.

"Well, I did."

It's been different having someone hanging with us who doesn't know the secret that Elzie and I are carrying. We find ourselves talking around the simplest things, having to be careful we don't say something that'll give us away. I like Cindy, but having her here gives me a whole new respect for those spandexed superheroes with their secret identities.

"I'd think," Elzie says, "that you'd end up embracing whatever your animal spirit was."

Marina nods.

"Because no matter what it was," Elzie goes on, "it would still be a gift. It wouldn't make any difference how small or insignificant your animal shape might seem from the outside. Or what kind of a bad rep it has in terms of how people look at you."

That's when I remember that I have no idea what kind of Wildling Elzie is. I keep meaning to ask her, but I only think of it when she's not around. What if she's something small like Laura was and somebody takes a potshot at *her*?

"Do you really think it's a gift?" Cindy asks. "Wouldn't it just make your life a complicated mess—and I'm not talking about what happened to poor Laura. I mean the general day-to-day business of living."

"Life's probably always going to be complicated," Marina says. "It doesn't matter if you're a Wildling or an ordinary teenager."

"I suppose," Cindy says, but she doesn't look convinced.

MARINA

What happened to Laura changes the whole weekend. Where normally we practice at least a couple of times—we've had some of our best practices on Sunday afternoons—we don't take our instruments out again. We don't go skateboarding or even hang out together. I think Desmond spends at least Saturday night with Cindy. I don't know what Josh does. He's probably hanging out with Elzie.

It's not like I was best friends with Laura, but the shock and the senselessness of how she died really gets to me.

On Saturday I spend most of my time alone in my room. Mamá has tried to talk to me about what happened to Laura, but nothing she says helps. I know she really believes that God called Laura home and now she's up in heaven with Our Lady of Grace and Los Santos—but you can't tell me that this wasn't way before her time. I keep going back and forth between being really angry and really sad.

A few of my blog subscribers knew Laura pretty well, so they're a mess, just trying to deal. I wish I could say or do something concrete to help them. I wish I could turn back time and save Laura.

In the end, all I can do is monitor the comments—listen, sympathize and remind people to try to stay safe. It doesn't seem like enough.

I wake up just before dawn on Sunday and decide to check out the waves with my board. I walk down the street away from my house, heading for the boardwalk. I feel as though a mental fog is lifting. I love this time of day. It's so full of possibilities. There's just me and the other early birds—a handful of joggers, a few surfers on the far side of the pier, people walking their dogs, the old Chinese man who does his Tai Chi on the beach every morning, no matter what day of the week it is.

I'm wearing my wetsuit with the top unzipped and rolling my surfboard behind me. I go south, as far as I can get from the pier without trespassing on government land. The swells are small, but I just want to get out into the water and be by myself.

It's going to be a beautiful day. There's still a bit of the night's coolness in the air, but I can tell by the sky that it's going to be clear and sunny. And hot. But right now I need my wetsuit. I zip up and kick off my sneakers. The sand is cool and grainy against my soles. I'm just about to head down to the water when I hear footsteps behind me.

"Hey, sweetcheeks."

I turn around to find Chaingang crossing the beach toward me and I have to shake my head. Only *he* would be wearing a pair of shades at this time of day. If I didn't know he was a Wildling, I'd be wondering how he can even see with those on in this poor light.

"Don't call me that," I tell him when he reaches me.

He pauses, then smiles. "Why not? You don't think you're some tough chica like your sister, do you?"

"How would *you* know?" I'm acting like a jerk, but I can't seem to help myself.

He lowers his shades and studies me for a long moment. I know it's just one of his poses, but I can't help but feel like he's giving me his full attention all the same.

"You're right," he says. "I don't."

"Maybe I'm just as tough as her. Maybe I'm tougher."

He nods. "Yeah, you probably are."

"What are you doing here anyway?"

Another pause. "I thought we should talk."

"About what?"

"Me reaching out to Josh. I started to think later that maybe you might've wanted to do that yourself."

When I shake my head, he lifts his eyebrows.

"You're not planning to tell him, are you?" he says.

"It's awkward. How am I supposed to explain why I didn't tell him earlier?"

"The longer you wait, the harder it's going to get."

"You think I don't know that?"

He holds his hands up, palms out.

"I didn't come to fight," he says. "Or point a finger. I just came to apologize if I stepped over the line."

I really don't get Chaingang. He's done time, then went right back to the gang when he got out of juvie. Yet, when he talks to me, all of that seems to fall away to reveal some sensitive guy and it just doesn't compute with that other stuff. Plus I can't seem to bury this weird resentment that he's going all sweet and sensitive with Josh, too. I know I should be okay with it, but I'm not. I don't know why.

"You didn't," I tell him.

"So we're good."

"Sure. Now I'm going to catch some waves."

I turn without waiting for his reply and head for the water. I can feel him just standing where I left him, watching me go, but I don't look back. I paddle out to where I can catch one of the little swells. When I turn around and look at the beach again, he's gone.

JOSH

The aftermath of the shooting seems to leave a pall over all of Santa Feliz. Elzie is restless, so we do a lot of walking. She says it helps ground her. I find it does the same for me, too.

On Sunday evening we've wandered up as far as the old Santa Feliz Beach Boardwalk, which is an abandoned amusement park north of the pier. We sit on a bench and look through the chain-link fence at the old rusting Ferris wheel, the Tilt-a-Whirl and the other rides. There's something both sad and fascinating about the place. Every kid who lives in Santa Feliz has snuck in at one point or another, but once you're inside, it's a bit of a disappointment. The rides are small, everything's broken down and there's scrap lying around everywhere. It's only when you're looking at it from the outside that it holds on to any of its faded glamour. Especially at night, when it's all just dark shapes against the sky.

"I'm not sure of the protocol here," I say to Elzie, "so don't get mad at me if I step out of line."

She gives me a curious look.

"I was just wondering what kind of animal you are," I say.

"Why? Are you afraid I'm a rat?"

"No, no. I'm with you and Marina on this. I think we appreciate whatever we get—once we get over the shock of it happening in the first place. But it's going to be more dangerous to be some shapes than others, don't you think?"

"Because of what happened to Laura Connor."

I nod. "When you're her size, how are you supposed to defend yourself against a guy with a gun?"

"So you're worried about me."

"I know you can take care of yourself. It's just ... yeah, I guess I'm sort of worried."

"I think that's sweet."

I sigh.

She bumps her shoulder against mine. "There's nothing wrong with being sweet."

"I thought girls liked the bad boys."

"Not me. And since you asked, I'm a jaguarundi."

"A jaguar-what?"

"A jaguarundi. I'd never heard of it before, either. It's like a big cat that likes to swim. Sort of a smaller version of a mountain lion—except for the swimming part."

"*My* animal shape is a mountain lion."

She smiles. "I know."

"So we're compatible."

"We're compatible on a lot of counts—don't you think?" she says with a wink.

"I ... yeah. Yeah, I do."

Except I'm still confused about how she doesn't want to actually call our relationship a relationship. Though maybe that's my fault, too. I haven't actually said anything to her since she first told me she didn't want any kind of commitment and then it turns out she wants to hang around with me every day. Right now doesn't seem like a good time to get into it.

"What happened to Laura," she says. "That was just a horrible, tragic fluke. It's hard to accept it happened, but I don't think those boys were deliberately going after Wildlings."

"I guess not. It's weird. I'm the Wildling and Des isn't, but I think he's more pissed off than I am. I'm just sad. A little freaked out, but mostly sad. I mean, she was our age and she had the whole Wildling thing thrown at her, which is tough enough. But then this happens."

She squeezes my hand. "Sad's exactly what it is."

We sit for a while, looking at the shadowed rides on the other side of the fence. The roller coaster's like an old *Mario Brothers* video game compared to the *Halo* of the roller coasters they have in amusement parks today, and the Ferris wheel only has fourteen or fifteen cars that don't go much higher than thirty feet. But I remember climbing to the top one time and sitting up there in a chair, rocking back and forth, the whole beach spread out before me all the way down to the pier and beyond. I may not have been very high up, but I felt like I was on the top of the world.

"I bet this place was cool in its day," she says. "Cheesy, but cool."

"My mom says we came here when I was a kid," I say. "When I was five or six."

"Do you remember it?"

I shake my head. "Not really. I get confused between my maybe memories of it and similar places I've seen in movies and on TV."

She smiles. "I never went, but my dad has a photo album of when he worked here as a teenager."

She sighs then and I realize that talking about her dad reminds her of how her family turned their back on her.

"So this whole business of shifting from one shape to another," I say, to change the subject. "How do you think it works?"

"What do you mean? You just decide which you want to be—human or animal—and there you go."

"No, I mean the physics of it. Cory told me that if you don't concentrate on what you're wearing, when you change back to your human shape, you're buck naked."

"That happens to all of us at first."

I nod. "But how does it all *work*?"

"I don't think science has anything to do with it," she says. "The government researchers think it must have something to do with genetics, but apparently they can't find anything unusual in our DNA. Cory talks about old bloodlines, but I don't think he means that literally—it's more that we inherited these animal souls or whatever. Auntie Min says it must be a gift from the Thunders—you know, the old-time mystery gods.

"Me ... I think something magic came here to Santa Feliz," Elzie continues. "Some spirit or force decided to connect a bunch of us with our animal brothers and sisters. And now it's our responsibility to share what we learn with the rest of the world."

"How does that fit in with getting rid of all the humans?" I have to ask.

"You're never going to let that go, are you?"

She doesn't look mad like she did when we first met on the pier, but I still feel the need to let her know I'm not starting an argument.

"I'm just trying to understand," I say. "That's all."

"Me too," she says. "I know things are messed up and I know we have to fix them, but I don't know how we're ever going to do it."

"I get that," I tell her.

"At least the ferals are trying to do something about it," she says.

"I know. I just don't think their plan is necessarily the best way."

"I have my own reservations."

I wonder how people let the world get to where it is now. Greed, power and religion, I guess. Even the hippie generation managed to screw it up, most of them ditching their peace, love and flowers ideals in favour of personal wealth and comfort. I'd like to say I'd do better, but my carbon footprint's nothing to be proud of.

This is depressing, so I change the subject again.

"The first time I met Cory," I say, "he did this thing where he was still human, but he had a coyote's head."

"I've seen a hawk Wildling do that, too. It's kind of creepy."

"Yeah. But I wonder if *we* can do that."

She laughs. "You are such a boy."

Okay, I've managed to change the mood, but I'm not sure I want her laughing at me.

"I just think it's interesting," I say. "And being able to freak people out with a Wildling head on a human body might give you an advantage if you were cornered or something."

"So long as they don't have a gun."

"Sure. But it makes you think, what else can we do? If it's all about magic, then it seems like anything's possible."

"There are probably rules."

"Yeah," I say. "There are *always* rules."

She nods. "Like having to eat after a change. I can't believe how hungry I get."

We fall silent again. The traffic from town seems very far away. There's just us and the deserted rides in the amusement park. Waves lapping against the shore. I love that sound. It's the soundtrack to my life. Lying in bed with my window open at night, the beach is close enough that I can hear them roll in as I fall asleep.

"Do you want to know the only magic I know?" Elzie says.

I turn to her. "Sure."

"You and me."

She slips her hands around my waist then onto my butt and pulls me in for a long kiss.

"How's that for magic?" she murmurs.

"The best kind," I tell her.

91

That night I Google jaguarundi. I look at pictures and they do look something like a mountain lion. They have short legs, long bodies, long thick tails and flattish heads with small rounded ears. None of that says Elzie to me, but when I look in a mirror, I don't see a mountain lion—except for that one time when I watched myself change, and that's not the same thing at all. Jaguarundis are good climbers, great swimmers and they're active during the day. They're also an endangered species, which brings back my nervousness.

I remind myself of what Elzie told me—that it was just a fluke that Laura got shot—but it's not particularly comforting. I mean, how do you prevent something so random? The only way you could fully protect yourself would be to never leave your house. That wouldn't work for Elzie because she doesn't have a house and she wouldn't stay in it twenty-four/seven if she did.

That gets me wondering about where Elzie *does* stay. She's always clean and dresses with style—thrift shop style, but she looks good. How do you manage that if you live on the street?

So where *does* she live? How can I not know where my sort-of girlfriend lives? What does she do when we aren't together?

I could drive myself crazy with these questions. I know that. But I also know myself well. Now that they're on my mind, I can't let them go.

I switch from the Google window to check my email. All the usual spam. The only interesting thing is an update from my Wild Surf subscription telling me they have a new demo up on their site, but I don't feel like listening to it at the moment.

I'm about to shut off my computer when I remember what Marina said about using the Internet to find some more info about Wildlings. I type "Wildlings" into the Google window and about a million entries come up. Most links on the first few pages are about what happened to Laura. That's the last thing I need to read right now. There's got to be something about Wildlings that doesn't focus on the shooting or link to that hawk video. I try adding "blog" to the search and my screen still fills up with way too many entries. They all seem to be about Laura, too.

It's late. I should just go to bed. I glance down the screen, scanning until a LiveJournal link makes me stop. The title of the blog is *My Life as an Otter*, which is just charming enough to catch my attention, so I click on it. The profile picture shows a pen and ink drawing of an otter. It takes me a moment to recognize it. I go over to the handful of books I've had since I was little and pull out a well-worn copy of *The Wind in the Willows*.

Sitting on my bed, I flip through the pages until I come to the image I'm looking for. I glance at my computer screen. The profile picture is a detail from the illustration in the book I'm holding.

The blogger's user name is Nira. If I were Sherlock Holmes, I'd deduce that somewhere in Santa Feliz, there's a teenager named Nira who's an otter Wildling and likes *The Wind in the Willows*—the original, judging from the illustration she used for her profile picture. Judging by the name, I'm guessing the author's a she, but I suppose Nira could be a guy's name, too.

There are links to other blogs. "Wildling Words." "Where the Wild Things Dream." "Cousins' Corner." "I Am a Teenage Wildling." I opt to stay on this page and read through Nira's post.

This will sound terrible, but as sad and horrified as I am about Laura Connor's death, one of the first things I thought afterward was here we go again. Yet more focus on the negative aspects of Wildlings.

The news media and blogosphere are already rampant with it:

When did Laura Connor become a Wildling?

Did anyone close to her know?

Why would she "choose" to be a rat?

Does this mean there are other Wildling vermin out there?

Why didn't she turn herself in to the government? She could have prevented this tragedy.

Should the government step in and put them all in camps?

And only later, questions more specific to this tragedy:

Did the boys know Laura was a Wildling?

Why would parents let teenagers out with a .22 rifle?

Could this be part of some gangster war—a settling of accounts between rival Wildling factions?

It's always bad stuff that makes the news. An attack, a tragic death, or more fear and speculation on the danger/cause/weirdness of it all.

Nobody ever talks about what an opportunity it is.

This is our first real chance to get some understanding and insight into the animal world. But lots of people don't want to see that happen. I'm not just talking about the religious Right and all those nut jobs that can't stand change. There's the whole meat industry, for starters. If you can have a conversation with an animal, can you really then turn around and eat it? Or the NRA. Give up hunting and fishing?

Okay, some Wildlings are predators. They eat meat. But I say, so what? Out in the wild, so do bears and mountains lions and wolves and such. The difference is they're killing to survive—it's the natural order of things. They're not killing for fun. For "sport."

The thing is, this is our chance to actually communicate with animals. But do we embrace the opportunity? No. We freak out.

Don't get me wrong. It's an awful awful thing that happened to Laura Connor. But what if those boys who were out shooting birds and rats could have met and talked to her, knowing that her Wildling aspect was a rat? Would they still think shooting rats was fun?

I don't know. I don't know those boys and I don't have any answers.

Right now I just feel sad for Laura and her friends and family. I wish I could have known her as a Wildling and as a girl. But I understand why she hid her animal aspect. And I understand what drove her to go running wild in a place she thought was safe. Sometimes I feel like the otter in me is going to burst out of my skin if I don't find some safe place to let her out.

Take care, my friends. After what happened to Laura, I can only wonder, is any place safe for us?

I know exactly what she means about the otter wanting to burst out of her skin. The mountain lion in me doesn't push and stretch only when I'm scared or angry. It's there all the time. I can feel the way it catches a scent that attracts it, or notices some movement in a hedge or up in the dried fronds of a palm. The way that it yearns to run free. But I don't see how or where I could do that. It's not like I'm something small like a rat or a lizard that nobody's going to notice. And the truth is, I'm a little scared, too. What if I lose control and someone gets hurt? Then I'll be just another one of those negative Wildling stories on the news.

I like this blogger. I read through what she wrote a second time before I go all the way back to her first post, dated a few months earlier:

The first wave I ever went paddling for, I thought for sure I'd catch it. The procedure seems so simple. Get on your knees, push your shoulders up and slide your body back, spring quickly to your feet, putting them a foot apart and under you in one motion. It's tricky, but doable when you practice on the beach.

But out on the water, that wave just slipped away. By the time I got to my feet, the wave had gone on and I just stood there on my board, slowly sinking into the water. I tried and tried again and, when I finally did catch my first swell, all I could think was, what happened? How'd I do this?

Every surfer goes through those painful days. I don't even recall my first ride very clearly, when the wave pushed me for long enough so that I could actually stand for a few seconds. But I do know that was the day that I got hooked. I think of that whole day as Wave No. 1. I remember lying in my bed that night and reliving the experience. I promised myself that every session I was going to ride at least one swell.

It took awhile, but when I finally got to the point where I could do just that, I felt so lucky. It made it all worthwhile: the paddle out, the turtle rolls, the constant paddling against the current.

What does any of this have to do with being a Wildling?

Nothing and everything. It took me a long time to get comfortable in this new skin—just like it took me a long time to get comfortable standing on my board, riding a wave to shore. It took me longer to feel lucky that I'm one of the few who, by some fluke of fate, gets to live two lives.

My job now is to integrate them the best I can. To still be a girl when I'm an otter and to let the superior senses and strengths of the otter enhance the girl.

Celebrate who you are, my Wildling friends. Be careful, but be joyful. We've received a tremendous gift.

I sit back and stretch my arms over my head. Well, she's definitely a girl and I think I'd like her even more if we met. We've got a lot in common. She's a Wildling. She's a surfer, so she must dig the whole surf scene. I wonder if she likes surf music. I'll bet Marina knows her and doesn't even realize that she's a Wildling.

Judging from the date of her first post, I see that she's been a Wildling for a relatively long time.

I'd love to know who she is. I want to read more of her blog, but I'll do that tomorrow night. Right now I've got to get to bed. The morning comes awfully quick when you go to sleep this late.

☙❧

Monday morning I find Marina and Desmond waiting for me in front of Desmond's house. I'm still feeling a little off and I guess they are, too, because we're pretty quiet as we make our way to school. We start off walking, carrying our boards.

"Do either of you know a girl named Nira?" I ask after a couple of blocks.

"Who's she?" Desmond asks.

"Some girl who's got a blog about what it's like to be a Wildling. One of us probably knows her."

"What makes you say that?" Marina asks.

I shrug. "She's a Wildling, so she has to be from Santa Feliz, and since it's only teenagers who are getting changed, she must go to our school. Where else would she go?"

"You said her name's Nira?"

"Yeah. But she's probably only calling herself that for her blog. It could be anything. She might be on the surf team. Has anyone been acting differently? Kind of, I don't know. Otterish?"

"That's her animal shape?" Desmond asks. "An otter?"

I nod. "A sea otter."

"I can't think of anyone," Marina says. "But I'm sure you're right that she'd use a pseudonym. If she's smart."

"Oh, she's way smart," I say. "I'd love to meet her, so I'm going to keep my eyes open—*and* my Wildling radar."

"That really works?" Desmond asks.

Marina gives me a thoughtful look, but I just shrug.

"Sort of. If she goes to school here, I figure I can find her."

"Unless she's like Elzie," Desmond says. "She could have been visiting and changed, and then gone back to wherever she's from."

"I didn't think of that."

"Which is why I'm the brains of this outfit."

Marina and I both whack him at the same time.

ა~⁊

I'm in English when I hear my name on the school PA system. For a moment, it doesn't register. Then Mr. Cairns tells me I'm excused to go to the office and I realize it was me that was asked to report to Principal Hayden.

I glance at Marina.

"What did you do?" she mouths.

I shake my head. I have no idea.

Everybody stares at me as I leave class and it's a long walk to the office. I feel guilty even though I know I haven't done anything wrong. Then I think of how I talked to Chaingang last week. Maybe one of the teachers noticed and now I'm about to get a lecture on gangs and drugs. They don't try to save the kids who are obviously already lost—like Chaingang—but they're all over anybody else they think is heading for trouble.

When I get to the office, I'm still trying to figure out what I'll say if they ask me about Chaingang. I step up to the counter and the school secretary lifts her head. Mrs. O'Shay usually has a smile for everyone, but right now she looks really serious. This can't be good.

"They're waiting for you in the office, Josh," she says.

They're waiting for me? What they? I assumed I was here to see Principal Hayden. Nobody said anything about a *they*. Of course, nobody said anything about anything.

"Wha—" I have to clear my throat. "What's it all about, Mrs. O'Shay?"

She gives me a sympathetic look, but only says, "You should just go in."

I might have some fierce mountain lion sitting inside me just waiting to pop out of my skin, but my hand's shaking as I turn the knob on the door to Principal Hayden's office. I've only been called to the office once before— when Zane Gibbons and I got caught messing around with firecrackers under the bleachers on the soccer field. Principal Hayden's sitting behind his desk, just as he was that time, but today he looks puzzled instead of pissed off.

A man in a dark suit is standing by the window with his back to me. When he turns, my heart sinks. It's the FBI guy from the pier—the one who went chasing off after Elzie. He smiles at me, but his pale-blue eyes are cold. I get the feeling they don't miss anything and I wonder what they're seeing when he looks at me.

"I'm Agent Matteson," he says.

He doesn't show me his badge, but I guess the school already verified his credentials or he wouldn't be allowed to talk to me. They're pretty hard line about who they let onto the campus.

"And behind you is Agent Solana," Matteson goes on.

When I turn, I see the other agent from the pier—the one who stopped me just before I took off. He doesn't smile, but he doesn't give off the same scary vibe that his partner does.

"You never called," he says.

I go blank until I remember the business card he gave me.

"I didn't have anything to tell you," I say.

Matteson moves from the window and sits on the edge of Principal Hayden's desk. I don't think Principal Hayden likes it, but he doesn't say anything.

"That's what we're having trouble with," Matteson says.

"I don't understand."

"This is serious business. I'd think that as a good citizen, you'd want to help out however you could."

"Help out with what?"

"How about we start with some names?" Solana says from behind me.

"I don't know what you're talking about. What names?"

I look to Principal Hayden for help. He meets my gaze for a moment before he looks away and just sits there with his hands on his desk.

"Of Wildlings," Solana says.

Matteson nods. "That's as good a place to start as any." He takes a pad out of the inner pocket of his suit coat. "Give us a list of all the Wildlings you know."

"I don't know any Wildlings."

"Come on, Saunders," Solana says. "We all know better than that. We saw you hanging out with Elizabeth Moore and Danny Reed down at the pier a few days ago."

Elzie's name is Elizabeth Moore?

"And that's not even taking into account," Matteson adds, "that somebody you know turned into a mountain lion in your house and attacked you."

"I wasn't attacked," I say. "That thing just showed up and I took off. I don't know anything more than that."

"We think you do," Solana says.

Matteson steps up to me. He's tall and broad across the shoulders. He's intimidating and he knows it.

"We know you're involved, kid," he says, "so I'm going to give you a piece of advice. Come clean now, while you can. If you don't, I promise it'll go that much harder on you down the line. Let it go too far and you'll find yourself in a place you don't even want to visit."

I don't reply to him. Instead I turn to Principal Hayden.

"I want my mom to be here," I say. "This isn't right. They're treating me like a criminal and I haven't done anything. Besides, when did Wildlings become against the law?"

"Aw," Matteson says, looking over my head at his partner. "He wants his mommy."

"That's enough," Principal Hayden finally says. "I won't have you threatening or mocking my students."

I see the flash of anger in Matteson's eyes before he shuts it down and smiles. He holds up his hands, palms out.

"Okay," he says. He steps back so that he can look at both the Principal and me. "I was out of line. But that doesn't change the problem we have. Wildlings can be dangerous—we all know that. After what happened to that poor girl last Friday, we're expecting them to deliver some kind of payback. All we're trying to do is stop it before things get out of hand."

"I thought they didn't shoot her on purpose," I say. "I heard it was a rat they shot."

Matteson nods. "A rat that turned into a girl."

"So why would anybody be looking for payback?"

"Think of it this way," Solana says from behind me. "White kid shoots a black kid. Does anybody see it as two kids, or does it become a race thing? Maybe the black kid was a banger that nobody in his community cared for. But if a white kid pulls the trigger, it becomes an issue. That black kid? Now he's a martyr. Next you get protest rallies, everybody up in arms, more violence."

"Do you see where we're going with this?" Matteson asks me.

I shake my head.

"We want to nip this in the bud before anybody else gets hurt."

"But I don't get your logic," I say, "and I don't know any Wildlings."

"Joshua, those kids at the pier ..."

"I didn't know they were Wildlings until you guys went after one and he changed into some kind of a deer. And I never knew the girl with the dreads was one until you just told me."

Matteson looks over my head at his partner, then shrugs.

"You've got Agent Solana's card," he says. "Call him if you change your mind. But don't wait too long. Principal Hayden," he adds with a nod in the Principal's direction.

He gives me a last lingering look, then he and his partner start for the door. I don't follow them out of the office. But I wait until they're gone before I ask Principal Hayden, "Are they allowed to do that?"

He shakes his head. "Agent Matteson was right. He stepped out of line." He hesitates, then asks, "I'm sorry, Josh, but I have to ask. Are you sure you can't tell them anything?"

"I don't *know* any Wildlings."

"I don't think either of those men are bad people," he says. "They appear to be genuinely concerned about preventing more innocent people being hurt."

I nod. I don't believe it, but I don't want to make any waves. I'm feeling lucky that they didn't take me away with them.

"Can I go now?" I ask.

"Of course. Mrs. O'Shay will give you a hall pass."

As soon as I leave the office, I head straight for the boys' washroom. I go into one of the stalls and sit on the seat, my phone in hand. If I get caught doing this, they'll confiscate it—Sunny Hill is really strict about any kind of electronic devices being used inside the school—but I have to get a message to Elzie. Phones are supposed to stay in our lockers, the same as our skateboards. Nobody leaves them there, but we all turn them off so we won't get caught.

I hesitate before writing anything. Can texts be intercepted the way they say calls on a cell phone can? I don't want to take a chance, so I just keep it simple and vague.

dont come 2 school 2day, I thumb. *meet me @ d's.*

But if they're investigating me, they'll be able to figure out that "D" stands for "Desmond." I backspace and change it to *meet me @ the usual.*

We hang out in Desmond's garage a lot of the time, so I'm sure she'll figure it out.

I press "Send," turn off my phone and stick it in my pocket. Then I flush like I had some real business in here and leave the washroom, heading for my class. The bell rings almost as soon as I take my seat again.

৩৵৻

"What was that all about?" Marina asks as we leave Mr. Cairns's classroom.

I shake my head. There are too many other kids close by, just as curious as she is about why I got called to the office.

"I'll tell you at lunch," I say.

"But—"

"Not now. Did you finish your calc homework?"

Luckily, she gets it. It's a little harder to quell Desmond's curiosity.

"Dude!" he cries as he catches up with us, pushing his way through the crowded hall. "Called to the office—I couldn't be more proud. What did you do?"

If you don't get a detention at least once a week, Desmond figures your life is too safe.

"Nothing," I tell him. "It was just a misunderstanding. I'll tell you about it at lunch."

"You're just going to leave me hanging?" He turns to Marina. "Did he tell you?"

She shakes her head. "He'll tell us both later. At lunch."

She's trying to give him the eye, the same as I am. But he's oblivious to the fact that we're surrounded by kids and maybe I don't want to have everybody and their uncle hear what happened.

"Come on," he says. "Lunch is almost an hour away. Enquiring minds need to know."

"Enquiring minds are just going to have to wait," Marina says, then she leans in closer to him and adds, in a whisper that the mountain lion in me lets me catch, "So shut the fuck up already."

"Jeez," he says with a hurt expression, but he lets it go.

∽∾

We take our lunches outside to the soccer field and sit on a bench in the stands, where we can talk without being overheard. There's a good breeze coming in from the west and I lift my head. There's so much to read in the smells I'm taking in. I let my nostrils flare until I realize that Marina's giving me a warning look.

"What?" I say.

"People don't do that," she says. "But I'm guessing Wildlings do."

And if I'm trying to hide the fact that I'm one ...

"Right," I say. "Thanks."

"So what's the big secret about your getting called to the office?" Desmond wants to know. "What did you do?"

"It was nothing I did. There were two FBI agents with Hayden when I got there—the same ones from the pier when I met Elzie. They grilled me about Wildlings."

Desmond's eyes go wide. "Are you serious?"

"Do they suspect you?" Marina asks.

"I don't know. It's hard to figure out what they're thinking. But they're pretty sure that I know some Wildlings and they want me to give up their names."

"What did you do?"

"I lied. What was I supposed to do? Tell them about Elzie?"

Not to mention Chaingang. And how about myself? No thanks.

"Oh no," Marina says. "Elzie doesn't know. Is she meeting us after school today?"

"Not anymore. At least I hope not. I texted her to go to Des's place, but I had to be kind of vague about it. You know how they say that you can tap

101

into a cell phone signal?"

"I don't think that applies to a text," Marina says.

I turn to Desmond. "Still think I'm being paranoid?"

He gives a slow shake of his head.

"I can't figure out how they know who I am," I say. "I never gave my name when the one agent stopped me at the pier that day. So how did they know to come looking for me here at school?"

"Dude," Desmond says. "Your face was plastered all over the news."

"Oh yeah."

"But you know what?" he adds. "I think you're okay. They're just fishing. If they actually had anything on you, they'd be pulling you in for some serious questioning."

"He's right," Marina says.

He nods. "Of course I'm right. I'm the smart one."

He holds his hands up in surrender as we both go to punch him.

ϟ

I'm nervous as hell when the bell rings to mark the end of the school day. I hurry to my locker, grab my backpack and board and head for the front entrance at a brisk walk. I'd go faster, but I don't want to get stopped by a teacher for running in the halls. Desmond and Marina fall in beside me. Marina puts a hand on my arm, slowing me down.

"Don't be so obvious," she says. "If there *are* FBI agents watching, we need to be totally casual and act like it's any other day. And don't you," she adds, turning to Desmond, "go looking all over the place for them. That'll just draw their attention."

"Well, duh," he says. "You think I don't know that?"

"But what if Elzie didn't get my text?" I say.

Marina turns back to me. "Then we'll have to get her away from the school as quickly and nonchalantly as we can. If she's outside, I'll go to her while you guys head off someplace else. We can hook up later at Desmond's. Just stay cool and we'll get through this."

She's right, of course, but thankfully Elzie's not waiting for us outside.

"Guys ... three o'clock ... dark sedan on the other side of the school buses," Desmond says. "Tinted windows. Engine idling. Who drives a car like that except for a cop?"

Marina and I take turns having a look as we continue down the walk to the street. I have no idea what an undercover police car would look like beyond the black SUVs I saw before. I don't like the fact that whoever's in it can see us but we can't see them.

"Could be," Marina says. "Let's split up. Desmond, come with me. Josh, I'll text you if the car follows you. If it does—"

"I know. Act normal, stay cool," I say.

When we reach the street, Marina and Desmond drop their boards to the pavement. They push off and head south while I go north, carrying my board. I fall in with a big group of kids heading to the mall. My phone vibrates in my pocket as we get to the end of the block. I pull it out and glance at the screen.

cop following u.

MARINA

The plan to split up is our only way to know whether Josh is being followed. Sure enough, as soon as Josh heads north, a man in a suit gets out of the sedan and falls in behind a big group of kids. Josh is lost in their midst. They're pretty much all going to hit the mall. I hope there's safety in numbers.

It's weird that in a town with a great big beautiful ocean just a few blocks away from school, they go straight from being indoors all day to indoors again at the shopping center. It's not that I've never done it, but the mall gets old pretty fast for me unless I'm there with Mamá. I like picking out clothes for her.

Desmond elbows me. "Holy crap! Are you seeing this? That cop's on Josh like a Valley Girl chasing her purse dog."

"Don't stare at them," I say.

I push off and wheel down the street, Desmond following. When we get to the corner, I pull out my phone to text Josh. I don't know what he'll do about it, but I figure he should know he's being followed.

"Okay," I tell Des. "I let Josh know about the cop. Let's go hang at your place.

"You got it, *amiga*," Des says, pushing off again.

୬◆ஐ

"I'm starved," Desmond says when we get to the garage. "Want to come in for some toast and peanut butter?"

"Nah, I'm good," I tell him. "I'll just hang out here and watch for Elzie."

What a day this has been. I guess I should've expected that Josh might come across my blog, but it still came as a shock. I feel strangely proud that he thinks Nira is cool and smart. I wish I could take credit, but that would blow my cover right out the door. Now I have to hope that he doesn't figure out that Nira is me.

I don't have to wait long before Desmond comes back, a satisfied grin on his face. A daub of shiny peanut butter on his lower lip only adds to his silly smirk.

"What's up with you, Wilson?" I ask.

"I'm just loving life, surfer girl. I'm thinking about Josh giving that cop a taste of what it's like to have *real* power. I just wish I could be there to watch."

"*Really?* You need to stay here on Earth with rest of us. There's no way Josh is dumb enough to change in front of that cop. I don't know what he plans to do, but I hope like hell they don't disappear him or anything."

That sobers Desmond, at least for the moment.

"So where's herself?" he asks.

"No clue," I say. "Let's just play some music for awhile, see if either of them shows."

"Sounds good to me," Des says, strapping on his bass.

It's a Fender Precision, just like Nokie Edwards plays, which is why he got it. It's hard to go wrong using the same gear The Ventures did on their early albums. I have to admit that I've got a pair of Canopus drumsticks myself—the official Mel Taylor model, of course.

It's hot outside so it's hot in the garage, which doesn't have any AC, but we don't care. The two of us jam for well over an hour, having fun, but missing the sweet sound of Josh's Les Paul riffing over top of the rhythms we're laying down. Desmond switches to his keyboard from time to time, but it's still not the same.

There's been no sign of Elzie, so I decide to text Josh again to tell him she's a no-show.

JOSH

I was scared when the two agents had me in Principal Hayden's office. And I was nervous for Elzie when I was rushing for the front entrance after school. But right now, I'm pissed off. Not enough to do something stupid like change in front of everybody. But enough to give these guys a run for their money.

I continue down the block, heading for the Santa Feliz Shopping Center. It's just me and a lot of other kids, going to hang out in the mall and stuff our faces in the food court so we won't have any appetite for dinner—or at least that's Mom's take on it.

We stop at the streetlight and I pretend to text while we wait for it to change. The wind's coming from behind me. I test the air, sifting through all the various scents, but not obviously, because I remember what Marina said.

The girls smell like perfume and shampoo and body washes, with a faint natural scent under it. The boys are stronger—there's more B.O. and if they're using a cologne, they're using too much. But male or female, they all have the smell of Sunny Hill High on them. All except for one. He smells of aftershave and the car he was just sitting in. I can even smell the faint metal and oil scent of the gun he's got under his jacket.

The light changes and the crowd streams across the street. I let myself get jostled enough to steal a quick glance back in a way that seems natural. The man in the suit isn't either Agents Matteson or Solana. My nose already told me that, but now I have a visual for him, too.

I quicken my pace as we all cross the mall parking lot in a long ragged line of laughing and talking kids with one lone FBI agent trailing in the rear. When we get to the entrance, I step to one side and bend down to retie my shoelace. Mr. FBI has to keep going. I let him go through the doors, then I follow. The air conditioning is cool on my skin after the heat outside.

He hasn't gone far. I pass him where he's standing by the window of the

107

Dollar Store, studying their merchandise. I walk by without looking and hear him fall in behind me. His shoes make a soft scuffing sound on the marble, distinct from everyone else's footfalls.

I've usually got the barrage of input that comes with being a Wildling clamped down so well that I forget just how useful it can be.

I haven't quite figured out how to lose him. I just know that it'll be easier here in the mall with all the other kids and shoppers around than it would be out on the street.

And then it comes to me.

After school, the busiest spot in the mall for guys my age is the gaming store, Spyglass Games. When I get there the usual crowd is inside, trying out games, flipping through the used bins and new titles. I walk to the back of the store, where Barry Stewart is working on an order.

Barry lives a block over from me and he's a full-on computer geek. When Des and I have problems with our computers, Marina's the one who deals with what needs to be fixed. But when she's stumped, or when the electronics are more complicated, we see Barry. Half the kids in school do— the jocks, the stoners, everybody. So even though he's tall and gawky, with a perpetual bad haircut and Buddy Holly glasses, nobody picks on him. Not even the Ocean Avers, because they've got electronics same as everybody else. If Barry can't fix it, then it's time to get a new one anyway.

He looks up when I crouch down beside him.

"Saw you on the news, man," he says. "What was up with that?"

I didn't realize it had been that long since we'd last talked. He's a senior, so we don't really hang out at school, and the rest of my life has been so crazy I just haven't been over to his place since I first changed. We've done some really cool home recording and mixing at his place. Like I said, if it involves computers, Barry's your man.

"I still don't really know," I say. "You remember me telling you about Steve—my mom's latest, now her ex?"

"Yeah. Sounds like he was a piece of work."

"Well, it was something he brought into the house. I don't know how he got mixed up with Wildlings, but as soon as that mountain lion showed up, I was out of there."

"That's what I heard. So what can I do for you?" he adds with a grin. "Are you finally going to bite the bullet and get yourself *Rock Band*?"

I laugh. "Have they got a Ventures module yet?"

"What do you think?"

"I think I'll stick to playing my Les Paul."

"No kidding," he says with a chuckle. "Still can't get you to come over to the dark side, eh?"

I've been keeping tabs on the Secret Agent Man while we're talking. He's still at the front of the store by the new releases rack, acting like he's trying to decide which game to buy.

"Mind if I use your washroom?" I ask Barry.

They're normally for staff only, but we've been friends long enough that he just nods.

"Sure. You know where it is?"

"Back of the storeroom."

Where there's also a back door that they use for receiving shipments.

"Just don't go looking through the new used stuff," Barry says. "Julio's got them in some weird order that no one else can figure out. He goes ballistic if anyone touches them."

"Not a problem."

I glance casually to the front of the store. Secret Agent Man has his head turned for a moment, so I take the opportunity to slip into the back room. Julio won't have to worry about me messing up the used games since I'm going right for the back door. But I have to say, if the chaos in here is his idea of being organized, I don't want to see where he lives. It's probably worse than Danny Reed's car.

The door opens with a creak and I step out. But before I can push it closed behind me, something catches the metal edge.

"You sure this is the smartest idea?"

The mountain lion caught and noted Cory's scent before he spoke. I turn to find him leaning on the door jamb, still holding the door ajar.

"I thought it was a pretty smart way to lose the FBI," I say.

He nods. "Except that it tells them that you know they're following you."

I give him a blank look.

"It tells them you've got something to hide," he says, "because you've gone to the effort to lose the agent."

"I need to see Elzie and I don't want to lead them to her."

"You don't need to see her. You *want* to see her. Not the same thing."

When I start to protest, he holds up a hand.

"It's okay," he says. "There's nothing wrong with wanting to see your girlfriend. But is it worth really putting yourself on the Feds' radar?"

"I'm already on their radar."

Cory shakes his head. "Right now, they're checking out possibilities. But deliberately lose the guy tailing you? That'll put your file right at the top of the heap. They'll be all over your life with a fine-toothed comb."

"I've done nothing wrong."

He raises an eyebrow.

"Okay, I get it," I say. "Being fingered as a possible Wildling would be enough to put me in their bad books. But why are they more interested in me now than last week?"

"Well, that's kind of my fault."

"You *told* them about me?"

"Don't be an ass. Remember when I ran into you and Elzie at the old naval base?"

"Yeah, you were scouting it out because they were keeping some friends of yours in there."

"Right. And last night, with the help of a couple of other friends, we broke them out. They had seven cousins locked up in there. They're all long gone now, except for Jez, who's sticking around to help me out. That's the good news."

He waits a moment and I realize he wants me to ask the question.

"So what's the bad news?"

"The bad news," he says, "is that now they know that some of us don't like what they're doing and we're messing with their game. There's already all kinds of extra security out there, so it'll be a lot harder the next time we want to break someone out."

"So that's why they came to question me today at school—I'm one of their suspects."

"Pretty much. They're being proactive. Trying to get a line on everybody they think is a going concern."

"So what am I supposed to do? Just forget about Elzie?"

He shakes his head. "She's a smart girl. So you be smart, too. Go do whatever you'd normally do after school. She'll get in touch with you when it's safe."

"Normally I'm seeing her."

He gives me a look.

"Okay," I tell him. "I'll be smart."

I turn to go back into the mall, but pause to ask, "How did you know to find me here?"

He smiles. "I didn't. I've been watching the Feds—mooching around to see how much they know, how many agents they've got in the field. I just happened to see Agent McCloud start following you—and it's a good thing I did. You could have really screwed things up for yourself."

"There should be a handbook for all this crap."

"There is," he says.

"Where do I find it?"

"It's not an 'it.' You need a more experienced cousin to take you under his wing."

"Is that an offer?"

He shakes his head. "Like I told you before, I'm too busy to be babysitting a virgin—especially one with the wrong politics."

"What's that supposed to mean?"

But I know. He thinks that because I'm with Elzie, I've aligned myself with the ferals.

"Just get back inside," he says. "And the next time something seems like a good idea, think it through first."

His know-it-all attitude is starting to bug me, but I take his advice and think it through before I tell him off. I have to admit he's right. I *was* about to screw up. And like he did from day one, he's only trying to help me.

"I get it," I tell him. "Thanks." I start to go back inside, then turn around. "But how could you be following us in there and yet be waiting outside this door?"

"I figured you'd try to make a break for it. Your plan was pretty obvious when you slipped into the back room."

"That still doesn't tell me how you got out here ahead of me."

His head shimmers and he flashes me a quick coyote grin. "I have my ways."

I nod and let the door close behind me. Inside, I go into the bathroom, flush the toilet and wet my hands, like that was all I was doing. When I come out into the store, I'm drying them on my jeans. I don't even look at the FBI agent. I just sit on the floor beside Barry and shoot the breeze for a while. My phone vibrates with a text from Marina.

just gang of 2 @ garage

I say bye to Barry and leave the mall.

∽∾

Secret Agent Man, a.k.a. Agent McCloud, follows me all the way back to

Desmond's place. He's carrying his jacket over his arm, has his sleeves rolled up and his tie in his pocket, but he still doesn't look like he belongs anywhere except for doing secret agent stuff.

Desmond and Marina are in the garage when I get there. If Elzie had shown up in the meantime, I'm sure Marina would've texted me. I don't like to show the Feds anything about my life, but Cory told me to do what I'd normally do and this is it.

"She wasn't here when—" Desmond begins, stopping as I hold up my hand.

I find a piece of paper and write: *Could the place be bugged?*

They both look at me with wide eyes. Desmond starts to say something, but I put a finger to my lips.

I write: *We can't talk without some noise.*

"Let's play some music," I say aloud.

I pick up my guitar, turn on my amp, check my tuning. Then I stand right beside Marina at her drum kit and start to play the theme song from that old British TV series *Danger Man*: "Secret Agent Man." I can play that song in my sleep. I think Johnny Rivers sang it and yeah, I know he didn't write it. Not a lot of people wrote their own material back in those days. But they still put their own stamp on it. Our version's kind of a Ventures/garage rock take that keeps the slinky spy vibe.

Desmond laughs at the song choice. He and Marina fall in, bass and drums locking down the rhythm, but at a low volume, like I'm playing. Desmond steps closer so that he's on the other side of Marina and we can all talk without shouting.

"Do you really think they put a bug in my garage?" he asks.

"I have no idea," I say. "Maybe I'm just being paranoid. But that FBI guy definitely followed me all the way to Spyglass Games and then back here to your place."

"It's like being in a James Bond movie."

"No, it's like having your life go down the tubes and there's nothing you can do about it."

I go on to tell them about meeting Cory and what he told me.

"I don't mean to take sides here," Marina says when I'm done, "but Cory was right."

"I know."

"What are you going to do?" Desmond asks.

"There's nothing I can do except what Cory said: be cool and try to act as normal as I can. Right now, I just want to make some noise."

Without waiting for either of them to respond, I thumb the volume control on my Les Paul way up and start playing the chunky chords for "Louie Louie." Desmond shrugs and falls in with the simple bass line. Marina grins and pounds on her drums.

We play through a bunch of songs until Desmond's mom finally comes into the garage with her hands over her ears and tells us to put a lid on it.

MARINA

From Nira's LiveJournal blog, *My Life as an Otter*:

Congressman Clayton Householder. Take note of that name, my friends. This man might be the biggest danger that we face. He's been on a crusade against Wildlings ever since the first one of us showed up. The media love him and with all the press that he gets, he just may succeed in getting everyone else to hate us, too.

For those of you who haven't seen what's trending on Twitter and the other social media, let me fill you in. Clayton Householder is a religious zealot who claims that the kids who've changed to Wildlings must have done something to bring God's wrath down upon their heads. He says his job is to stop this "sinful disease" from spreading.

So he's lobbying the legislature to pass laws that will allow the government to capture all the Wildlings and contain the "disease" by imposing a quarantine on all of Santa Feliz.

That's right, kids. Quarantine means if there are good curls down in San Diego or Mexico, you're not going to be riding those waves. And say your favourite band is playing a gig in L.A. or Long Beach—you're not going to be catching that show. Of course, if you're locked away in some hellhole, it's not as though you'll be surfing or catching shows anyway.

Look, it's been proven that what we have is not a virus, so a quarantine isn't going to "solve" anything. And you don't see Wildlings going around attacking people. You're way more likely to have a banger messing up your face.

I've so had it with the bad rap that Wildlings are getting. It seems to me that we're being persecuted for having something extra that other people don't have. I don't know exactly what this is or why it happened, but I am one hundred percent certain that what we have is good, not bad. I wish we didn't have to hide it and we sure shouldn't have to feel ashamed of it.

Fortunately, not all politicians are as whacked out as Householder. It's early days still, so talk to your parents about his witch hunt. If that quarantine happens, it's going to affect them as much as us, so ask them to call their congressional representative.

But speak discreetly, my Wildling friends … until all danger has passed, keep the secret of your gift to yourselves.

JOSH

I read through a bunch more of the archived *My Life as an Otter* blogs after dinner, when I'm supposed to be doing my homework. A message pop-up tells me that Nira has just posted a new entry, so I click on her latest blog about Congressman Householder.

Man, this keeps going from bad to worse. One wrong move could put me in that same holding facility that Cory broke into last night to rescue his friends. I'm glad Mr. Delaney gave me an extension on my history essay because of my "trouble at home," but with something like this hanging over my head, it's hard to care much about English homework or that overdue essay.

Actually, up until this latest post, I haven't concentrated very hard on the blog, either. Mostly, I've just looked for clues to see if I can figure who the mysterious otter girl really is. She's pretty circumspect. Her blogs manage to be really personal without giving away any information about her identity.

I might be better at finding those clues about Nira if I weren't so distracted worrying about Elzie. It's almost midnight now and there's still no word from her. My phone's sitting between my keyboard and the monitor. I keep waiting for it to vibrate with either a call or text.

Maybe I'm being watched somehow. I'm tempted to sneak out to see if I can spy FBI agents skulking around, but I promised Mom I'd tell her if I was going out and it's not like I can tell her the truth. She was so cool about letting me off the hook last week and I really don't want to lose her trust. It's bad enough I can't tell her about this whole Wildling business.

My window's open. I get up from the computer and lean on the sill. I let the night air fill my nostrils and see how many scents I can identify. Maybe I'll smell an agent out here.

It's weird how *much* there is to smell. I never really paid attention to it before. The night's full of sounds, too, if you take the time to concentrate. I suppose it helps if you can tap into a mountain lion's senses, but really, I think we mostly go through life half asleep—oblivious to all the little details of the world around us. I like being able to notice all these things. It's definitely one of the gifts that comes with being a Wildling.

That makes me think of Nira again. Maybe I should try to send her a private message. But just as I start to turn back around, something catches my attention beyond the window.

It starts out as a feeling, more than actually hearing or smelling anything. I pop the screen and lean out a little, really opening my nostrils, smelling and listening. That's when I hear a giggle. The backyard is dark, but my night sight cuts right through the shadows to find Elzie crouched low along the side of the house. I'm so happy to see her, my heart does a little leap.

"You should see what your face looks like when you do that," she says in a loud whisper.

I smile and lean further out to look at her. "What are you *doing* there," I whisper back.

"Stand back from the window," she says.

I barely have time to get out of the way before a large cat comes bounding through the opening. It lands in the middle of the room, transforming back into Elzie. A nude Elzie.

"Whoops," she says as she strikes a sultry pose.

There's a rapid transformation into her Wildling jaguarundi shape, then back to her own, this time dressed. I know she did it on purpose just to get a rise out of me—figuratively as well as literally. Her gaze goes to where I've got a stiff tent pole under my pants. She grins.

"Happy to see me?" she asks in a normal voice.

I nod, but put a finger to my lips.

She steps close to whisper into my ear, "Are you worried about your mom hearing me?"

Her warm breath in my ear tickles. It also makes the bulge in my pants push harder against the fabric.

I shake my head and whisper back into her ear, "Maybe the room's bugged."

"Oh, you don't have to worry about that," she says in a normal voice. "If the room was bugged I'd know. The transmitter has to send out a signal and Auntie Min taught me to identify it. Checking for that's the first thing I did when I got outside your house because—you know the Feds have a car parked down the street, right?"

"I figured they might. They questioned me at school and they've been following me around ever since."

"Do you have anything to eat?" she asks. "I'm starving."

I go into the kitchen and bring back a bag of tortilla chips and some salsa.

"Yum," she says and digs in.

"Why didn't you call me or send a text?" I ask.

"I didn't know who you'd be with."

"I'm not going to be with some other—oh. You mean the FBI."

"Yeah, they've been heavying people all over town. They showed up under the overpass and would have taken everybody in for questioning, except they all scattered while the cops were getting out of their cars."

"Cory told me he broke some people out of the holding facility at the naval base. He thinks that's why the FBI is being so aggressive."

She nods. "And all this talk about quarantining Santa Feliz probably has them scrambling to be in control of the situation."

"I heard about that. Do you really think it'll come to a quarantine?"

"Not unless a bunch of Wildlings get out of control." She pauses, then adds, "Or if the authorities decide they can prove that what's happened to us is communicable, instead of accepting what it really is."

I give her a blank look.

"I keep telling you," she says. "It's a gift. From Mother Earth, or Gaia, or God, or the Creator, or whatever spiritual force it is that guides the world. Auntie Min calls it the Grace, but I'm never quite sure if she's talking about a person, a place, or maybe some combination of the two."

"Auntie Min sounds really interesting," I say. "I would have liked to have met her."

"Why can't you?"

"You just said everybody scattered."

She nods. "Yeah, but Auntie Min won't go far. This is her holy ground. They'll all end up back there after the cops split."

"Her holy ground? You mean Santa Feliz?"

"Not exactly. It's more like the land that Santa Feliz is built on."

I think about that for a moment.

"She's not a Wildling, is she?" I say.

"If you mean, did she get changed in the last six months like us, then no. She's one of the old ones, like Cory—or at least, they're a lot older than either you or me. How old, I don't know. Auntie Min says that there were animal people here when the world first began and some of those first Wildlings are still around today."

"Do you believe that?"

Elzie shrugs. "Why not? What's happened to us is pretty extraordinary."

That's an understatement. But *immortal* Wildlings? I think that's a bit of a stretch, but I don't say anything to Elzie. I don't want to set off an argument.

"This is really good salsa," she says. "What kind is it?"

"Homemade. My mom got the recipe from Marina's mom."

"Mmm."

She dips a couple more chips into the salsa and puts them both in her mouth, chewing with relish.

"Is Auntie Min the leader of the ferals?" I ask, hoping this won't lead to anything confrontational.

"She isn't a feral," Elzie says after she swallows, "and we don't really have a leader. We aren't really that organized. I don't think any of the Wildlings are. If we *could* organize, maybe it'd be different. Maybe we could force the government to accept us as people, instead of trying to round us up and lock us away."

"Do you think that's possible?"

"Why not? Once upon a time, women couldn't vote and your ancestors were slaves. But we fixed that, didn't we?"

There are still misogynists and racists out there, but I know what she means. It's better now. A lot better. Not perfect, but maybe perfection's impossible. You can't just make laws. You have to change the way people think and that can't be legislated.

"But I doubt Wildlings will ever get into organized group lobbying or anything," Elzie goes on. "The change is more of spiritual state—I'm sure you know what I mean. Even Auntie Min says that every individual has to find their own path into the Grace."

"The Grace," I repeat. "I like that term."

"Me too," she says. "Sometimes late at night, when I'm in my jaguarundi shape and running at top speed down some deserted beach, I can feel what she means. I get this whole Zen thing happening inside."

She sees something in my face and punches my shoulder.

"What?" she says. "Didn't you ever feel like that?"

"Hey, I'm not mocking you."

"No, but you looked like you were about to. I know it sounds woo woo."

"It's not that. It's—I've only ever changed once. Twice, if you count doing it for a moment and then freaking out and switching back."

"You're kidding."

I shake my head.

"Well, we'll just have to fix that," she says. "We can easily get past the guys watching us."

"I can't."

"Why not?"

I take a breath. Okay, here comes the big turn-off.

"It's my mom," I say. "She doesn't know I'm a Wildling and I promised her I wouldn't go out without telling her first."

"But if she never finds out ..."

Her voice trails off and she cocks her head to study me for a moment.

"You guys are really close, aren't you?" she says.

"Yeah. Since my dad walked out, all we have is each other."

"At least you've got that."

I put my arm around her shoulder.

"You've got me," I tell her.

She snuggles into me for a second, then pulls away, smiling.

"I do, don't I? So we'll stay in. What do you want to do? Wait!" she adds before I can say anything. "I've got an idea."

Then she grabs my arm and pulls me down onto the bed. We fall in a tumble of limbs and the headboard bangs into the wall. We lie silent, waiting to hear if Mom heard anything. Luckily her room is way down the hall.

Elzie puts her mouth against my ear again.

"Whoops," she breathes, like she did before, only this time she removes her clothing piece by piece.

Then she turns my face so that we can kiss.

MARINA

I leave my room and go sit beside Mamá in the living room. Wouldn't you know that creep Householder is holding forth on the religious channel. He's a great big man in his fifties and older people seem to think he's handsome. I don't see that. I just see a disgusting old bigot who has way too much power and sway over people.

"We live in a beautiful world," Householder is saying on the television. "We live in the best country in the world. But, friends, right now, right here in the U.S. of A., we have a contagion that threatens everything we hold dear. A virus waits to strike like the serpent did in the Garden. The Devil possesses our innocents and changes them into monsters that will turn on you and your family to rip out your throats and consume your flesh.

"Good people, we have a sacred duty to remove these vermin from the garden of God …"

"Mamá," I say. "You don't actually believe what he's saying, do you?"

"I'm not sure what to think, *mija*. He's very close to God, so I'm interested in what he has to say. But it's hard to think that the Devil has entered all of these poor children."

"I don't think God or the Devil have anything to do with it. I'll bet none of those kids had a choice about what happened to them. We shouldn't judge them for something that's not even their fault. No one really knows why it's been happening—at least, not yet—but it's got nothing to do with God and it's not a disease."

"But God watches over everything," Mamá says. "I thought that he had chosen to bring Laura Connor up to heaven with him, but perhaps Congressman Householder is right. Only the Devil himself would turn poor Laura into a rat and then kill her. I fear for you and Ampora. Have you been saying your prayers?"

Mamá and I don't see eye to eye on religious matters, but otherwise, we're pretty close. My sister Ampora and me, not so much.

My parents' divorce really split our family. Ampora sided with Papá and she still won't speak to me, even though I kept Papá's name and we go to the same school. She's proud of our Mexican heritage. I am too, but I don't know much about it.

When Mamá remarried, she pretty much turned her back on the past.

"We're Americans now, not Mexicans," she told us—and embraced my step dad's gringo culture—although she held tight to her religious upbringing.

We all lived in the barrio before the divorce. I was young enough when my parents split up that I only vaguely remember the barrio as a scary place. But Ampora thrives in it. As far as I know, she never got jumped into a gang, but she's embraced the whole gangsta music and bandas fashion scene. She thinks surfing is for dorks, so you can imagine what she thinks of me. And being as judgmental as she is, she probably hates Wildlings, too—although not for the same reason as Householder.

"Yes, Mamá," I say, to make her happy. "But I'm sure that what happened to Laura had nothing to do with God or the Devil. I think she was just in the wrong place at the wrong time. None of it was her fault."

"Perhaps, *mija*, perhaps. I hope you pray for her soul."

"Of course I do. But what Congressman Householder is preaching is racism. Treating people like second-class citizens because they're different just leads to what happened to the Native people and Mexicans when the Spaniards came, and the way some people still treat us today."

"How can you be so sure?" Mamá asks. "Congressman Householder seems to be a man of God."

I press my point. "And a bigot. Think about it, Mamá. A quarantine will keep everybody stuck here in Santa Feliz—not just kids. You won't be able to visit Abuela and Abuelo, or Tía Rosa."

"I hadn't thought of that."

"Please tell me you'll get in touch with our own congresswoman and tell her that you don't agree with Householder's ideas. We need to fight that kind of thinking."

Mamá gets a line in her brow that tells me she doesn't much like the prospect of a quarantine.

"Tonight I will ask for God's guidance in my prayers," she says. "You know that you can do that, too, don't you? You might also pray for your little stepsisters, that this terrible curse doesn't fall upon them."

I don't let my face show how much it hurts that my own mother can feel like that about what I've become, even if she doesn't *know* I'm a Wildling.

All I say is, "Of course. And I'll pray for you as well. I know God will tell you that it's not right to cast judgment on those who are innocent. I really hope you'll call Congresswoman Cohen and ask Papá to call her, too."

JOSH

When I wake up the next morning, Elzie's gone. I don't know when she left and there isn't a note. I see a light blinking on my phone, telling me I have a text. I reach over from the bed and look.

had 2 leave b4 light so i wouldnt b seen. talk 2 u soon. kiss kiss.

I grin like a fool as I go take a shower. I never got around to asking Elzie where she sleeps or what she does during the day, but right now, I don't really care. Not even seeing the undercover cops sitting in their car at the end of the street can wreck my mood. I've still got a goofy grin when I meet up with Desmond and Marina to go to school.

"Aw, man," Desmond says. "I know that look. You totally got some last night."

Marina elbows him. "Don't be gross," she tells him before turning to me. "So how is Elzie? Obviously she got your message, but is she okay?"

I tell them what she told me about how the police rousted the homeless people under the freeway overpass, looking for Wildlings.

"They shouldn't be allowed to do that," Marina says. "That's just wrong on so many levels."

"No kidding," I say.

"Is that where she lives?" Desmond asks. "Under the overpass?"

"I have no idea. I never seem to get around to asking her where she lives or what she does when she's not with me."

"That's kind of weird."

"I usually have other stuff on my mind."

Desmond smiles and gives me a push. "No kidding, stud-boy. You had so much of that other stuff on your mind today that you forgot your board. Now we all have to walk."

I realize he's right. I did kind of float out of the house in a happy cloud.

126

"Where does Cindy live?" I ask, to change the subject.

"She—uh. Okay. I don't know yet. Point for you."

"We'd better get going," Marina says. "Des, can I stash my board in your garage till after school?"

"Sure. Man, I should've never sold my old board," says Desmond. "Walking is way too slow."

"Suck it up, baby," says Marina. "I think we humans were meant to walk occasionally."

They put their boards in the garage and we all head down the street. It doesn't take long before we realize we've got company several houses behind us.

"I really hate those guys following you," Marina says. "Following you and staking out our houses. Doesn't the government have better things to do than harass a bunch of kids?"

"Apparently not," Desmond says. "Hey, did you ever figure out who your secret blogger is?"

Marina looks over as I shake my head. "No, but I read some more of her blogs before Elzie came over last night. I like the way she thinks. I'm going to try private messaging her some time."

"Don't bother," Desmond says. "She'll never respond. She'll think you're either a cop or some perv."

"Yeah," Marina adds, "and unless you've picked up some mad computer skills to hide your identity, the FBI will be able to trace your email right back to you."

"You think they're monitoring her blog?"

"What do you think? If they're disappearing Wildlings and following you around, wouldn't they be doing that, too?"

Desmond taps my shoulder to get my attention. "Hey, what's going on at the school?"

There's a crowd of kids gathered on the walkway at the school entrance. There are so many of them that they spill over onto the lawn on either side. That's unusual enough, but when we get closer, we see another bunch of kids clustered right up at the front doors arguing with Principal Hayden. It takes us a moment to realize that they're all wearing bits and pieces of animal costumes. There are lots of perky cat ears, drooping rabbit ears, insect antennas and various animal tails. One girl's wearing a faux leopard-skin jacket. Another has a striped black and yellow sweater that makes her look like a skinny bumblebee.

"This is insane," Desmond says. "What is this, a Fuzzies convention?"

"I think you mean Furries," Marina says.

"Whatever."

He taps the closest guy on his shoulder and Terry Seals turns around.

"What's happening, dude?" Desmond asks.

"You didn't hear?"

"Why do you think I'm asking?"

"Dillon Harner killed himself this morning. He hanged himself in his dad's garage."

"Oh, crap," Desmond says. "Really?"

I hear what they're saying, but I can't quite process the words. They don't make sense. Dillon would never do this. He has too much to live for. He's one of the best musicians I know. We hang out in the music room trading guitar licks a couple of times a week when we have the same spare. He plays his classical guitar and I use one of the school's cheap Strat knock-offs. He's taught me Segovia and Gilardino on the electric, while I've turned him on to The Ventures and Dick Dale—both of which sound surprisingly cool on a classical guitar. At least, they do the way Dillon plays them. He loves music as much as I do and he's brilliant at it.

Weekends he's in Long Beach with his mother and the rest of the time he lives with his dad here in Santa Feliz. His dad's a guitarist, too. He seems to overcompensate for the breakup, filling all their evenings with father–son jam sessions, which is why I only see Dillon at school. Except for his dislike of Wildlings, Dillon was a happy guy. Nothing fazed him.

How the hell can he be dead?

"That doesn't explain what's going on with the costumes," Desmond is saying to Terry.

"Are you okay?" Marina asks me.

I shake my head. The day's already warm, but I can't shake the chill that's crawled up into my chest.

Susie Wong, who's standing beside Terry, turns then. Her eyes are red from crying and she's holding a cloth shopping bag.

"He sent texts to a couple of people," she says to Desmond, "telling them he was a Wildling. That he couldn't take what was coming."

"He was a Wildling?" I say.

He hated Wildlings. How could he be one? And how could I not have known? We were just working up a version of The Astronauts' "Baja" last week. We even talked a bit about the mountain lion in my house business—

although I didn't tell him the truth. We played more than we talked.

Where the hell was my Wildling radar? I could have talked him out of doing something this stupid.

"What did he think was coming?" Marina asks.

Susie shakes her head. "I don't know. I didn't get the text—Nancy Hajjir did and she told me. She said he was afraid he was going to be outed."

"Would he really have been scared enough to kill himself?" Marina says.

"Are you kidding?" Terry says. "It'd be a freak show. You've seen how the media goes for the throat whenever they get a lead on a new Wildling. There haven't been many recently, so they're hungry for fresh blood. Rehashing old stories doesn't sell ads."

I find myself nodding, even though I somehow managed to sidestep most of that attention myself.

Susie touches the cat's ears on the hair band that she's carrying. "Nancy says we should show our support for Dillon and all the Wildlings by wearing animal ears and stuff. To honour Dillon's memory. But Principal Hayden says we can't wear them on campus."

Terry nods. "Anybody who does is going to get a suspension."

"So we're trying to get everyone to wear something. He can't suspend the whole school, can he?"

I still can't get past the idea that Dillon was a Wildling and killed himself because of it. I glance to the street, where the FBI agent who was following us should be. For a moment I can't see him, then I spot him beside a dark car parked down the block, leaning in the window of the passenger's side. As I watch, he gets into the back seat and the car takes off.

My mountain lion hearing lets me in on the conversation that Hayden and some of the students are having by the front door. He's telling them that this can all be discussed in the special assembly he's called for first period. Everybody's supposed to go to the auditorium.

I can't do it. As the rest of the kids take off their bits of animal costumes and start to file inside, Marina gives me a tug on my arm.

"We have to go inside," she says.

I shake my head. "I'll be along. I just need a couple of minutes."

"Josh, I'm sorry. I know he was your friend, but you couldn't have known."

"No? If I'd just recognized him for what he was, I could have talked him out of it."

"I don't think suicide is ever that simple," Marina says.

But maybe this is. He hated Wildlings, so I guess he hated himself, too. Except that couldn't be the whole story, could it? If I could have just talked to him. If I'd told him I was one ...

"Well, we're not going to know now, are we?" I say.

"Josh ... please don't go there."

"Don't worry. I'm not going to do anything stupid."

I want her to say something like "I know you won't," but she only nods and says, "Okay."

"What's going on?" Desmond asks when he sees we aren't following him and Terry and the others.

"Nothing." Marina tucks her hand into the crook of his arm when he returns to where we're standing. "Come on, let's go."

"What about you, Josh?" he asks.

"He's coming in a minute," Marina says before I can. "Now let's go."

She gives his arm a tug and Desmond lets himself be led away.

I'm alone now except for the few stragglers hurrying for the front door. They give me curious looks, but nobody stops. I look up and down the street. There's no sign of the dark car that the FBI agent got into. I don't see any of them anywhere.

I need to talk to another Wildling, but I don't know where to find Elzie or Cory and I don't know any others. Or maybe I do, but just like with Dillon, I'm unable to recognize them. I feel utterly useless. I could call Elzie, but talking on the phone about this doesn't seem right. Besides, what could Elzie say to make any of this better? She doesn't even know Dillon. Didn't. As in the past. I can't believe this.

My gaze drifts to the picnic tables under the palm and eucalyptus trees. I do know one other Wildling. Chaingang.

I doubt he wants to talk to me again. I remember him saying how we weren't going to have meetings or hang out together. But he also said if I needed a helping hand, he'd be there for me. This probably isn't the kind of thing he was talking about, but what have I got to lose? If he was serious, it's not like he's going to beat me up or even have one of his gang do it for him.

He looks up as I approach his table. I can't get a take on his mood because of the shades and the stillness of his face. Up close, he seems bigger than I remember.

"Can I talk to you?" I say.

"Well, at least you waited until the Feds drove off. Wonder what spooked them?"

I shrug.

He nods as if I said something. "I'm guessing something else came along to turn their crank. Or maybe they don't want to be so obvious with this many kids outside looking around. Losers. They haven't exactly been invisible."

"Did you hear about Dillon?" I ask. "Dillon Harner."

"Yeah. Not the greatest news to start the day."

"I just don't get it. Someone said he killed himself because he was a Wildling."

"I heard the same thing. But I also heard he got in touch with the Feds and admitted he was a Wildling. You know, followed what those stupid PSAs have been telling kids to do. Then he found out they were planning to take him away this morning."

Could this morning get any weirder?

"Why didn't he run?"

Chaingang takes off his shades and regards me. "That kind of life, bro—it's not for everybody. I don't know if I could live on the run, cut off from everything and everyone I know."

"You? But you went away to juvie."

"Yeah, but with my connections, it was like a holiday. Meals, a bed, Internet. I had pretty much anything I wanted, except for girls. This'd be different."

"I don't understand."

"I can do my time," Chaingang says. "The judge lays down the sentence and they put me away, but I can see the end—you know what I'm saying? Sooner or later they have to put me back on the street. This Householder crusade is revving up and the Feds seem to be running with it. Who knows what weird-ass shit they'll do to you, or if you'll ever see the outside again?"

"Some guys rescued a bunch of Wildlings the other night. The FBI had them locked up at the old naval base."

"Yeah, I heard about that, too. Now the Feds are in everybody's faces."

"But not yours."

Chaingang shakes his head. "Not yet. But that doesn't mean it's not coming."

"This is so messed up."

"Tell me about it. Word of advice. If the Feds pull you in, don't let them see you change. Not even if they lock you up. Don't ever change where anyone can see, and that means watching out for traffic cams and shit like that, too."

"What if you don't have a choice?"

"You're not listening to me," he says. "Let them lock you up and wait it out. Because when it all falls apart—and bro, it will fall apart— you'll be in the right and the whole world will see that they're on a witch hunt. Public opinion will see them as the bad guys instead of us.

"But change on camera, or anyplace they can see you and it's game over. Then you're the freak and there's no denying it."

I nod, mostly because he expects it.

I'm still trying to come to terms with what Dillon did. He took the only way out that he thought would allow him any control over his life.

There were other choices. If only I'd known. If I could have just talked to him.

"We used to play music together," I say. "In the band room during our spares."

Chaingang nods. "And?"

"I never even knew he was a Wildling. If I had, I could have done something."

"The kid was messed up," Chaingang says. "He was like some closet gay going out bashing gays, you know what I'm saying?"

"Yeah, I see that now. But maybe if I could have talked to him ..."

"You need to let this go," he tells me, his voice firm.

"I can't."

He shakes his head. "It's not on you, bro—don't you get that? It wasn't your decision to make. It was his."

"You don't really believe that."

"Yeah, I really do. You can honour his memory. You can regret the choice he made. You can bang your head against a wall. But it's done."

"Can you teach me how to tell if someone's a Wildling or not?"

"You already know," he says.

"I didn't know Dillon was one."

"It's complicated if you knew someone well before you changed. They're going to smell and seem the same, the way they always did. With strangers you can catch the high wild scent that sets a little something off in your head like there's a signal ringing in the distance."

"So somebody like my friend Desmond could be a Wildling?"

"He's not."

"No, of course he's not. We're best friends. He'd have told me."

The school bell rings. Everybody's gone into the auditorium so that Principal Hayden can give his speech about what a terrible loss this is and how there'll be counsellors for those who want to talk about what we're feeling. Just like last week's special assembly for Laura.

"Go inside," Chaingang says.

"I don't feel like it."

"Yeah, except the Feds' car is just coming around the corner and I don't want them to see you talking to me."

"Oh, right," I say as I dart for the front door. The mountain lion has me move so fast that my hand's almost on the doorknob before the words are out of my mouth.

"Careful, bro," Chaingang says.

Though his voice is soft, I hear it clearly. I look back, but he's got his shades back on and he's sitting there on the picnic table staring off into nowhere just like always.

I open the door and slip into the school before the Feds can see me.

I try to sneak into the auditorium, but Principal Hayden immediately notices me from where he's standing behind the podium on the stage. His gaze tracks me as I ease the door shut and take a seat at the rear. He keeps right on talking the whole time. Nobody else seems to notice me coming in late except for Marina, who turns in her seat as if she's got some kind of Josh-radar. She flashes me a sympathetic smile, then faces the front.

I do my best to pay attention to what Principal Hayden is saying, but it all sounds like the same platitudes as last Monday's assembly. After awhile Hayden starts to talk about how wearing bits of animal costumes sends an inappropriate message to the community—trivializing the very real problems that Wildlings face—and suggests that we wear ribbons or armbands instead.

I shift in my seat, waiting for him to finish telling us that counsellors are available if we want to talk to someone about Dillon. One thing's for sure. No counsellor can bring Dillon back.

I doubt I'm the only one who's relieved when we're finally dismissed to go to our classes.

"So where'd you disappear to, Saunders?" Desmond asks when he and Marina catch up to me after the assembly.

"Nowhere. I just needed a moment to think before I came in."

Marina touches my arm softly. "Maybe Dillon had some bad habits, but he had a good heart. I didn't know him as well as you, but anybody could see that."

She's being nice, not coming right out and saying anything about how he was always badmouthing Wildlings, but maybe she didn't see it. Lots of people don't see crap like that unless they're on the receiving end.

Desmond looks like he has something to add, except he's restraining himself.

"What?" I ask.

"Nothing, man."

"Come on. I know that look."

Desmond sighs. "I don't want to come off like some big jerk. The thing is, I get what you're feeling and what happened with Dillon is a real bummer, but I have to say, I don't understand why he did it. Being a Wildling would be so awesome—like the total opposite of wanting to kill yourself."

"I don't know how he felt about being a Wildling," I say, "but we know how he hated them. That had to be hard. And someone said he found out that the FBI was coming to take him away. That's what he couldn't face. Being locked away and studied and never being free again."

"Disappeared," Marina says quietly.

I nod.

"That sucks," Desmond agrees. "But why did he stick around for as long as he did? I'm not trying to get rid of you, Josh, but why do any of you stick around? If it happened to me, I'd be so gone. I'd just take off. I'd go as far as I could from Santa Feliz and start my life over."

I nod. "And never see your mom and dad again? Or your little sister? Because to be safe, you'd have to cut all ties with them and your friends and everything you care about."

"Yeah, but—"

"And what would you do for identification? How would you get a job, a car license, a bank account?"

"I don't know. I guess I'd have to go underground and buy those things."

"Using what? Meanwhile the FBI'd probably still be trying to track you down. So you'd be on the run on top of everything else."

"Dude, you make it sounds like a curse."

"I don't know if it is or it isn't," I tell him. "I just know that no one wants to give us enough room to find out."

We arrive at our classroom. Marina and I have English this period. I'm not sure what Desmond has. I catch his arm before he can go.

"I know you think it's really cool," I say, "and a lot of the time, a big part of me agrees with you. But today's not one of those times."

Desmond nods. "Sorry, dude. We should have saved this convo for another day."

"No," I tell him. "This is also when I really needed to be reminded of the awesomeness."

He grins and we bump fists. Then I follow Marina into the classroom.

MARINA

It seems a long time until lunch. It's been hard enough to focus on everyday things ever since Laura was killed. This is worse. Josh seems really low and I'm worried about how he seems to be blaming himself for not picking up on Dillon's state of mind. I would love to be there for him, but after English, we both go to our separate classes. Eventually the long morning drags its way to the noon bell.

Josh is waiting for me outside my chem class as I exit, and we walk to the lunchroom to hook up with Desmond.

"He's going to let it slip, you know," I say as he falls into step beside me.

He knows exactly what I'm talking about and shakes his head. "Come on. This is Desmond. He knows how serious this is."

"Except he tends to talk first, think later. I don't think he'll do it on purpose, but—"

"Don't worry. He'll be cool."

I sigh. "*Why* did you have to tell us?"

"You're my best friends. How could I not tell you?"

I feel awful. Maybe I should have done the same, but maybe if I had, I'd be locked up by now. How can Josh be so sure that Desmond won't blow it?

Josh sees the doubt on my face. "What?" he asks.

"I just don't know. Maybe you shouldn't have. This is way more serious than any secret we'd normally share."

He shakes his head. "It's just different. Anyway, Dillon kept it a secret and look what happened to him."

That shuts me up.

Desmond joins us just as we get to the lunchroom. I brought my lunch so I go grab a table while Desmond and Josh stand in line to buy theirs.

I don't want to be nosy, but Josh's shoulders are slumped with despair, so I tune in to what he and Des are saying to each other.

"What's with Gess?" I hear Desmond say to Josh. "He's totally giving you the evil eye."

We all look over to where Desmond is jerking his thumb.

Erik Gess is a tall white guy, so blond his hair's almost platinum. He's a big deal on the boy's track and field team, an A student, and he's the president of the Sunny Hill High Purity Club. They're like the nationwide Pure Love Club—you know, no sex, no drugs, no alcohol. Whatever. People are free to make their own choices and if they want to have an abstinence club, so be it.

But on our campus, Erik and his pals take their mandate for purity a little further than the nationwide club does. They're as white bread as they come. No blacks, no Mexicans, no Asians, no Arabs. It's nothing that would ever be said aloud, but anyone who belongs to a minority in Sunny Hill knows better than to try to join the Purity Club.

Erik is glaring at Josh as though he's Satan personified. I have no idea why he looks so pissed off. It's not as though Josh has done anything to him.

Josh looks at Erik, then over at me. He sees that I'm picking up on this weird vibe.

"Who knows," he mutters to Desmond as he turns back to the food counter. "Maybe he got up on the wrong side of the bed this morning."

"I dunno. He looks *seriously* pissed."

Josh shrugs. "Guys like him are always pissed about something or other."

The cook hands Josh his order and he pushes his tray toward the cash.

"Yeah, and today it's you," Desmond says.

"Right. Just what I need. So I'll just stay out of his way."

Josh and Des go through the cash, then join me at the table. Erik's animosity is like a physical presence in the room, but the three of us manage to ignore him all the way through lunch. As usual, when we finish eating, we go outside for some fresh air. I don't know about Josh and Desmond, but whenever I get outside, I feel like I can finally breathe again—doesn't matter what the weather is. That's only become more pronounced since I started sharing my skin with the otter.

We're outside for only a couple of minutes when Erik's voice booms behind us.

"Saunders!"

We turn around to find him standing a few feet away with a couple of his track team buddies.

"You need to listen very carefully to me," he says to Josh.

"I don't know what this is about," Josh says, "but one of my best friends killed himself this morning. Whatever your problem is, I don't have the time or energy to deal with it right now."

"Yeah?" he says. "Too bad, because I'm not in the mood to have another drug dealer in the school."

"Say what?"

"You heard me."

"If you have a problem with dealers, go talk to the Ocean Avers."

"Yeah, you'd like that, wouldn't you? Have your competition do the dirty work for you. Rough me up. Then you can all sit around and have a laugh while you're getting high."

"Are you nuts? What even makes you think I'm dealing?"

"You were seen talking to Chaingang this morning—and it's not the first time. What are you doing? Working out your territories? Or do you just buy your dope from him?"

I see Desmond's jaw drop, but I manage to keep my cool.

"You need to give this a rest," Josh tells Erik.

"Yeah, or what?"

He gives Josh's shoulder a shove.

"And don't go looking for your gang friends to help you here," he says. "Just because Chaingang's selling you dope, doesn't mean he gives a rat's ass what happens to you. You're no Ocean Aver."

He starts to push him again, but Josh grabs his hand and holds it in place. I see the shock register on Erik's face when he realizes he can't move it. Josh squeezes his fingers and he winces.

"Are you ready to back off now?" Josh asks.

Erik strains to break free, but he's not going anywhere. Josh may be smaller than him, but being a Wildling makes him a lot stronger.

"I said, are you ready to back off now?" he repeats.

"Yeah, sure."

But as soon as Josh lets him go, Erik takes a swing at him. It all happens so fast that it's hard to tell exactly what happened, but the next thing we know, Josh has Erik slammed up against the wall, his hand on his throat pinning him in place. Gess looks scared now, but that doesn't seem to faze Josh.

"Whoa," Desmond says stepping up to them. "You don't want to go all mountain lion on him."

I can't believe he just said that. From the look on Desmond's face, neither can he. Josh stares at Desmond then lets Erik go. Gess staggers and puts his hand up to his throat.

"He went all mountain lion on me first," Josh says, trying to cover up, like 'going mountain lion' is some kind of slang we use.

But Erik doesn't buy it and neither does anyone who was close enough to see the fight. It's clear what they're thinking. Josh shouldn't have been able to deal so easily with Gess. He's got the height and weight on Josh and he should have had the strength. He has to be in good shape to do so well in track and field. Josh is just Josh and everybody knows it. Just like everybody knows the news stories about the mountain lion that was in his house.

"You're one of them," Erik says, backing off a step. "You're a Wildling."

The look on his face says he likes Wildlings even less than non-whites and drug dealers. No big surprise there. The Purity Club worships guys like Congressman Householder.

"Don't be crazy," Josh says. "I'm not a dealer and I'm for sure not a Wildling." He takes a step toward Erik. "I mean, *look* at me. Do I look like some powerhouse Wildling?"

Erik backs away, not wanting to engage in another showdown. He turns to his friends and they all retreat back toward the school door.

"This isn't over," Gess calls back over his shoulder.

Everybody that's outside is staring at Josh.

"Dude," Desmond starts. "I—"

I elbow Des in the side before he can go on.

"You're such an ass," I say, pitching my voice loud enough that it will carry. "People are going to think he really is a Wildling."

"I'm not," Josh says.

"Well, *we* know that."

I don't know how many people are buying it, but when I focus my hearing, the other kids are talking more about the fight and how Erik backed off after Josh used some kind of kung fu on him. A few are wondering about Josh being a Wildling, but more of them wonder if Josh is really dealing. I hear one guy say to his buddy, "I wonder if his shit's cheaper than what the Avers are pushing."

The bell rings for us to return to classes. Everybody starts to go back inside, but Josh hesitates. I come up alongside him and slip my arm into his.

"I think you're okay," I tell him quietly. "Nobody's really sure of what they saw. It's not like you changed—it was just a stupid fight. And everybody knows Erik's an ass. They're not going to listen to him."

I hope I'm right.

JOSH

Marina couldn't be more wrong.

Right after the first period of the afternoon, I'm walking by the administration offices on the way to my next class when Principal Hayden takes me aside. I can't look at Mrs. O'Shay as he ushers me into the office and closes the door. This time I know why Hayden wants to talk to me and I'm embarrassed that she's seeing me here in the office again. Hayden doesn't waste any time once we're inside where—thankfully—it's only the two of us this time. Nobody's called in the Feds yet.

He sits down behind his desk and waves me to a chair.

"I've heard something disturbing," he says, looking at me over steepled fingers, elbows on his desk.

"Does this have anything to do with Erik Gess?" I ask.

He nods.

"I'm not dealing drugs, sir. I don't even do drugs. I tried some hash once and all it did was make me sick."

I realize I'm doing that thing that the cop shows on TV always say you shouldn't: blathering and giving away far too much information when I should keep my mouth shut and see what Hayden has to say. But my nervousness has turned me into a motor-mouth.

"You're admitting to drug use," he says.

"I said I tried it once and I didn't like it. And it wasn't at school."

I want to knock myself on the back of my head because I'm still doing it.

"And it made you sick," he says.

I sigh. "Yes, sir."

"But that hasn't stopped you from selling it."

"I'm not a dealer."

"Then why does Erik say you are?"

"I don't know, sir. You'll have to ask him."

Principal Hayden nods. He regards me for a long moment.

"Tell me about this other matter," he says.

I'm learning, because all I say is, "Sir?"

"Erik says you're a Wildling."

"I'm not."

"And yet this is the second time you've been in this office because of something related to Wildlings."

I want to say, and what's wrong with Wildlings? Are we suddenly against the law? But this time I stay smart and keep my mouth shut.

"Well?" Hayden asks.

"What more do you want me to say, sir?"

"Why would Erik say that?"

I hesitate for a moment. I just want this to go away, but I can tell by the look in Hayden's eyes that he's going to keep after me until he gets some answers. The last thing I need is for him to get on the phone to the FBI.

"Sir, he's a racist and he picked a fight with me," I say. "I used some self-defence moves I saw on YouTube. Erik didn't come off well in the fight and I guess this is just his way of saving face."

"How so?"

"Look at me. I'm a head shorter. If he tells everybody I'm a Wildling, then he doesn't look like a wuss for letting a little guy like me stand up to him the way I did."

Hayden gives a slow nod.

"Do you know we have zero tolerance toward violence in this school?" he says.

"Yes, sir. And zero tolerance toward bullying, too."

Hayden looks at me, but doesn't say anything. My heart's sinking. The last kids who had a fight on campus each got a couple of weeks' suspension. If that happens, how am I ever supposed to explain it to Mom?

"So are you telling me you were trying to defend yourself?" he asks finally. "That he started it and you were only protecting yourself from his attack?"

"Sir, I'm upset today and I lost my temper. I have to accept the consequences."

He gives me a long considering look before he says, "That's a mature attitude, Josh. I appreciate a student who understands and accepts responsibility for his actions."

I don't know what to say to that, so I just offer up a "Yes, sir."

"You're getting a week of detention," he says. "Lunchtime *and* after school."

"Yes, sir."

"Mrs. O'Shay will give you a hall pass."

"Yes, sir."

I get the pass and head off to my class. As I walk down the hall, I hear the announcement over the school PA: "Erik Gess. Please report to the office immediately."

I don't really care what happens to Erik, but I'd rather he didn't have the chance to plead his case against me all over again. There's nothing I can do about it, though.

❧

I sit through class wishing I were a fly on the wall in Principal Hayden's office. The only positive thing is that I don't get called back to the office. Which means I'm either in the clear or Hayden is still grilling Erik. Or worst-case scenario, he's already called the FBI and letting them handle it.

When class is over, Marina and I head for the library because we both have a study period. As we make our way to a free study station, I see Rachel Armstrong sitting at a table by the windows with a couple of her friends. They pretend indifference when I catch them checking us out, but Rachel gives me a high-wattage smile before she looks away.

"Well," Marina says when we sit down.

"Well what?"

"From the way she was flirting with you, looks like you actually might have a shot with Rachel. At least, for as long as it takes for her to satisfy her curiosity about you."

"Meow."

"Oh, please. We both know she's as shallow as she's cute."

"How do we know that's not just a stereotype?"

"Come *on.*"

"Okay. So maybe I have a shot with her. The funny thing is I'm not really interested anymore."

Marina's eyebrows shoot up.

"Elzie is more than enough for any one guy," I say. "I don't need to go looking elsewhere."

She smiles. "Spoken like a good boyfriend." Then her smile fades and she leans forward, elbows on the table, chin supported.

"What happened when you went to the office?" she asks.

"I got a week's detention."

"For?"

"Fighting."

"Why'd he let you off so easy? Jimmy Ford and Dave Lawson each got two weeks' suspension when they got caught."

"I know. He said it was because I owned up to it and didn't try to make excuses. I think he might be cutting me a bit of slack 'cause of Dillon, too, though he didn't say that."

"Huh. And what about Gess accusing you of dealing and the Wildling stuff? Did any of that come up?"

"I'm pretty sure he doesn't think I'm dealing and he doesn't seem to have made up his mind yet about the Wildling business."

"So that's good, right?"

I shrug. "He called Erik back to the office."

"The whole school heard that. Why do you think Rachel's suddenly interested in you? You've gone from some guy she's maybe noticed in the halls to the guy who stood up to Erik Gess."

"I'm also the guy who might be a Wildling."

She smiles. "Well, yeah, there's that, too. But I don't think anyone's taking it too seriously."

"Erik did. What if he convinces Hayden that I am?"

"The cops would be on your ass by now."

"I guess."

She opens her history textbook.

"We should at least be pretending to study," she says.

I glance at Ms. Fyad standing behind her desk. I don't think the school librarian cares what we do in here, so long as we aren't loud. But I crack my history book all the same. The words blur on the page in front of me, no matter how much I try to concentrate.

It's weird. When I'm keeping busy, I can almost forget how the day started. That business with Erik after lunch, talking to Marina right now, worrying in class about what Erik might be saying to Mr. Hayden ... it all distracts me. But as soon as there's a down moment, it all comes rushing back: the big black cloud of Dillon having killed himself. Some friend I ended up being.

I guess my face is showing what I'm going through because Marina bumps her textbook against mine to get my attention.

"You know," she says, as though we hadn't stopped talking, "this Wildlings business goes back forever."

It takes me a moment to get out of my head and focus on her voice.

"What?" I say. "Random kids turning into animals?"

"No, stories about animal people. They show up in folktales and mythologies from pretty much everywhere in the world. They just don't call them Wildlings."

I sit up. "What do they call them?" I ask.

"Shape-shifters, skin-walkers, cousins, animal people—stuff like that. I ran across a cool site the other night that has all these stories from the Kikimi tribe in Arizona. They're about crow boys and antelope girls and this scary guy they call Old Man Panther. I'll send you the URL."

"Okay, but what about what's happening here in Santa Feliz? Has anything like this happened before?"

"You'd think it must have, but it didn't show up in any of my searches."

"Cory told me that the Wildlings—he calls them cousins—have kept their lives secret for hundreds of years. Then kids here started changing and it got all over the news. Now suddenly the whole world knows about it."

Marina leans across the table. "But what if this happened in the past, before information could go viral? They didn't have the Internet back in the old days. The government could have covered it up, like Roswell."

"Except everybody's heard about Roswell," I say, "and who knows what really went down there. But for sure the Wildlings outbreak isn't a secret—it's all over the news."

"Right," she says. "So we probably need to talk to one of those older Wildlings. Ask them if this has happened before."

"Cory said something to me when I saw him at the mall. That I should look for a mentor to learn more about who I am."

"Was he offering?"

"No. I asked, but he told me my politics were wrong."

"Your politics?"

"Because I hang with Elzie, he thinks I'm into this whole feral return-the-world-to-its-once-pristine-state thing."

"Yeah. She's talked to me about it, too. Do you think she *really* wants that?"

Josh cocks his head and looks at me. "Wow, I'm surprised that she'd throw that one out at you, given the implications of so-called putting the world back to the way it was before humans came along. But she doesn't seem to have it all worked out in her head."

"I know. She's pretty hazy on how all that could happen. But she believes that something has to be done and I'm with her on that, so long as it doesn't harm people."

I nod. "I love that Elzie has such strong convictions about making the world a better place. And she's got way too big a heart to ever hurt anybody."

Marina glances over my shoulder and grins.

"Hey lover boy," she says, "your other girlfriend is still staring at you."

"Shut up."

"Maybe you should go over and talk to her. Or do you want me to?" She puts on a breathy Valley Girl voice and adds, "So, like, Josh, he *really* likes you but he's, like, so *shy*, so he asked me to, like, ask you if you—"

"If you weren't my friend, I'd have to smack you."

She laughs. "And get in trouble with the Principal again. And yet you're smiling."

I am. But that's Marina for you. She always knows how to take your mind off your problems, either by finding something else interesting to talk about or, if that fails, being goofy.

I haven't thought about what happened to Dillon for at least ten minutes.

And I'm feeling much more optimistic about this whole business with Erik and him trying to out me to the Principal. If something were going to go down, it would have happened by now. But the intercom's silent and the only people who seem to be paying me any attention are Rachel Armstrong and her friends.

MARINA

As we go to our last class of the day, the rumour mill out in the halls is in full swing. Everybody's looking at Josh, but strangely, they don't seem to be so concerned about whether or not he's a Wildling.

Snatches of conversation tell me they're not ignoring the possibility that he's been outed, but are more interested that he supposedly has primo dope that he only sells to certain A-list people. They're also excited about him standing up to Erik and wondering why Gess got a two-week suspension, while Josh only got five days of detention. They think he must have some in with Principal Hayden, and half the kids I'm eavesdropping on say he's probably a customer of Josh's. The other half think Josh has paid Hayden off.

Where do they get this stuff?

There's also some gossip about Josh having used some kind of hot new kung fu on Erik, which is so preposterous I don't even know how that started.

But Josh being a Wildling? Nobody in earshot—and I can hear conversations that are some distance away—has entirely bought that, except for the kids in the Purity Club. And you'd pretty much expect them to side with Erik.

Josh is walking with his head down, looking perturbed about all this new attention.

"Give it a couple of days," I say softly at his side. "There'll be some new drama and you'll be old news—just like last time."

"Gimme old news," says Josh.

I laugh. "Yet another good song title."

We get through the last class, everybody impatient and watching the clock until finally the bell rings. Now we can get out of here and Josh can stop being on display.

Except I remember he's got detention.

"I'll wait for you," I tell him. "I want to get a head start on my history homework and if I go home, I'll just end up wasting time on the computer."

We both know I'm not telling the truth, but from the grateful look on his face, I can tell he appreciates the support.

"Thanks," he says, with a soft smile.

My heart wants to melt. He's my favourite person in the world. I'll do whatever it takes to get him through this. Normal may never come our way again, but I want to be there with him for whatever does.

"Come get me in the library when you're done," I say.

"You got it, surfer girl."

I obsess about it all the way to the library. Did he call me that because I love to surf, or was it a reference to The Beach Boys' "Surfer Girl" song which is sappy, sure, but so romantic?

I know he's got Elzie now, but she's not here. She can't be here.

But I am.

JOSH

Desmond catches up to me on my way to detention.

"I know I screwed up," he starts, but I don't let him finish. I need to shut him down before he makes a worse mess of things.

"We're cool," I say under my breath. "Just ... you know. Next time try to think before you open your mouth."

"There isn't going to be a next time."

That seems unlikely, but I let it slide.

"Do you have detention today, too?" I ask.

"Nope. I'm the clean-cut one in our little group. Why would I have detention?"

I roll my eyes.

"Marina's in the library," I tell him as we reach the door to the detention room.

He nods. "Maybe I'll go keep her company. Later."

He gives me a punch in the shoulder, then heads off. I walk alone into the room, feeling like a character in some old Western movie entering the saloon, where everybody's gaze turns in the direction of the newcomer. I see Henry Still—one of the Ocean Avers—sitting by the windows and he flashes me a grin. Nobody's sitting near him. I hesitate for a moment, then take the desk in front of him.

"Yo, Saunders," he whispers. "Way to put that prick Gess in his place. He's had it coming for awhile."

It's kind of funny. Henry and I were friends in elementary school, but then in middle school, he got jumped into the Avers and it wasn't cool for him to hang out with me anymore. He went from being a guy I played pickup baseball games with, or we'd mess around on our boards, to a guy who sneers whenever he sees me coming down the hall. Where he used to have a cool retro-Afro, now he's got a buzz cut with designs shaved on the sides of his head. A half-dozen tattoos and a gangbanger attitude complete the change.

Today—whether it's because all the Ocean Avers must know that Chaingang's been talking to me, or because of this business with Erik—it looks like I'm okay for him to relate to again.

"The guy's a tool," Henry goes on. "Brothers are good enough to put track and field in state finals, but then he turns around and says how there ain't going to be no homeys in Heaven."

"No talking!" Mr. Waggoner calls from the front of the room. He's frowning at Henry and me. "Unless you want another detention on top of this one."

"My bad, Mr. Waggoner," Henry says. "It won't happen again."

"See that it doesn't. I'm tired of seeing your face in here."

I look out the window for a moment—doing my usual check for government cars and men in black—then open my history textbook. I might as well give this essay another go.

MARINA

I'm at our usual table, facing the wall at the far end of the library with my textbook open, but it's pretty hard to concentrate on history when I feel like we're *making* history here in Santa Feliz. As world events go, this Wildling phenomenon must rank right up there with any of the big stories. There's never been anything like this before—unless it *has* happened in the past and it got covered up.

Elzie told me that some of the older animal people, like this Auntie Min, have been around for centuries. How's that even possible? More to the point, will it happen to us? Will we just stop aging? Ever since I took up the drums, it's been so hard to wait to be old enough to finally play in the bars, but I've never liked the idea of turning into an old person like our teachers and parents.

Living forever. How weird would that be? It'd be like you were a vampire without the icky blood-drinking or having to hide away all day from the sun.

Jeez, what if there really *are* vampires?

There's so much we don't know. We really do need to seek out a more experienced animal person—though I suppose I should call them what they call themselves. Cousins.

A big hand ruffles my hair from behind. I twist around to see Desmond standing there, grinning like a fool. We haven't been out of a group setting all day and it's been hard to keep suppressing the fury I feel toward him for outing Josh. I knew he was going to mess up, but I'd still been hoping like hell that he wouldn't.

"Cool takedown on Gess, dontcha think?" Des says. He plops his big frame into the seat beside me. "Erik's been cruisin' for that since middle school. I love that it was Josh who set him straight. Did you see his face? It was hilarious."

I can't believe what I'm hearing.

"You can't possibly be proud of what you did," I say. "All you did was add to the crap that Josh's already had to deal with today. You owe him a huge apology."

Desmond licks his index finger and chalks one up in the air. "Already done, dude. Josh says we're cool. No biggie."

"Come on. Do you really think it's as simple as that? Josh could get beaten up by Erik's gang of jocks or disappeared by the Feds or expelled from school. And stop calling me dude."

"Hey, ease up," Desmond says. "I call everybody dude. And didn't you see how strong Josh is? I'll bet he could take on all of Erik's dorkmeisters at once. *And*," he finishes with a satisfied smirk, "Hayden went easy on him, so he's cool in school."

"This isn't some big joke, Des. It's a massive problem for Josh and he's already really hurting about Dillon."

"Yeah, that sucked."

"Try to respect how Josh wants to handle this. He needs our support, not the clown brigade."

Desmond pushes his long blond mane back with his fingers, finally looking contrite.

"I know I wasn't cool," he says. "That's why I told Josh I was sorry. It really isn't going to happen again, you know. I've got it under control."

"You'd better."

My anger is still bubbling under the surface, just waiting to vent, but I try to calm down. No one is perfect and discretion isn't one of Desmond's strong points. And I can't stand the hangdog expression he's wearing now.

I take a deep breath.

"Listen," I say. "It's been an insane day and we're all just trying to deal. Sorry for getting on your case, but it's hard to watch Josh going through all of this. You know how he likes his low profile and he says he just wants to have a normal life. That's starting to seem less and less possible."

"Like I told Josh, I'd probably try to start over somewhere else if I were him. But man, it sure would suck if he really did take off. Love ya, dude, but The Gang of Two just doesn't quite cut it."

"I'm with you on that, *dude*," I say.

Then I punch him on the arm.

JOSH

Henry falls in beside me as I'm leaving the detention room on my way to the library. I'm not sure I suddenly want to become pals with him, but there's no point in being rude.

"So what's the deal?" he asks.

"What deal?" I say, slipping my backpack onto my shoulder with one strap.

"You know, you and Chaingang."

I shrug. "There's no deal." He gives me a knowing look, but I stick to the story I gave Desmond and Marina. "He was just asking me about my band."

"I forgot about that band of yours. You guys ever play anywhere?"

"Just in Desmond's garage."

"And you're still into surf music?"

"Yeah, but also spy and hot rod."

He shakes his head. "Why would Chaingang give a rat's ass about any of that crap?"

"How would I know? You should ask him."

That shuts him up.

When we get to the library, he tips a finger against his brow and gives me a little salute with it.

"Good slam on Gess," he says and saunters off.

Marina and Desmond are close enough to see.

"Apparently, I'm his new hero," I tell them at Desmond's raised eyebrow, "for taking Erik down a peg."

"Good for you," Desmond says. "But he's not going to help your rep."

"What rep?"

"The one that says you're dealing dope."

"I didn't think of that," I say.

Marina gives me a sympathetic look. "Life's way too complicated."

"No kidding," I say. "Right now I just want to get out of here and forget this place."

Desmond nods. "Music or boarding?"

"How about just vegging in the backyard? Your place, mine, Marina's—I don't care."

"Sounds like a plan," Desmond says as we walk down the hall.

He pushes open the front door and we all step outside. Desmond stops so suddenly that I bump into his back.

"What's going—?" I start.

But then I see them. A half-dozen men in dark suits are waiting for us, holding Tasers in that classic pose I've seen on way too many TV shows and movies like *Men in Black*. I don't know how many times we killed ourselves laughing over that movie. Turns out it's not so funny when it's happening for real and the weapons are aimed at you.

How did this become my life?

The day started bad with the news about Dillon and that business with Erik at lunchtime sure didn't help.

Now it feels like the ground's disappearing underfoot.

"Joshua Saunders," one of the men says. "FBI. We have orders to take you in. Surrender yourself and no one has to get hurt."

I don't see Matteson or Solana or any of the agents I'd recognize. These are all strangers, their eyes hidden behind mirrored sunglasses.

I have a wild impulse to change into the mountain lion, to just take off and leave them in my dust. But then I remember Chaingang's advice.

Don't ever change where they can see.

And I remember what happened to Elzie's friend Danny, how easily they took him down, even in his Wildling shape. Yeah, supposedly it was put on, but it still showed me how easily it could happen for real.

Marina grabs my arm. "Oh, Josh ..."

I shake off her grip. Moving away from my friends, I drop my backpack on the pavement and put my hands in the air. I step forward and it's like I've hit the slow-motion button on an old VCR. I'm being careful to not make any threatening gestures, but they open fire with their Tasers anyway. Three of them.

I hear the *whuft* of the nitrogen cartridges in the handsets as they're discharged.

One. Two. Three.

I lose count.

But I can see the darts coming for me, trailing tiny electrical wires.

My body jumps involuntarily as the electricity hits me.

Every nerve feels on fire.

My vision strobes.

There's a high-pitched whine in my ears.

And then it all goes black.

MARINA

When I see Josh jerking on the ends of those Taser wires, I almost lose control and shift into my Wildling shape. Not that a sea otter could do much good against six FBI agents. But that isn't the point. For one moment, I'm purely in my animal brain, seeing a pack mate in need and desperate to help and I just know I have to do *something*. I can't bear seeing Josh go down, twitching on the pavement like a landed fish.

I don't know how he keeps from shifting into his animal form. I wouldn't be able to stop myself. Maybe the Taser charge is too strong. I smell the charge in the air, the electricity arcing through his nervous system, burning as it goes ...

Desmond grabs my arm as I lunge forward.

He isn't stopping the Wildling in me. He's stopping the girl whose skin I wear. I'm stronger than him, though he doesn't know it. Faster, too. I know I could shrug him off and attack the agents, but there are too many of them and I don't want things to escalate. If I attack, it's possible some of the other kids might follow suit and then more people will be hurt.

So I let Desmond hold me back while I helplessly watch Josh twitch on the ground. It's all I can do not to run and throw myself on top of him to protect him from the FBI.

There aren't a lot of students around the front of the school at this time of day. Most of them just stand around in shock, but several have their phones out, recording the action. While some of the men in suits run up to Josh, a couple of the other agents try to grab those kids and confiscate their phones, but there are too many of them. As soon as the FBI agents begin their approach, the kids scatter in all directions. I know what that means. In minutes, Josh's capture will be on the Internet, where it'll go viral.

Didn't these stupid agents even consider that? The PR fallout is going to be huge because people aren't going to see brave FBI agents taking down a fierce and dangerous Wildling mountain lion. They'll see bullies in suits Tazing some helpless school kid.

No—not just some kid. They'll see Josh. My friend, whom I never even told that I'm a Wildling, too. And it's all because of Desmond and his big mouth.

I have to contain my frustration and anger toward Des, though. There's something more important to worry about. Once this incident goes viral, the FBI will immediately go into denial mode. They'll hide Josh somewhere so deep and far from view that we'll never be able to find him. Whatever we do to help him, we'll have to do it fast.

We watch as two of the agents grab a now-limp Josh under the arms and drag him down the walk to a black van parked at the curb. The other agents get into a pair of black SUVs parked in front of and behind the van. Moments later, the little cavalcade pulls away.

"This is all my fault," Desmond says as they drive off.

"Yeah," I tell him. "It is."

He turns to me with a hurt look, but I don't cut him any slack.

"You *knew* how important it was to keep this quiet," I say.

He nods. "Yeah. I'll take the fall for this. But first chance I get, I'm going to find Erik Gess and beat the crap out of him."

"That won't solve anything."

"No, but it'll make me feel better. He needs to know that ratting anybody out is not cool."

"Ironic, since *you're* the one who really ratted Josh out."

Desmond looks mournful, but just as he's about to say something, some of the kids who took off come drifting back. They mill around Desmond and me, jabbering like monkeys.

"Did you see?"

"Holy crap!"

"Who did they grab?"

"Saunders."

"Who *were* those guys?"

"The one who had the fight with Erik at lunch?"

"I think they were cops."

"Holy shit. I've already got thirty hits on my upload."

"What do the cops want with Saunders?"

"Too bad no one got it from the start."

"I heard he's a Wildling."

"I thought that cop was going to get me for sure."

"So now it's against the law to be a Wildling?"

"My dad'd kill me if I lost my phone. I just got it last week."

"Jeez. First Dillon and now this."

I try not to pay attention to them. Instead, I make a beeline to where I saw something fall when the agents zapped Josh. Bending down, I retrieve Josh's phone.

"What've you got there?" Desmond asks.

I hold up the phone. "It's Josh's. I saw it go flying when they Tazed him."

Desmond picks up Josh's backpack from the walk where it fell.

"There's this, too," he says.

He makes the backpack as small as he can and stuffs it into his own while I scroll through Josh's contacts. I stop when I find the one I'm looking for and thumb the call button.

"What're you doing?" Desmond asks.

"Calling Elzie."

He starts to say something else, but I hold up a finger because the call has gone through.

"Hey there, what's up, lover boy?" Elzie says.

Her voice is light and warm with humour and affection.

"Sorry," I tell her. "It's Marina. The FBI has Josh."

The change in her voice is immediate.

"What? What happened? When did—"

"Is there someplace we can meet?" I break in. "I don't want to do this on the phone."

"How about in front of the old amusement park?"

"I'll be there in ten minutes," I tell her.

"Be where?" Desmond asks as I pocket Josh's phone.

"I'm going to see Elzie," I say. "You should head home."

"What do you mean?"

"There's nothing you can do now."

"But you two can? Are you really that pissed at me? Can't you see it was a mistake?"

This is where I should be telling him about the otter in me, except I've already seen how well that went with him knowing about Josh, so, no. I don't think so.

"I can't have this conversation right now," I tell him. "I have to meet Elzie."

"I *said* I was sorry and wouldn't do it again. Josh said we were cool. What more do you want?"

"I know, but this has nothing to do with that. Can't you please let it go for now and I'll come by your place later?"

"I just don't get what the big secret is."

And then I realize that not having him come along might be the very thing that gives me away. Elzie won't out me. If she hasn't told Josh or Desmond by now, it's not going to happen.

"No secret," I say. "Come along then. But you do realize that Elzie's going to be royally pissed at you, right? Next time you need to open your mouth, think first."

"I get it," he tells me. "Trust me, this isn't a lesson I'm going to forget."

I feel like yelling, too bad you couldn't have thought of that earlier, but I hold back. Instead, I set out at a brisk jog. Screw Des. He can keep up or not.

But I don't have it in me to be mean for long. After a few blocks, I slow down so that he can catch up instead of half-jogging a block or so behind me, trying to follow. I'm not even breathing hard, but he's really winded.

"Holy crap," he gasps. "I wish I had my board. You are in excellent shape."

A few years ago, when Desmond thought his considerable charm would work on any girl he met, that might've been a come-on. Back then he was mooning over me while I was mooning over Josh. Somehow, Josh remained oblivious to it all and after awhile Des and I settled into the easy friendship we have now. The three of us are great together.

Sometimes I have to watch myself, though. I can still be caught off guard by something—like the tilt of Josh's head back dropped by a setting sun, the dying light haloing his hair. That quick grin when he actually catches a wave, or pulls off a particularly tricky lick on his guitar.

But Josh has never looked at me in the same way as he looks at Elzie and there's nothing I can do to change that. Not without maybe screwing up our friendship, the band and pretty much everything.

I should try to go easier on Desmond. I know that deep down he's even more upset with himself than I am. That's got to be hard. Desmond can't help his unbridled enthusiasm and it's a big part of why Josh and I love him.

"You should come out running with me in the morning," I say to Desmond, "instead of lolling around in bed the way you do."

He's still too out of breath to make with a smart comeback. Or maybe he's just being careful because of the way I lit into him earlier.

⟡

When we arrive at the old amusement park, Elzie's already waiting for us on a bench. As soon as she sees us, she jumps up and starts running toward us.

The hot sunny weather we've had all week has gone grey this afternoon—just like my mood. Out past the ruin of the carnival, I can see the ocean. The wind has picked up, carrying the smell of brine and fish inland. The swells are good—not huge, like they are running in front of a storm, but solid.

I don't even feel a twinge that I'm not out there on my board.

As we approach Elzie, I think about how I've never really liked this place the way that Josh and Desmond do. Those broken down rides and abandoned buildings look lost and sad in the daylight and way too creepy at night. But right now I'm happy to be here.

No, that came out wrong. How can I be happy with Josh in Federal custody? I'm just glad to be meeting Elzie here, because maybe we can come up with a way to get Josh back.

I give Elzie a hug when we meet. As always, she looks like a million dollars. I know she shops only in thrift shops, but I *never* find things like she does.

Her usual radiant smile is replaced by worry. "Tell me everything," she says.

"It's awful," I begin.

"Hey, let's grab that bench," Desmond says. "Marina went like a bat out of hell to get here and I need to catch my breath."

Elzie fidgets on her end of the bench while Desmond and I go through what happened. Her gaze grows dark as we relate the events of the day and darker still when Desmond admits how the mountain lion remark blurted out of his mouth. I have to give him credit. He doesn't whitewash it.

"What the hell is wrong with you?" she demands of Desmond. "Can't *anyone* be loyal anymore?"

"I know, dude. I get it now. He's my best friend and I totally betrayed him. I didn't mean to. It just, like, slipped out. I'm such a jerk. You guys must hate me."

My own anger dissipated during our jog. I can't blame Elzie for being upset. I needed to vent just like she does, but now I'm feeling kind of sorry for Desmond. At least he's taking responsibility for messing up.

"We don't hate you, Des," I say. "At least, I don't hate you."

Elzie seems somewhat appeased by Desmond's obvious regret. "What happened next?" she asks.

I tell her how the FBI agents were waiting for Josh when we left the school. She jumps to her feet when I describe how the agents took Josh down with Tasers, even though he was only trying to surrender.

"Those bastards!" she cries. "I should have been there."

"And then they'd have *both* of you."

She shakes her head. "With two moving targets and civilians all around, they wouldn't have taken the chance of hitting a bystander. We would have gotten away."

"Weren't you listening?" I say. "Josh surrendered and they *still* Tazed him in front of everyone. He hadn't even shifted or *anything*."

"Yeah," Desmond adds. "And they didn't give a crap who saw."

"He's right," I say. "Kids were videoing with their phones, but the agents barely even tried to confiscate them. It was almost as though they didn't really care. The footage is all over the Net now."

Elzie frowns. "There's only one reason why they'd make such a public display of capturing him."

I realize she's thinking about Danny Reed, her friend who went to work for the FBI using the subterfuge that he'd been "snatched" to go away with them. I don't know how she can even think that Josh would do something like that, but Desmond jumps in before I can call her on it.

"Uh-uh," Desmond says. "*No way* was Josh selling out like your friend did."

"Then why were they so blatant about it?"

"They're the FBI," Desmond says. "A bunch of goddamn all-powerful sons of bitches. They probably were making an example of him—trying to scare Wildlings into turning themselves in, rather than get taken by force. It won't matter about that evidence all over cyberspace. They'll just claim that there's missing footage that shows Josh was a threat. Or that he's a big-time drug dealer."

"I don't know … it's a lot like what happened with Danny."

"Maybe," I say. "But come on. This is Josh, the original good guy."

Elzie gives a slow nod and sits down again. Her shoulders are slumped, but both hands are clenched into fists.

"This Erik Gess," she says. "He needs to have his lights punched out."

"Totally," Desmond agrees.

I don't argue with them. I'm relieved she's directing the brunt of her anger toward Gess. He's the one who started it all anyway.

"We need to focus on rescuing Josh," I say. I turn to Elzie. "Can you get hold of Cory? Like, now?"

Elzie gives me a puzzled look. "What for?"

"Didn't he already break some people out of the FBI's holding facility?"

"Yeah, but because of Cory's little rescue mission, the Feds will have that place locked up so tight nobody's going to get in or out. Hell, they probably didn't even take Josh there. Now that they know the place is on our radar, they've probably already got him on a plane to who-knows-where."

"We don't know that for sure," I say. "There could still be time to get him back."

Elzie gives an unhappy nod. "I hope so. But I'm not so sure Cory will have anything to do with it if I'm involved."

My stomach is in knots. This is taking way too long.

"We need to get help from somewhere and fast," I say. "We can't do this on our own."

Elzie looks away, past the old rides. For a moment I don't think she heard me, but then her eyes meet mine.

"Let's go see Auntie Min," she says.

"Cool," Desmond says. "What kind of an animal is she?"

"Des!" I say. "I don't think that's something you just ask anybody."

"What? Why not?"

"Your animal skin's a personal thing," Elzie says, "and so's the decision about whether or not you'll go public with it."

"So being a Wildling's like being gay?" Desmond asks.

I think for a moment that he's being serious, but then I catch the smile in his eyes. The silly goof is irrepressible. I elbow him at the same time as Elzie does, so we get him from both sides.

"Ow!" he cries.

"You can be an ass now," Elzie says, "but let's see how funny you end up being with Auntie Min."

"Why?" he asks. "Is she scary?"

Elzie nods. "Formidable is a better word. It's not that she doesn't have a sense of humour. She just doesn't put up with crap from anyone." She stands up and turns to look at us. "So let's get out of here already."

Desmond and I jump up and follow Elzie's quick pace down the boardwalk.

JOSH

I come to, lying in a fetal position on the floor of a van. The after-effects of the Tasers leave me feeling more disoriented than anything else. My body is soaked in sweat, I have tears in my eyes and both nipples are on fire. My arms and legs are tingling and twitching involuntarily. The tremors seem to be diminishing, but the fact that the agent on my left is still aiming his Taser at me stops any notion I might have to sit up. I'm not sure I could yet, anyway, but I am recovering quickly. I wonder how long it would take if I weren't a Wildling.

I look up at him sitting on a sideways bench in front of me.

"I want to call my mom and a lawyer," I say.

"Shut the fuck up," says the agent on my other side.

I can't see him because of my position, but I assume his Taser is pointed at me, too.

"Stay where you are, you little freak," warns the cop I just spoke to. "Move one hair and we'll fry your ass again."

I can tell he's really hoping I'll move.

I find it hard to believe that the FBI would treat a kid like this. I think about Chaingang and what he might have gone through before he went to juvie. Either the cops treated him better or he's way tougher than I am. Probably the latter.

I have no idea how long I was out cold. I think I read somewhere that loss of consciousness from being Tazed doesn't last very long, so I assume I woke up pretty quickly after being dumped here on the floor of the vehicle.

There are no windows in the left side panel that I can see. I try to use my Wildling hearing to figure out what's going on beyond the vehicle so that I can figure out where they're taking me, but the sounds of the motor and the wheels on the pavement echo through the van. I can't clearly make out other noises. I'm pretty sure they must be bringing me to the naval base. I'll know when we hit the gravel road that they're taking me there. Maybe Cory will be able to break me out.

But a few minutes later the van starts to slow right down and I hear what sounds like a massive garage door reeling up. Judging by the echo, we seem to be entering some sort of cavernous place and then we're driving downward. My body starts to slide forward involuntarily, but the cop behind me jams his foot hard against my shoulder to stop the momentum. Under my skin, the mountain lion wants to tear off that foot, but I remember what Chaingang told me and I play it cool.

The incline levels back out and a few moments later, the van comes to a stop. The cop on the left pulls a black hood out of a bag beside him and tugs it roughly over my head.

"Don't try to be a hero," he says. "Make a move and you burn—got it?"

I feel a little panicked when the bag cuts off my sight, the mountain lion grumbling deep inside, where only I can hear it. I'm trying to make sense of this. How do the Feds get away with this shit? When I get out of this, I am so going to expose these sick creeps and sue their asses.

The back door of the van clicks open.

"All yours, Doc," says the agent who just threatened me.

I feel him move aside and then there's someone else bending over me, holding my left bicep. The cloth over my head is making me claustrophobic as hell and it's hard to breathe properly. The mountain lion wants to rip into the hand with its claws. I'm seconds away from letting it out when I feel the prick of the injection and sink into oblivion.

MARINA

I'm so relieved to be actually on our way to see this Auntie Min. I think about Josh and where they might have taken him. I hope that they haven't put him on a plane somewhere. And I pray that he'll resist the urge to change. I don't know that I could.

"Remind me," Desmond gasps as we jog east through town, "why we didn't bring our boards to school today?"

Elzie and I are having no trouble keeping to a nice stride, but poor Des is really being put through his paces today.

We're almost at our destination now. We went through some chi-chi neighbourhoods along the way, but here, rundown adobe houses with big dusty yards have replaced all pretence at classy residential housing. Yard decorations run to junked cars, broken plastic toys and old appliances. The sidewalk is littered with debris from the unkempt palms.

When we reach the lights at Rio Grande Drive, we cross the four lanes of traffic, then turn south to where the homeless have set up their camp of cardboard boxes and lean-tos below the freeway overpass. I've driven by this place lots of times with Mamá and my step dad, but this is the first time I've been up close.

The smell hits me first. I thought it would be rank—some horrible stew of garbage and urine—but it smells sweet, like walking through one of the fruit orchards up north when the trees are all in bloom.

The other weird thing is the silence. You can hear the traffic, but it's not much louder than the sound of the tide from my bedroom. It's quiet enough to hear the birds and the wind in the ragged trees, and I don't think it's just my Wildling hearing that's letting me notice this.

But the visual chaos is anything but peaceful. As we follow in Elzie's footsteps, we pick our way through old mattresses, rusting appliances, broken furniture, and an acre of plastic bottles, pop cans, wrappers and other litter.

It's odd that the city doesn't haul this garbage away, but my step dad says they leave it alone because the town council likes to group all the homeless in the same place. That way they don't have to worry about them camping out in alleyways or on the beach.

There certainly are a lot of people here today—a couple of dozen, at least. I guess the ones that got away after the police crackdown have all drifted back. They may be unkempt and dressed in raggedy clothes, but they also look tough. I try nodding to one or two, but they just watch us pass by with expressionless gazes. I get Wildling *pings* from some of them, but most are ordinary people—or at least as ordinary as anyone can be who lives in a place like this.

The *ping's* a funny thing—a weird combination of a barely-there scent, a tickle and a tiny bell sound. It's just this little low-key awareness that settles somewhere deep in your head.

So I'm surprised when the *pings* I'm getting ramp up as we approach a sofa at the top of the slope by the freeway's pylons.

Though the sky is still mostly grey, a shaft of sunlight beams down and bathes the old woman sitting on the sofa. A pillow supports her lower back, her legs are propped up on a weathered fruit crate and she looks to be about a hundred years old. But not frail-old. More like some old turtle or elephant that just seems more powerful with age.

Her hair is black, without a trace of grey, and her is face brown, like mine. It looks coffee coloured against her white blouse, but her features are more Native American than Mexican: broad face, a flat nose, wide-set eyes.

Those eyes. Her penetrating gaze tells me she's anything but a bag lady, for all that she sits here on a junked sofa under this overpass, with a red shawl around her sloped shoulders and the folds of her blue cotton skirt falling to the ground.

I don't need the super-*ping* coming from her to know why Elzie would describe her as formidable.

The ground seems strange and spongy underfoot—as though it's not entirely solid anymore—and I feel like a little girl who still has everything to learn about the world.

She gives me a slow smile, as though she knows exactly what I'm thinking and approves of my acceptance of my place in the order of things. That smile says that I can't learn until I've realized my own ignorance.

"Hey, Auntie Min," Elzie says as we approach the sofa.

Her casual greeting breaks the spell. Auntie Min's gaze remains deep, but it's mild at the same time. The ground feels solid again, no give, unless I step on a squishy piece of garbage.

Elzie flops down beside the old woman. I can't believe she'd do that uninvited, but there are so many things I don't know about the older animal people.

Desmond and I look around. Desmond spots a couple more old wooden fruit crates and drags them over for us to use as stools.

"These are my friends," Elzie says. "Marina and Desmond."

Auntie Min nods a greeting as she looks from me to Desmond. Her gaze rests on him for a long moment.

"Why did you bring a five-fingered being to see me?" she asks Elzie.

Desmond looks confused. "Five-fingered being?" he starts, but Elzie lifts a hand and wiggles her fingers.

"Humans," she explains. "Wildlings only have hands in their human shapes, so the old cousins call you a five-fingered being."

"So why's she only looking at me?" he asks. "What about Marina?"

When Elzie doesn't reply, he turns to me. I almost see the light go off in his head. Oh crap. I didn't see this coming.

"*Seriously?*" he says. "You're a Wildling, too? Is *everybody* one except for me?"

"It's not like you think," I tell him.

"How's it not like I think? We're supposed to be friends. Josh told us as soon as it happened."

"And look where that got him," I say.

I want to pull the words back into my mouth when I see the hurt in his eyes, but it's too late.

"I guess you just knew I'd screw up," he says.

I shake my head. "I didn't know that for sure. I trusted you to *try* to do the right thing, but I didn't think it was fair to put the burden of my secret on anyone but me."

"Why don't you just admit that you don't trust me? That you've never trusted me?"

"Because it's not true."

"I noticed you said 'try,' not 'do.'"

"Oh, for God's sake, Des. Get your head out of your ass. It's not about you, it's about me and my own fears."

Elzie clears her throat. We both look at her.

"Not really the time or place to bicker," she says.

"Really?" Auntie Min says with a twinkle of amusement in her eyes. "I'm finding it pretty entertaining."

"I'm sure you are," Elzie tells her, "but right now we've got big trouble."

Auntie Min cocks an eyebrow. "Tell me what happened," she says.

Elzie tilts her head toward us. "Let them tell it. They were there."

Desmond and I take turns relating the story of Josh's capture. I see Auntie Min is paying attention, but she remains expressionless.

"I wish you'd brought him here before this happened," she says to Elzie, when we're done. "I haven't seen one of the Mountain Lion Clan in decades."

"Why not?" Elzie asks.

Auntie Min adjusts her shawl and shrugs. "The more the five-fingered beings intrude on our lands, the harder it is to stay safe from their weapons and traps. Members of the larger clans find it more difficult to hide than the little cousins do. A cactus wren or a lizard blends into the landscape easily, but it's not so simple for a mountain lion or a bear.

"The world has changed," she continues. "Everybody needs papers now, so the older cousins are no longer safe, even in our human shapes. These days we're likely to end up in jail because we can't prove we're citizens—we, who were here before any of the five-fingered beings arrived."

Elzie nods. "Jail is where Josh is right now and we need to get him out."

"Perhaps," Auntie Min says.

"Perhaps what?"

"If you were to ask my advice," Auntie Min tells her, "I might suggest you allow him to complete this journey on his own."

"What?" Desmond breaks in. "That doesn't make any sense."

Elzie and I nod in agreement.

Auntie Min regards us with a puzzled look.

"How is this hard to understand?" she asks.

"No one gets out of Federal custody on their own," Elzie says.

"But this is *his* journey," Auntie Min says, wagging her finger at us. "Not yours."

This isn't going at all the way I expected. I don't understand why Auntie Min is suggesting that we just abandon Josh.

I look over at Des, who, like me, is shifting uncomfortably on his crate.

"But what if we make it *our* journey, too?" he asks.

"Then it becomes something different," Auntie Min says. "It becomes a new wheel upon which you will all turn and the young lion loses his chance to learn from the challenge set before him."

"But if we don't try to help him," Elzie asks, "will he be safe?"

Auntie Min shrugs. "Our spirits grow strong quickly when we face adversity. Perhaps he'll be safe. Perhaps he'll use this experience to prepare for a greater danger yet to come."

My heart leaps into overtime. "He's already been captured by the FBI," I say. "What's the greater danger?"

"I'm no shaman, young otter. I can only suppose—the same as you."

Des turns to me. "Otter!" he cries. "Dude, I should've known."

"Later, Des," I tell him, returning my gaze to Auntie Min.

"You said you can only suppose," I continue. What is it that you suppose might happen to Josh?

"I can't read the future. If you want to know how the future will unfold, you must look to the Thunders. Only they know how to read the days to come."

"Who are the Thunders?"

"They're kind of like what we'd think of as gods," Elzie explains, "except nobody calls them that. Apparently they're big-deal spirits who've been around forever—way longer than Auntie Min or Cory."

Auntie Min laughs. "Cory! Oh that boy still has to learn how people need to make their own choices."

I think about the lousy choice that Dillon made and how it's too late for him to learn anything. Killing yourself makes you dead. Period.

"What if those choices are mistakes?" I ask.

Auntie Min shrugs. "We learn more from our mistakes than from our successes. Who are you or I to steal the opportunity to learn from another being?"

"But what if somebody else gets hurt because of a mistake we make? Or what if someone chooses to end their own life? How can they possibly learn from that choice?"

"Those are good questions," she replies enigmatically, without further elaboration.

I give Elzie a look. She shakes her head as if to say, don't bother—she won't answer if she doesn't feel like it.

I'd like to see if Auntie Min has the answer to something else I've been wondering about ever since the otter woke up under my skin.

"Okay," I say. "Can you at least tell us this. Why is this happening now? Why are we changing? Why here? Why us? We're just kids."

173

She studies me just long enough for me to think she's going to ignore this as well.

"It's not our place to question the big Thunders," she finally says, "and why their wheels turn as they do. Our role is simply to take what we are given in this world and make Beauty."

I make an obvious scan of the ugly mess around us. "Do you *really* believe that?" I ask.

"I don't say things that I don't believe."

I wave my right arm toward the piles of trash all around us. "You seem so wise and powerful. Why do you live like this?"

"Live like what?"

"Homeless. In poverty."

Elzie rolls her eyes, but Auntie Min only laughs.

"I'm not poor," she says. "I have the land under my feet and the sky above my head. I have the company of friends and students. I have a place to lay my head, food to eat, water to drink. How is that a life of poverty?"

"But all this concrete and pollution ..."

"... are like a dear friend wearing an ugly set of clothes. It will pass. And nothing can change what lies under the skin of the world. The spirit that burns in its heart remains unchanged."

"So," Desmond breaks in, "about Josh. You're saying that if we help him escape, his life becomes our responsibility—right? That whatever he does or doesn't do from then on—good or bad—it's partly on us."

Auntie Min nods. "At least someone is paying attention."

I give Desmond a considering look.

"What?" he asks.

"I'm impressed," I tell him.

"Don't be," he says. "There was the same kind of a deal in a samurai movie I saw awhile back."

I smile. "Now *that's* the Desmond we all know and love."

He raises his eyebrows.

"So we're good?" he asks.

"You tell me," I say. "Are we?"

He gives me a slow nod. "Yeah. I guess. But I still can't believe you held back on being a Wildling." He holds up a hand before I can say anything.

It's clear that he still feels hurt and that makes me even more anxious about having kept my secret from Josh. Now I'll have to tell him soon. Except for my crush on him, there've never been any secrets between Josh and me until this happened. When I get the opportunity to tell him that I'm a Wildling—*if* that comes—I have no idea how he'll react.

But first we have to get him away from the Feds.

I look back at Auntie Min. "So are you saying that we shouldn't interfere with anything?" I ask. "That even though our friend got kidnapped, even though people are destroying the planet, we should just sit back and let it all happen?"

She shakes her head. "You must do what is strong and leads you into Beauty. For some, it is contemplation that brings them grace. For others, the path to Beauty lies in confrontation and striving. Only you can tell what path you should choose."

"But you said we shouldn't try to rescue Josh."

"No, I said that you should consider letting him complete his journey on his own. But if you twine your path with his, remember this. Having stolen his chance to learn and grow strong, you must be strong for him. Not simply for a day or a week, but throughout your lives. As your friend Desmond already knows, it's a grave responsibility that shouldn't be taken lightly."

"So what would you do?" I ask.

"If a friend of mine were in the same circumstances," she says, "I would do everything in my power to set him free and damn the consequences."

I can't believe she just contradicted herself that badly.

"Then why did you tell us not to?" I ask.

"I didn't. I simply asked you to *consider* those consequences."

Elzie lets out an exasperated sigh and gets up from her side of the sofa. "Unless you've got some practical advice as to how to set him free, we need to get going."

Auntie Min nods. "I will ask the little cousins to look for your friend. As for advice, if you must intervene, you could do worse than to ask the grasshopper mouse for help."

"Who?" Desmond says.

"It's okay," Elzie replies before Auntie Min can. "I know who she means."

"What's a grasshopper mouse?" I have to ask.

"It's a mouse that's more like a wolf or a coyote than a mouse," Elzie says. "They're carnivorous and can howl like a wolf. They live—"

She breaks off as Auntie Min suddenly lifts her head. The old woman's nostrils flare slightly, reading the air.

"We have company approaching," she says.

I watch Elzie rise up on the balls of her feet, trying to see who's coming. "Who?"

"Your friend Daniel."

JOSH

I'm floating in an impenetrable haze. The mountain lion is trying to wake me up, pressing to get out. There is screaming in the distance ... a girl ... a blood-curdling sound beyond anything I've ever heard. The air is charged with panic ... and something else ... an intermittent series of pings. I know what they mean. There are other Wildlings here. Is the girl one of them? What is happening to her?

I need to wake up. Am I dreaming? I have to find out if this is a nightmare or real. An electronic beep that I hadn't noticed before quickens, matching my pulse. There is rustling beside me. A sharp sting in my arm. Nothingness.

MARINA

Elzie scowls and spits in the dirt. "Daniel's no friend of mine."

"He comes ahead, but there are others following him. Five-fingered beings."

"Isn't this the guy that ran off to the Feds?" Desmond says. "Shouldn't we be worried about him showing up?"

"That little weasel? Not likely. I've been dying to get my hands on him."

Desmond frowns. "Weasel? I thought his Wildling shape was a deer of some kind."

Elzie gives him a look.

"Oh," he says. "Not an *actual* weasel."

I can smell them coming now, too. I don't recognize any of the scents, but one continues to approach, while the rest hang behind. Then the wind shifts and I lose them. But by then, I have a visual of a boy I don't know making his way through the trash to where we're sitting. He has short brown hair and a dark tan. The tails of his white golf shirt hang out over beige trousers and he has brown loafers on his feet. In his right ear is a Bluetooth receiver.

"Jesus," Elzie says when he reaches us. "Look at you. They cleaned you right up, didn't they?"

He shrugs. "Nothing wrong with looking nice."

"Nice? You look like you're on your way to a friggin' golf course."

He doesn't rise to the bait. "I need to talk to you."

"So talk."

"Alone."

"If you think I'm going anywhere with you, you're living in dreamland."

His gaze drifts from her to Auntie Min, then to Desmond and me.

"I'm here to offer you a job," he says when his gaze returns to Elzie.

"The way you offered Josh a job?"

"Josh. You mean the kid who got kidnapped from Sunny Hill this afternoon?"

"Like you had nothing to with it."

"We didn't. The Bureau Chief is catching major crap for letting it happen on his watch."

"See?" Desmond says. "I told you they'd play dumb."

"I swear. We didn't take him. Someone else did."

"Yeah, like there's a whole other government branch calling themselves the FBI, running around in their black SUVs, wearing suits and shades."

"Think about it. If that had been our operation," Daniel says, "the guys would have been wearing vests with 'FBI' splashed across them in big bold letters."

He studies Desmond for a moment, before adding, "You're not one of us. Who are you?"

"None of your business," Elzie says. "So what's this job you're offering me?"

"Identifying and tracking down Wildlings, then helping them adapt to the change their lives have taken."

"And you lock them up to help them 'adapt' according to the government's terms," she says, using air quotes.

"It's not like that," he says. "But we have to consider the safety of those kids and the general public as well—"

"*This* is what you've become?" Elzie breaks in. "From an idealist to a government lackey?"

"Give me a break."

"Why? So you can spout more bullshit propaganda at us?"

"Christ," he says. "When did you become so naive?"

"*I'm* naive?"

"Working for the government," he says, "is a way for us to get it all done—all those things we talked about. I'm on the inside, Elzie. I can actually help people and the environment, instead of just talking about it the way we used to."

"What makes you think the government gives a rat's ass about ordinary people or the planet? All they care about is staying in power and not making waves. Unless it's to get rid of something that might upset the status quo. Like *us*."

He shakes his head. "It doesn't work that way."

"No, it's probably way worse than that."

Daniel sighs. "Why do you have to make this so hard?"

"Because I'm true to myself. I don't want to be like you—pretending you're living in la-la land, fighting the good fight—when it's all crap. You're ratting us out for your own benefit. Simple as that."

"It's not like—"

"So what happens now? You call in those FBI buddies who are hiding just out of sight and take me away?"

"I don't want it to come to that. I went out on a limb for you, Elzie. I told them you'd make a great member of the team."

"Really? You must be smoking some really primo stuff."

He sighs and looks back at Desmond. "Look, I don't know who you are," he says, "or why you're hanging around, but *you* need to get out of here. The rest of you are coming with me."

Either he doesn't notice the dangerous flicker in Elzie's eyes or he doesn't care.

"So," she says. "Do your friends know that I can take you down before they can do one damn thing to stop me?"

"You can try," he says.

She starts to move forward, but Auntie Min grabs her wrist and pulls her back onto the sofa. Instead, she stands up herself.

"This has been very amusing so far," Auntie Min tells Daniel, "but you appear to have forgotten who I am."

Her voice is mild. Standing, she's not even as tall as my own five-four. But Daniel still takes a step back.

"I'm wired," he says. "The rest of the team has heard everything we've been saying. If you do something stupid now, you're only going to make things worse for yourselves."

The wind has shifted since he arrived, but I don't need it anymore to track the rest of his team. Behind him, I see three of them approaching—wearing those distinctive FBI vests he mentioned a moment ago—and I assume there are more behind me.

We're so screwed.

We're all on our feet now.

"Get out of here while you can," I tell Desmond out of the corner of my mouth. "No point in all of us being taken."

Elzie nods in agreement, though her hard gaze never leaves Daniel. Desmond, as I should have expected, stays rooted to the spot.

I feel my Wildling side straining to break free—an instinctive need to defend my pack, like we're all floating on the ocean and the sharks are circling in. It's all I can do to leave the decision of fight or flee to Elzie and Auntie Min. But taking off seems less and less of an option as the Federal agents draw closer.

We have maybe a minute before we'll all be dancing on the ends of the wires from their Tasers. Except they're carrying rifles. It takes me a moment to realize that they must be tranquilizer guns. I suppose that even the FBI isn't going to Taze an old lady and a bunch of kids—not after the flak they must have caught with capturing Josh.

Auntie Min regards Daniel evenly. As mild as her face is, the air feels charged with static electricity. "You seem confused," she tells him.

He takes another step back, though she still hasn't even given him so much as a dirty look. He clears his throat.

"What do you mean?" he asks.

"You seem to think I care about the concerns of the five-fingered beings, or the cousins aligned with them."

He shakes his head. "It doesn't matter if you care or not. You still have to come with us."

She smiles. "Don't you remember who I am, young antelope?"

She's so unthreatening that he seems to get some of his bravado back, though he maintains his distance from her.

"Sure," he says. "You're Auntie Min—the old woman who thinks she's queen of the homeless."

The FBI agents are almost upon us. This is it. We are caught unless Auntie Min can pull a miracle out from behind a sofa cushion or out of her sleeve. But all she does is hold out her hands to Daniel.

"If that's all you remember," she says, "then put your handcuffs on me and take me away."

"Auntie Min!" Elzie cries. "What are you *doing*?"

All I can do is stare.

"Shit," I hear Desmond mutter beside me. "My mom's going to kill me."

Mamá isn't going to be happy with me, either, but that's the least of my worries. Bad enough I'm about to be arrested by the FBI, but what about when Mamá finds out I'm a Wildling? Or maybe they're going to disappear me and then she'll think I've just run away. Either way, it'll break her heart. And what about Josh? Who will save him now?

"*Really?*" Elzie says. "We're not going to run?"

"Why would we run?" Auntie Min says, keeping her gaze on Daniel. "We have done nothing wrong. We have broken no laws."

"There's nowhere you *can* run," Daniel tells us.

He's right. The FBI agents surround us now. Daniel turns to them.

"You'd better tranq them now," he says, "before they change and take off. I don't know what their shapes are, but—"

"That's enough, Reed," the lead agent says. "We'll take over from here."

He has the handsome good looks of a leading man from one of those telenovelas I catch Mamá watching from time to time. Under his vest he wears a crisp white shirt and tie and well-tailored pants with a sharp crease.

"But—" Daniel begins.

"I said stand down," the agent tells him.

"That's right," Elzie says. "Be a good little puppy and do what your master says."

Daniel shoots her a dirty look. Auntie Min doesn't even acknowledge the presence of the FBI agents. All of her attention is still on Daniel.

"You might consider this, Daniel," she says. "The Thunders gave you a great honour by waking the old blood in you. But they expect you to prove yourself worthy. Ask yourself this. Are you living a life of worth?"

"You don't scare me," Daniel says.

His eyes tell a different story. I'm not too comfortable with the question myself. What exactly is a life of worth? It probably doesn't include hiding your Wildling aspect and keeping a secret blog. So how would these Thunders judge *me*?

The lead agent steps in between Daniel and Auntie Min.

"Ma'am," he says. "I'm Special Agent Solana. The Bureau Chief has asked us to bring you all to headquarters."

"Why?" Elzie says, her voice rising in anger. "What did we do? And what have you done with Josh?"

"Hush now," Auntie Min says. "These men mean us no harm." Her gaze finally leaves Daniel and fixes on Agent Solana. "Do you, Señor Solana?"

"No, Señora. The Chief only wants to talk to you."

"What's going on here?" Daniel says. "This was supposed to be my—"

Solana cut him off. "We have new orders." He turns back to us. "If you'll come with me?"

Auntie Min now holds her hands out to him.

"You can put your hands down," Solana tells her. "You're not being arrested."

"Then why do we have to go with you?" Elzie demands.

There's a wild, panicked look in her eyes and I realize that she's just as scared as Desmond and me. The difference is, she's on the offensive while we're just trying to make ourselves invisible. Neither strategy is doing much good. The only positive thing I can see is that the agents are no longer threatening us with their tranquilizer guns. Their rifles are slung over their shoulders, with the muzzles pointed to the ground.

"Because I'm asking you nicely?" Solana says.

"Hush now," Auntie Min tells Elzie. "The sooner we do what the nice gentleman asks, the sooner we'll be done with it."

Solana and a tall blonde woman lead the way back to their cars. I fall in step beside Auntie Min. She takes my arm and leans on me as though she needs my support. I'm not fooled, but I suppose the Feds are.

"Now listen to me," she says so softly that only I can hear. "Unless our lives are threatened, you have to keep that otter of yours under your skin, where it can't be seen. Don't show them what you have become and don't admit what you are."

"But they already know we're Wildlings."

"No, they have nothing they can prove. We will get through this so long as we don't give them fuel to treat us as anything but the five-fingered beings we present ourselves to be. You can pretend you're scared—that would be natural, given the circumstances—but no matter what they promise or how they threaten, do not allow them a glimpse of your true nature."

"I don't have to pretend to be scared. And what about Daniel? He can tell them which of us are Wildlings."

She squeezes my arm. "Don't worry. I don't think they put much faith in Daniel. You'll do just fine. Now make sure you let Desmond know what I said."

"I think he'll keep his mouth shut this time. What about Elzie?"

"She knows what she needs to do. She might complain bitterly, but she'll do the right thing."

❧

When we get to where the three black SUVs are parked all in a row, I make my way to Desmond's side and whisper the message that Auntie Min has asked me to give him.

"Come on," he says in a low voice that doesn't hide his annoyance. "You don't think I haven't already figured that out? I'm not going to screw up

185

again."

"I know," I tell him, but it's more for his sake than because I believe it. The truth is, I can't be sure. "Auntie Min just asked me to tell you," I add.

I turn away from Desmond and call over to Solana, "Can I send my mother a text? She's going to be worried."

He stops on his way to the lead car.

"Of course," he says. "You can have her meet us at the office if you like." He nods toward a man standing nearby. "Agent Bryden will give you the address."

He keeps on going without checking what I'll do. Daniel joins him as he gets to the driver's door.

Now I'm really confused. If I can ask Mamá to meet us at the FBI headquarters, they're not planning to make us disappear, are they? They haven't tranquilized us. They haven't searched us or taken away our phones. They haven't put us in handcuffs. And now it's okay for me to text Mamá? So what *do* they want from us?

"Are you sure you want to do that?" Desmond says under his breath as I take my phone from my pocket. He hugs me as if we're an item and puts his mouth to my ear. "You're going to spend an hour just trying to explain how you've ended up here. I mean, dude. Do your parents even suspect you're a Wildling?"

I shake my head slightly.

"And you want to open that can of worms with all of this going on?"

I shake my head again. "You're right," I murmur, pulling back from him.

And he is—if Agent Solana is really as benign as he seems to be. I glance over to where Solana and Daniel are having a hushed conversation by the side of the lead car. If I were an ordinary girl, they'd be too far away for me to hear, but the otter under my skin has excellent hearing.

"—under control," Daniel is saying. "I didn't need you to step in and take over."

"I know you're trying to prove yourself," Solana tells him, "but this was your first field assignment and these orders came directly from the Chief. He wants these people in his office and he wants it handled with kid gloves."

"But *why*? I can tell him anything he needs to know about Wildlings."

"Maybe so. Why don't you take it up with him?"

"He doesn't like me," Daniel says.

I have to smile. Does anybody?

"I can't help you there," Solana says. "But if you want him to respect you, a good place to start might be not arguing about his orders."

As I listen, I go ahead and send Mamá a text telling her I'm with Desmond and not to wait for me for dinner.

JOSH

A buzzing sound fills my ears. My entire head is vibrating. My body aches and I can't seem to move my limbs. I'm vaguely aware of someone's foul breath as they lean over me, doing I don't know what. There are other sensations. A regular beeping sound—faint, but persistent. Have I heard it before? Something is fastened to my left middle finger. I try to raise that hand, but it remains stubbornly beside my body. I'm on my back. My bed feels hard. My head seems to be cradled by some metal support. Where is my pillow?

I struggle to regain consciousness, to wake up from this bad dream. Am I naked? Why do we dream stuff like this? I'm almost there. I'll awake in my bed at home and this weird nightmare will be over. I summon all of my meager strength to wake myself up. My eyelids start to flutter open and I'm instantly blinded by bright fluorescent lights beaming down on me. Instinct has me shut my eyes. I don't know if I could've kept them open anyway.

The mountain lion is straining to wake up inside me. There's an inherent sense of danger all around and strange antiseptic smells begin to seep into my consciousness. I can't subdue my Wildling sense of smell to block it out and I begin to gag involuntarily. Vomit rises from my stomach and wrenches my body, but I can't even turn my head to get rid of it. I'm drowning in my own puke. Why won't my eyes open?

"Give me a hand here," a female voice says. It sounds faint and garbled. "Quick, we're losing him."

Now my jaw is being wrenched to the side and vomit suctioned from my mouth. Something hard is being forced down my throat and I gag once more. A breathing tube. And again, the prick of an injection.

The mountain lion and I fall back into the void once more.

MARINA

They split us up for the drive. Daniel is in the front car, Auntie Min and I in the second, with Desmond and Elzie in the last. It's a short trip.

There was never an FBI field office in Santa Feliz before the Wildlings outbreak—there'd been no need. But now they've taken over the old Bayside Realty building by the marina, which has been empty since all the mortgage foreclosures made them go out of business. I know all of this because Julie Harrison's mother worked there until Bayside closed. Julie and I used to go by after school every couple of weeks and wait for Mrs. Harrison to finish work. Then she'd drive us down the coast to Tiki Bay, where we'd surf until sunset. The only obvious difference between then and now is that the Bayside sign is gone and the parking lot is filled with black sedans, SUVs and vans.

A crowd of reporters is milling outside the front doors, while the street is lined with news vans.

"Damn," I hear Solana say over the car radio. "We'll go in the front and keep them busy. The rest of you take our guests in through the back."

The lead car pulls into the front parking lot while we continue down the street, the car holding Desmond and Elzie following us. I look back to see the reporters swarming the first car until we're around the block. There's a newly erected tall chain-link fence all around the back lot, which makes me think of prison. One more turn and we pull up to a gate, where a guard lets the car through. We park by the back door of the building and the agents hustle us from the vehicles.

"They're going to split us up," Desmond whispers to me as we're led into the building, "so let's stick to the same story. We were just hanging out. If they want anything else, just give them the silent treatment."

I roll my eyes. *Good luck with that*, I think, but I don't say it aloud.

But we aren't put in cells or even in separate interrogation rooms.

Instead, we're all ushered into a large office on the second floor with a fabulous view of the marina. A large white man with a shaved head is behind the desk, peering at a laptop. He glances up, but doesn't rise when we're brought in. His dark suit is looking a little rumpled, the top button of his white shirt is undone, and his tie is hanging loose. Dark rings under his eyes tell me that he's tired and his five o'clock shadow might've been a fashion statement if he didn't look more like an accountant than an FBI agent. But although he only gives us a quick once-over before returning to whatever is on the screen of his laptop, I sense he's the kind of person who doesn't miss a thing.

He motions distractedly toward a sofa and a pair of chairs along the wall. We head over to the seats.

I watch the man at his keyboard. The screen casts a faint blue glow onto his face.

"Sorry," he says. "I just need to finish this."

Beyond the window, the masts of the boats in the marina look beautiful in the evening sun. I don't want to be here. I want to get Josh back. Then I want to return to Auntie Min's camp, where I can learn more about the old cousins and the new Wildlings. When she was talking about us, I didn't feel like a freak. I felt special. Like we have a purpose, even if we don't know exactly what that purpose is. I don't know how we're supposed to find out what it is, but I'm *so* ready to learn.

After several minutes, Agent Solana and another man in a suit enter the room. They lean against the wall near the door. The new man's cold blue eyes give us a once-over before he turns his head toward Solana.

"What've we got here?" he says in a voice so low that I only hear it because I'm a Wildling.

I instantly dislike the newcomer. It's not just his creepy pale eyes. It's the way he carries himself. He's big and broad-shouldered with just a hint of swagger. And he clearly doesn't like us.

"Beats me," Solana replies, leaning over to speak in the other man's ear. "The Chief just said to bring them in and to be nice about it. Boy, did that ever put a bug up Reed's ass."

"Who gives a shit? The kid's an asshole. Using Wildlings to catch Wildlings was a lousy idea—I said it from the start."

"Apparently we're not catching them anymore," Solana says. "Lindel wants us to—"

He breaks off because the man at the desk shuts his laptop and looks across the desk at us.

"Again," he tells us, "I'm sorry for making you wait. But ever since that boy got abducted at the school, there's been hell to play. Parents and the media are going nuts and politicians are after our heads." His gaze drifts over us. "Some of you are his friends, correct?"

Desmond and I nod uncertainly. Elzie gives him a stone face. Auntie Min has taken out a bracelet of Hopi fetishes and is playing the carved animal figures through her fingers as though it's a rosary, except she's smiling, rather than looking serious the way Mamá does when she's saying her Hail Marys. Auntie Min doesn't seem to be paying attention to anything but her bracelet.

"My name's Jason Lindel," he goes on, "and I'm the Bureau Chief here in the Santa Feliz office. I'm hoping we can help each other."

"To do what?" I find myself asking.

"To get your friend back."

"Well you could just try releasing him," says Elzie, sarcasm dripping from her voice.

"What would make you think we have him?" asks Lindel.

"We were there," I say. "The FBI Tazed Josh and took him away."

"That wasn't the FBI who abducted your friend. It was someone else."

Elzie gives a derisive snort, but he ignores her, his gaze on me.

"Anything you can tell us could help," he says. "Something he might have said, or that you might have noticed. Has he been in trouble lately? Have there been any suspicious strangers hanging around?"

"Oh, come on," Desmond says. "There's been nothing but suspicious strangers hanging around."

So much for the silent treatment. Des, I plead inwardly, please don't tell them too much.

Lindel nods. "Can you describe these strangers?"

Desmond hooks a thumb to where the two agents lean against the wall by the door.

"Guys like that," he says.

"So these men who took your friend—you've seen them before."

"Dude," Desmond says, "your agents have been following him around for days now."

Lindel's gaze goes briefly to his two men before returning to Desmond.

"And you know this because …," Lindel checks a note on his desk, "… Joshua told you this?"

"I know it because I'm not blind. Your men have been hanging around the school for days now. They're in our neighbourhood, following us everywhere ..."

I think the Bureau Chief is being very patient, but I'm also proud of Desmond. He's keeping himself in check, but he's standing up to the cops who Tazed Josh and hauled him away. For my part, I just want to go hide somewhere—and I'm the Wildling.

"If our men have been watching you," Lindel says, "it's only for your protection. "

None of us believe him. Really, what else is he going to say?

"Let me get this straight," Elzie interrupts. "You're *seriously* pretending you had nothing to do with Josh getting grabbed?"

"I can assure you Ms. ...?" He lets the question hang until he realizes she's not going to answer and then goes on. "We had nothing to do with it his abduction. The Bureau doesn't operate like that."

"Oh sure," she says. "Just like you didn't pretend to snatch Danny."

Lindel pauses. "I see why you feel that way, but apparently, Reed asked us to. It was a bad judgment call—especially in light of what happened today."

"We didn't know those men at the school," I find myself saying. "But they identified themselves as FBI."

"Why are we here?" Elzie breaks in. "And don't give us that bull about trying to help each other. Twenty minutes ago, Danny Reed said he was arresting us."

Lindel glances at his agents. "Solana?"

"Reed did say that to them," Solana tells his chief. "He seemed to think he could get them to give up information. He also tried to recruit this young woman," Solana adds, motioning toward Elzie.

Lindel nods. "I'm going to want a full report on that."

"Screw you and your reports," Elzie says. "Either be straight with us and tell us what you've done with Josh, arrest us, or let us go."

Lindel rubs his face with his hands, then looks at us again.

"I think we need to start over," he says. "As I said, my name is Jason Lindel and I've been hired to lead the FBI's Santa Feliz field office. Either the brass think I'm good at what I do and can get things under control here, or I've pissed somebody off and this posting is my punishment. I've been here a week and I'm still playing catch-up. The men by the door are Special Agents Matteson and Solana.

"The Wildlings problem—" He holds up a hand, palm out, before Elzie can protest. "Okay, *issue*. Can we just accept for the sake of argument that there is one?

"The Wildlings issue has become a problem," he goes on, "because it's escalating out of control. We've got kids being shot, suicides, a population that's getting more antsy by the day, and pressure from various political and religious groups to put a fence around the whole place, lock it up tight, and throw away the key.

"And now we've got some unknown party abducting a kid from right in front of his school—which, I have to tell you, is probably just the start of a whole new mess of headaches."

"Josh isn't a Wildling," Elzie says.

"Fine," Lindel says. "To be honest, from the evidence I've seen so far, it could go either way. What hasn't changed is that he's been taken by persons unknown and we need to find him. I wanted to have this meeting with you to see if we can put our heads together and figure out what to do next."

I hear Matteson's small grunt of disapproval, but I like the way Lindel levels with us and doesn't talk down. Maybe he's telling the truth. The guys who Tazed Josh weren't wearing FBI vests. But for the moment, I'm reserving judgment. I don't know who to trust.

Lindel studies us for a moment before he says, "So now you know who we are ..."

He lets his voice trail off. I wait a moment to see if anybody else is going to speak.

"My name's Marina," I say finally. "Desmond and I are in a band with Josh."

Desmond holds up a hand when I mention his name.

"Thank you," Lindel says.

His gaze turns to Elzie. She gives a theatrical sigh.

"I'm Valerie," she says.

Lindel waits a moment. He knows she's lying. We all do. But he doesn't call her on it. Instead, his gaze goes to Auntie Min.

"I'm no one," she says. "Just an old homeless woman who happened to be nearby when all this excitement began. But you may call me Señora Mariposa."

Just for a moment, I think I see something shimmer in the air behind her as she speaks. It's a ghostly image of a giant moth, its wings a mottled brown and black with startling bands of white, and tiny iridescent turquoise highlights appearing here and there like stars in the night sky. It's there and gone so quickly that I think I've imagined it.

Lindel is looking right at her, but he doesn't seem to have noticed. Neither did the others on the sofa beside me. But I hear Agent Solana shift his feet. I turn to see that he appears pale and uncomfortable, though Matteson has the same bland expression that Lindel wears.

Mariposa means butterfly, but the shape behind Auntie Min was a moth. I wonder if it's some kind of projected aura of her animal shape and why Solana could see it.

Señora Mariposa. Mrs. Butterfly.

I sort of remember a movie or something with that name. *Madame Butterfly*. But that's an opera, isn't it? Then something else comes to mind.

When I was really young, before Mamá tried to reshape us into brown-skinned gringas, she would tell Ampora and me stories that her own mother had told her. Old folktales from the desert peoples of Sonora, where Mamá's family originates. There was one about a butterfly. A scary one ...

And then I remember. *Mariposa de la Muerte*. The black witch moth. Depending on who was telling the story, they were either harbingers of death, or the souls of the dead. In Mamá's story, they were the familiars of a powerful *brujá*.

I look at Auntie Min, then glance over to Agent Solana again. Is that who she's saying she is? I have no idea why I've even thought of that old story of Mamá's, but I can tell that Solana saw what I did and he doesn't like it. Has he heard the same stories from his own mamá? He sees me staring at him, so I turn away.

"Chief?" Matteson says.

Lindel nods to him.

"Reed says the old lady's a Wildling—'old school,' he called her."

Lindel looks back at Auntie Min.

"I thought it was only teenagers who had been changed," he says.

It's hard to figure out who he's talking to. Matteson? Auntie Min? Himself?

"That's what we've been assuming," Matteson says. "There've been no been no reports of adults having changed."

Solana nods. "But there've always been stories about animal people—long before this Wildlings business came up. Werewolves, Navajo shape-shifters, Kikimi crow people."

"Right," says Matteson. "And Santa Claus lives at the North Pole and flies around the world delivering presents on Christmas Eve."

Lindel sighs. "But if kids can turn into animals, who knows what else is hiding out there?"

"Just because one impossible thing is true," Auntie Min says, "that doesn't mean everything is."

Lindel studies her for a long moment. Finally he nods.

"So why did you agree to come here?" he asks.

She smiles. "Because the nice Señor Solana asked me to."

Lindel's gaze goes to Solana, who can only shrug.

"She was there when Reed approached the others," Solana says. "You told us you wanted to question anyone who might know something. And as Matteson just said, according to Reed, she's one of them."

"This arrangement with Reed needs a serious revisit," Lindel says, before he returns his attention to us.

"So here's where I stand," he tells us. "I've got the media and my bosses on my case. Everybody's demanding answers when all I've got are questions, but the longer I don't come up with some results, the worse it's going to get.

"But that's not what's important at this moment. Right now, persons unknown have grabbed your friend Josh, and I don't care if he's a Wildling or not, we need to get him back. Safe and unharmed. So if there's anything you haven't told us, *anything* you can do to help, now would be the time to step up and be heard."

"You're seriously saying you want *our* help?" Desmond asks. "Dude, we're just a bunch of kids. What're we supposed to do?"

"Exactly my point," I hear Matteson mutter under his breath.

Lindel spreads his hands across the desk. "Yes, you're just a bunch of kids," he says. "But this is all about kids, isn't it? Adults aren't affected by whatever it is that remakes an ordinary teenager into a Wildling." He glances at Auntie Min before adding, "At least, so far as we know."

"Okay," Desmond says. "Just saying you guys aren't responsible for what happened to Josh—and to be honest, I still don't buy that—the question you've got to answer, dude, is this. Who's got the most to gain from you taking the rap for it?"

"I highly doubt that anyone's trying to frame the FBI," Lindel begins.

Desmond shakes his head. "Come on, dude. Seriously?"

I've never seen Desmond quite like this. Calm, sure of himself, disarming and just a little bit cocky. Usually he's the one who gets hot under the collar.

"Kid's got a point," Matteson says. "Why else would they pull a stunt like that in the middle of the day with all those school kids around? They had to know that someone was going to record it, throw it up on the Net and we'd take the heat."

"Okay," Lindel says. "So who could it be and why would they do it?"

Matteson shakes his head.

"The other thing we have to work out," Solana says, "is why they took that kid. It's one thing to bring in a tame Wildling like we did with Reed, but this is a whole other ball game. I've watched the footage. I don't think Josh is that good an actor. He looked scared. And those men were violent. You don't Taze someone who is compliant."

"And he's not a Wildling," Elzie puts in. "None of us are. Danny Reed is full of shit. He's just a loser who wants to act like he's some big important cop."

Matteson rolls his eyes, but Lindel nods.

"We're not here to debate who's what," Lindel says. "Our priority is to get Josh back and find the perpetrators so that this doesn't happen again.

"Now, if no one has anything to add, you can all go. But please, if something comes to mind, even the smallest detail, call us immediately. Agent Solana will give each of you his card."

"So we can go?" Elzie says. "Just like that?"

"You were never under arrest," Lindel says. "We're not your enemy."

Agent Solana hands each of us his card and escorts us down to the back door.

"I'll have someone drive you to wherever you need to go," he says.

Auntie Min pats his arm. "Oh, that won't be necessary. I'm not that feeble."

"Yeah," Elzie says. "We want to walk."

Solana nods. "Try to avoid the press out there. The guard will let you out the back gate. Think about what Chief Lindel told you. We want to get Josh back as much as you do."

"We will," I say.

"But if you send Danny after us again," Elzie adds, "you'd better make sure he's got an army with him, because the next time I see him, I'm going to pop him one."

Solana tries not to smile. "It's not wise to make threats, young lady. But by the time the Chief gets through with him, Reed is going to have a lot more on his mind than you."

"Just give him my message," Elzie says, undaunted.

Auntie Min takes her by the arm before she can go on.

"Help an old lady home," she says.

"I thought you just said you weren't feeble."

Auntie Min looks at Solana and shakes her head.

"Young people," she says.

Then she sets off, not so much leaning on Elzie for support as walking her away from the building. Desmond falls in behind them. I would follow, except that Agent Solana touches my shoulder.

"Back in the office," he says. "What happened there? When she said her name, I thought I saw ... I don't know. Something. And I know you did, too."

I hesitate for a moment, then nod. I know I shouldn't trust him, but I find myself liking Solana, so I decide to be honest.

"I don't know," I tell him. "It was weird. Like there was a big moth behind her." I wait a moment, then add, "You've heard the stories."

"Of course I have. I grew up in the barrio—not here in Santa Feliz, but the stories don't change."

"Mamá told me that *Mariposa de la Muerte* can pull aside the veil between the worlds."

"In the ones I heard, she was the Angel of Death." He looks down the street. "You don't think she's really ...?"

He can't bring himself to say the words and I don't blame him. It seems so implausible.

"Maybe she just did it for effect," I say. "To freak us out."

"If that's the case, it's working. I felt like I was seven years old again and listening to Tía Margarida's spooky stories."

I see that Desmond has stopped and is waiting for me, looking mildly annoyed.

"Your partner doesn't like us," I say to Solana, before I go to catch up to Des.

"Agent Matteson takes his job seriously," Solana says. "To serve and protect are more than just words to him. In the Bureau, we know that the kids who've changed aren't evil, but ever since it began, there's been a hell of a lot of collateral damage. It's our job to keep people safe and that includes Wildlings. And your friend Josh."

"Then why are you harassing Wildlings?"

"We're not. We're simply trying to protect everyone from harm.

Sometimes that means taking dangerous people off the streets and doing what we can to teach them not to hurt anybody, or themselves."

"I don't know ..."

"Just think about it."

I want to defend Wildlings, but that would risk exposing my secret. So I leave it at, "I will," and hurry off to join Desmond.

"Getting all chummy with the fuzz, are we?" says Des as I get to him.

"I don't know," I say. "Maybe it really wasn't them who took Josh. I mean, three guys Tazed him even though he was surrendering. He's just a kid. Even with all the bad cop stories you hear, that seems way over the top."

"So if it wasn't the cops, then who the hell was it?"

"I don't know, Des, but we've got to find out and we've got to save him."

JOSH

I wake up disoriented. I'm lying on my back. On the other side of my closed eyelids, everything looks white—like I'm under a bright spotlight. I have this vague sense of déjà vu.

My mouth is dry, my throat is really sore, and my tongue feels swollen, too big for my mouth. There's a dull ache in my head, just behind my eyes. My whole body is tingling with that pins-and-needles feeling you get when your foot or your arm goes to sleep. I smell strong cleaners and antiseptics, glass and steel. I'm lying on some kind of thin mattress. I can hear the soft murmur of machines but there's only one person close by. A little *ping* of recognition tells me it's another Wildling. It's no one I know.

I have a vague recollection of hearing screams, and another of being strapped to a table, but the last thing I remember with any clarity is getting an injection in the van. I can't even begin to guess how long ago that was, where I am, what's going to happen next. I'm thinking I should play dead a little longer. Just because I can't smell or hear anybody close by, doesn't mean I'm not being watched.

I decide I don't care.

I open my eyes and sit up, and immediately wish I hadn't. Everything goes spinning around me and I think I'm going to hurl. I put out a hand to the mattress to regain my balance and my whole arm feels clunky—like it belongs to someone else. I manage to get it in place before I topple over. I find if I don't move, the spinning and nausea finally start to go away. The pins-and-needles feeling takes longer. The headache sticks around.

The other Wildling is in the cell behind me. His breathing is so even, I think he's asleep.

The cell I'm in—I don't even know if I can call it a cell. It's more like a glass box. I can't tell where it opens, or how. There's a row of them in the direction I'm facing. Five more, all empty except for mattresses and stainless steel toilets. No pillows or sheets or even a blanket. No taps, no sinks.

That reminds me that I'm thirsty. Wanting something to drink makes my stomach rumble, but the nausea's too recent for me to want any food.

Beyond the glass cubicles, the rest of the room seems to be some weird combination of a science lab and a hospital operating room. It's all gleaming steel, the walls white. Rows of fluorescent light above leave no chance of shadow anywhere except for under the operating tables.

I take the chance that moving won't give me vertigo again and turn around to find the Wildling sitting up on his mattress, looking at me. He's like me—just a kid—dressed in some kind of white cotton pants and a shirt. I'm dressed the same, I realize. That's kind of creepy. People I don't know and never saw took off my clothes and put me in these. That's even creepier.

He's a skinny white kid with a fading tan, sharp angular features and big blue eyes that have a world-weary look that doesn't really go with his age. It's hard to tell, but I think his hair is blond—his eyebrows certainly are. His hair is cut so short it might as well not even be there. It's not until I see his shaved head that I realize my own head feels light. I lift a hand and all I find is stubble as short as his. My dreads are gone.

I hear a growl. It takes me a moment to understand that it's coming from me. It's not my stomach. It's the mountain lion under my skin, reacting to my anger. I remember what Chaingang told me.

If the Feds pull you in, don't let them see you change. Not even if they lock you up. Don't ever change where they can see.

I push the mountain lion away so that it's not so close to my skin.

"Whu—" I have to stop and clear my throat. "Where are we?"

"I don't know. I'm Rico."

"Josh."

"How do you feel?" he asks.

"Like crap. Dizzy. Nauseous. Thirsty."

He nods. "That's the drugs."

"Drugs? What kind of drugs?"

"I don't know. Some kind of tranquilizer."

"I don't feel very tranquil."

"That's 'cause they're wearing off. They shot you up so that you wouldn't bust free."

"Do I look like I could take on a bunch of grown men?"

"They think you're a Wildling."

"Well, I'm not."

He gives me a thin smile and nods. "Yeah, me neither."

"How long have you been here?"

"I'm not sure. A few weeks. There've been others, but I don't know where they are now. A girl was locked up in your cell for awhile, but they took her away yesterday and I haven't seen her since. She ... she wasn't doing so good. They'd taken a lot of blood from her."

Chills crawl up my spine. "What do you mean?"

He shrugs. "Like I said, they kept taking blood ... and ... tissue samples. After awhile she kind of started to lose her mind. She was screaming a lot and really freaking out. Yesterday they moved her out."

"*I'm* freaking out," I say. "How can our own government treat us like this?"

"I don't think this is a government lab."

"Then what is it?"

He shakes his head. "I have no idea. But they're pretty determined to figure out what makes a Wildling tick."

He shifts his position and I see he's missing his right leg from the knee down. He catches me looking at it.

"Like I said, they've been taking blood and tissue samples ever since I got here," he says. "A couple of days ago, they decided they needed something more substantial."

I can't look away from where the cloth of his pants goes flat past his knee.

"Are you ... are you saying ... did they ...?"

It's so insanely horrible I can't seem to get it out. My stomach does a flip and I taste bile. I want to throw up.

"Yeah," he says. "They cut it off two days ago. I think that's what made Jenny really lose it. She knew what was coming."

"Jesus. How can you be so calm?"

He shrugs. "I went crazy when I first got here, but it didn't do me any good. Now I'm just trying to make it through, one day at a time."

I can't imagine ever being able to do that. Right now, all I want to do is let the mountain lion take over. It could smash its way out of this glass cage and rip apart anybody who got in the way of our getting out of here. Screw Chaingang's advice.

But what if I can't break the glass? What if I change and all it does is give them what they want?

I force myself to breathe slowly.

"Why would they cut off your leg?" I finally manage to get out.

"Like I said, they needed a bigger tissue sample. They're also interested in seeing if my leg grows back."

"That's insane."

He shrugs. "Some lizards can grow back their tails. Since I don't have a tail, they're curious to know if the leg'll grow back instead. But that was just an afterthought. They took my leg because of their experiments." He points to a refrigerator unit I hadn't noticed before. "They store it in there when they're not working on it."

Now I really want to hurl.

"That ... that doesn't make any sense," I say.

"They think my Wildling shape is a lizard. I think one of the others told them that."

"But you're not a Wildling," I say for the benefit of the invisible audience that might be watching.

"No more than you," he says. "We're just really unlucky kids."

"I can't believe that this is happening. What about our civil rights?"

"I guess they figure we're Wildlings so we don't have any. And we don't know whose lab this is. Could be government. Could be some mad scientist."

I shake my head. "No, look at all of this equipment. It's got to be worth a fortune. This isn't somebody working on his own."

"It doesn't really matter who it is," he says. "We're still stuck here."

Not if I can help it, but I don't say that aloud.

MARINA

Desmond and I have caught up to the others and we're now several blocks away from the FBI field office. It looks like we've eluded the media by taking a circuitous route along back streets. No one seems to be following us.

Now we're heading back toward the sea, rather than the overpass. I have no idea why, or where we're going. There's been so much rolling around inside my head that I've just followed Auntie Min's lead, but I'm getting more worried with every step.

The sky is barely starting to turn that lovely combination of pink, orange and purplish blue that we so adore in Santa Feliz. There are bunches of people who sit by the ocean and actually applaud the sunset nightly. Normally I love it, too, but today it just reminds me that in another hour or so, it will be dark and we're still no closer to finding Josh.

"We should never have stopped to listen to Danny," Elzie is saying. "I should have kicked his ass the moment he showed up and we could have motored out of there along with everybody else."

The homeless people and Wildlings under the overpass really did do a quick disappearing act as soon the FBI arrived.

"But we learned such interesting things," Auntie Min says.

"Yeah, nobody knows zip. Big whup."

"That, too," Auntie Min says. "But it seems we have unexpected allies. Or, if not allies, then at least five-fingered beings who are willing to listen to reason."

"Who cares?" Elzie says. "What we need to focus on is finding Josh."

"Oh, I've been working on that," Auntie Min says. "Let me go check on how the search is going."

She walks across the street to the far side of a convenience store parking lot. The raggedy jade hedge there seems to be filled with birds—mostly sparrows, finches and doves. On the telephone wires above, a pair of crows loiter in that nonchalant way crows excel at. Auntie Min walks up to the hedge and pauses, apparently having a conversation with some invisible presence.

"What's she doing?" Desmond asks.

"Looks like she's talking to the birds," Elzie tells him.

"Yeah, right."

"Well, could be she just wants us to think that," Elzie adds. "She's a master of subterfuge."

Desmond rolls his eyes. "And what are the birds saying?"

"I don't know. Tweet, tweet?"

"Very funny."

"But it really does look like a conversation," I add.

We all cross the street, but wait on the sidewalk, keeping a respectful distance. I turn to Elzie and Desmond.

"I'm worried," I say. "Auntie Min doesn't seem real down with the idea of rescuing Josh and it's driving me nuts standing around like this."

Before they can respond, Auntie Min heads back across the parking lot toward us.

"I've got news," she says when she joins us. "Do any of you know of a company called ValentiCorp?"

"Sure," Desmond says. "They're in that big shopping center out on Cerritos Drive. You can see it from the freeway. Computerland is in there, and Target and a bunch of other stores, but ValentiCorp is that huge place in the middle. You can't miss it."

Auntie Min nods. "That's it."

"So what about them?" Elzie asks.

"That's where they took Josh—a half-dozen men in black vehicles wearing black suits. Does that sound right? Sparrows aren't good at counting."

"What?" Desmond says. "Dude, wait a second. That doesn't make sense. What would some big company want with Josh?"

"I don't know anything about ValentiCorp," I say. "What do they do?"

"Come on, you know," Desmond says. "It's that tall shiny black building right in the middle of the complex—all glass and steel—with the fancy-pants gold lettering on top. The logo must be at least twenty feet high. I'm almost sure it says 'Research and Development' under their name."

"Yes, I know the building," I say. "But what kind of company are they?

Research and development of what?"

"Who knows? Whatever it is, it can't be good if they're willing to abduct people. I've got a bad feeling about this. It looks more and more like the FBI were telling the truth after all."

Auntie Min nods. "We have to get him out. This is bigger than I originally thought."

I let out a breath I wasn't aware of holding. I'm so relieved that she's changed her mind and wants to rescue Josh. We need all the help we can get. I think of the men who kidnapped him. Who knows how many more of them are in the building.

"How will we get him out?" I ask. "Should we call Agent Solana?"

"Not yet. I'm still considering our best approach." She gives me a bright smile, which, for some reason, makes me uneasy. "I have to collect a few things first, so you go ahead. I'll meet you there."

"It'll take us forever to get out to Cerritos Drive from here," Elzie says.

"If you were walking the whole way," Auntie Min agrees. "But I sent one of the crows to fetch Theodore. He'll give you a ride."

I can't help it. I look up at the wire. There's only one crow there now.

"Don't dawdle," Auntie Min says.

She turns and crosses the parking lot again. She seems to be just walking, but she moves with Wildling speed now. In moments, she rounds the hedge.

"Wait, Auntie Min," Elzie yells, darting after her and stopping dead when she gets to the other side of the hedge.

"She vanished," she calls back to us.

"People don't just vanish, dude," Desmond says.

"Most people don't get messages from birds, either," I tell him.

"Let's get moving," Elzie says when she trots back over to us. "If Auntie Min really sent a message to Theodore, he'll find us along the way."

"Do you know him?" I ask as we head off in the direction of Cerritos Drive.

"Yeah, he's that grasshopper mouse Auntie Min was telling us about before Danny showed up."

"Aw, man," Des says as we start to pick up our pace. "Are you two going to put me through this *again*?"

"Have we found Josh yet?" I say.

"Point taken. But dude, when this is over, I'm going to sleep for days."

Elzie and I just smile at each other and keep to a brisk trot. Dusk is coming on fast.

"There's something else," I say as we motor along. "Did either of you see something weird when she called herself 'Señora Mariposa'?"

They shake their heads.

"There was this big moth in the air behind her," I tell them. "I mean *huge*." I stretch my arms out wide.

"Wow, I didn't see that," Elzie says.

"Yeah, me neither."

"Well, Agent Solana did. So is it something about him that let him see it, or was it something Auntie Min did?"

"Who knows," Elzie says. "Like I said, she's got mysterious ways. I think there are all kinds of secret things the old ones can do—things that maybe we can do, too." She turns to me. "Doesn't it feel to you like they're keeping stuff from us?"

"I wouldn't know. She's only the second of the original animal people that I've ever met."

"Was the first Cory?" Elzie asks.

I shake my head. "I've never met him. This guy named Jez showed up the first time I changed and gave me some of the basics the way Josh says Cory did with him. I could have died of embarrassment."

Elzie laughs. "Because you were stark naked."

That catches Desmond's attention and he adds a little speed. "Really? You have to get naked to change?" He grins at me, then adds, "That's cool."

"It's not cool when it's happening to you," I tell him.

"Maybe not from your viewpoint," he says and dances back as I go to punch him.

❧

We've put maybe a dozen long blocks behind us when I hear an unfamiliar sound. Trucks and cars have been passing us, but this is different. Motors, for sure, but this is a lot of them. Noisy. Like ...

I turn and my heart does a little skip of fear when I see that it's a gang of bikers, maybe a dozen strong, headlights on, coming down the street in our direction. Of course, that's exactly why they ride in a bunch like that—to make people nervous. Then I recognize the guy riding in front and realize they're Ocean Avers. That surprises me, because this is bandas territory and the Mexican gangs don't take kindly to invasions on their turf.

"Isn't that Chaingang?" Desmond asks.

I nod. And then something clicks. We call him Chaingang, but his real name is Theodore Washington.

"He's the grasshopper mouse?" I say.

"What're you talking about?" Desmond says, but Elzie is nodding.

"Oh, Jeez," I say, clapping my hand over my mouth, half in surprise, half in shame. I knew that Chaingang is a Wildling, but I never asked him what kind. It seems like everyone's being outed today. Now I feel like a traitor, having blurted that out in front of Desmond.

"Aw, come on," Desmond says. "Chaingang's a Wildling, too?"

But now the bikes are pulling up at the curb beside us and we don't answer him. We don't really need to.

Chaingang puts a motorcycle boot down on the pavement to steady his big chopper and pulls down his sunglasses to give us a once-over. The rest of the gang is strung out along the curb, engines idling. It's impossible to know what they're thinking, but I only catch the ping of one other Wildling among them. Bunched up as they are, I can't tell which of them it is.

"What's with the civilian?" Chaingang asks Elzie, nodding his chin at Desmond.

She shrugs. "Auntie Min likes him."

"She would." He turns to me. "Hey, sweetcheeks. Caught any good waves lately?"

I can't help but smile. "I don't know, big boy," I say. "How's probation treating you?"

He grins and puts his shades back on. "Better than juvie. Hop on. We're your ride."

"Are they all Wildlings?" Desmond mutters behind me.

I shake my head and get on the back of Chaingang's bike. Elzie and Desmond hesitate a moment, then get on behind a couple of the others. Chaingang revs his motor.

"Hang on," he says, doing a wheelie as we head down the street.

The bikes pull back out behind us. I do have to hang on to Chaingang or I'll lose my seat. He gives a little chuckle, obviously enjoying that I have to hold on so tight.

I'm not sure exactly what we're going to do, but this is Wildlings' business and there are too many other people involved. Five-fingered beings, civilians. It doesn't matter what you call them. Involving them could make everything blow up in our faces. I especially don't like so many people knowing I'm a Wildling—because Chaingang probably told his gang why they're here. I've gone five months under the radar and now way too many people know my secret.

I think about Josh—how we need help to rescue him—and I know we don't have another choice. This is how it has to be. But it makes me nervous as hell.

JOSH

"So are we being monitored?" I ask Rico.

He points to tiny cameras mounted where the walls meet the ceiling. They've been placed so that no matter where we are in our cells, we can be seen.

"The researchers clocked out an hour or so ago," Rico says. "I'm sure those cameras are recording everything and there's probably a guard somewhere who looks at a monitor every once in a while, but we'll be on our own for the night."

"I need to get out of here."

I get up from the mattress. Another wave of vertigo hits me and I have to close my eyes, swaying where I stand. When it passes, I walk over to the glass wall and rap on it with a knuckle.

"It's not glass," I say.

"No, it's some kind of plastic. Thick. Probably hard to break, even if the person trying was really strong."

Something occurs to me. I tap on the plastic again.

"We probably shouldn't be able to hear each other through this," I say.

"We don't. We're reading each other's lips."

I give a slow nod. "Right."

But I'm sick of pretending. So what if the world knows I'm a Wildling? Better that than having some freak show scientist cut off *my* leg.

"Have you tried to escape?" I ask.

I don't care who's listening now. Let them play back the tapes in the morning. I plan to be out of here before anybody comes back to work.

Rico shakes his head. "Even if I could get out of this cell, I'd never get out of this room. The doors all need key cards to unlock them. I know there are guards and I know we're underground. The odds suck."

213

"Underground? This is So-Cal. Nobody builds underground." Then I understand. "We're not even in California anymore, are we?"

Rico studies me for a long moment.

"We'd *know* if they'd taken us away from our land," he says finally.

We would? But as soon as he says it, I realize he's right. Somewhere, out beyond the space this building takes up, I can feel the tug of some big comforting presence. Even if Rico hadn't told me, I'd have known what it was. And beyond it, I can sense the bigger mystery that's the Pacific.

I press my fingers against the plastic wall. It's hard and thick, but I'll bet the mountain lion could get through.

"I'm not staying here," I tell Rico. "If I can get us out of these cells, I'll take you with me."

"You're pretty confident."

"No, I'm scared out of my mind and desperate. But I think I can do it."

He gives me a slow nod. "If you can get us to the ground floor, I can take us to someplace they'll never find."

"Okay," I say.

I step back, studying the wall for the best place to rip it apart.

"Wait," Rico says.

I turn to him. "Why?"

"Give the place a chance to quiet down. Let the guards settle into their usual routines."

It makes sense, I suppose, but I don't want to wait.

"How long?" I ask.

"A couple of hours should do it."

"I don't know. I'll see if I can wait that long. But if I can't ..."

Rico gives me a feral grin and there's a dark look in his eyes that makes me wonder if he's really my age or if he's more like Cory, and just looks my age.

"Oh, I'll be with you," he says. "Just as fast as I can drag myself along behind you."

MARINA

Chaingang's twists, turns and wheelies make the ride feel kind of like street surfing. If I weren't so freaked about Josh, I'd probably find this even more fun. I have to grab on tight, but I love the adrenaline rush.

We're almost at the shopping complex now. My step dad says this neighbourhood used to be all open orchards—kind of a community fruit bowl back in the day. Then in the sixties, the land got bought up by developers, who built block upon block of cheap housing. It wasn't so bad at the time—my step dad grew up in those 'burbs—but like everything else here in So-Cal, it eventually got all rundown. I guess it's like that everywhere. Why can't we take care of stuff?

Then ValentiCorp came on the scene and the whole area got bulldozed and "rejuvenated," which means it's now block after block of condos, two- and three-stories high, plus big box stores and chain restaurants. In the middle of it all stands the tall ValentiCorp office structure with its corporate logo on the roof, surrounded by acres of parking lots.

As we pull in off the street, I realize that I've never really looked at the building before. It's almost dark out now, but the whole structure looks like a behemoth made of steel and black glass windows. It's ridiculous. Nine stories of windows. You wouldn't think anybody in their right mind would build something like that here, but it's withstood two earthquakes now, one of which did a lot of damage to the other businesses in the complex, but none to ValentiCorp.

Chaingang brings us to Computerland—one of those huge generic electronics stores. The bikes pull in around the far side of the building and we can't see ValentiCorp anymore. The riders shut off their machines. The sudden quiet is such a relief.

"Wait for me here," Chaingang tells his guys.

When Elzie and Desmond dismount the bikes that they're riding on, he motions them to follow us. He and I ride slowly back around the corner, to where three people stand on an island of grass and palm trees that separates one section of the parking lot from another. He parks the bike and we both get off. Desmond and Elzie join us.

I see Auntie Min, but I don't recognize either of the men with her. The strong Wildling *pings* they give off as we walk up to them tell me that they, like her, are old ones.

If we actually resemble our animal shapes, one of the strangers would be some kind of slinky animal, maybe from the weasel family. Or some kind of reptile. He's wiry-thin, his skin dark and parched-looking, his hair cut short except for a width of longer spikes that stands up in a stiff swath. I'd call it a Mohawk, but it's not quite tall enough. It reminds me more of a lizard's crest. His eyes are two dark pools that make me want to turn away when his gaze rests on me. I'm afraid they'll swallow some part of me.

The other is younger, also dark skinned, with longer dark hair. He's handsome and appears to be not much older than me, and his eyes are kinder, if a little sly. He's looking over at the ValentiCorp building, which is quite far off—about the distance of a football field from where we stand—but still imposing.

Auntie Min makes introductions. "Marina and Desmond, this is Cory," she says, placing her hand on the younger man's shoulder. "He's interested in helping your friend Josh."

"Thank you," we both say at the same time.

Cory smiles and nods toward us, then looks back at the building as though he's studying every aspect of it.

"And this is Tomás, who is visiting from the Los Angeles area. Elzie and Theodore, I don't believe you've met Tomás before, either."

Tomás barely acknowledges any of us. His attention is on ValentiCorp, too, where it towers in the distance. Several spotlights light up the structure and make it look even more dramatic than it does during daytime.

Desmond follows their gaze. "Ridiculously huge, isn't it," he says.

Cory nods. "With a lot of guards. They look like ex-military, or cops."

"Wow, dude, great eyesight," Desmond says.

My own Wildling vision lets me see what Cory means. Though it's not obvious from this distance, men are stationed around the building. Now I understand why Chaingang has left the rest of the Ocean Avers well out of sight. Motorcycle gangs attract attention and he doesn't want to tip off the guards. Or maybe he just doesn't want to mix Wildlings and gang business.

As for our little group, we're certainly an odd mix, but hopefully the dim light obscures us. We're probably too far away for them to pay us any mind.

"What's the plan, anyway?" Chaingang asks.

"This is where they brought Josh after he got snatched," Elzie says. "We're getting him out."

Chaingang removes his shades and cocks an eyebrow.

"We are," Elzie tells him.

"Yeah, well good luck with that. Black Key Securities has the contract for that place. Lots of bodies and fancy high-tech crap. You'd need an army to get in there or ..."

He stares intently at one section of the building. I realize he's using his own night vision. "Those vents between the first and second floors look big enough to let someone with a real small Wildling shape sneak in. Maybe they could take down their alarms from the inside."

"Exactly," Auntie Min says.

"But then you'll still need to get your people in. How're you planning to do this?"

"Well, *you've* got the army," Cory begins.

Chaingang just shakes his head. "Not happening. I brought my crew to get us through bandas territory in one piece. You're talking about Wildlings business and I won't involve them."

"Then we at least need someone with a small Wildling shape," Tomás says.

He, Auntie Min and Cory all look at Chaingang with obvious expectation. Then I remember. His Wildling shape is a grasshopper mouse.

"And how, exactly, would *you* know anything about me?" Chaingang asks Tomás.

Tomás frowns but makes no response.

"Hey," Cory says. "Take it easy. He's okay."

"He'd better be," Chaingang says, "seeing as how you've already given up my secrets to him."

Tomás bristles. "I don't need to be vetted by anybo—"

Chaingang cuts him off with a raised palm. "Don't kid yourself," he says. "If I don't know you, you need to be vetted." Returning his attention to Cory and Auntie Min, he adds, "But it doesn't matter. I'm not going in there."

Though he's only half Chaingang's size, Tomás isn't going to back down.

"I didn't take you for a coward," he says.

Chaingang turns to him. He moves at his usual slow and deliberate speed.

"You don't *get* to take me for anything," he says, his eyes dark with anger, "because you don't know dick about me."

Elzie, Desmond and I have been following all of this, but we haven't spoken up. Now Elzie does.

"But you're the only one who can get small enough to slip in through those vents," Elzie says.

I think he might bite her head off the way he did with Tomás, but he only gives her a small, humourless smile and shakes his head.

"I like Josh," Chaingang tells Elzie. "Really, I do. He's stand-up all the way. And I'd have his back if not for the fact that this is a no-win situation. We can't get him out. If we go in, we're just giving ourselves up, too, and that doesn't help anybody."

"I thought being Wildlings made you guys into some kind of superheroes," Desmond says.

Chaingang studies him for a moment. Bad move, Des, I think. Chaingang's already in a grim mood. Antagonizing him isn't going to help anything.

I put my hand on Chaingang's arm and give him a pleading look. He looks back at me, then gives a slow nod.

"Sure," he says, holding my gaze for all that he's talking to Des. "I get how it seems that way. Wildling blood makes us faster and stronger when we're in human shape, which is cool, yeah. I'm down with that. But all it does when you're in animal shape is let you still think like a human. If you're just some little rodent or lizard, being a Wildling doesn't give you any advantage."

"So why did you come?" Elzie asks.

Chaingang looks over at her and then at Auntie Min. "That crow you sent reminded me I owed you a favour. He didn't say *what* the favour was." He looks away from Auntie Min and back at me. His face softens. "Besides, I have some other friends here."

I feel kind of warm and fuzzy inside, enjoying the same gentle attention that Chaingang has shown me before, but then I remember how bitchy I was to him on the beach. And all because I thought he'd been just as nice with Josh. God, am I really that shallow? I can't repress a shudder at the thought.

Chaingang gets a pained look and seems to pull himself up, away from that soft place. I realize I've just sent out the wrong signal and want to correct it, but the moment has passed because he looks around at the others and continues talking.

"Look, this is just a bad idea," he says. "They'll have cameras everywhere. Even if you manage to get Josh out, they're going to know too much. They'll know that it's not just kids who are Wildlings. That we can fight back. We need those aces in the hole, because things are going to get a whole lot worse around here before they get better."

I don't pretend to understand exactly what's going on. I know it makes sense to keep a low profile. Just being here out in the open makes me really uncomfortable, even surrounded by people like Chaingang, Auntie Min and Cory. But what I do know is that we can't abandon Josh.

"Could I do it?" I find myself saying. "Is a sea otter small enough to slip in?"

"And then what?" Chaingang asks. "Do you know how to disable their security system? Can you take down a squadron of armed guards when they come running?" He shakes his head before I can answer. "I don't think so."

He turns to Auntie Min.

"If you don't care about giving up our secrets," he tells her, "then you should be willing to give up some of your own. I know you old-school Wildlings can do all kinds of things that we can only guess at. It wouldn't surprise me if you had your own way in."

"Don't push your luck," Tomás says.

"You're really starting to piss me off," Chaingang tells him, taking a step in his direction.

Auntie Min frowns. "What is the matter with the two of you? We're all on the same side."

"Are we?" Chaingang asks. "Josh is a good guy, but what's the big deal about rescuing *him*? Other Wildlings have disappeared and I haven't seen you do squat to get them back."

"Not true," says Cory, looking pointedly at Chaingang. "We figured out a way to get a bunch of kids out of the Feds' place the other night, and seems to me one of them was a friend of yours."

Auntie Min interrupts. "Josh is Mountain Lion Clan," she says.

"And I care about that because …?"

"All the children who have been changed so far are little cousins," Auntie Min tells him. "Snakes and rodents, small birds and a few medium-sized animals. He is the first of the old clans to appear among you. So far, he's the *only* one."

"Still don't know why I'm supposed to care."

"We need strong leaders to see us through the times to come. Leaders who are part of both worlds, but powerful in a way that most of us are not. Those old clans—raven, mountain lion, bear, eagle, hummingbird, wolf— they command the respect of the little cousins *and* they have the capacity to force the five-fingered beings to treat us fairly and with dignity. Now that our existence has been revealed, we will need them for our dealings with the human world."

Chaingang shakes his head. "I don't know what it was like in your day, but that's not how the world works anymore. Power doesn't come from who or what you are. It comes from the money and resources you have access to, what armies you can put on the field."

"Perhaps we can change that," Auntie Min says. "Would that not be a fine thing? And don't you want to be standing with us when we do?"

Chaingang sighs. "I'm more for you than against you, but I don't really trust any of you—" He tilts his head toward me. "Except for maybe Marina."

Elzie and Desmond both look at me and raise their eyebrows.

Again I get that soft squishy feeling inside. I'm flattered that Chaingang trusts me, but I'm embarrassed that it seems to be coming from a place of attraction, rather than because I actually earned it. And I feel strangely like I'm cheating on Josh, which is weirder than hell.

Chaingang turns back to Auntie Min. "The Wildling in me tells me I need to give you props, Auntie Min, so I do. And we've got some history. Cory here did do me a solid by getting one of my crew out of that fed zoo they had out at the old naval base. But you—" His gaze shifts to Tomás. "You're just some little prick I don't want to know who's walking around like he's got an alpha's *cojones*. You think you're making with a thousand yard stare, but I've done my time. I know guys who would eat you for breakfast. And just FYI, you're way too old to pull off that old school punk look."

"In L.A.," Auntie Min says, "Tomás serves the same function as I do here."

"Now see, you say that like it's a good thing, but I just see it as no better than the Feds or ValentiCorp or any other opportunist who comes sniffing around looking to see how they can turn a profit out of what's happening to us here."

"Hold on," Tomás says, "I am just here to help. All of the cousins have only your best interests in mind."

"But maybe we don't want the handout," Chaingang tells him. "I don't know your history, but my people came over here as slaves and we know all about struggles and broken promises. We had to fight for everything we've got right now and for a whole lot of us, what we've got is pretty much next to nothing."

"You've seen how the government is treating Wildlings," Tomás tells him. "Ours is not such a different fight. They give lip service to our rights as citizens, yet detain us for nothing. They ignore our civil rights, just as they did yours."

"And you think *Josh* can change this? *He's* your big hope?"

"Not at this moment," Auntie Min says. "But he could be. One charismatic leader could turn the tide. He could be accepted by both sides. Who's going to look to an old woman like me as a leader, or a gang member like you? But a good kid like Josh? With a white father and a black mother and Wildling blood?"

Tomás nods. "He's like a poster child for the cause."

"And what if being your figurehead isn't something Josh wants?" Elzie asks. "What if he just wants a normal life?"

"Normal isn't up for discussion," Cory says. "He lost that when he changed."

Elzie just scowls.

"We didn't want this either," Tomás says. "We've managed to go about our business unnoticed for thousands of years. But just as you can't change being a Wildling, neither can we go back to our own status quo."

"We stand to lose everything," Auntie Min adds.

Chaingang studies them for a long moment.

"Okay," he says. "So you're saying there's no other way into that building?"

"Not without frightening the humans even more," Auntie Min says. "If they knew everything that we do, they would stop at nothing to keep us all under their control."

"And you're not going to share what that is?"

"Not yet," she says. "It's too dangerous for you to know right now. Let's get Josh out, then we'll talk again."

Chaingang turns to Elzie and me. "So are you in?"

I nod. "I was never out."

Elzie nods as well. "Let's go," she says.

"Okay. I don't suppose anybody has a floor plan for the building?"

The older cousins shake their heads.

"Yeah, I suppose that would make it too easy."

"You need floor plans?" Desmond says. "Dude, that's what the Internet is for. We'll just go into that store and 'try out' one of their computers." He makes air quotations as he speaks. "Marina's almost as good at surfing the web as she is riding a wave."

Chaingang looks at the computer store before turning back with a grin.

"I knew you had to be good for something, bro," he says. "Why don't the two of you go for it. We'll wait for you here."

JOSH

I don't feel like talking with Rico while we wait for things to settle down. Everything he's told me is so horrible that if I hear any more, I'm going to lose my nerve. But when I lie back down on the mattress, my mind fills with even more worries. Not just about this place and getting out, but what's happening outside.

What's Mom thinking? I've never pulled a no-show on her before. She's going to go crazy when she hears I've been grabbed, even if it is by the Feds, which now seems like a remote possibility.

What if these people came after her, too? And Desmond and Marina—they were outside the school with me. What if they tried to stop what was happening and got hurt in the process? They could be dead and I'd never know it.

Where is Elzie? Did they catch her, too? How long can she keep fighting after everything she's been through?

When you don't know what's going on, it's way too easy to blow everything out of proportion. If only I didn't have all this time to think.

I look over at Rico stretched out on his mattress, staring at the ceiling. He's doing the same thing. One hand protectively cups his knee where his leg was amputated. I watch for a while, but he never even blinks.

"Are you sure there wasn't anything wrong with your leg?" I find myself asking. I don't know why—I guess I want a different answer than the one I already got.

He turns his head. "No. It'd be easier to accept if they did it to save my life, but like I said, we're just lab rats to them. They think I'm a Wildling. I told them I'm not, but they don't believe me. Before they cut off my leg, they told me I was doing a service to mankind—that if they can crack the Wildling code, they'll be able to cure all kinds of illnesses. But I get the feeling that what they're really aiming for is to breed themselves a bunch of pet Wildlings."

"Oh my God. What makes you think that? Why would they want to keep them as pets?"

"It'd be more like they want to breed them so that the new Wildlings would do what they say."

"But *why*?"

He sits up, wincing when he bangs his knee in the process.

"You're not really that naive, are you?" he asks.

"I don't know," I say. "I've been told that it's just a matter of time until different factions try to get Wildlings to join them. Government, industry, gangs. I guess that makes sense, since they'd be useful for spy and strong-arm stuff. But breed them—like pets?"

"They think that way they'll be assured of loyalty."

The concept sickens me.

"How could they even do that?" I ask. "I heard that nobody has the first clue about what makes a Wildling. Supposedly, Wildlings are genetically the same as humans, right down to their DNA."

Rico shrugs. "That's what these people are trying to find out: what makes Wildlings different. Or maybe they're trying to redo something. I heard a rumour that researchers have been working on crossbreeding animals and people for years, and that's how come the Wildlings first started showing up here. They messed up—lost the formula or something and it got loose in the general population."

"Do you believe that?"

Rico just shakes head. "I don't know. There are too many stories. Another is that this is a last-ditch effort by the old spirits to reclaim their lands. The Indians lived in harmony with animal people for a long time, but ever since the Europeans showed up, they've been steadily losing their sacred bonds with the land.

"The ironic thing is that everybody wants a piece of it except for those who've actually become Wildlings. A lot of kids just want to turn back the clock to how things were before they changed."

I think about that. Life was simpler before, that's for sure, and I definitely wouldn't be in this mess right now. But the longer I've had the mountain lion under my skin, the more comforting it feels. The more normal. I like how it amplifies everything. My hearing. My sight. My endurance.

I realize I don't want to go back to the old normal anymore. Like Nira says in her blog, we should revel in our gift, not turn our backs on it.

Once again, I find myself wishing I were just waiting out this couple of hours in silence, but Rico goes on. "I guess sooner or later, somebody'll figure it all out," he says. "The people holding us here have a lot riding on it. It's not just about developing perfect servants, soldiers and spies. Think about the aging population. Baby boomers are getting near pension age. Imagine the big bucks waiting for anybody who can provide a way for them to feel young and strong again."

"You think it would actually work like that for old people?"

Rico smiles. "It doesn't matter what I think. What matters is what people like the ones holding us think. If they believe it's a possibility, they'll throw everything they've got into it—including kidnapping kids like us."

He's probably right. I feel myself sliding into depression. Maybe Elzie and the ferals are right, too—that it's such a huge mess that we *should* just get rid of everything and start over. But then I think of my mom and my friends and I know I could never get behind anything that would hurt them or other innocent people.

For sure there are a lot of unethical humans, but not everybody's like that. It's just a small percentage. Unfortunately, that percentage always seems to hold all the cards—and they probably will unless we can figure out another way to deal with them.

I'm still trying to keep my spirits up, but let's face it. This has been the worst day of my life. It started with finding out that one of my friends had committed suicide and now look where I am.

"It's a pretty shitty world," I say.

"No, it's a great world," Rico says. "Only a few shitty people screw it up."

He holds up a hand suddenly.

"You hear that?" he asks.

As soon as he says it, I do. It sounded like the clang of a door. And now I hear footsteps. Two pairs.

"This doesn't make sense," Rico says. "They never come in here at night. Maybe it's because you're new and they were watching to see what you'd do."

"What do we do?"

"Nothing. Play it cool. Maybe just the guards saw us talking and they're only coming to check up. Soon as they see we're still safely locked up, they'll leave."

I stand up. I don't want to play it cool. I want to set the mountain lion loose on whoever comes through that door.

"And if they don't?" I say. "If it's somebody coming to experiment on us?"

"They always gas you first," Rico says. He gives a nod in the direction of the ceiling. "It sprays down from nozzles up there."

I look up. "I don't see anything."

"They're up there. Trust me. They're built right into the ceiling."

The footsteps are right outside the main room now. Something whirs inside the door, then it hisses open and they step inside. A man and a woman.

MARINA

"Did you hear what he called me?" Desmond says as we go into Computerland. "He called me 'bro.'"

I have to smile. Trust Desmond to focus on that.

"I wouldn't make too much of it," I say.

"No, I think it's a sign of respect, you know? He didn't call anybody else 'bro.'"

"Nope. Guess that means you're in the gang now. Have fun with that."

"Ha ha," Desmond says, bumping my shoulder. "If anyone's in the gang, it's you. He obviously wants to jump your bones."

I ignore that and steer us over to the laptop displays. "Why do you care what anybody thinks of you anyway?"

"I don't. But, you know. I'm not a Wildling like you guys, so it's kind of cool that he likes me."

It's not busy, so a sales rep approaches us before I can check to see if any of the laptops are online. Normally I wouldn't mind talking to him. He's cute—almost as tall as Desmond—with wavy brown hair that keeps falling across his eyes, no matter how often he uses his fingers to brush it back. He smells good, too. Clean, no cologne. His nametag reads "Evan."

"Can I help you find something?" he asks.

"Hey, dude," Desmond says. "What can you tell me about this Toshiba?"

I drift away as Evan starts to describe the machine. Halfway down the aisle, I stop at another laptop. I wake the screen from sleep mode and do a quick check for the online icon, then open a browser. Down the aisle, Desmond is playing especially dim with the sales rep, who's doing a great job of not sounding annoyed.

A few Google searches later and I have nothing. I find a schematic of the whole commercial area around the complex, but nothing for the ValentiCorp building itself. I try rephrasing my search, but have no better luck.

I shouldn't be surprised. If they can hire all those security guards, they certainly won't have anything easily accessible online.

I rejoin Desmond and lean against him.

"I'm bored," I say.

Desmond is quick to get the hint. He gives Evan a "what can you do?" raise of his eyebrows.

"Thanks for your time, dude," he says. "I'll be back."

Evan hands him his card, which Desmond sticks in his pocket and we saunter off.

"Nothing?" he asks when we're out of Evan's hearing.

"Not even close. It was a good idea, but I guess it was a long shot that they'd have something like that online."

"Some companies do, for their employees. I'll bet it's in their own computer network."

"Yeah," I say, "behind some firewall that we'd never be able to crack."

We stop and look at each other.

"Barry," we say at the same time and trade high-fives.

Desmond takes out his phone and makes the call.

"Barry," Desmond says when the connection is made. "I need your help, dude."

"Wait a minute," I hear Barry say, thanks to my Wildling hearing. "Tell me what's up with Josh. I saw you guys in a YouTube video of the FBI taking him down. Where the hell do they come off thinking they can pull crap like that?"

"It's not the FBI."

"They've been saying that on the news, but come *on*. You don't buy that crap, do you? Those guys were totally Feds."

"Except they weren't. They were from ValentiCorp. They kidnapped Josh and we need you to help us hack into their computer system."

"Are you shitting me?"

"I wish."

"What do they want with Josh?"

"They think he's a Wildling," Desmond says.

"Yeah, and I'm bopping Joanie Jones. Seriously, man, no joke, why are you calling?"

"I just told you."

229

"You *really* want to access ValentiCorp's servers?"

"We need a floor plan of the building," Desmond says, "so we can figure out where they're keeping Josh and how we can get in there."

"Not going to happen. Their security's like an impenetrable vault. I mean, think about it. They're always dealing with military contracts and shit like that. They've got firewalls up the doo-dah."

"You make it sound like you've already tried to get in."

"I might have taken a run a time or two—just to see if I could."

"So you can't help."

"I didn't say that. We can't access ValentiCorp's servers, but the Santa Feliz Zoning Commission? That'd be a piece of cake. You don't get to build something that big without filing a gazillion schematics and blueprints."

"How fast can you get in?"

"I'm already in. I've been working on it as we speak, m'man. Now, let's see. Crap, these are big files. How much free storage have you got on your phone?"

"How would I know?"

"Pathetic," Barry mutters, then adds, "Where are you right now?"

"The Computerland building across the parking lot from ValentiCorp."

"Give me fifteen. I'll bring what you need on a laptop. Hang on ... *this* is interesting. Have you ever been to Disneyland?"

"Dude, that's like asking me if I've ever been to the pier."

"Yeah, yeah. Well, you know how Disney has that huge service space underneath, with a whole network of access tunnels and stuff?"

"I've heard about it," Desmond says.

"ValentiCorp has the same deal under their parking lot. It stretches right under all those box stores like the one you're in."

"What does that mean?"

"It means we can probably get in through a back door."

"He can't come with us," I tell Desmond.

He holds up his hand to me. "That's great," he says into the phone. "Get here as quick as you can."

"Fifteen minutes," Barry says.

Desmond snaps his phone shut.

"He really can't come," I repeat. "We might have to change shapes at some point. He can't be part of that."

Desmond smiles. "Yeah, I guess there's that thing you have about us seeing you naked."

"Desmond, I'm not kidding and you have no idea what you're even talking about. My point is, too many people already know who shouldn't."

"Okay, I was just making a joke. I get it. You wish I didn't know because you think I'm going to betray you."

"No, I don't. That just came out wrong. You know what I mean. You know how Barry loves to talk."

"What else could I do?" Desmond says. "We need those plans. Let's wait for him to bring what we need and then we can deal with it."

৩◦৶

There are a couple of long benches outside Computerland, where shoppers can take a break, I guess. When Desmond and I exit the store, Auntie Min and Tomás are sitting on one bench, Elzie, Cory and Chaingang on the other. ValentiCorp can still be seen in the distance, spotlights emphasizing its towering height.

Desmond plops himself down on the seat between Elzie and Chaingang, then leans toward Chaingang and says, "We're on it bro. Best computer geek in town's coming over here to help us."

Chaingang gives Desmond a considering look, then gets up.

"Getting a bit crowded around here," he says. "I'm gonna send my crew off. Let 'em get a bite to eat."

He saunters around the corner and I take his seat at the end of the bench.

I hope Barry gets here quick and that we can keep our Wildling identities under wraps. He's too connected to the Net and geek-land for comfort.

"Barry's great," I say, "but let's not share any of our, um, personal stuff, okay?"

"Well at least it's not just me that you don't trust," Desmond says.

I elbow him in the ribs as we watch the motorbikes pull out and Chaingang walking back toward us. The bikes go in the opposite direction from ValentiCorp.

When Chaingang gets back to where we're waiting, he pauses, looks at the empty space beside Tomás, then shakes his head and comes back toward our bench, where I'm sitting. I slide over toward Des, so there's just enough room for Chaingang to sit on the end beside me. Desmond snickers and I elbow him a little harder this time.

"Like the man said, it's a bit crowded," I tell Desmond. "Scoot over a bit and give us some room."

"Nah, it's cool now," says Chaingang.

Desmond can't suppress another silly grin. I give his arm a little push and he shifts toward Elzie, giving me a bit more space.

Chaingang leans across me and looks down the bench toward Cory. "Hey, coyote boy," he says. "How come the old lady didn't mention you when she was talking about the old-school clans?"

Cory shrugs. "Nobody trusts us. We're like the crow clans and the buzzards—carrion eaters, so we're always on the outside."

"Raven's a carrion eater, too, but they all seem to give him big props."

"Yeah, but he made the world. Bad-mouthing him would be like talking back to the Thunders."

I give Chaingang a little push and he sits back straight again.

I look at Cory. "Those Thunders—are they even real?"

"What do you mean?" Cory says.

"Do they actually exist, or are they more like mythical gods or something?"

"They're the big mysteries," he says. "Some say they're pieces of the Creator, some say they're his voice."

"Is one of the Thunders this guy called Raven?"

He shakes his head. "Raven just made the world. Something had to make him first."

"You buy all that?" Chaingang asks him.

"Well, you know," Cory replies, "I once asked my uncle that same thing and he said it didn't matter what he believed. What mattered was what I believe."

"So what *do* you believe?" Elzie asks.

"That instead of that every-man-for-himself mentality dividing the world up into smaller and smaller pieces, we should come together to protect and share what we still have."

Chaingang frowns. "Are you a communist?"

"Communists think the state owns everything. I'm saying no ownership. We're here to take care of each other."

"But we don't," I say.

"No," Cory says. "We don't."

Just then Barry pulls up in his old Honda. It's only been twelve minutes since he hung up. I know the exact time because I've glanced at my watch a hundred times in the interim. He bounces out of his car and hurries over to us, laptop under his arm.

"Hey, Marina!" he calls. "So are you part of ..."

His voice trails off as it registers that we're a larger group than he expected. His eyes go wide when Chaingang looks up at him.

"What does he know?" Chaingang asks.

Oh crap. Chaingang wasn't here when I suggested we should use discretion around Barry. Desmond and I exchange worried looks.

"Um, that we're trying to rescue Josh?" I say.

Barry holds up his free hand in a peace sign.

"Look, man," he says. "You know me. Didn't I fix your little brother's Game Boy last week? But you don't want me here, I'm gone."

Chaingang shakes his head. "My bad. I'm feeling a little edgy today. Show us what you got."

"Sure," Barry says.

But he's still glancing around, taking in Auntie Min and Tomás and Cory, and I can tell he's more than a little freaked out. I stand up and take his arm.

"Chill," I tell him. "We're all here for the same reason."

He nods. "Right, right."

But his gaze keeps flicking from face to face, then quickly looking away.

"Let's see those plans," I say. "Sit here. I'll go around behind you."

"Right."

He takes my seat and puts his laptop on his thighs, fingers fumbling as he tries to get it open. Chaingang lays a meaty hand on his shoulder.

"Do you know why I'm here?" he asks, his voice mild.

Barry shakes his head. "It's cool. I don't need to know anything."

"I'm here because I told Josh I'd have his back. I give you props for coming out here to help us, so now I'm telling you the same thing. Anybody messes with you, give me a call. We'll have Ocean Avers all over their ass."

"R-really?"

"Really, bro."

Desmond gives me a significant look, but I just roll my eyes.

"So let's see what you found for us," Chaingang says.

Barry nods. He opens his laptop. Desmond, Elzie and Cory get up and join me behind the bench to look over Barry's shoulder. At first, it's just a mess of complicated blue lines, but then he changes the view and I understand what we're looking at. There's ValentiCorp in the middle, surrounded by parking lots and box stores.

"Here's where it gets interesting," he says.

He makes an adjustment and now the image is in 3-D.

"What the hell is that?" Chaingang says, leaning in closer.

He points to this big angular diagram under the parking lots.

Barry seems uneasy about Chaingang leaning over him. "It's ... it's a huge service area, just like under, you know—"

"Disneyland," Desmond finishes for him.

Chaingang frowns. "Who builds something like that in earthquake country?"

Barry looks toward the ValentiCorp tower.

"The same people who built that," he says.

"Point taken."

Chaingang moves his finger above the screen, tracing out what looks like one of a series of big corridors running all the way from ValentiCorp to a bunch of the box stores. It's as though the building is in the center of a spider web.

"Are these what I think they are?" he asks.

Barry nods. "Access tunnels. Big enough to drive a truck through." He points to a large building on the east side of the lot. "See the service bay on that side of Pep Boys?" His finger touches the laptop's screen. "I bet that's an entrance to this tunnel."

"That's not part of Pep Boys' automotive bays?"

"Nope," Barry says. "Those are on the other side. ValentiCorp just rents them one part of the building. Makes a perfect cover for their own entrance at the other end."

Chaingang nods. "So it would be the same for all the rest of these corridors we see."

Barry nods. He points at the screen again, finger hovering over one side of ValentiCorp.

"Here's where they have their own above-ground delivery bays," he says. "I'll bet they use the others outside of business hours—when they don't want anyone to see certain shipments."

"I don't get it," Elzie says. "What kind of shipments? What are they even doing in there?"

"I have no idea. Research and development—whatever that means. It could be anything. They've got a public website, but it focuses on stuff related to this retail complex. There are vague references to government research contracts, but no specifics. I heard they do contracts for the military, but I don't know what."

"Can you do anything about their security system?" Chaingang asks.

"Maybe. I've been running a protocol to get through their firewall ever since I got off the phone with Desmond, but they've got some serious encryptions and I haven't been able to get in yet. Makes sense, if they've got military contracts."

"I thought you said you tried to get into their site before," Desmond says.

"Yeah, but I know stuff now that I didn't then." Barry throws Des a smirk. "I've developed some code that theoretically can get me into anything, given enough time."

"Time's something we don't exactly have," Chaingang says. He studies the screen a little longer. "So what are you saying? That the best we can do is sneak in through one of those secret entrances?"

"Pretty much. And then you'll still have to get by their security cameras and guards."

Chaingang gives another nod. "Not a problem. We can do it the hard way."

Barry can't know what he means, but I can guess. We're Wildlings. Stronger. Faster. Chaingang expects us to take on the guards with whatever small advantage the animals living under our skins can give us.

"I guess," Barry says. He hesitates, then adds, "Can I ask why you're not calling the cops? SWAT would be able to storm the building legally—you know, without our having to go through all this spy stuff."

"They'd have to go through a whole chain of command," Cory says. "Find probable cause, get a judge to sign off on a warrant."

"And by the time they finished dicking around," Chaingang says, "Josh could be long gone."

He doesn't add, *or worse*. Like maybe dead. He doesn't have to.

"So no cops," Chaingang continues. He looks around at us. "Let's get ready. Who's in?"

Far to the west of us, the sun has set over the ocean. Surfers have gone home after catching their last few waves. Lovers are walking hand-in-hand along the boardwalk. Skaters are messing around in the lit parking lot by the pier. It seems like a whole other world. Twenty-four hours ago, that was *my* world—well, except for the lovers part. Now I'm part of some half-assed commando unit that's probably going to get itself killed.

"I'm still in," I say.

Everybody else speaks up except for Auntie Min and Tomás, who've remained on the other bench. I'm surprised. I had no expectations with Tomás, but I thought Auntie Min was a tough cookie and I'd like to have her with us.

"I'm coming, too," Barry says.

That really surprises me. I know why Desmond is coming—and we wouldn't be able to stop him anyway. But Barry? And he doesn't even know about the Wildlings under our skins.

"Why?" Cory asks.

"Josh is my friend. He'd do the same for me. Hell, he'd probably do it for somebody he didn't know if he saw they were in trouble."

Cory smiles. "Good answer."

Chaingang stands up. He takes out his phone and makes a call. A few moments later we hear his crew's motorcycles approaching again. By the time Chaingang has swung his leg over the seat of his own machine, the other Ocean Avers come cruising to where we are. Stragglers on their way to their cars from the various stores pause to watch the gang arrive. I glance over to ValentiCorp. The guards way over there are paying attention, too. Alert. The shoppers are nervous. I can smell their fear from where we stand.

The Ocean Avers pull up in a ragged line behind Chaingang's chopper.

"Let's saddle up," he tells us. "Buddy up and play nice."

As we start for the row of motorcycles, Chaingang calls over to me.

"What's the matter, sweetcheeks?" he says. "Lost your love for me?"

I aim myself in his direction, relieved that he's already forgiven me for that look I gave him earlier.

"Don't call me that, babyface," I tease as I get on behind him.

He laughs and revs his engine. He waits until everybody is in their seats except for Auntie Min and Tomás, then he gives the signal and we're off.

The bikers take us out of the shopping complex. Chaingang leads his crew back toward the beach, but turns off onto a side street once we can't see the stores anymore. The Ocean Avers with passengers follow him. The others keep going in the other direction.

"I thought you weren't involving your crew," I say.

I don't have to lean forward. I know Chaingang can hear me just fine, the same way I can hear his reply.

"They're strictly transport," he tells me.

A few more turns and Chaingang pulls over again, killing his engine. He puts the chopper up on its stand. The other bikers let off their passengers, then continue on down the street.

"We're close to the Pep Boys now," he says. "Don't bunch up. We already created enough ruckus with the bikes. Ritzy neighbourhood like this, we don't want to make anybody nervous."

Following his lead, we walk in pairs on either side of the street until we join up again, slipping in behind a jade hedge that separates the garden wall of a row of condos from the sidewalk.

Peering through the waxy leaves, we can see the Pep Boys building. It's starting to hit me that in another few moments, all hell could break loose.

"You ready for this?" Elzie asks, glancing over as we crouch behind the hedge.

I turn my head slowly to glare at her. "Sure. Don't you think I'm up to it?"

I'm insulted that she assumes I can't handle it. Being circumspect has never been my strongpoint.

"No, no—of course you are. Forget that I said anything. I was out of line."

I have to bite my tongue from saying, damn straight.

But to be honest, she's touched a raw nerve. I'm not the bravest person in the world. Sure, I've ridden some big waves and when Josh was being kidnapped, I was ready to go all mother-bear fierce. But that's instinct kicking in. I'm not like Elzie, who always seems ready to take on anybody. And I'm sure not like Chaingang, who's probably carrying a gun and God knows how many knives on him. Not that he needs weapons, considering his size. I saw him fight a couple of guys at school once and he decimated them. Really. It was brutal. And that was before he became a Wildling.

"Okay," Chaingang says.

An electronic beep from Barry's computer interrupts whatever Chaingang was about to say.

"Hang on," Barry says. "This is good."

He crouches down and opens his laptop. A couple of keystrokes later he looks up, grinning.

"I'm in," he says. "Here, look. This is the camera feed that's monitoring the street in front of us."

We all crowd around. The screen is split into a number of black and white windows. They show interior hallways, stairwells, the underground service space, the parking lots. The views in the various windows keep changing. Barry hovers his cursor over one and it fills the top portion of the screen. The rest of the views scroll right to left below it.

I give the expanded window careful study. There's the street we've come down. There's the hedge. But I can't see us. We're hidden from the camera's view.

"Look!" Elzie says, stabbing a finger at one of the smaller views.

Barry brings it up. We seem to be looking at a hospital or infirmary. There's a line of cubicles, separated from each other by floor-to-ceiling glass. Each one has a mattress on the floor and a stainless steel toilet. The camera feed shows two figures in adjoining cubicles, sitting on their mattresses. It's impossible to make out any features.

"Is that Josh?" I ask, pointing to one of them.

Elzie and I both press against Barry, trying to get a closer view.

"I can't tell," she says. "He doesn't have Josh's dreads."

"They could have cut them off," Desmond says.

I'm still trying to figure out the room itself. It looks sort of like a hospital. But it also looks like a laboratory. It's hard to see from the camera angle, but I think there's the edge of an operating table at the bottom of the screen.

"Why would they have a place like that in an office building?" I say.

"Research and development," Cory says.

I turn to look at him. "Seriously, what's that even supposed to mean?"

"They want to figure out what makes them tick," Cory explains. "What makes a Wildling. You can't find that out in a jail cell. But in a lab like that?"

My heart goes into overtime.

"Wildling?" Barry says, but no one answers him.

"*Is* that Josh?" Chaingang asks.

Nobody can confirm it.

"Hard to know, but it makes sense that it would be him," Cory says. "Or that he'd be in the same area. The body shape is right."

"Okay," Chaingang says. "It's probably him. That's good. Half the battle was figuring out whether or not he was even in there." He holds up a hand before Cory can respond. "Yeah, I know Auntie Min already told us. But I needed to see for myself what they've got going on in there."

"And now?" Cory asks.

"Now, assuming that's him, we need to get him out," Chaingang says. He turns to Barry and adds, "Where is that room?"

"But ... um ... okay, let's see."

Barry does something with his cursor and a small window pops up with an identifying code.

"Fifth floor," he says. "But that's the fifth floor going *down*—like basement levels."

The big access tunnels underneath are one thing, but this is *really* weird. I don't know any building with a basement around here and certainly nothing like this.

"Let's see what's in front of us again," Chaingang says.

Barry reduces the image of Josh and brings back the street view from the Pep Boys building.

"Can you shut the cameras off?" Cory asks.

"Do we really want to? That'll let them know they've had a breach and the whole place might go into some kind of shutdown mode."

Chaingang nods. "How about redirecting the feed from just that camera? Can you do that?"

"Let me see."

He starts tapping keys. I have no idea what he's doing, but after a few moments, he smiles.

"Somebody walk out there," he says, motioning toward the street.

Desmond gets up and pushes through the hedge before I can grab his arm. It should be a Wildling doing this. Somebody better equipped to handle it if things go wrong.

My gaze fixes on the screen. The street looks bare, even though Desmond is right there, out on the sidewalk. A couple of cars go by and Desmond slips back to join us.

"What did you do, Barry?" I ask.

"I've got it repeating a loop of footage. Unless someone notices, you can't tell what's happening now on the street."

"Good job, bro," Chaingang tells Barry. "See if you can rejig the rest of the cameras along that corridor."

"No problem. I've got the protocol down now. But I can't do anything about human eyes. Anyone around here or down there will see you."

"Let us worry about that," Chaingang says. "Give us fifteen minutes, then shut everything down. Cameras. Security. Locks. Lights. The works."

"You'll just have gotten under the building itself by then."

"Yeah," Chaingang says. "But in the dark, the advantage is ours."

Barry frowns. "I don't get it."

I touch his arm. "It's okay, Barry. Just do what he says."

But Barry isn't stupid. He looks around at us.

"You guys are all Wildlings, aren't you?" he says.

Everybody goes tense. Chaingang's eyes narrow.

"No, no," Desmond says. "It's not like that, dude."

"You think I care?" Barry says. "What happened to Josh isn't right. Those guys need to be stopped and now at least I know you've got a fighting chance."

The tension holds a moment longer, then Chaingang smiles and extends a fist to Barry. They bump knuckles.

"Fifteen minutes," Chaingang says.

When Barry nods, Chaingang gets to his feet and looks around at the rest of us.

"Let's do this thing," he says.

He pushes his way through the hedge and the rest of us follow, jogging across the street toward the big garage door on the right side of the Pep Boys building.

JOSH

The man and woman are both dressed in white lab coats. The man's short and slender—or maybe he only looks short because the woman's so tall. She's over six feet and scarecrow thin. Her hair's short and the eyes behind her glasses are scary cold. He looks like one of those old dot-com guys—thinning hair pulled back into a small ponytail, blinking in our direction like we're a line of code that's not doing what it's supposed to.

They seem surprised to see me standing, Rico sitting up, both of us watching them come in.

"Are they supposed to be awake?" the man asks.

The woman shrugs. "No, but I'll take care of it."

"This is it," Rico says as she walks toward a bank of computer monitors.

He's standing now, too, balancing steadily on one leg.

"When I give the word," I tell him, "go to the far side of your cell and bang as hard as you can on the wall."

He lifts an eyebrow, but nods.

I focus on the mountain lion under my skin. I bring up the memory of that moment in my bathroom, how I called it up. There's no room for error. I've thought about this a hundred times since it happened, looking for the Wildling in me, weighing its presence, seeing what I'd have to do to let its body replace mine. I just hadn't actually taken the final step again. I'd felt like I was under a microscope, watched everywhere I went. And I'd been too scared.

I'm still scared, but now I don't have a choice. I've got one chance to do it. If I screw this up, I could be joining Rico in the one-leg brigade.

"Now!" I tell him.

He lunges over to the side of his cell, launching himself against the hard plastic, then bangs on it with both hands. He adds a scream that they probably can't hear. The two researchers immediately look in his direction. I grab that momentary distraction and let the constraints go.

I don't know why I was so worried. The change is instantaneous—just like it was before.

I feel strong. Powerful. I fit inside the mountain lion as though I've always been under its skin.

I'm also angry as hell.

For being in here—caged in their private zoo. For what they did to Rico. For what they want to do to me.

I bunch my leg muscles. Turning my anger into energy, I throw myself at the plastic wall, claws extended, ready to rip it to shreds. But I don't have to. The force of my impact makes the wall pop out of whatever was holding it in place. It comes crashing down and I'm riding it like it's a board, leaping off just before it smashes onto the floor. It takes down tables and cabinets along the way and sends their contents flying in a jangle of broken glass and metal implements that clatter across the marble floor.

The man screams. He drops to his knees and starts scrabbling for the door. The woman keeps her cool. She turns, finger stabbing out at some control on the keyboard by the computers. She's fast—I'll give her that—but I'm faster. I bat her away with one paw, not even thinking about my strength. I hear something snap. Her neck, maybe. She flies across the room. There's another snapping sound as her back hits the edge of one of the stainless steel surgical tables. Her body drops to the floor and settles in unnatural angles, blood trickling from the corner of her mouth.

I want to taste that blood, but then I hear the man. He's at the door, trying to escape.

It takes me one leap to reach him. My jaws are open, extended wide so I can take his head between my teeth. I can almost hear the bones of his skull shattering under my bite. But before I can crush his head, something slithers between us.

I register scales. A flat head. Dark unblinking eyes.

I'm slow on the uptake, but the mountain lion in me immediately recognizes the rattlesnake ready to strike. Before I can assimilate the information, I've already jumped back out of the snake's striking range. I roar my displeasure.

The snake becomes Rico. He's wearing jeans and a T-shirt, high tops on his feet—feet plural because he has both legs now. I don't understand and that makes me angry again. How did he get out of his cell? How'd he get his leg back? The growl starts up low in my chest.

He hold his hands up, palms out, before it develops into another roar.

"Easy," he says. "Easy. Cousins don't eat cousins."

The man behind him scrambles to his feet. Rico turns just long enough to sweep his legs from under him. As the man falls back onto the floor, arms flailing, Rico faces me again.

"Why don't you let the boy come back?" he says to me.

The boy? What boy?

But then I get it. I will the change. A moment later I'm standing there in my own shape.

"Aw, come on, man," Rico says. "I don't need to see your junk."

The hospital clothes I was wearing a moment ago didn't come back with me when I left my Wildling shape behind. I'm stark naked. In normal circumstances, I'd be mortified, but my gaze goes to the dead woman and I can't pull it away. I don't even bother to cover my dick with my hands. There's a weird whine in my ears and I'm finding it hard to breathe.

Dead.

At my hand.

Not hand. *Paw.*

I killed her like it was nothing. Like it was an afterthought. Just swept her out of my way.

I drop to my knees and throw up until I can only dry heave.

I lift my head and my gaze immediately locks on the woman's body again.

I hear water running, then a wet cloth lands with a splat on the floor in front of me.

"Wipe your face," Rico says. "We don't have time to screw around."

"She ... I ..."

"Yeah, she's dead. She also cut off my leg without even thinking twice. Get over it. It's not like you killed a nun."

I finally look away from the body to him.

"Your leg ..." I begin.

"It was gone, now it's back. I know. I'll answer your questions if we get out of this place, but can you just focus for a minute?"

I nod. I pick up the cloth and wipe my face. The cool rough cotton helps settle me.

Don't look at the body, I tell myself.

"They keep the clothes in that cabinet," Rico says, pointing.

I walk over to the cabinet on shaky legs. I pull out a white shirt and drawstring pants, put them on. It's hard to concentrate. I'm numb and everything seems unfocused. I start to button the shirt, then realize that Rico has a scalpel in his hand. He's holding the man up by the scruff of his lab coat.

"You get one chance to answer my question," Rico says.

He lets go and gives the man a push. The man's eyes are wild with panic as he falls back against the wall.

"I didn't do it," he says, voice pitched high with panic. "You know I didn't do it. It was her idea. I was just ... please ... I didn't want any of that to happen."

Rico slaps him. "Shut up. I don't care who was here or who gave the order. Just tell me what happened to Jenny."

"Juh—Jenny?"

"The girl who was in here with me."

"I don't know anything—"

He breaks off as Rico moves the scalpel in front of his eyes.

"Remember what I said about you getting one chance to answer?" Rico says.

"She's down the hall!" the man cries. "She's just down the hall! Second door on your right."

"Your key card opens her door?"

"Yes, yes."

"That's all I need to know," Rico tells him.

Then he slices across the man's neck and pushes him away so that the sudden spurt of blood doesn't get all over him.

"Jesus Christ!" I yell. "Are you nuts? What did you do that for?"

I run toward where the man's clutching his neck, blood spurting out between his fingers. Rico blocks my way. I don't know what I'd do anyway. Try to stop the bleeding, I guess.

"He's a monster," Rico says. "He doesn't deserve to live."

"And what does that make us?"

Rico shakes his head like he can't believe me.

"Trapped animals," he says.

He picks up the man's key card. There's blood on it, which he wipes away on the man's pant leg. The man has stopped twitching. He slumps where he fell, blood pooling on the floor around him. I look away, bile rising back up my throat.

"You coming?" Rico asks.

I shake my head. "You're nuts. I'm not going anywhere with you."

"So you're going to stay here and let them run their experiments on you? Since I'll be gone, I guess they'll only have you to cut up."

"No, I—" I'm so confused. "I don't know what I'm going to do. But I'm not going to go around killing people."

"Fair enough. If we're lucky, we won't run into anybody else."

He turns away and slides the key card down its slot. The inside of the door whirs and when he pulls on the handle, it opens. I look back at the chaos we're leaving behind. Dead bodies. Broken glass and lab equipment. The wall of my cell crushing the tables and cabinets it landed on. The front walls of the cells on either side standing askew off the floor. Which, I realize, is how Rico got out.

"Tick-tock, tick-tock," Rico says. "If you want to get out of here, we need to get to the ground floor and we need to get there fast."

"And then what?" I ask.

He shrugs. He turns away, letting the door close. I have to sprint to catch it before it locks again. When I slip through, he's at the second door on the right, sliding the key card through its slot.

"I thought we had to go?" I say.

"Not without Jenny."

The door unlocks. He turns the handle and pushes it slightly open, but then just stands there. He doesn't go in. He doesn't even try to look at what's inside. Instead he leans his head against the doorjamb.

"What's the matter?" I say.

"You don't smell it?"

I didn't. But as soon as he says it, I do. A foul, ripe odour mixed with something sweet and cloying. I don't recognize it.

"What—what is it?" I ask.

"The dead." He pushes himself upright and squares his shoulders. "You might want to stay out here," he adds, then opens the door and steps inside.

I don't want to follow him, but I do. I need to know everything, even though I wish I wasn't part of any of it. Killing that woman. Watching Rico kill her companion.

For a long moment, I don't know what I'm looking at. It's a much smaller room than the one we were held in, but just as sterile. Marble floors. White walls and ceiling. One wall is taken up with a bank of large steel drawers, the other has a long table with a computer and microscopes on it. It's cold in here—cold enough that I can see my breath, but for some reason, I don't feel the chill on my skin. The only chill I feel is inside. It's like I've got ice water running through my veins instead of blood.

In the middle of the room is another operating table. There are lights above it—turned off at the moment. Beside it is a small metal table on wheels that holds a bunch of surgical equipment. On the table ...

I want to look away, but I make myself join Rico where he's standing at the table, looking down at the body.

"Is—is this ...?"

"Yeah," he says. "This was Jenny. She was alive when they took her away. Scared out of her mind, but alive."

Making myself look at her is one of the hardest things I've ever done. I want to pretend I'm watching one of those CSI shows on TV. That this isn't real. But it's all too real.

They've cut her open and removed her organs. Just peeled the skin and tissue back, leaving this awful cavity. The organs are in basins on a second wheeled metal table. The top of her head is gone, her brain taken out and placed in another basin. Thin slices have been cut from the main part and are laid out in the basin.

She's not a person anymore. She's just meat.

I feel sick again, but there's nothing left in me to throw up.

"This ... this isn't right," I say

"No shit, Sherlock. Still feeling bad about those freaks we put down in the other room?"

I shake my head, but I'm not sure I really mean it. Then Rico bends down to kiss the dead girl's brow. The pain in his eyes when he straightens up makes me flinch. I've never seen hurt like that and something hardens inside me. I realize I *am* sure. I'm not at all sorry about what happened to the researchers.

Rico walks over the bank of steel drawers. I don't want him to open them, but he does. One after the other. By the time we've gone through them all, we've found the remains of half a dozen other kids.

Rico slams a fist against the metal, leaving a dent.

I don't say anything. I want to hit something, too.

Rico trembles with anger and turns away. He crosses the room, where he picks up one of the computer monitors and smashes it on the floor. Microscopes and the rest of the computer equipment soon join it.

"We're not fucking animals!" he yells.

He kicks at the broken pieces, then drops to his knees. He looks up at me.

"They don't even know or care if we're human or not," he says. "Cousin, human, they'll take us apart just to see how we work. And even if they figured out the difference, they wouldn't give a shit, except for the time they wasted on the ones that weren't cousins."

I don't know what to say.

He stands up finally and gives the computer tower another kick. It's already cracked in two. The impact of his foot sends pieces flying. Drives, motherboard, circuits.

"So much for their research," he says. "Let them try to salvage something from that."

I wish I could let him believe that it's all been destroyed, but he needs to know the truth.

"The data's all still there," I tell him. "They can still pull it off the hard drives."

"What does a hard drive look like?"

I'm no geek, but even I know that. So how come he doesn't? Still, I point one out to him.

"It looks like there are three of them," I say, "but it won't make any difference. They'll have backups stored off-site."

"Fuck!"

His eyes are crazed looking. He picks up the first drive and hurls it across the room. The other two follow in equally violent succession. They smash the wall with such force that the pieces scatter in a wide radius. If the bodies of either of those researchers were in this room, he'd probably pick up the scalpels and start stabbing them.

He looks down at the floor and takes a deep breath, collecting himself. When he looks up again, the craziness has been pushed to the back of his eyes.

"Okay," he says. "We can't do anything about that. And we can't give the dead a proper burial. All we can do now is try to get our own asses out of here."

As he heads for the door, I weigh my options. Do I want to go with the crazy guy who can turn into a snake and kills people without warning? Or do I want to stay here and take my chances?

My gaze returns to the body of the dead girl.

"Tick-tock," Rico says from behind me.

I make up my mind and join him at the door. Moments later we're running down the hall, looking for a stairwell because Rico says an elevator will just trap us all over again. My skin prickles along my shoulder blades. My bare feet slap the floor. I keep expecting alarms to go off. There are cameras everywhere. Why haven't the alarms gone off?

We find the door to the stairwell at the end of the hall. Rico swipes his stolen key card and hauls the door open. As we start up the stairs, the alarms finally go off. Their high-pitched clarion is so loud that it hurts my ears.

"We just need to make it to the ground floor," Rico says.

He picks up his pace before I can ask why, moving with a Wildling's speed.

I stay right on his heels.

MARINA

My phone rings as we make our way across the road in front of Pep Boys. I reach into my pocket, annoyed that I forgot to turn it off, then see that it's Barry.

"Hang on," I tell the others.

"Oh, Jesus," Barry says as soon as I answer. "You guys really need to see this before you go in."

"See what?"

"Just get back here."

I look at Chaingang to see what he thinks. I know that he, Elzie and Cory can hear both sides of our conversation.

"Who was that?" Desmond asks.

Chaingang sighs. "Just tell him we're coming."

"It was Barry," I tell Desmond as we turn around again.

"What does he want?"

"He didn't say."

We hurry back, moving fast. Desmond trails behind, trying to keep up.

"This better be good," Chaingang says as he pushes through the hedge ahead of the rest of us.

But judging from the smell of fear on Barry, whatever it is, it isn't good.

"All hell's broken loose over there," he says. "Look at this."

He pulls up a camera view on the laptop.

"What are we looking at?" Cory asks.

"It's an autopsy room."

A trashed autopsy room, I think, as I take in the image. There are pieces of some kind of machine scattered all over the floor, but I can't quite figure out what it was.

Barry points at the metal table in the middle of the room. I lean in closer to figure out what's there, then quickly turn away. My stomach lurches.

"She was just a kid," Cory says.

I feel scared and sick. I wish I'd never seen that image, but I'll never be able to forget it now.

Barry nods. "Yeah. And it gets worse. Let's see if I can play this back. I saw them smashing up that computer, then backed the video up to what had been recorded a few moments ago, in the first room we saw."

He hits a couple of keystrokes then mutters a few choice words under his breath when the screen shows an interior view of the building's foyer.

"Just a sec."

A few more keystrokes and we're back looking at the room with the weird glass cells, except it's from a different perspective. We can see more of the room now.

"Is that …?" Desmond begins.

"Josh, yeah," Barry says. "They shaved off his dreads."

Poor Josh. It took him a long time to grow those dreads. He'd never let them shave him willingly. Now I notice that Josh isn't alone. There's a one-legged kid in the cell beside him.

"Fine," Chaingang says. "So we've confirmed that it's him. Now if we can just get back on track …"

His voice trails off. Josh and the other kid are both standing up now, staring at a door at the far end of the room as it opens to let in a couple of people in white lab coats. A tall woman, a shorter man. The kid we don't know suddenly makes this amazing one-legged leap to the side of his cell and starts banging on the glass. At the same time, Josh shifts into his mountain lion shape and lunges for the front of his cell.

"Aw, crap," Chaingang says.

Barry's right. It gets far worse after that. We watch transfixed as the wall of the cell collapses under the mountain lion's weight. Instantly, Josh snaps the woman's neck with one swat of a huge paw. Everyone is struck dumb as the rest of the scene plays out. Even Desmond has lost his quick tongue.

Barry swallows hard.

"I called you as soon as—well—right after Josh *changed* and all this other stuff happened …"

Maybe he'd already guessed about Josh, but he's white as a sheet and his hands are shaking. By now, he certainly suspects that the rest of us gathered here around his laptop are also Wildlings. Having seen two violent deaths play out right in front of his eyes, and imagining that the rest of us might have similar powers, I'm surprised he's holding it together as well as he is.

As for me, I'm all light-headed and my legs feel like Jell-O. I've just witnessed two murders. I don't know the other kid, but why did Josh change and why couldn't he control the lion? But then I think of that poor girl on the autopsy table. Maybe they were coming to do the same thing to Josh and his companion. Maybe they had no other choice. But it's still impossible to relate it to the Josh that I know.

"You were right to call us back, bro," Chaingang says. "Where are they now?"

"Dude, are you sure you want to go near that snake or that mountain lion?" Desmond says. "I kind of doubt they need our help ... bro."

Chaingang ignores Desmond. "Barry," he says again. "Where are they?"

Barry shakes his head as though waking from a dream and looks at Chaingang. "I was able to see them in the autopsy room after that. The other dude trashed the equipment. They left right after that, but I don't know where they went. That's when I called you guys."

"You've got to kill the cameras," Chaingang says. "All of them."

"I don't know if I can."

"Now. Just try, before—"

We all freeze as alarms start to wail in the ValentiCorp building. Or at least, all the Wildlings hear it.

"What's the matter?" Desmond says.

"There's going to be cops all over the place," Chaingang says.

Cory nods. "Kill their power," he tells Barry. "Backup generators, too."

"I'm trying, man."

Chaingang points a finger at Desmond. "You stay here. The rest of you, let's motor."

"Come on, dude," says Desmond. "Don't leave me out. I'm in all the way."

But he's already talking to Chaingang's back.

I touch Desmond's arm. "We know," I tell him. "but you won't be able to keep up."

Cory and Elzie are already gone. I run after them. As we tear across the parking lot, I hear Desmond far behind us. "Wait up!" he cries, to no avail.

As Chaingang races across one of the medians separating the various parking lots, he scoops up a big stone without even breaking stride. I think it's a poor choice for a weapon, but just as we're about to pass a big cherry-red SUV, I find out what the rock is really for. Chaingang smashes it into the driver's side window, then throws it aside. Opening the door, he sweeps the glass from the seat and pops out a piece of the dash from under the steering wheel.

"What the hell are you doing?" Elzie yells. "We need to get our butts over there!"

"Josh and the snake kid are going to need a distraction if they're going to get out of there," Chaingang says. "*This* is the distraction."

The SUV's engine roars to life.

"Oh yeah," Chaingang says with a grin as he gets behind the wheel. "I've still got it. Grab a seat, ladies and gent."

He pops the locks open and the rest of us pile in. I'm still closing my door when the SUV takes off. Chaingang pushes it at high speed right toward ValentiCorp, weaving to avoid parked cars and other medians. In the distance, I catch the first sound of an approaching siren. It's still far away, but it's soon joined by others. They'll be here in a minute.

"What's the plan?" Cory asks from the shotgun seat.

"Well," Chaingang says, "I'm going to drive through their front doors and see what happens."

"Works for me."

Elzie and I gasp at the same time, then quickly fumble for our seatbelts. Once we're strapped in, I reach for Elzie's hand. I think maybe she's too cool to need comfort, but as soon as my fingers find hers, she locks on to mine in a tight grip.

A couple of the security guards appear, running from the side of the building as we roar up to the front. They draw guns from shoulder holsters and we all duck as they begin to fire. Except for Chaingang. He just laughs.

"Payback time, fuckers!" he yells.

I have time to think, great. He's gone nuts and we're all going to die.

Bullets hit the car, pinging from the metal, shattering the windows. Then we're past them, up on the curb, heading right for the front doors. More men appear. There's more gunfire. They all scatter as Chaingang drives right for them.

Then we smash through the doors, spraying glass and metal, and we're in the foyer. The SUV skids on the marble floor. Chaingang yanks the steering wheel left, so that we're pulling three-sixties right there in the foyer. We take out a reception desk, a waiting area filled with sofas, tables and floor lamps. There's a momentary lull in the gunfire as the security guards dive out of our way.

Then suddenly the building goes black and the alarms that have been screaming are cut off. There's only the roar of our motor. The headlights of the SUV pierce the sudden dark. As we rotate, they pick out a side door opening and two figures in white pants and shirts who dart out. I see them for a flash, then the SUV spins some more and they're lost to my sight.

The gunfire starts up again as guards begin to shoot down on us from the mezzanine above. A couple of bullets come right through the roof of the SUV and it's a serious miracle that none of us are hit.

"Straighten out!" Cory yells. "Drive for that wall!"

He points to the far side of the foyer where I'd seen the two figures in white a moment ago. They're still there, but now the SUV's headlights are picking out an impossible sight behind them. There's a weird flickering in the air—like a heat shimmer—and on the other side of it, I can make out a pristine, moonlit landscape. Instead of the glass walls that should have been there with a parking lot behind them, we're looking at a place that can't possibly exist.

The two figures run right into the shimmer.

"What the hell?" Chaingang says.

"Just follow them!" Cory shouts.

If I'd been behind the wheel, I don't know that I could have done it. But Chaingang stomps his foot on the gas and we drive straight to where the two figures disappeared. I hear somebody screaming their head off and realize it's me.

JOSH

I'm counting exit doors as we race up the stairs.

The first door has a big red "4B" on it. Fourth floor basement.

Still a ways to go. Two more turns on the stairs.

Third floor.

Just as Rico reaches the landing, the door flies open. The alarm is suddenly louder and a security guard steps out. He has long enough to register our presence, then Rico grabs him by the lapels of his jacket and flings him right over my head, down the stairs. I hear the sound of breaking bones as he lands, but we're already up the next flight.

The door below automatically shuts, muffling the screaming sound of the alarm until a second later, it opens again. Voices are shouting. One pair of crepe-soled shoes pursues us up the stairs. The other heads down to their fallen comrade.

We're at the door to the second floor now. Just one more to go.

The guard following us can't come close to matching our speed. We're not even breathing hard and he's already struggling for air. But he manages to radio our position to someone else.

The ground floor door bangs open above us. Two guards fire in our direction. Rico leaps high, I drop low and the first shots miss us. Then Rico's on them. He propels one back through the door, the other toward me. The guard tries to latch on to me as he goes by, but I grab his flailing arms and use his momentum to throw him down onto the man still coming up the stairs after us. Then I follow Rico out the door.

It's insane on the ground floor. We come out into the foyer to the wailing of the alarm, an SUV pulling three-sixties on the marble floor, and enough gunfire to make it sound like a small war. But they're not shooting at us. It's the SUV that has their attention.

"Follow me!" Rico cries.

As we take off toward a bank of windows, all the power shuts down. Lights. Alarm. It's dark, except for the SUV's headlights spinning counter-clockwise. There's a lull in the gunfire. The roar of the SUV's engine is deafening.

I don't know what it is that Rico does, but a shimmer fills the air in front of us. For a moment, the windows of the foyer and the parking lots outside are hazy and indistinct, then I'm looking out at a completely different landscape. It's night out there, but the mountain lion's gaze tells me that there isn't a man-made structure as far as the eye can see. The smells that come to me are rich and wild. There's not a trace of concrete or gas or metal.

Then we're through the shimmer and dry grass is crunching under our feet. I stop, stunned, until Rico barrels into me and throws me sideways onto the dusty ground. A moment later the red SUV from the foyer of ValentiCorp roars by, right where I was standing, throwing up a cloud of dust. It skids to a halt a dozen yards away and the engine shuts off.

I leap to my feet and look back the way we came. I'm expecting guards to be running in our direction, firing as they come. But they don't come. I can't make out the shimmer anymore because of the dust. I need to use my other senses, but what my nose and ears tell me, I don't believe. It's not until the dust clears that I see they're telling me the truth.

The building we came from is gone. Ditto, the parking lots that had surrounded it. All of Santa Feliz.

It's dark out here except for the moonlight and there is absolutely no sign of human habitation.

"Okay," I say. "Now I'm seriously freaking out."

"Save it for later," Rico tells me. "We've got company."

Right. The SUV.

"Did *they* bring us here?" I ask.

Rico shakes his head. "I brought us here. They just swooped along in our wake."

"And *where* are we?"

"Later."

I'm getting awfully tired of his laters, but I let it slide for the moment. The wind's coming from behind us, so I haven't a clue as to who's in the SUV. But considering how my luck's been of late, I'm expecting the worst.

Rico doesn't seem concerned. He's standing casually by my side, but I'm not fooled. He's poised for anything. I've seen how fast he can go into action.

His gaze is steady as he takes in the vehicle. It's pretty beat up. All the windows are blown out and the metal is riddled with bullet holes, the paint scraped off the sides in long streaks and fenders bent. It looks as though it's had the wrath of God laid on it.

"The enemies of our enemies," I mutter. I think I heard it in a movie.

"Maybe," Rico says.

Then the last person I expect to see steps out of the driver's door.

"Chaingang?" I say.

He grins. "Wassup, bro?"

The passenger door opens and my own smile gets bigger as Cory gets out. But if they were unexpected, the two slim forms that pile out of the back seat pretty much floor me. Marina and Elzie.

"Holy shit! What are you guys *doing* here?" I cry as I run forward.

"And where the hell is 'here'?" says Chaingang, looking around.

I ignore him for the moment and hug both girls. I thought I'd never see either of them again. The relief of having them here threatens to overwhelm me.

"Well, we thought we were saving your ass," Elzie says.

Marina smiles. "But it turns out you didn't need saving."

I can't stop grinning. But then I realize there's something different about Marina.

"You've changed!" I say.

She and Elzie exchange a quick look.

"Um, yeah," she says, looking up at me.

"When did that happen? Is Desmond a Wildling, too?"

She shakes her head. "So far as I know, Desmond's still human—much to his continued disappointment."

"But he's safe?"

"I hope so. He didn't make it anywhere near the building, so he should be good."

Elzie reaches up to rub my scalp. "Now we're twins," she says, her eyes twinkling. I grab her hand and hold it in mine for a moment. I'm so grateful that she's okay. We look into each other's eyes and then Chaingang steps up and Elzie and Marina release me.

Chaingang smiles and we bump fists.

"Nice to see you, bro," he says, "but you'd better tell me what's going on here. Like I said, where are we?"

"Later," says Rico.

Chaingang scowls at him. "I wasn't talking to you."

"Hey," I say, putting my hands out. "I don't have a clue either."

Cory comes over to join us. "We'll get into that soon," he says, "but first things first. What did I tell you about keeping a low profile?"

"Yeah," says Chaingang. "Back there, they've got all the footage they need to put you away forever. "

Cory scuffs the ground with his boot and shakes his head. "Way to go."

"Hey," I begin. "At first I wasn't going to do anyth—"

"I get it," Cory says. "You didn't really know any better. But I was talking to Rico."

"You guys know each other?" I ask.

Rico shrugs. "Sure. Coyote Clan and rattler go back a long way," he says. "He's been around stirring that pot since day one."

He looks at Cory. "Once our mountain lion boy here dropped his human skin, there wasn't much point in pretending anymore. And I've got to tell you, I wasn't looking forward to having them saw off my other leg."

"You would have gotten it back."

"How *does* that work?" I ask.

But neither of them pays attention to me.

"Maybe so," Rico says. "But it still hurts like a son of a bitch while they're doing it. And what they did to Jenny, you know—that little soft-spoken cottontail always hung around with the deer girls? Never had a bad word for anybody?"

"They cut the top of her head off and pulled out her brain. And I'm pretty sure she was still alive when they did it. She screamed for a long time—until she didn't. So don't tell me I was supposed to hang in there."

Cory gets a pained look.

Remembering the gruesome scene of Jenny on the autopsy table, I find that hard place inside me getting a little colder, a little stronger. I'm not sure if that's a good thing or not.

Once again I put one arm around Elzie's shoulders, the other around Marina's. They both shiver, listening to Rico. Marina turns her head into my shoulder. Elzie's shoulders tense up under my arm and I know she's angry.

Cory nods. "Truth is, I don't care how or why you guys broke out. I'm just glad you got a little damage in while you were doing it. It's long past time we had some payback."

"But the old woman is going to be pissed," Rico says.

"Oh, yeah," Cory agrees.

"Well, I don't care. Maybe it's time she volunteered to be the experiment."

"You know it wasn't her idea."

"But she agreed to it."

"Enough," Chaingang breaks in. His voice is quiet, but it demands attention. "Which one of you is going to tell us what the hell's going on here?"

"Yeah," Elzie says. "Like Chaingang said, where are we?"

"And how'd you grow your leg back?" I add.

Cory nods and puts both hands up. "I understand that you've got questions," he says. "But let's do this in proper cousin style. Build a fire, make a truth circle."

Chaingang frowns. "The hell's that?"

"It's something cousins do when we need to share, to make sense of things."

"I've got a better idea," Chaingang says. "How about we skip the New Age bullshit and you just answer our questions?"

"It's not up to you," Cory tells him. "You're not the only one here."

I want answers to all those questions, too, but something about this pristine place makes me feel we should follow the lead of the older Wildlings. If they've got a ceremony for this kind of thing, maybe it's best to follow it.

"Let's give their way a chance," I say.

Chaingang turns to me. "Oh, and are *you* calling the shots now?"

I shake my head. "No, I'm just saying. I mean, what would it hurt?"

"Josh is right," Marina says, looking at Chaingang. "I think maybe we all could use a truth circle right now."

Chaingang frowns, but he looks at Marina, then his face softens and he nods in slow agreement.

"Okay, I get it," he says. "But I gotta tell you, this place has me feeling antsy. I guess I can wait a little longer, but do your thing and then let's get going."

Rico rubs his hands together. "Excellent," he says. "So do you have any food in that big-ass car of yours?"

"Something was rolling around under the cover of the hatch. Let's go check," Elzie says.

Marina and I follow her to the SUV. As we walk, Marina explains to me how Chaingang hot-wired it in the parking lot. It looks like a mom owned the vehicle because, miraculously, when we roll back the hatch cover, the storage space is packed tight with cloth bags full of food. A bunch of apples have come out of one bag and are scattered everywhere, and a carton of milk caught a bullet and leaked itself empty, but otherwise, everything seems to have survived the firefight.

Whoever owned this vehicle was really practical and orderly. They probably have four perfect kids. Besides all that food, there's a pile of thick fleece throws in the back and each is monogrammed: Mom, Dad, Kirsty, Katie, Kieran, David. Marina bundles them up in her arms.

All that food makes my stomach growl. I hadn't even thought about it because there'd been so much going on, but now I realize how hungry I am. That's what shifting your shape does, I remember.

Elzie turns and tosses me a bag of chips.

"After what I saw on the surveillance cameras," she says, "you'll probably want to start in on this."

What she saw? I remember the sounds as the mountain lion's paw broke that woman's neck, then her back snapped. I stare at the bag of chips and although I'm famished, the last thing I want to do it eat. Then I think of what they were doing to Wildlings in that place and know that if I had the chance for a do-over, I wouldn't do anything differently.

"You *saw* what happened?"

She nods. "We all did." Her eyes are sympathetic and she puts a hand on my arm.

"You didn't have a choice," she says.

"You know that's not true. There's always a choice."

"Well, sure, if you wanted to end up like those kids we saw in the autopsy room ..."

Another shiver creeps up my spine at the memory of Jenny and all those drawers filled with dead kids.

"But *how* did you see all of that?" I ask.

"Barry hooked into the feed of their surveillance cameras," Marina says.

"Barry? What was he doing there? Is he okay?"

They both nod.

"He told us about all the tunnels that ValentiCorp has under that complex," Elzie says. "That's how they got you into their building."

"But he wasn't with us," Marina adds, "when Chaingang went, you know, all Arnold and drove us right into the front of the building."

Elzie nods. "Yeah, I didn't think we'd make it. I'm surprised none of us got shot." She taps the chips I'm holding and adds, "Eat."

I give in to my hunger, rip the bag open and start to make short work of the chips.

MARINA

Viewing the grisly scene at ValentiCorp already made me feel ill, but now my stomach is in even more knots. I've worried for months about telling Josh that I didn't trust him enough to reveal that I'm a Wildling and now time has run out. I'll have to find the courage to admit my mistake and face the consequences.

If Desmond felt as shocked and hurt as he did, Josh is going to feel ten times worse. I wish I could turn back the clock. If I had a second chance, I would never betray our friendship.

We're all sitting around the fire on the fleece throws that I brought from the car. I seem to be the only one without much of an appetite. Everybody else is hungry, but there's plenty of food. The grocery bags hold steaks, pork chops, hot dogs and spare ribs, and we cook it all, poking sharpened sticks into the meat and holding it over the fire.

Loaves of bread, boxes of cookies and cereal, milk, bottled water and pop—a respectable amount of it disappears quickly.

No one talks much while they're eating. I don't know what anyone else has on their mind, but I'm trying not to think about the coming truth circle.

I wonder where we are and what happened to Santa Feliz. This place is amazing. The clean scents of plant life and the breeze from the nearby ocean waft over the smells of the fire and the food. The air is incredibly clear and the stars and a quarter-moon make a vast canopy of light above us. Ours is the only other light for as far as I can see—one small crackling campfire in a sea of darkness.

Finally, the last food wrapper has been burned in the fire and all the Styrofoam containers have been bagged, ready to go back into the car. Elzie starts to say something, but Rico raises a hand to stop her.

"Let's do this right," he says.

Cory nods and rises. He pulls a little bundle of tightly bound sage and sweetgrass out of his pocket. Turquoise and red strings hold it together. I've seen these inside Mandala, the New Age store on Main Street.

Cory takes the stick he was using to cook with and lights it from the fire, then holds it to one end of the sweetgrass bundle. The bundle flames up and he blows it out so that it starts to smoulder, reminding me of the heady smells in the shop.

First Cory directs the smoke toward himself, running his free hand through the smoke toward his chest and then over his head. Then he walks around in a circle behind us. As he goes, he stops four times and holds the smouldering grasses high above his head. The second time he stops, I realize he's marking compass points. North. West. South. East.

I glance across the fire at Chaingang and he rolls his eyes, but doesn't say anything. Cory makes the circuit four times, then returns to the blanket where he was sitting and rubs the smouldering end of the bundle on a rock until it's extinguished.

"We have broken bread together," he says, "and given our respect to the four directions. Let there only be truth in this circle that we share."

"Let there only be truth," Rico repeats.

The two of them look at the rest of us. After a moment, we repeat the words in a ragged chorus.

"Is there going to be more of this?" Chaingang asks. "Because I've gotta tell you, this touchy-feely stuff is really not my bag."

"What we're doing with this circle," Cory says, "is showing our respect. Respect is a pretty big thing to the Ocean Avers, right?"

Chaingang shifts on his blanket and nods.

"So were showing respect to the grandfather Thunders who live in the four directions—and also to the land, the sea, the sky and the fire. And we're showing our respect for one another. Wherever our individual ways take us after tonight—here and now, in this circle, we offer only respect to each other. And we speak only the truth."

"That too touchy-feely for you?" Rico asks Chaingang.

Chaingang smiles and shakes his head, but he flips a quick "screw you" finger in Rico's direction. Looks like respect might be a challenge for Chaingang.

"So whatever we ask someone," Elzie says, glancing at me, then Josh, between us, "they have to answer with the truth?"

Cory shakes his head. "We're not here to confront each other or to bare our souls. We're here to share information and strategies."

I let out a sigh of relief. Maybe I won't have to do this so publicly.

"Can we start with where we are?" I ask. "And how did we get here?"

"That's easy," Cory said. "These are the spiritlands—they're a step sideways from what you thought of as only one world."

At our blank looks, he laces his fingers together and moves the fingers of one hand. "Think of *this* as the world we came from"—He wiggles the fingers of the other hand—"and *this* is where we are now. It's almost like they take up the same space, but they're two individual places. Once you learn to see from one into the other, it's easy to move between them, the way Rico did to bring us here."

"You expect us to buy that?" Chaingang says.

Cory shrugs. "You're here, aren't you?"

"You can really do that from anywhere?" I ask. "In either world?"

"Sure."

I look over at Rico. "Then why did you stay locked up?" I ask.

Rico's face is calm. The light of flames dances across his features. "Two reasons. If we'd simply disappeared, they'd know we can do that."

"But they cut off your *leg!*" I say.

"Yeah. And I might have said screw it at that point, but we were underground and there was no place for me to come out over here. If I'd tried, I would have ended up trapped under a hundred feet of dirt and rock. I needed to be on the ground floor."

"So how have you kept this … other world … a secret for so long?" Josh asks.

"We haven't, exactly," Cory says. "It's there in all kinds of folklore and fairy tales. And that's where it stays, because nobody truly believes in it. The other thing that clouds the waters is that these spiritlands change. The deeper you go into them, the more complex they become—they transform, like a work in progress."

"And everybody starts to see them differently," Rico adds. "Although once, this world and yours were the same place. That is, until one of Cory's ancestors decided that the best way to get rid of the five-fingered beings was to roll up their world like a carpet and hide it away. But that didn't quite work out the way he expected—which is what usually happens when Coyote gets a wild notion. Instead, the world split in two, so now we have both worlds."

Chaingang shakes his head. "You're shitting us. Are you really saying that happened?"

Rico shrugs. "This is a truth circle."

"Come on, bro," Chaingang says. "How do you roll up a world?"

"Hey, maybe we should try that again," Elzie says. "I like the idea of getting everything back to how the world was before we all came along and screwed it up. This place rocks."

"We don't have to," Cory tells her. "The spiritlands are already here, untouched by the five-fingered beings."

"The problem we have right now is damage control," Rico says. "How much of what went down at ValentiCorp was caught on their security cameras and what are they going to do with that information?"

"From what we saw on Barry's laptop," I say, "they're sure to have recordings of everything."

Chaingang nods. "So we have to go back in and get it."

"We don't make that decision," Cory says. "That's up to Señora Mariposa and the other elders."

Chaingang grunts with displeasure. "So you've got bosses and governments telling you what to do, just like us," he says. "Tell me the truth—did you guys *do* something to change us into Wildlings?"

"Not that I know of," Rico says.

"I doubt it," Cory adds. "We were doing fine, staying under the radar like always, until this whole Wildlings thing happened and messed it up for all of us."

Chaingang nods, but I can tell he's not a hundred percent sure that the elders aren't responsible. If they were, would they even admit it?

"I find it disappointing," Chaingang says, "that even in your world, some big-assed set of people gets to call all the shots."

"It's not that, so much as a matter of respect," Rico says. "Cousins aren't inclined to get together to get things done. But elders—especially ones like Señora Mariposa—have so much history bound up in both worlds. We need their perspective and their wisdom."

"What is she, *really*?" I ask. "She seems, I don't know, bigger than the rest of us—and not just because she's an elder."

"Señora Mariposa has been living where she has for a very very long time," Cory says. "She understands the needs of the land and the cousins living on it, plus she's very attuned to the five-fingered beings who share that space with us."

"But you do what she says."

Cory shakes his head. "Not exactly. We listen to what she says. And if it makes sense, we try to follow her advice. Her decisions are based on what's good for everybody, not just herself. There are discussions—sometimes they even get a little heated—but most of the time, her advice is right. Or else we wouldn't listen to her."

"Okay," Chaingang says, "so where does that Tomás guy come in? I'm down with Auntie Min. She can be annoying, but she's always done okay by me. But that guy—he pisses me off."

"He pisses a lot of people off," Cory says. "He's been in L.A. too long, I guess, but his heart's in the right place."

"So you trust him."

Cory looks around himself and shifts on his blanket. "Actually, I don't really know him."

Chaingang laughs. "Oh, come on. You're Coyote Clan. Even *I* know that you guys have an opinion on everything and everyone."

Instead of answering—or even taking offence—Cory pokes at the fire with a stick. Rico gives him a curious look.

Cory glances at Rico, then his gaze goes to where Chaingang is sitting and he sighs.

"I don't *know* anything," he says, "but I don't trust him. He worries me. A lot of the old cousins were angry when the whole Wildlings business blew up in Santa Feliz and, to be honest, I wonder how far they might go to address the problem."

"What does that mean?" Josh asks.

"It means," Chaingang says, "that *we're* the so-called problem and they want us to go away. They're probably coming up with some plan of their own to get rid of us."

"Figures," Elzie says, hugging herself. "I don't know why I've ever trusted anybody."

Josh gives Elzie a squeeze and looks at Rico. "You told me that cousins don't eat cousins," he says.

Rico nods. "Yeah. That's a given."

"But it's okay to kill us?"

Cory breaks in. "Hey, I didn't say that."

"You didn't have to," Chaingang says.

"Don't start jumping to conclusions," Cory says.

"I'm not jumping on anything," Chaingang says. "I just get a bad feeling from that dude."

"Is Auntie Min really a part of this?" Elzie asks.

"We don't even know that there *is* a 'this,'" Rico tells her, "but she'd never be a part of anything like that."

Chaingang nods. "Uh-huh. And you know this because?"

"Because she's Señora Mariposa. All you new cousins are part of Santa Feliz and it's under her protection. So *you're* under her protection."

Elzie looks at Cory. "But you also said she doesn't have any real power on her own."

"No, I didn't say that." Cory says. "Don't misread me. She is far more powerful than you can imagine. I just said that this particular circumstance has her in a bind. Why do you think she wants Josh on her side?"

Josh's eyes open wide and both arms drop from our shoulders. He jumps to his feet.

"Me?" he says. "What good would *I* do?"

"Relax. Sit down. You're Mountain Lion Clan—the first of the old clans to appear since all of this started. She thinks you could be the leader that will make sense of everything and bring us all together."

Josh drops to his haunches. "Yeah, right."

"Think about it," Rico says. "You come from a powerful clan that has the respect of the older cousins, but you're also a new Wildling, so the kids in your town will know that you understand what they're going through. Plus you're a mixed-blood human, so you're touching on a lot of bases."

Cory's nodding. "That's what Señora Mariposa said."

Josh looks a little panicked. He sits back down and puts his hands on either side of his head.

"You're starting to freak me out here," he says.

"Give some thought to Señora Mariposa's idea," Cory says. "Her main concern is the land and she sees you as the way to resolve this situation."

But Josh is slowly shaking his head, staring into the fire.

"This is crazy," he says.

"Looks like you blew it, bro" Chaingang says.

"What do you mean?"

"I know you had no choice, but how's what happened down at ValentiCorp supposed to make Wildlings look all warm and fuzzy? It plays right into the bad rep that guys like Congressman Householder are trying to lay on us. Quarantine, here we come."

"Damn right I had no choice," says Josh, bristling.

"Listen, ValentiCorp isn't going to let those images go public," Cory says. "They have way too much to lose."

"Ever heard of editing?" Chaingang asks.

Cory nods. "Yeah, but the FBI would be on to it. ValentiCorp couldn't edit those recordings without leaving a trace of their handiwork behind. Any decent forensics lab could identify it."

"Yeah, for sure they're going to hush this up," Rico adds. "They were *killing* kids, for Christ's sake. They'll want to keep a lid on this as much as we do."

"Whatever," Chaingang says. Then his eyes go hard. "But let me tell you, just because we need to stay under the radar doesn't mean I won't be extracting some payback for what they did to those kids."

"I just want my life back," Josh moans.

"Not going to happen, bro," says Chaingang. "Not if you're supposed to be the guy that rallies the troops."

Josh looks at me, then Elzie, and shakes his head. We each lean in toward him in sympathy.

"Okay," Cory says. "Let's focus on where we're at right now. We know the Feds are on our case. They're acting benign, but they're still pulling kids in off the street and holding them. We know ValentiCorp is probably going to keep grabbing kids for their experiments. They might also try to relay information to put us in a bad light without incriminating themselves. And then there's the elders and whatever they're planning. We know what Auntie Min wants, but as for Tomás and the others, that remains to be seen."

"That about covers it," Rico says.

"So what do we do now?" Elzie says, "Can we even be sure that the government isn't in on what happened at ValentiCorp? Who in God's name *can* we trust?"

"Ourselves," Cory says. "Each other. Right now we're all we've got."

"Oh, that's just *dandy*," Elzie says, shaking her head. "Let's hope nothing comes between any of us." She turns and stares pointedly at me.

Josh looks back and forth at the two of us, obviously confused.

"I agree," Cory says. "And now I'm going for a run."

He shifts into his coyote shape and before anyone can respond, lopes off into the night.

JOSH

I'm suddenly exhausted. Totally wiped. After the day I've had, I guess it's no surprise. It's all I can do to keep my eyes open.

Chaingang takes out his phone.

"No bars," he says. "Big surprise."

He puts it back in his pocket and lies down.

"Keep it down, kids," he tells us. "I need my beauty sleep."

"There isn't that much sleep in the world," Marina says with a wink.

He chuckles. Closing his eyes, he's gone in moments.

Rico shakes out his blanket, then moves it closer to the fire. A moment later, he's asleep as well.

Elzie rubs her hand again on my stubbled head. "You look cute," she says. Her own hair has just started to grow back. It's a soft fuzz, haloing her pretty head in the firelight.

I touch my own. "Not a look I was planning on."

She flicks a nail against the fabric of the white shirt I grabbed from the lab.

"And seriously," she adds. "Tomorrow we're going to practice how you keep your clothes on when you change back."

"I wasn't really worrying about that at the time."

Her eyes go warm with sympathy. "You should get some rest," she says. "You must be beat."

"I am."

I think she's going to lie down beside me, but she stands up and stretches.

"I'm going down to the ocean," she says. "I want to see what it feels like swimming without somebody's trash bumping into my face.

"No," she adds as I start to get up. "You need to sleep."

I nod.

"I'm going to turn in, too," Marina says.

Elzie raises her eyebrows and gives her look that I don't understand.

"Later," she says.

Marina and I watch her go.

"So what's up with you two?" I ask her.

Marina pushes her hair behind her ears and sighs. "Nothing, really."

"Come on. I can tell it's more than nothing."

"You're not going to like it."

"I don't like much of anything that's happened to me in the past twenty-four hours, but I'm dealing with it. I'm pretty sure I can handle a girl fight."

"It's not that," she says. "It's about my being a Wildling."

All the tension drains out of me. What a relief. If that's all this is, I can deal with it. It doesn't explain the weirdness between the two of them, but I don't mind to provide a listening ear to Marina. After all, she just changed. I know how disconcerting that is.

I reach over and touch her under the chin.

"Come on," I say sympathetically. "Don't let it freak you out too much. It might not seem like it now, but it's actually pretty cool, once you get used to it."

"I know."

It takes me a moment to process what she's just said and, even then, I'm pretty sure that I must be wrong. I have to be wrong. This is Marina, my best friend. We don't have secrets about anything.

"What do you mean, you 'know'?" I ask.

"I know how you get used to it."

My chest feels like it's encased in a metal band squeezing the air out of my lungs. I dread asking the question, but I do.

"Just … how long … have you been a Wildling?"

She's staring at the ground, unable to look me in the eye. "Around five months," she whispers.

"Five *months*?"

She nods.

"You've been a Wildling for five months and you never told me?"

Her shoulders are slumped and she looks miserable. "I didn't know how to. And then the longer I didn't, the more impossible it seemed."

The imagined metal band tightens a notch. "I told you right away."

"I know."

"You and Desmond were the first people I told. I came to you as soon as I could."

"I *know*. How do you think that makes *me* feel?"

"Oh, I'm *so* sorry. I didn't know it was all about how *you* feel. I'm not sure I know *you* at all anymore. The Marina I knew would never have kept something this big from me."

Her face goes from slack to a pained grimace. "Please don't be mad," she says.

"I'm not. I'm just really really hurt and confused. If you can keep something like that from me, what else are you hiding?"

Her eyes are shiny and her lower lip is trembling, but I don't feel the urge to comfort her. She takes a raggedy breath.

"I'm Nira," she says. *My Life as an Otter* ... that's my blog."

Another notch tighter. This is just too much. She totally pretended she knew nothing about it when I told Desmond and her about having found it.

"I don't get it," I tell her. "I thought we were friends."

"We *are* friends."

"Then why have you been lying to me all this time?"

"I didn't lie! I just didn't tell you everything."

I think about her giving me advice, like to surf online for more information, or that day in the library, when she was talking about Wildlings and shape-changers like it was just something she'd researched.

She tries to straighten up, without much success. "Do you tell me everything?" she asks.

I look her in the eye. "Yeah, I do."

I watch a tear trickle down her cheek as she looks away. It seems to take forever to travel down to her chin. Any other time I'd be comforting her the way I always have whenever something's gone bad in her life—like when her folks split up or when her sister hassles her—but I just can't muster the sympathy.

Her shoulders slump again. "I guess I'm just not as good a person as you," she says.

"That's bullshit. What it really means is that our friendship wasn't as important to you as it was to me."

Her face searches mine unbelievingly. "That's not true!"

"Did you ever stop to think how much you could have helped me when I first changed?"

"I *know*. I already said I screwed up when I didn't tell you right away.

And then I just didn't know how."

"When I changed might have been a good time."

She stares back down into her lap. "I just ... couldn't. It had already been months since it happened to me. I felt ashamed that I hadn't told you. I knew you'd get mad."

I stand up. "I told you. I'm not mad. But I don't see how we can be friends after something like this. How am I supposed to trust you about anything?"

"Please, Josh. Please don't say that."

"Is this what was going on between you Elzie?"

She looks up at me and nods. "She said I should tell you."

"She was right."

"Except now, the thing I was most scared of is happening. I'm losing my best friend."

The tears are rolling one by one down her cheek.

I shake my head. "No, *I'm* the one losing my best friend. You didn't think of me that way or you would have trusted me enough to tell me a hell of a lot sooner."

"Please stop saying that."

"Jesus," Chaingang says. "Would you lovebirds keep it down? People are trying to sleep."

"Screw you," I tell him. If he punched me out right now, it would be a blessing.

He grunts and rolls over.

I find myself wondering if I was even talking to Chaingang. Maybe I meant Marina. Hell, maybe I was talking to myself. I don't know. I can't stand to see her crying. I feel like crying myself. But this is too big a thing. It hurts way too much. And I can see it's really hurting her, but she had a chance to make it right and she didn't take it. Me, I just got blindsided and lost my best friend to a lie. I feel that hard place inside of me get colder. Maybe Elzie's right. You can't trust anyone.

"Josh ..." she begins again.

I can't do this anymore. I can't talk it out. I don't know if there can ever be an out with this.

I turn and walk away from the fire.

"Josh, don't!" she cries.

But I can't go back. Everything's too screwed up for me to go back.

✌✌

I walk until I can't see the fire anymore. The land slopes to the sea and I follow the incline down into the marshlands, skirting the wet ground until I come to a stretch of sand that leads down to the ocean. We're closer to the shore than I expected. I walk along the edge of the tide in my bare feet. Kelp and eelgrass litter the sand. After awhile I just stand there letting the waves lap against my ankles. I stare out into the forever of the ocean and my breathing settles into the rhythm of the tide.

I look up at the stars. I can't tell if they're the same as the ones in the world we left behind. I just know they're brighter than I've ever seen, even with the moonlight, and there are thousands upon thousands of them.

I think about Mom. She's got to be so worried. All she knows is that a bunch of guys Tazed me outside of school and then drove off with me in a van.

I hope Desmond and Barry got away before anything bad could happen to them.

Then I think about how all of this started up because Desmond couldn't keep his mouth shut. That pisses me off, too. But at least he didn't lie to me.

I focus on the waves as they wash against my calves. Tide's rising. I let the steady rhythm empty my head and take me away.

The water's just below my knees when I hear the soft pad of footsteps on the sand behind me. The wind's coming from her direction, so I know who it is.

Elzie comes up and wraps her arms around my waist. She lays her head against my back. I don't know where I went in my mind, but the press of her body feels good and helps bring me back. She grounds me. Right now, being in this place and with everything that's gone down, I really need to be grounded.

"I guess she finally told you," she says.

"Yeah."

"So how are you doing?"

"On a scale of one to ten? Maybe zero."

She sighs. "I should have let her do it in her own time."

"No. I needed to know. Besides, who says she'd *ever* have told me?"

Elzie just holds me a little tighter. The soft touch of her body helps ease the tension in my chest.

"Did she tell you?" I ask.

"No."

"Then how did you know?"

She shrugs. "I just did—the way Wildlings always know each other."

"*I* didn't pick up on it."

"That's because she'd already changed. You knew her as a Wildling before you changed so she didn't seem any different."

"But she did tonight."

"Maybe it's because of where we are. This place feels so different—like everything is sharper and crisper."

"When did you find out?"

"At the skate park—the first time we met."

"But you didn't tell me."

"It wasn't my secret to tell," she says. "I didn't agree with what she was doing."

"This makes me feel like such a dumb-ass. It really sucks."

She turns me around and looks into my eyes. "Would you have told me if our positions were reversed? If it was my best friend who was the Wildling?"

I don't really have to think about it. "Probably not."

We don't say anything for a while. We move back from the rising tide, but we stay on the beach, looking out over the ocean. It's strange seeing it so empty. There are no freighters slowly going by in the distance. No lights from big oilrigs way offshore, like there are in Santa Feliz. It's—I don't know— pure.

Elzie is beside me, her arm around my waist.

"How did you leave things with her?" she finally asks.

I shrug. "Not great. She was crying ..."

"And you just walked away?"

"What was I supposed to do? She *lied* to me. She was my best friend and right when I really could have used her help, she abandoned me."

She bumps my hip with hers. "That's not fair."

"Tell me about it."

"No," she says, "I mean it's not fair for you to put that on her. Just because she kept the fact that she's a Wildling a secret, doesn't mean she abandoned you or didn't care about you."

I take the hand that's on my waist in my own and turn to face her. "You can't be serious."

"When you told her, she was supportive, wasn't she? Right from the start."

"Well, yeah, but—"

"And she's the one who put everything in motion and risked her life to get you away from ValentiCorp."

"Jeez, make me feel worse, why don't you?"

She puts her other hand on my shoulder. Her gaze holds mine.

"I'm not trying to, Josh. You guys have been tight for a really long time. I just don't want you throwing away your friendship. The way things are going, we need all the friends we can get."

"But how am I supposed to trust her?"

She leans her head against my chest.

"I don't know," she murmurs. "Me and trust aren't exactly bosom buddies."

She straightens up and turns to look out at the ocean.

"Marina messed up," she says. "I'm not going to pretend she didn't and you can't either. But remember, you guys have a lot of history—good history. Is it really worth it to hang on to this feeling of betrayal and lose all of that?"

"She lied to me for five months. It's a huge deal."

"Of course it is. But only about that one thing. Sure, it happened to both of you, but she decided to keep it private when you didn't." She turns to face me again. "Where's the rule that says she's not allowed to keep some stuff to herself? What makes you right and her not?"

"Nothing, I suppose ..."

She taps her forehead lightly on my shoulder. "Just don't close the door on your friendship. And listen, it's *me* saying this, which ain't easy."

"Okay," I tell her. "I'll try not to close the door."

She takes my hand. "Come on, let's walk for awhile. Can you believe how beautiful it is here?"

I let myself be distracted and nod in agreement. It's not just the absence of the Pacific Coast Highway and parking lots and condos and all those other artifacts of civilization that inevitably follow the coastline—though that certainly helps. Without the light pollution, the sky is a deep dark velvet as far as we can see, and we can see a long way. The air is a rich stew of brine and marsh and wet sand, without a trace of smog or exhaust. But mostly, it's the space. I'm so aware of how it unrolls around us in all directions and seems to go on forever. And because of that, it feels like we can, too. That something inside us can expand and reach its full potential with nothing to stop it.

I try to explain the feeling to Elzie and she nods.

"I know just what you mean," she says. "We should stay here."

I smile. "And do what?"

She stops. "I'm serious. Why go back to a crappy world where nobody cares about anything but themselves?"

"Okay, but—"

"Look at what just happened to you. We're just freaks there—one more resource that everybody wants a piece of. Here, we could be anything."

I want to ask, what about our friends and family, but I don't. It's not the same for her as it is for me. And maybe it's getting to be less like that for me, too, considering what's happened with Desmond and Marina. I mean if your best friends can mess things up this badly ...

But then I think of Mom.

"I don't know that I could do it," I say. "There's too much for me back there. It's what I know."

"There could be a world of heartache waiting for you, too," she says.

"That's a chance I'll have to take."

"Maybe that's the difference between you and me," she says. "I'm drawn to things I don't know or haven't experienced yet."

Because you don't have any roots in our world, I think, but I don't say that, either.

"Go for a swim?" she asks.

Now that's something I don't have to over-think.

We strip off our clothes and race for the ocean. The water's cold and hits like a shock, but it's so clean and invigorating. It clears my head and for a little while I feel happy and carefree.

When we get back on shore, she turns to me with a grin. She's saying something, but it's hard to focus on it because she looks so beautiful standing there naked, with the water dripping from her. I feel myself go hard and she pokes me with a playful finger.

"Did you hear anything I said?"

"Sure, I—" Then I shake my head. "No, not a word."

She pokes me again. "Idiot. I said, let's change."

"What? Right here?"

"Josh, this is the perfect place. Our animal shapes are part of who we are. You need to learn how to have fun with the mountain lion in you."

"I don't know ..."

But she's already gone. The jaguarundi that lives under her skin bats my leg with a teasing paw, then takes off down the sand. I wait a moment, appreciating this other side of her beauty as she runs. Strong and lean. Then I let the mountain lion out and chase after her.

We spend hours wrestling and racing each other. I feel as though my heart's going to burst with the joy I feel. At one point, I have to run up to a bluff and lift my head, roaring at the sky and stars.

Elzie's right. Everything about this feels free and beautiful.

MARINA

I don't think I've ever felt this low. Not even when Mamá and Papá broke up. I kind of knew back then that they shouldn't stay together because they'd been fighting constantly, but I was still incredibly sad. This is way worse.

I'm curled into a little ball and my entire body is shaking with grief. My tears won't stop and I desperately need a tissue. This fleece isn't the most absorbent fabric they've ever made.

"Hey, little girl," Chaingang says gently from across the fire. "Don't let it get you so down. He'll come around."

"No, he won't," I manage to say, my voice hitching.

"Sure he will. He just needs some space. Want to come and sit with me?"

I can't believe he'd hit on me when I'm in this state.

"Screw off," I mutter.

"Hey, I didn't mean it that way. Sometimes you just need a shoulder to cry on, that's all. Who do you think I am?"

I feel ashamed. What is wrong with me? Oh yeah, everything.

"Sorry, I just need to try to get through this," I say. "But I don't know how."

"He'll forgive you."

"I don't deserve his forgiveness."

"Listen, pretty girl. Just try to get some sleep. You'll feel better in the morning.

ༀ

But I don't. I've been awake for about twenty minutes now and although I'm no longer crying, I feel as bad as ever. Josh and Elzie are nowhere to be seen. Maybe I'll never see them again.

Chaingang and Rico have been trying to distract me and cheer me up, but all it does is make me feel worse. I can tell they think that I'll snap right out of it if they're nice to me. They don't seem to understand that I can't just turn off or compartmentalize my sad feelings. I'm not prone to depression, but when I'm really unhappy, I'm not one of those people who can just pretend that everything's okay. I need to go through this. I just wish I wasn't going through it so publicly.

A few minutes later Josh and Elzie walk back into the camp, hand in hand. Josh can barely look in my direction. Elzie lets go of his hand and comes to sit beside me, leaning her head on my shoulder in sympathy.

I could never tell her, but the worst part of all of this is knowing that any chance there might have been of Josh and me hooking up someday is gone forever. He's with her now, but I still had a pathetic little ray of hope. That's gone now. And it's not that I wish them ill. But you know ... people drift apart. That could happen and maybe next he'd pick up on how much I care for him.

See what I mean about pathetic? But now there's no chance at all, because he hates me. I hate myself a little, too, for feeling this way.

"Come on," Elzie murmurs. "He'll get over it. It's Josh. I might not know him as well as you do, but I do know he's loyal to a fault. He's not going to throw away years of friendship over something like this. It's not like you were being deliberately malicious."

"But that's just it," I say. "He *is* fiercely loyal and he expects the same from his friends. Take Henry Still—no, I know you don't know him—but he was this guy that we hung out with back in elementary school. Then he got jumped into the Avers and he and Josh hadn't talked until yesterday in detention. Now Henry's suddenly all proud of Josh for getting into a fight with Erik Gess."

She raises her head and gets a fierce look on her face. "Who I'd still like to punch myself."

"Yeah, but the point is," I go on, "Josh never forgave Henry for turning his back on us. I'm sure he still doesn't. *That's* who Josh is. He'll do anything for a friend, but betray him and he cuts you right out of his life."

"I'm still saying he'll get over it."

"Maybe we'll talk again," I say, "but we won't be real friends. Not like we were."

She puts her brow on my shoulder. "Oh, for God's sake, why not?"

"Because he can't trust me to be straight with him anymore. And really, why should he?"

She lifts her head, looking back over my shoulder. "Here he comes now. Why don't you ask him if that's the way he feels?"

I feel the depression inside me well up in another dark wave. There's a new knot in my stomach.

"Please don't push this," I say. "Promise me you won't."

She studies me for a long moment and I can't shake the feeling that somehow she's looking right into my soul, reading everything that Josh means to me and how I've wished it could be more, but now it's never going to be. I want to turn away, but I can't move.

I flinch when she reaches out a hand to touch my cheek.

"Oh, I'm so sorry," she says. "I had no idea you felt this way toward him."

I finally manage to break away from her gaze.

"So now you're a mind reader?" I ask, staring at the ground.

She lifts my chin with her hand.

"No," she says. "It's there for anybody to see. I just wasn't looking."

I cross my arms over my chest and squeeze myself. "Don't worry," I tell her. "I would never get in between the two of you. I've never gotten in between him and anybody he's been into, and he's *really* into you."

"Maybe you should," she says.

"What do you mean?"

She gives me a sad smile. "Maybe in the days to come, he's going to need somebody who's more than just a friend."

JOSH

I'm really uncomfortable about going near where Marina and Elzie are leaning in toward one another, but Cory has just handed me something to help break the ice. I take a deep breath and walk in their direction.

I hold up the paper bag. "Anybody want coffee and muffins?"

"Seriously?" Elzie says, jumping up. "Coffee and muffins? I'm famished! Where did you score those?"

"I didn't. Cory went over to the other side and brought them back."

"I might have to marry him."

She reaches for the bag but I pull it away.

God, she's cute. "Don't I get any say in that?"

"Sure you do. You get to stand up at the point when the priest asks if anybody knows a good reason why these two people shouldn't get married, then you say you love me and carry me off into the sunset. Now gimme."

I laugh and hand her the bag. Elzie takes a coffee out for herself, then rummages further to pick out a muffin. I go a little closer to where Marina sits staring at the ground.

"So I've been thinking," I say.

She raises her head and those sad brown eyes look into mine.

"Last night," I say. "I didn't handle that as well as I could have. As I *should* have."

"It's okay. I kind of blindsided you."

"No, it's not okay. We've been friends for long enough that I should have been able to cut you a little slack over something like this."

I can see a bit of the tension leaving her shoulders. "But you were right," she says. "I totally should have told you."

I shake my head. "As Elzie pointed out to me last night, what happened to us—everybody's going to handle it differently. I went to you guys because

284

that's what I always do. You decided to deal with it on your own. That was your call and with something this personal, I have no right to tell you what you should or shouldn't have done."

She looks at me intently. "I so wanted to tell you. I just didn't know how."

"It doesn't matter," I say. "Let's just put it behind us, okay?"

"Just like that?" she says, scanning my face, as though she can't believe what I'm saying. "Everything goes back to the way it was before?"

I'm not one hundred percent sure that's possible, but I nod anyway. "Let's try."

I take another step toward her, opening my arms. She leaps up and meets me halfway. Our hug is short and awkward, but it has Elzie cheering in delight.

"Ta-da!" she says. "God, I love a happy ending."

Marina gives her a small smile. "Me, too."

But both Marina and I know that nothing's going back to exactly the way it had been before. I want it to, but I feel a touch of wariness toward her that I wish wasn't there.

Marina still looks meek, but she tries to put on a brave face with a forced smile. Maybe I'm the only one who can tell it's forced.

"I think my work here is done," Elzie says with a satisfied grin. "Should we go join the others at the car?"

She hands the bag back to me, then links her free arm through mine and tugs me back toward where the SUV's parked. Marina falls in behind us. Elzie's chatter flows over us as we continue up to the higher ground where the others are waiting.

MARINA

I'm a bit self-conscious as we join the others, who are standing by the car. I can tell they're wondering how our little emotional drama is playing out.

Cory and Rico don't really know either of us. I assume they've just dismissed what happened between Josh and me as teen theatrics. We might look like we've put our hurt behind us, but under our masks of reconciliation, we're walking wounded. They just don't pick up on it.

Chaingang does—I know right away by how he looks at us—but if he has an opinion, he keeps it to himself.

As for Elzie, I can't decide if she's just pretending that everything is okay, or if she really can't see the truth.

The important thing is, I'm not the center of attention anymore.

"I found a place where we can bring the SUV back across," says Cory, pointing south and west. "Think we can drive it about a quarter mile in that direction?"

"Shouldn't be a problem," Chaingang replies.

"You see any of our people while you were over there?" Rico asks Cory.

"No, but I didn't stick around. They've got cops all over the place."

"Any word on the bodies we left behind in the lab?" Rico asks.

"No idea."

❧

Their conversation ebbs and flows around me, but I don't contribute anything. I wonder what's going to happen next. I don't know if my cover was blown or not. Maybe I've been lucky. Except for Desmond and Barry, maybe it's just Wildlings and the older cousins who know about the otter, and I can go back to my old life.

What am I thinking? Too much has changed.

No matter what Josh says, I know I've lost my best friend. Just hanging out, the band—that's all gone. Josh is going to try to lead the Wildlings— whatever that means.

I might still have Desmond, so long as he got through last night okay, but it's not the same. Like he said before, The Gang of Two just doesn't cut it. And now he knows my secret. I just hope he can keep his mouth shut.

Barry's even more problematic. He's always been a talker with all those geek buddies online and in the store, but hopefully he'll understand how serious this is.

And what about the Ocean Avers who came with Chaingang yesterday? How much do they know?

I wonder what Mamá is doing. I've never stayed out all night before and she'll be beside herself, especially given that she'll have heard about Josh's abduction by now.

I think again about Auntie Min's plans for Josh. Being the saviour of the Wildlings seems like an awful lot to put on the shoulders of someone who's so new to what he's become that he still changes back buck naked. Does he really understand what they'll be asking of him? They may as well put a big target on his chest.

He's slouched beside Elzie, head resting against hers, thoughtful and quiet, like I am. Once I could have just asked him what he's thinking. Now I have to guess and my guess is that he's just going to go along with the plans of the older cousins.

But he surprises me. Almost as though he can read my mind, he straightens up and looks over at Cory and Rico.

"You know what I don't get?" he says. "I can't figure out the point of your lives."

Cory looks confused, but Rico bristles, clearly insulted. "What do you mean?" he demands.

Josh shrugs. "Well, until I got changed, the things that were important to me were hanging with my friends, playing music, skateboarding, trying to do okay in school, being with my mom—stuff like that. But you guys live and act like you're in an army or a gang. It's all about conflict. Don't you have other things you care about? What exactly are you fighting for?"

I have to smile. That is so the Josh I know. And maybe he isn't totally going along with this idea of him being their leader.

Chaingang also looks toward Cory and Rico with one of his slow nods. Sometimes—with his eyes hidden behind his shades and the way his face can go so still—it's hard to tell if he's even listening.

"I'd be interested in hearing what you've got to say about that, too," he says. "Because I've got to tell you, I've already got a crew. I don't exactly need to join another to make my life complete."

Rico's so tense that I half-expect him to turn into the rattlesnake. His gaze darts back and forth between Josh and Chaingang, and at first I don't know which of them is going to get the brunt of his anger. But then he juts his chin toward Josh.

"We're fighting for our survival," he almost spits. "You were down there in the lab with me and you still have to ask that?" He starts to moves forward.

"Hang on," Cory says, grabbing Rico's forearm. "I get it. I see what he's asking."

Rico yanks his arm away, but holds his ground and lets Cory continue.

"Okay," Cory says. "Up until six months ago, I was living on a buddy's ranch out in the Sonoran Desert, trying to get this old GMC pickup of his running. That's what I like to do. Work on cars and trucks. Carter's an old desert rat—I don't mean that literally. He's human, but he spends a lot of time out there in the badlands. We'd go out and find stuff and bring it back to his ranch and try to fix it up." He smiles. "The place looks like a junkyard."

He nods at Rico.

Rico crosses his arms and shrugs. "Me? I like to surf. Before this happened, I just followed the waves, from here down into Mexico."

Chaingang snorts. "A surfing snake? That, I'd like to see."

He's smiling, but there's derision in his voice.

Rico clenches his fists, glares at Chaingang and takes a step in his direction. "Anybody ever tell you that you've got a big—"

"Rico means when he's in his human form," I say, inserting myself between the two of them before they can start another round of alpha meets alpha. "And I know what he means. That whole faster/stronger thing also translates into fantastic balance. Ever since I changed, I have to work at falling off my board. I *own* those waves."

Rico nods and visibly relaxes. "Tell me about it."

"So you had different lives," Josh says, "and you're only doing this because you have to."

"Pretty much," Cory says. "The outing of Wildlings impacts us, too, you know. Soon they'll be grabbing us up along with all you Wildling kids."

"They're already doing that," Josh says.

Rico shakes his head. "No, I *let* them grab me. We wanted to see what was happening to the kids that the Feds were rounding up. We didn't realize they weren't the Feds until it was too late."

"Okay," Josh says. "But why not just live *here*, where they can't get you?"

Cory shakes his head. "We like our human skins. Here, you have to hunt for your food and make your own shelter. Resources are plentiful, but the deeper you go, the stranger it gets."

"Yeah, reality's a bit more … fluid … here," Rico adds.

"But you were happy—back then before the worlds got split up. Nobody bugged you."

"Hey, *we* weren't around that far back," Cory says. "We only know about the old days from what the elders have told us. And so much great stuff has happened in the last couple of hundred years."

He ticks items off on his fingers. "Cars, books, music, movies, surf boards—why would we want to leave? He lifts his cup off the hood of the car and smiles. "And a good cup of coffee? Humans might not be perfect, but they get a lot of things right."

"Besides," Rico adds. "Why should we have to leave? We were there first."

"There should be room for everyone," Cory adds.

"But people are selfish," Josh says.

Cory nods. "Right, but not everybody's like that. It's just the usual jerks who see a buck to be made, or want to make sure *their* little corner of the world stays pure and untouched by anyone else. But they spoil it for the rest of us."

"You got that right," Chaingang says.

"Yep, we can all relate to that," Elzie puts in.

"Okay," Josh says. "That I understand. So I'll do what I can to help. But keep in mind that I'm still going to live my own life, too."

"You can try," Rico says, shaking his head in doubt.

Cory motions toward the field in front of us. "Everybody ready?" he asks. "Let's get a move on. And take a look around—we don't want to leave anything behind."

Elzie and Josh gather up the blankets, while Rico and I collect the used coffee cups and wrappers and stuff them into the paper bags that Cory brought over from the other side. We put everything into the hatch of the SUV.

Cory is talking to Chaingang, pointing across the landscape, presumably toward the place where he'll cross back with the vehicle.

Chaingang has some windshield washer fluid and a cloth that he must have found in the console. He's wiping the entire car, the inside of the hatch, seats, door handles, anywhere we might have left a fingerprint. Then he climbs up into the driver's seat and pulls the door closed.

"Let's rumble," he says, through the glassless window.

"Most of us will go over on foot." Cory explains. "Chaingang will bring the vehicle. I'm going to double-check the co-ordinates one more time—to make sure no one's parked a car or is hanging around where we're coming through on the other side."

Chaingang nods. He leans over the steering wheel and reaches under it with his fingers. The motor coughs into life. Cory pushes down on the hood with his elbow as he passes the front of the car, but it won't close all the way.

"Don't worry about it, bro," Chaingang tells him. "It's not like I'm going to be driving at high speeds. I'll be fine so long as I can see."

Cory sets off again. The rest of us trail along a short distance behind. Chaingang drives the SUV at a crawling pace behind us. We proceed until Cory holds up a hand and leans forward. For a moment his head disappears and it's just his torso standing there.

"Show off," Rico says, laughing.

Cory steps back and his head reappears.

"All clear," he says. "Soon as we get over to the other side, we all just go our separate ways—everybody got that? Move fast, but don't run. And try not to look guilty. We could run into anybody. We can meet up later to figure out what we're going to do next. I'll find you."

"How come the air's not shimmering like it did last night?" I ask.

Cory shrugs. "It usually doesn't. It must have had something to do with the car's lights shining right on it. Come on, let's go."

We all start to walk toward the spot where Cory stands waiting. It's a good distance from where we came through last night.

Josh reaches for Elzie's hand, but she moves it out of his reach.

She looks at him with a pained expression. "I'm not going," she says.

That stops all forward momentum. For a long moment, no one says anything. We're all waiting to see what Josh's reaction will be. But he doesn't look surprised. A little sad, maybe, but he seems to have known this was coming. He lets his hand drop.

"You don't want to stay here," Rico says to Elzie, breaking the silence. "It's harder than you think."

"Oh, I do," Elzie tells him. "I'll tell you what I *don't* want to do is go back and live in the margins again."

"This place has its own challenges."

She nods. "I'm sure it does. But it doesn't involve noise and pollution, or guys in black suits running around trying to stick you in a cage, does it?"

"Maybe not," Cory says from where he waits a few feet in front of us. "But I'm warning you, it's not all peaceful like this. You have to work to stay alive. Time and space shifts underfoot here. In some places, it's what you see here, but take a couple of wrong steps and you could end up walking around in other people's dreams—literally."

"Seriously," Rico says. "It's a weird and dangerous place, and nobody knows all the ins and outs of it."

"And you're going to be trying to figure it out all on your own," Cory adds.

Elzie turns toward Josh and puts her arms on his shoulders. "Am I?" she asks with an exaggerated wink.

Oh, please don't put him in this position, I want to say. Don't make him have to choose between his mom and everything on the other side and you.

Then she laughs and lets him go, and I realize that she isn't really expecting him to come. She already knows the answer. And I understand that this is just another one of those cases of lopsided love, where one person cares way more than the other does. It isn't that Elzie doesn't care for Josh. I believe that she does love him, but true to her feline nature, she's unpredictable and curious. Purring and cozying up one minute, off doing her own thing the next.

"Don't worry," she tells him. "It's not forever. I might get bored and come back. Or you might realize that the world's too messed up for anybody to fix and you'll come looking for me."

"I still have to try to fix it," Josh says.

"I know. It's part of your charm. Be noble, like Don Quixote, tilting at windmills. Just promise me you'll be careful, too, because these particular windmills might come back and smack you on the ass."

She slaps his butt playfully, puts a hand on the back of his head and gives him a fierce kiss. Then she shifts into her jaguarundi shape and bounds away.

We watch her go until she's nothing more than a speck on the horizon.

"She didn't even say goodbye," I find myself saying, then wish I could pull the words back into my mouth.

But Josh just gives me a weak smile. "She doesn't like goodbyes," he says.

The Josh looking back at me is the one I've known forever. For one long moment he seems open to me and I can see all the hurt he's holding: the trouble Desmond brought to us, my betrayal, Elzie leaving. Then he looks away and it's gone, as though a door has slammed between us.

He walks forward to where Cory's opening the way back to our own world. He doesn't look in the direction that Elzie took, but I do.

I feel another twinge of guilt. It's not my fault that she left, but now he's all on his own.

JOSH

"Hang on, Josh" Chaingang says from the car, about fifteen feet away from me.

We've all just come through in the service area behind the Target store at the shopping center. The Target logo on the closed doors of the five loading bays back here tells me where we are, but thankfully, none of them are in use at the moment.

Cory chose well. It was a good spot to cross over. There are no windows on the rear walls of this building. It's large and there's no one around, no one to see us literally appear out of thin air. There are security cameras, but they're pointed at the loading bays, not where we are.

Our companions are already in motion, disappearing to their respective destinations, so it's just Chaingang and me left here beside the remains of a car that looks like it was in the middle of a war zone—which, it pretty much was. Not a good place to hang out if you're trying to keep a low profile.

I glance around again. Any minute somebody is going to have a look back here and see us.

Chaingang hands me the bags of trash that we brought back from the spiritlands.

"Get rid of this as soon as you can," he says. He's working quickly, wiping down the steering wheel, door handles, anything he's touched.

I want to take off like the others, but I hang back.

"Is that it?" I say.

"Afraid not, bro. That last piece of advice I gave you didn't seem to do much good, but I'm going to try again."

"I know," I tell him, looking around nervously. "Don't change where anybody can see it happen."

He shakes his head and lowers his shades so that I can see his eyes.

293

"Come on. We're out of here," he says.

We walk quickly away from the car, following the fence that separates this part of the complex from the street behind it. Dumpsters are dotted at various intervals along it—some for recycling, some for garbage. I go to toss the bags into the closest one.

He puts up his hand.

"Not there," Chaingang says. "It's too close to the car. Wait until you're in front of the store. They always have big trash cans there."

"Okay, see you later."

"Hang on," he says. "I want to talk to you about Auntie Min and the rest of them—whoever these elders are. They're going to try to change you. It'll be just some little thing here, another there, but I'm telling you, bro, if you don't watch out, the guy standing in front of me won't even exist anymore."

"And you know this how?"

He taps a finger against his temple. "Experience. You don't think I've been more than one social worker's pet project? Changes are good for everybody, they tell you. What they don't say is that if you don't pay attention, you'll wake up like a puppet with somebody's hand up your ass, telling you every little thing you can say or do."

"Yuck. Thanks for putting that picture in my head."

"You're welcome," he says without irony. "So take a good look at it whenever they ask you to do something."

I nod.

"What changed your mind?" I ask.

We're halfway to the corner of the building. I'll feel so much better when we're nowhere near that wrecked car.

"About what?"

"Wildlings pulling together. When I first talked to you at school, you said that stuff about having each other's backs."

"I never changed my mind about that, bro. What are you talking about?"

"You told Cory you didn't want to join in on anything."

He nods. "Right. I don't want to be in *their* gang. Cousins, elders, whatever they are. I don't trust their intentions. Hell, I can't even be sure that they didn't do this to us in the first place."

"I doubt it. It seems to have put a pretty big cramp in their lifestyle."

"Maybe," he says. "But we don't know their endgame, do we?"

"What's that supposed to mean?"

He shrugs. "Maybe it just happened. Maybe they're just taking advantage of the situation. But for sure we don't have the whole picture. There are too many unknowns."

"I guess. But if the stories are true about the elders, then don't we have a responsibility to help them? And if not them, what about the world in general? Maybe we can actually do something to stop this environmental nosedive we're in."

Chaingang shakes his head. "That crap always sounds good from a pulpit or on paper. It's all political bullshit. Try to do something and it all goes to hell."

"I've still got to try."

We've reached the corner of the building. ValentiCorp is in plain sight, yellow tape and barricades surrounding it.

"Want a ride somewhere?" Chaingang asks. "My bike's not far from here."

I shake my head. I haven't told anybody what I'm planning to do. I've pretty much lost the only people I might have confided in and I don't see much room for me in their lives anymore. Elzie abandoned me for that other world. Marina's better at taking secrets than sharing them. And Desmond ... well, he's Desmond. Big heart, big mouth.

But I want as much of my life back as I can get and there's only one way I can see that happening.

"No, I'm good," I tell Chaingang.

He pulls me back behind the corner of the building and I almost drop the trash bags. He studies me for a moment. "You're not planning to do something stupid, are you?"

"Why would you say that?"

"You've got a look about you." He hesitates, then goes on. "You need to know, bro. What happened with the girls was harsh, but don't hang on to it for too long. Make friends with that hurt and it's going to settle down inside you and never go away. I've seen it happen too many times before."

"I'm doing okay."

"Yeah. That's what worries me."

"Don't. Later."

I can feel his gaze on me as I walk away from him toward the entrance of the Target store.

"Later," he says.

I drop the bags into the big trash can by the shopping cart return at the front of the store. As I walk, I notice all the weird stares I'm getting from people. I might be clean from last night's swim, but the white pants and shirt I took from the lab are streaked with dirt and they don't fit well. My feet are bare and I've got a head full of stubble. I must look like a street person or some guy in a religious cult. Or maybe like somebody who's just escaped from a loony bin.

At least nobody's asking me if I want any help. If anything, they're avoiding eye contact and walking a little more quickly. They're probably scared that I'll hit them up for spare change. Or that I'll start ranting and yelling or something, the way street people sometimes do.

But here's something else new—at least for me. I can smell that fear on them. It's weird and not particularly pleasant, but at the same time, I have to stop myself from strutting a bit as I walk because the mountain lion part of me kind of enjoys making them feel that way.

I look again across a couple of parking lots to where the ValentiCorp building stands gleaming in the sun. The place gives me the creeps. It's not quite noon, but it's already hot. Not enough to burn the bare soles of my feet, but I can feel it on the asphalt. Beyond the yellow tape and the cop cars scattered around the front, I can see that they haven't even boarded up the entrance yet.

I'm looking for someone in charge as I approach the police cars. On TV, the detectives are always in suits, but too many people around here are wearing suits. The one thing I don't want is to get nabbed again by one of those guys from ValentiCorp.

I see a couple of familiar faces. I don't know what Agents Solana and Matteson are doing here—investigating, I guess—but this will make everything a lot easier.

I head toward where they're leaning against the hood of their black SUV, arms folded as they lean in toward one another, talking and checking out what's going on in front of ValentiCorp. Solana notices me first. He glances my way, then does a double-take and elbows his partner. They both start to push away from the car hood, but by that point, I'm in speaking range.

"Boy," I say with a loud sigh. "Am I glad to see you."

MARINA

Crossing back over is easier than I expected. I don't know why I thought it might be any more complicated than going to the spiritlands, but that time I was a passenger in a vehicle. This morning it's just a matter of everyone except Chaingang taking a step forward and we're out of the spiritlands and back at the ValentiCorp complex—this time behind the big Target store. A moment later, Chaingang comes through in the vehicle just a few yards to the left of us.

There's no one around, but we still get out of there as fast as we can. All of us except for Chaingang, who immediately begins to wipe his prints off the car, and Josh, who stays behind with Chaingang. That's not what Cory told us to do, but Cory's already jumped the fence behind the Target and disappeared along with Rico, who changed to a snake and went under it.

I don't know why Chaingang called Josh over, but as I look, I see him handing Josh those trash bags. I'm glad he thinks of all that stuff. I look at the wrecked SUV and my fear of being discovered near it has me moving out of there quickly.

I reach the back corner of the Target store and look out toward the parking lot. ValentiCorp rears in the distance, surrounded by police barricades and the proverbial yellow tape. There are a lot of cop cars over there, too. People in the Target parking lot seem oblivious—caught up in their own little worlds—just going about their usual shopping and walking back and forth with bags, shopping carts and noisy children.

Except for what's happening over at ValentiCorp, life looks completely normal. But normal feels strange right now, as though *this* is a dream and everything that happened yesterday was more substantial, though disturbing.

I could easily get lost in thought about that, but right now I need to come up with a story that might appease Mamá about why I didn't make it home last night.

Then I think of Julie, my old surfing buddy. She'll back me up. I take out my phone and look at it. Almost noon. Luckily I still have about an eighth left on the battery. It's enough. I start to jog toward home.

୭ৡ

When noon comes, I stop jogging and dial Julie's number. As usual, she's hanging around outside the school campus, where cell phones are allowed.

"Hey, girlfriend," I say. "I need a favour—parent business. Can you back me up on a story? I didn't make it home last night."

Normally, I would never dream of doing anything like this, but Julie's got a wild side and this is right up her alley. I feel bad for taking advantage of her, but I'm not the best schemer in the world and she's the only resource that I can come up with on such short notice.

"I never thought I'd see the day," Julie teases. "Welcome to the club."

We agree that I'll say I was with a bunch of friends out searching for Josh last night and that we knew our parents would be worried about the danger, so we didn't want to tell them what we were up to. We searched all night and then I was afraid to go home, so I crashed at Julie's for a couple of hours.

The searching for Josh and being afraid to go home parts of that story are true. I wish I had something better, but concocting lies isn't my forte. I hope I haven't given Mamá a heart attack worrying. I pray she hasn't called Papá. Ampora would have a heyday with this. If she finds out, she'll mock me forever, plus she'll rat on me if she so much as suspects my story is untrue.

Julie is dying to know exactly what I *did* do all night, but the most that I give her is 'you wouldn't believe it if I told you,' which just makes her all the more curious. But I say that my battery's dying, which it is, and that I'll tell her the juicy details in person when I see her at school. That'll be yet another complication, since I'll need to come up with a whole other story for her, but that's the problem with lies, I suppose. They complicate everything.

I start to run again, praying to all the *santos* I only half-believe in that I won't be grounded forever when I walk through the door.

JOSH

Solana and Matteson push off the hood of their car and close the distance between us.

"Are you okay, kid?" Solana says, holding my upper arm. "Do you need a medic or anything?"

"What happened to you?" Matteson asks. "Where have you been?"

I'm surprised that he seems genuinely concerned.

I remember the advice that Cory gave me what seems like a century ago now. The best way to lie is to have your story be mostly true. I point to ValentiCorp.

"I was in there," I say. "Guys that work there Tazed me when I was leaving school and when I came to, I was locked up in a laboratory five stories underground."

"*You* did that?" Matteson says, pointing at the twisted metal and broken plate glass that litters the area where Chaingang drove the vehicle through the doors.

Some of his former antagonism is creeping back into his eyes.

"As if," I say. "I don't know what happened over there. All I know is that I was able to escape in the confusion."

Matteson frowns. "But that happened hours ago."

I nod. "Yeah, it was night when I ran out of the place wearing this crap." I pluck at my shirt. "They took my clothes and dressed me in this. When I ran, I was still feeling kind of woozy—they shot me up with tranquilizers or something."

"Are you sure you don't need a medic?" Solana asks.

I nod. "I'm okay now. I didn't get far last night, but I managed to hide behind a dumpster before I collapsed. I only just came to."

Solana is giving me all of his attention, but Matteson's not as focused on me. I can almost see the cogs whirring in his head.

"The people who snatched you," Solana says. "You're saying they brought you here—to ValentiCorp?"

"Yes, sir."

"Would you stand up in court and swear to that?"

"Yes, sir. It's the truth."

He puts a hand on my shoulder. "Don't worry, son. You're safe now."

"I hope so," I say. "The other kids they took didn't ... they didn't get a chance to escape like me."

"Other kids?" Solana asks. "Did you know any of them?"

I shook my head. "It was awful ... I think they were all dead. They were in this kind of morgue. They'd been all cut up ... dissected."

The agents exchange glances.

"Goddamn," Matteson mutters and pulls out his phone. "Chief?" he says into it. "We just caught a break. We found the Saunders kid—yeah, he's safe. But get this. He's fingering ValentiCorp for the abduction and he says he's not the only one they snatched, but he's the only one who survived. That's right. He says there are kids' bodies in the building. I think that gives us enough probable cause to get a warrant, don't you? And since Black Key runs their security, we should run the faces from those abduction videos against Black Key's staff here in Santa Feliz."

He listens for a moment longer, then takes the phone away from his ear and looks at me.

"The Chief wants to know if you can hang on until he gets here."

"Sure, I guess ..."

"We'll be waiting for you," he says back into the phone.

He puts it back in his pocket and gives me a thoughtful look.

"You're not shitting us on this, are you, kid?" he asks. "It's not too late to come clean, if you are. But once we've got that warrant and go in there—if things aren't like you say, you're going to be in real deep shit."

"Jesus, Paul," Solana says.

Matteson turns to him. "The Chief's been out for blood ever since this whole thing blew up in our faces. Do you really want to take the fall if this goes sour? His job's on the line and that means our jobs are on the line."

"I get it," Solana says. "But after everything Josh has already been through ..."

"It's okay," I say. "I know how crazy this all sounds. I can't even guarantee that the bodies will still be there."

Matteson whips around to fix me with a dark look. "What?"

"Well, they've had all morning to move them, haven't they?" I say.

"We would have seen them doing that."

"Sure, except do you know they've got a network of maintenance tunnels under these parking lots—just like at Disneyland?"

"Aw, come *on*," Matteson groans.

"It's true." Remembering some of the details that Cory told me about last night, I point to Pep Boys at the far side of the parking lot. "One of them comes out at the big bay on the side of that building. There are more exits behind some of the other stores. They could have moved the bodies out through any of them."

He gives me a long, dirty look. "Yeah, right."

I don't say anything more. I just meet his glare.

"Crap," he says. "We'll need to cover those when we go in."

He gets back on his phone and asks for backup.

"Are you sure you don't need anything while we wait?" Solana asks. "Something to eat or drink?"

"Well, I wanted to call my mom last night, but I lost my phone."

"Here," he says and hands me his.

It's hard talking to Mom. I try to tell her what happened to me—sticking to the same story I gave the FBI agents—but she keeps asking me over and over again if I'm all right and then I have to backtrack to fill in the parts she missed, because she's too panicked to listen.

"Just a sec," I finally say. I hold my hand over the mouthpiece and turn to the agents. "Can my mom meet us here?"

They exchange looks, then Solana nods.

"Of course," he says.

"What if she doesn't give permission for him to come in with us?" Matteson asks.

"She'll be cool," I say. "And I'd like to ask her to bring me something else to wear."

"Crap," Matteson says. "If she sees him looking like this ..."

"Tell her where we are so that she can meet us," Solana tells me, "but don't say anything about bringing clothes. We'll get you fixed up."

I raise my eyebrows.

"Don't worry. We won't get anything that sucks."

I tell Mom where we are, then Solana takes me to Target. By the time she arrives, I'm waiting with the two agents dressed in baggy new skater shorts, a Wild Surf T-shirt, sneakers and a baseball cap to cover my lack of hair. I shouldn't have bothered trying to hide the fact that my dreads are gone. It's the first thing she notices.

She jumps out of the car and grabs me. "Honey, your hair! What happened? I've been so worried. What did they do to you? Where did they take you?"

The barrage of questions comes so fast that I have no time to answer. I don't know that I could. She's holding me so tight that it's hard to breathe. I realize she's crying.

"Calm down, Mom. I'm okay."

She gives me another hard hug, then she steps back. She pulls a tissue from her pocket and composes herself as best she can. But a tissue can't hide the dark hollows under her eyes, or how red they are from crying. She looks way older than I remember.

When I think of how it would have been for her if I'd stayed in that other world with Elzie, I feel a little sick.

Finally she turns to the agents. "Are you the men who rescued him?" she asks them.

"Your son rescued himself," Matteson says. "That's quite the boy you've raised, ma'am."

Wow, I think. Who knew he could brown-nose so well?

"Please," she says. "Call me Naomi."

He smiles. "Naomi it is, then." He takes her hand in both of his and holds it for a long moment before dropping it.

I give him a closer look and realize that he's not brown-nosing. He's flirting with my mom. How gross is that? Who flirts with a woman who's just gone through what she has? But then I realize I'm wrong about that, too. He's just being kind. Compassion is such an alien thing when it comes to how I see him that it didn't register.

"Maybe you should sit down for a moment," he says to Mom.

He lifts the hatch of the SUV for her and ushers her over. She pats the space beside her and I sit down. Her arm goes around my shoulders and she holds me tight. I can feel her still trembling.

MARINA

I'm making good time in spite of feeling exhausted. Physically, I'm not so bad, but emotionally, I've pretty much been steamrolled. Thinking back on yesterday almost makes my head spin. So much went down that it's hard to believe it could all take place in the space of a day. I'm going to be in huge trouble at home, but I'm actually looking forward to getting there. Sleep is what I want more than anything. And after that, the freedom of getting on top of some waves. That is, assuming I'll be allowed to get out on the waves. I've never pushed the envelope this far.

I jump when my phone rings. I'm surprised there's enough juice left. I pull it out to check the display and see that it's Desmond. Thank God, he's safe. As least, I assume so. Julie would have mentioned any trouble regarding Desmond. She's had the hots for him since grade ten and watches him like a hawk. He never even notices, big lovable lug that he is. I've thought of setting them up, but it would be too weird when they broke up, and for sure they'd break up.

I'm about to answer when I hear the roar of a motorcycle coming up the street behind me. I send out another silent prayer. *Please, please, don't let that be a cop.*

The motorcycle comes right alongside me and slows down. My heart is in my throat. I have to look.

"Nice locomotion you've got there, sweetcheeks."

I come to a dead halt. I am so relieved that I could hug him. "Jeez, you scared me half to death. I was sure you were a cop."

"Well, if I *were* a cop," Chaingang says, lowering his shades, "I'd want to arrest you and lock you up tight where I could keep an eye on you."

I can't help but laugh. It feels unbelievably good to laugh, to be back in Santa Feliz, to be standing here on the street with Chaingang, even to be

303

going home to face the music. And it feels good to have someone so obviously into me. It's not that I've never had guys hit on me, but this feels different. Deeper somehow. Perhaps it's only that shared camaraderie that we're both Wildlings and we've just gone through something huge. Maybe it's more than that.

"Hop on," he says, patting the seat behind him. "I'll drive you partway home—give you something solid to hang on to again."

I swing my leg over the seat and hold on tight.

JOSH

We've just finished telling Mom about my having been kidnapped by ValentiCorp when another black SUV pulls up. I glance across the parking lot and see a half-dozen others enter in a line, one after the other. The lead vehicle pulls away and drives toward Pep Boys. The rest continue along their way until they're out of my range of vision.

A big guy with a shaved head steps out of the SUV that stopped near us. By the way Matteson and Solana straighten up, I figure this is their boss. Mom and I stand up as he approaches us. He puts out his hand.

"Mrs. Saunders?" he says to Mom. "My name's Jason Lindel. I can't tell you how sorry we are for the worry you've had to go through."

"Thank you," Mom says as she shakes his hand.

He looks at me with what appears to be genuine concern. "How are you holding up, son?"

"I'm okay."

His body language and voice are easygoing, but his eyes have steel in them and they don't seem to miss a thing. He studies me for a moment, then turns back to Mom.

"Have the agents explained why we need your son's help?" he asks.

"Yes, but ... I've just got him back ..."

Lindel nods. "His safety is our number one concern, Mrs. Saunders. We won't bring him inside until we're sure the building's cleared of danger. But if he can just lead us to where he was held captive and—" He shoots an unspoken question to the agents and Solana nods. "—to where he found the bodies, it will make our job that much easier."

She looks reluctant and even horrified, but if there's one thing I know about my mom, it's that she'll do the right thing.

"As long as you're certain it's safe ... and Josh doesn't mind ..."

305

"Absolutely," Lindel says. "I guarantee your boy will be fine. He'll be of immense help to our investigation. We have to think of those other kids and their parents."

That cinches it.

"All right, then," she says.

"You've raised a brave young man," Lindel tells her. "Okay, let's get the vests on and do this thing."

Matteson hands me a tactical Kevlar vest with "FBI" emblazoned on it in big white letters.

"I thought you said there wasn't any danger," Mom says as I'm putting on the vest. It weighs more than I expected, but that's not a problem for me.

"It's just a precaution, Mrs. Saunders," Solana says. "We intend to take every measure available to us to keep your boy safe."

When the other agents and Lindel have their vests on, Lindel gives us all a once-over.

"Let's saddle up," he says. "You folks ride with Special Agents Matteson and Solana."

He gets back into the SUV he arrived in. Besides his driver, there are two other agents in the back seat. When we pull up in front of ValentiCorp, three of the other FBI vehicles are already parked there.

"Hang on," Matteson says as I go to open the car door. "The Chief needs to sort out jurisdictions."

I'm not sure what he means, so I open my window and let my Wildling hearing do its thing as three cops approach Lindel. He pulls a folded piece of paper from his pocket.

"Where's Neufield?" Lindel asks the nearest one.

"Chief!" the cop yells toward the building. A tall man with greying hair and broad shoulders turns around from where he's standing several yards from the building.

"Hello, Jason," he says, walking over to Lindel with his hand extended. "I hope you're here to take this headache away from me."

I recognize him from TV and the paper. He's Ted Neufield, the Santa Feliz Police Chief.

"Come take a look," he says as they shake hands. As they walk back toward ValentiCorp, Neufield introduces various officials along the way. There are officers from the County Sheriff's office, the Highway Patrol and a man in dark blue suit from Homeland Security. The FBI agents from the other three cars have followed behind and are waiting Lindel's orders.

"What do we have so far?" Lindel asks. '

"As you can see, a lot of damage to the front entrance and foyer of the building. Witnesses say it was a red SUV, but there's no sign of the driver, or even the vehicle that did it. Staff from some of the other stores say a bunch of motorcycles pulled into the complex shortly before this all went down, so it could be part of a gang war. Apparently there was a lot of gunfire. That's about all we know. We haven't actually gotten access to the inside yet. The security here is Black Key, so you know what that means."

"They've been stonewalling you."

"They claim there's structural damage inside and don't want to let us in until it's been checked over by their team. ValentiCorp is afraid of lawsuits if the place comes down. Einhorn—" He nods at the man from Homeland Security. "—says the company has a number of sensitive government contracts, meaning it could be an act of terrorism. That's why he's here."

"Where's the head of Black Key?" Lindel asks.

The Police Chief points to where three men are standing nearer to the damaged entrance. I recognize the man on the right as one of the men who grabbed me at the school. I wish I could release the mountain lion on him.

"He's the one in the middle," Neufield says. "Name's Clint Gaillard. Ex-marine, apparently."

"Thanks," Lindel says. "We'll take it from here."

"If this was a terrorist attack …" the man from Homeland Security begins.

"We don't know what it was," Lindel tells him. "But we do know that it was the site of a juvenile kidnapping and that puts it in our jurisdiction."

With that, he sets off toward the head of Black Key Securities, his agents following in a fan shape behind him.

"What's happening?" Mom asks.

"We're just gaining access to the site," Matteson says. "It shouldn't take long."

I'm not too sure about that. Even from where I am, my Wildling sight shows Gaillard bristling at the approach of the Chief and his agents. He's as tall as Lindel, but in much better shape.

Lindel looks into the trashed foyer of ValentiCorp, then waves the search warrant in the man's face.

"I'm going to need you and your men to stand down," he says. "We need access to the building."

"I'm sorry, sir," Gaillard says, "but I can't allow that without the okay from my bosses. We have concerns about structural damage."

"Bullshit about the structural damage. Any fool can see that no bearing walls have been affected. And speaking of fools, don't you see what *this* is?" Lindel adds, holding the warrant mere inches from the other man's face.

"I still can't let you—"

"Brackens and Johnson," Lindel says and two of his men step forward. "Cuff Mr. Gaillard. Read him his rights and then charge him with obstruction of justice."

"You can't—" Gaillard begins.

But the two agents are already on either side of him. They each grip an arm and propel him to the side of the closest vehicle. They push him down over the hood, pull his hands behind his back and snap on the handcuffs. One of them starts reciting his rights.

Lindel's attention is now on the two other Black Key guards who were standing with Gaillard. He holds the warrant up.

"Either of you care to join him?" he says, jerking his thumb over his shoulder toward Gaillard.

One man shoots a glance to where his boss stands in cuffs.

"I can't just—"

"Arrest him as well," Lindel tells his men as he turns to the remaining guard. "And how about you?"

The guard sighs. "You might as well arrest me, too. I don't have the authority to make that kind of decision."

Lindel motions to his men and they take the pair away to where Gaillard is standing under guard. Lindel looks toward the front entrance, where yet more of the Black Key guards are standing.

"I can do this all day," he calls over to them. "Right now, you're only facing obstruction charges, but if we find what I expect to find inside, you'll also be up on charges of accessory after the fact."

"What are you talking about?" one of the guards calls back. "*We* were the ones who were attacked."

"Arrest them all," Lindel says.

His men move forward.

"Man," Matteson says softly to his partner. "I wish I could hear everything that's going on. Do you see how many of those guys he's got in cuffs? I'm gaining a whole new respect for the Chief."

Solana nods. "He's pretty hardcore, all right." He turns from the front seat to look at me. "Do you recognize any of those guards?"

"Well, they're pretty far away," I lie, "but one of those three looks like one of the men who grabbed me from school." I point to the first three men who were arrested. "The one standing on the right."

"Let me tell the Chief," Solana says.

He gets out of the car and trots over to where Lindel is watching the remaining Black Key guards arguing with the agents arresting them.

"Saunders says he thinks he can finger at least one of them for the abduction," he tells Lindel.

Lindel nods. "Ask the Police Chief to bring us a prisoner van. We'll run the bunch of them against that video footage."

Solana heads off to where the local law enforcement officers are standing, watching the show. Lindel waits until the last of the guards is handcuffed, then he motions for us to join him.

"You should wait in the car," I tell Mom as she reaches for her door handle.

Matteson turns from the front seat. "He's right, Mrs. Saunders. It will be much more comfortable for you waiting here."

"But—"

"I'll be okay, Mom. Special Agent Matteson will be with me."

He gives me a surprised look and I wonder, how did we ever end up on the same side? Then I give Mom a quick kiss and step outside.

We cross the pavement to where Lindel is waiting for us.

"You're sure you're all right with this, son?" Lindel asks me.

I give him a quick nod.

We wait until the local police have the Black Key guards in custody and the rest of the FBI agents have joined us.

"Which way?" Lindel asks me.

I start to lead off, but he puts a hand on my shoulder.

"I doubt there's any danger," he says, "but I'd prefer to have my men take point. You just tell us in what direction we're going."

It's a very different trip back to the labs than it was escaping them with Rico. No one is trying to kill or recapture me this time, but I do worry the whole way down. What if the bodies are gone? What if somebody comes along and shows the FBI the surveillance footage of me changing into a mountain lion and then killing the woman researcher? What if they can tell just by looking at her body that I was the one who killed her?

I know it's ridiculous, but the deeper we go, the more vulnerable I feel. The press of the building seems to weigh down my shoulders. All the horrible

memories from this place crowd around in my head like the unwelcome
guests that they are.

Waking from the drugs. Rico's missing leg. Snapping the woman's neck.
Rico cutting her companion's throat. Jenny's desecrated body. All those cut
up kids in the metal drawers ...

I almost hope they're not there, because I don't know that I can bear to
see them again.

Two agents lead the way down the stairs with Matteson and Lindel
behind them. Solana and I are next, with another four agents bringing up the
rear. No one has a weapon drawn.

When a cell phone rings, we all start. The Chief fishes his phone out of
his pocket.

"Lindel," he says.

The mountain lion lets me tune in to hear what the caller's saying.

"We found the vehicle, Chief. A 2010 Chevy Suburban. Thing looks
like it just came back from the front lines—shot to shit, the windows all
gone."

"Where was it?"

"In back of the Target. The weird thing is, the locals already checked this
entire complex. I don't how they missed it."

"Any sign of the driver?"

"Nothing."

"How about the owner?"

"Reported it stolen last night around nine-fifteen."

"Okay," Lindel says. "Keep working it."

He stows his phone away just as we're coming down the fifth flight of
stairs.

"Through that door," I say.

My nose catches the smells of cleaners and disinfectants as soon as the
door opens. Our smell is still there, lying just under it—Rico and me, the
dead Wildlings—but it's faint. I breathe a sigh of relief. I won't have to see
the bodies again. But the relief is short-lived, replaced by worry. The FBI is
not going to be happy with me.

I point to the door at the end of the hall. "That's where I woke up—in
the lab behind that door."

"And the bodies of the kids?" Lindel asks.

I hesitate. I'm torn between wanting to tell them that everything's been
cleaned up and squeezing out a last few seconds of reprieve before they come

down hard on me.

Lindel misinterprets my silence.

"How are you holding up?" he asks, his voice gentle.

I decide to go with at least a portion of the truth.

"I'm okay," I tell him. "It's just harder being here than I thought it would be."

"You don't have to look at them again," he says. "Just tell us where they are."

I point to the morgue's door. "In there."

The two agents on point go in first, followed by Lindel and Solana. The rest of us wait in the hall. I can tell Jenny's body is not there. It's not just the lack of reaction from the agents. With the door open, I would have smelled it.

I realize I'm holding my breath and make myself exhale. I hear the first drawer open on its sliding wheels. No reaction. A second. Then the smell comes rushing out to me and I hear one of the agents gag.

"Jesus Christ!" Lindel says, his voice soft.

More of the drawers are opened and the smell of the dead gets stronger.

I hear one of the agents punch some numbers into his cell, then realize it's Solana when he says, "We need somebody from the coroner's office down here."

"What've you got?" the voice on the other end asks.

"Eight—no, nine bodies," Solana tells him. "It's bad. Most of them are teenagers."

I lean against a wall and slide down until I'm sitting on my haunches.

Matteson had gone to look in the room, but he's back with me now. "You okay, kid?" he asks.

I stare straight ahead and give a slow nod. "But they're not. They didn't get away like I did."

Matteson crouches down so that his head's level with mine.

"Don't let it get to you," he says. "Yeah, you survived and they didn't, but they were already gone before you were even brought here. This had nothing to do with you."

Lindel comes out of the morgue, phone in hand.

"There are cameras mounted everywhere," he says to whoever's on the other end. "I want to see their footage. I want the faces behind what happened to these kids."

"I'm already on it," the agent he's talking to says. "The power failure they had took down their computer system and screwed any chances for us to see last night's recordings, but I've got a tech bringing up the backups so we should be able to access everything else. What dates and times do you want?"

"No idea. Start with newest ones from these fifth floor labs and work back from there."

"Will do."

"You sure they don't have backups from yesterday?"

"Guy says they send those out to an off-site storage facility every morning, but when the computers crashed, they lost anything from after yesterday's backup."

"Well, get what you can," Lindel says.

He notices me on the floor, Matteson crouched in front of me. All I'm trying to do is hide my relief.

"You don't have to stay here much longer, son," Lindel says. "But if you can, I'd just like you to look into this lab that you told me about and verify that that's where they held you."

"Sure, that's not a problem," I say, hoping like hell that there won't be any evidence of what we did in that room.

But it turns out to be all right. Other than the broken, cockeyed plastic cells within the room, there's no trace of violence to humans. Someone even cleaned up where the male researcher bled out.

"Where did they keep you?" Matteson asks.

I point to one of the undamaged cells. "I was in that one for awhile," I lie, "but I was out in the main part of the room with a couple of … doctors … when the alarms went off and everything went haywire. I escaped at the same time as the doctors exited the room, but in all the commotion, they weren't aware of it."

That seems to satisfy both of them. I'm so grateful that they don't seem to think I had anything to do with the damaged cells. Maybe it hasn't occurred to them. Maybe they're just so shocked by what went on in the morgue that my confirmation about this room is just a formality.

"I want you to know that you did good work," Lindel says, patting me on the shoulder.

"I'll take him back up," Matteson says.

Lindel nods, then he returns to the morgue.

"You need a hand?" Matteson asks.

I start to shake my head, but his hand is already on my shoulder, steering me toward the exit.

"We'll let your mother take you home," he says. "Everything else can wait for a couple of days. I have the feeling we're going to be really busy here for awhile."

"I'd like that," I say. "Going home, I mean."

"I hear you. At a time like this, I wish I could do the same."

It's so weird, comparing the Matteson here with the one I first met. I have no idea what to make of him anymore. Which is he? Probably both.

"The worst thing about all of this," he says as we start back up the stairs, "is they're probably going to get off."

I give him a shocked look.

"Oh, yeah. ValentiCorp has been on the FBI's radar for years now about several questionable ventures, but all those government contracts get them connections that always stop us dead in our tracks. Until today, it's just been hearsay and suspicions—nothing we could really pin on them."

"But those kids ..."

"Don't get me wrong. Some stiff's going to take the fall for it. But in the long term? It's likely to be business as usual."

"You mean they'll go back to grabbing kids and—experimenting on them?"

He shrugs. "Honestly, I hope to hell not. But I do know that when you get to a certain level on the food chain, you get to live by a different set of rules. Something like what's happened here—with the added stupidity of trying to pin your kidnapping on the FBI—lets us step in. Right now, we have carte blanche to investigate, but you watch. Roadblocks are going to go up and next thing you know, we won't be able to do zip."

"Why are you telling me this?" I ask.

He stops on a landing to look at me.

"The Chief was right," he says. "You did a good thing here. But I don't want you to think it's over and drop your guard. We don't know what they wanted with you—with any of those kids. But sooner or later, they just might come looking for you and your friends again."

"We're not Wildlings."

"Yeah, and I'm not a cop. And I'm not a big fan of you kids running around putting yourselves and the general populace in danger. But I'm even less of a fan of what happened down in that lab. That's just wrong. I wouldn't treat my neighbour's dog that way and I hate that yapping little mutt."

"So can I ask you something?" I say.

"Shoot."

"How is ValentiCorp any different from the FBI pulling kids off the street and doing whatever it is you do with them on the old naval base?"

"How do you know about that?"

"Come on. You've got those PSAs running on all the local stations. I live here. Everybody knows that's where you're taking them."

He gives a slow nod. "Okay, here's the difference, so far as I've been told, and I've no reason to think it's not this way. When a Wildling proves dangerous or if they want some guidance … Don't look at me like that— we've had a few come to us, like your friend Danny."

"He's not my friend."

"Yeah, well I can't blame you for feeling that. The kid's a jerk. But the point is, all that's happening on the base is they're being kept in a safe environment and learning to control themselves. It's not Guantánamo Bay. It's more like a boarding school."

"If it's so nice, why do people want to escape?"

His gaze narrows, but he doesn't call me on how I know that.

"Like I said," he tells me, "some of these kids are dangerous and they were brought in to stop them from hurting the people around them. Or themselves. We have to keep them away from the general public."

I think of Dillon killing himself because he was so scared of being taken away.

I return his narrow gaze. "So how's that working out for you?" I ask. "Are you saving many from hurting themselves?"

Anger flickers in Matteson's eyes, but he keeps his temper in check.

"I'm not getting into a pissing match with you, kid," he says. "Not today. Not with what we found down there. But the free pass doesn't last forever. Keep your nose clean and you've got nothing to worry about."

"From you."

"From the Bureau. None of this is personal." He starts up the stairs again. "Let's get you back to your mother."

When we get back to the foyer, he stops me again.

"Wait here," he says. "I'm going to go out and give a 'press conference.'" He makes air quotes. "When you see the reporters gathering around me, go collect your mother and get out of here. If you're lucky, it'll give you enough of a breathing space to get home. I'd send an escort with you, but if I do that, I might as well hang a sign around your neck saying 'here I am.' Are you okay with that?"

"I don't really have much choice, do I?"

He shakes his head. "'Fraid not. Freedom of the frigging press and all."

"Is there any way to stop them from harassing me?"

"You could appeal to their sense of humanity." He gives me a humourless smile. "Just wait it out. In a couple of days, you'll be old news and they'll all be in a frenzy about something else."

That's starting to sound like a tired old refrain.

I wait while he goes outside and moves away from the front of the building to the barricades that the reporters and their cameramen are now pressing against. I suppose once word gets out that the FBI Chief is on a case, it generates all this fresh media attention.

When Matteson approaches them, I slip out, get Mom, and we walk to our car. She keeps her arm around my shoulders as we go. I don't know if it's to make sure I'm really here with her or to keep anybody from trying to take me away. Whichever it is, I find it comforting.

MARINA

Chaingang drops me off a couple of blocks from home. Bad enough that I'm arriving the day after having been out all night. I don't want to announce my arrival home via motorcycle to Mamá or the whole neighbourhood, for that matter.

I cover the last two blocks on foot, go around back and slip in by the back door. I tiptoe down the hall toward the kitchen and there's Mamá on her knees on the floor, all of her *santos* statues spread out around her, and every votive candle in the house lit in front of her. My framed high school picture is in the middle of it all. Her head is bowed and her eyes are closed. Her lips move in fervent prayer. She seems oblivious to the fact that it's stifling hot in here because of those candles.

"Mamá, I'm home," I say softly. "I'm okay."

She raises her head and opens her eyes. Her red eyes well up with new tears. It's clear she's been doing a lot of crying. I feel like a piece of crap for making her go through this.

"*Gracias, Dios*," she sobs and reaches for me.

I get down on the floor beside her and hug her for all I'm worth.

"You heard about Josh getting kidnapped from school?" I say into her ear.

I'm looking at all those saints and thinking I'm about to get struck down for telling my mother lies, but I go ahead anyway. It's not as though I can tell her the truth.

JOSH

Home feels good, normal. Normal is exactly what I need. Mom has put a macaroni and cheese casserole into the oven and we're both sitting at the kitchen table.

"They cut off all your dreads," she says, reaching over and rubbing her hand across my stubble. The gesture reminds me of Elzie and I feel a little pang of loss.

Tears well in her eyes. I know they're not about my hair. They're about me. About what almost happened to me.

"Tell me the truth now," she says. "Are you okay? Do you need to see a doctor?"

"I'm fine," I tell her. "Just really tired."

She nods. "I can't understand. Why did they take you? Why *you*?"

I suppose I could try to spin something out, but I stick with the truth.

"They think I'm a Wildling," I say.

She holds my gaze, searching for something. Then she asks the question I don't want to hear: "Are you?"

I hesitate, remembering Elzie's story about her family, but this is my mom. This is different. *We're* different. And while it's one thing to just not tell her because she's never asked me directly, it's a whole other thing to lie. I already did it once with that whole business with Steve. I'm not going to make a habit of it. Everything else might be messed up in my life, but I'm not going to add lying to my mom.

"Yeah," I say. "I guess I sort of am."

"And you didn't tell me?"

Her voice is quiet. I wish she were yelling at me the way she and Dad went at it toward the end. I wish she'd just get mad. But all she does is give me a disappointed look that hangs there in the air between us forever.

"I'm sorry," I say.

I mean it, but the words don't seem enough.

"Why didn't you tell me?" she asks. "How could you not trust me enough?"

"It wasn't that," I say. "I thought your knowing would put you in danger."

I hear Marina's voice in my head. This is the same conversation she and I had, except this time I'm the one who didn't tell the truth.

It's not my proudest moment.

I don't say anything more and Mom doesn't press me on it. I take a shower, change into some clothes of my own. We have a really uncomfortable dinner, during which we mostly just push the food around on our plates. I'm hungry, but every bite I take is hard to swallow and it has nothing to do with Mom's cooking.

She finally breaks the silence. "So who knows about this?" she asks.

I shrug. "Marina and Desmond. Elzie."

I feel another little wave of regret when I say Elzie's name. What happened with her is one more thing I've screwed up. I'm not sure how I screwed it up. I just know I did.

"Of course you'd tell *them*," Mom says. "Oh, don't look at me like that," she adds. "Do you think I was never a teenager? At your age, we always kept the big stuff from our parents."

Does she actually understand? Mom never ceases to impress me.

"So you're not mad?"

Her eyes flash. "Are you kidding? I'm furious. But before I have the luxury of letting you know exactly how furious I am, I need to understand this situation so that we can contain it."

"Oh."

My heart sinks. So I have that to look forward to.

"Only those three friends know?" Mom asks.

"Plus other Wildlings."

"What other Wildlings? Who are they?"

"I can't say."

"Can't, or won't?" she asks.

"Won't, I guess. It's not for me to out them."

"But you can just go ahead and tell them what you are, without a problem."

"It's not like that," I say. "Wildlings just *know*. We recognize each other whether we want to or not."

Our plates are pushed aside. She has her elbows on the table, her chin cupped in her hands.

"What kind are you?" she asks.

"A mountain lion."

"So it *was* you who attacked Steve."

I nod. "But not like you think. That was the first time I changed and I didn't even know I was doing it. Like I said, he hit me on the back of the head and the next thing I knew, I was a mountain lion, standing over him and ready to chew off his head. I took off because I didn't want to hurt him more than I already had."

"You have some control over the animal you turn into?"

"Yes. I'm still me—I just have a different shape."

She sits up and wipes at her face, as though doing that might make this all go away. She looks at me again.

"I don't know what to do," she says. "You'll have to go away for starters. You could stay with your grandparents until we figure out a better arrange ..."

Her voice trails off as I shake my head.

"I'm not going anywhere," I say.

"Now, you listen to me, young man."

I don't let her finish. I've never had to stand up to her in quite this way, but I have no choice.

"Look, I know I screwed up big-time by not levelling with you in the first place," I tell her. "But this is my problem, so I get some say in what happens next. Hiding me away isn't going to do any good—I'm sure of that."

I wait for her to lay into me, but all she does is ask, "So what do *you* think you should do?"

"Finish my school year. I'm going to try to reclaim the life that was stolen from me."

"How does that work with everybody knowing you're a Wildling?"

"But they don't. Hardly anyone does. No one's seen me change. Nobody can prove I'm anything but the kid I say I am."

"But that's just avoiding the issue as well. We have to figure out how to fix this."

I shake my head. "It's not a disease, Mom. There is no fix. This is what I am now. And I don't want to change it."

She slumps in her chair and we sit there for a while.

"Can you show me?" she asks finally.

"What? You mean change?"

She nods.

"I don't think that's such a good idea."

"Why?" she asks. "Is it too dangerous? If you can't control the animal, then how can you expect me to let you go back to school, where you might hurt someone?"

"No, I can control it. It's not what you think. It's just ..."

Embarrassing, I think. It's like she's asking me to drop my pants, which, although she doesn't know it, is kind of what she has done since I haven't had a chance to practice the change back. As soon as I come back to my human shape, I'll end up naked again.

But I find myself remembering that trick that Cory did the first time I saw him—how for a moment he showed me a coyote head on his shoulders, then he was human again.

I close my eyes and think about how I do the change, but instead of letting it take all of me, I focus just on my hand. I have no idea what I'm doing, but the next moment Mom gasps and I feel the difference.

My right arm now ends in a mountain lion's paw. Opening my eyes, I see Mom staring, her eyes wide. I can smell her anxiety, but not fear. That's good. At least she isn't scared of me. I lift my paw and flex the toes so that the claws pop out. I wiggle them for a moment, then I bring my human hand back.

"That—that's really something," she says.

Then she falls silent, just staring at my where my hand lies on the table.

"Mom," I say. "Could you just yell at me or something? I can't stand knowing you're so mad at me but you're just sitting there so quietly."

She reaches over the table and takes the hand that changed in her own. She covers it with her other hand.

"I'm not really angry, Josh. I think I had to see what you just did to really understand. I won't say I'm not disappointed that you didn't feel you could confide in me, but this—this situation—is so extraordinary that I can't say what's right or wrong in how you've been dealing with it."

"So—are we okay?"

She nods and gives my hand a squeeze, then she lets go and stands up.

"I need to think about all of this some more," she says.

"Please. You can't tell anyone."

"I know. But—I have a lot to process right now. I think we both need some rest."

She goes to her bedroom and quietly closes the door.

I sit there at the table for a little while longer. I think about Mom's reaction and how much more mature it was compared to how I dealt with Marina.

I am such a jerk.

❧

Mom falls asleep. I sit in the living room for a while and use my Wildling hearing, listening to her breathe. It soothes me somehow. Maybe I can still find some normal in my world.

I go to bed as well, but all I do is stare at the ceiling. I haven't even had time to really think about losing Elzie. Now that I do have the time, I don't want to, but she's right there in my head. Trying to put her out of my mind doesn't do any good. It's either her, or Marina, or that woman I killed at ValentiCorp.

Then I realize it's been less than forty-eight hours since Dillon killed himself and that makes me feel worse. I've pretended to Mom and everybody that I'm okay, but the truth is, everything feels like its spinning out of control and I can't stop the jumbled mess it leaves in my head.

I get up and start to pace my bedroom. That feels so claustrophobic that I take it to the rest of the house, walking from one end to the other. When that doesn't help either, I go out into the backyard.

The light pollution makes the stars seem dim compared to how they were in the spiritlands, but at least there's a breeze. I can smell the ocean and hear the waves breaking on the sand. I stand there for a long time, nostrils working, listening. It makes me think of Elzie again, but not in the same way as I did before. Now I remember running with her in my animal shape, how good it felt. How free.

I wonder how's she's doing over there in the spiritlands. Maybe she's the one who did the right thing. She gets all of this good stuff—the ocean, the beach, the stars and sky—without any people or the crap we build around us to get along.

I miss her, but I'm feeling calmer now and sit down on a lawn chair.

I don't get to be on my own for long.

I smell him long before I hear him.

"I was wondering when one of you guys was going to show up," I say as he slips into the backyard.

Cory drops onto another lawn chair. His eyes seem to glow when he

322

looks at me—like when animals get caught in a car's headlights. I wonder if it's the same for me. But then he blinks and the glow is gone.

"So what …" he says. "Are you out of your mind? Do you have any idea what you've done?"

"Yeah. I stuck it to ValentiCorp and took my life back."

"And if they show the video with you changing into a mountain lion and killing that woman?"

"They don't have it. They lost all of their surveillance video when the power went down."

"Did you ever think that they could be just saying that? That they're holding on to it and plan to pull it out at just the right time?"

"Then I'll take the rap."

"What about the rest of us?"

"You didn't do it."

"I mean what it *says* about us. That we are dangerous."

"They already think that. And we *are* dangerous."

Cory shakes his head. "The elders are going to be pissed off."

I think about Chaingang and puppets.

"I don't care," I tell him. "It's my life, not theirs."

"What you did—you know it's not going to make a lot of difference, right? It'll take years to go through the courts and even then, they'll probably get off. A couple of flunkeys do the time, but the big shots? They'll just find some other place, under another name and keep right on with their sick crap."

"That's what the FBI guy said. But it makes a difference to me."

Cory cocks his head and studies me for a long moment.

"Maybe Auntie Min's right about you," he says. "Maybe you are what we need. You're just going to do it your own way." He grins. "I like that. You sure you don't have some coyote in you?"

I have to laugh. "How would I know?"

We don't talk for a while. Turns out when he's not in my face about what I should and shouldn't be doing, he's pretty easy company.

"You know," he says, "you never asked me about those guys I helped get out of the old naval base."

"What's to know? You said they got away with that floor plan or whatever from you—but—now I'm thinking maybe you helped them get over to the spiritlands and back."

He shakes his head. "No, I did what I told Chaingang I did. The spiritlands *really* aren't something we want the five-fingered beings to know about. Not unless you'd like that pretty beach you saw covered in oil wells."

I pull a face.

"Yeah, I thought as much." He waits a beat, then adds, "Aren't you curious about what was being done to the detainees the Feds had locked up?"

My stomach lurches because I'm seeing Jenny in my mind's eye—or at least, what was left of her. I know Matteson claimed the FBI was just holding most Wildlings for their own protection, and a few others from hurting anybody else, but I don't really believe him.

"What—" I have to clear my throat. "What were they doing to them?"

"Nothing."

So Matteson told me the truth.

"Nothing?" I repeat.

"They were doing just what they said they've been doing. Taking them off the streets. The kids in there had full cable, nice rooms, decent food, a gym, but no Internet. It was more like a spa than a jail. The only thing they didn't have was their freedom. And that's why they took off when I gave them the chance."

"Maybe they were still setting up the labs."

Cory gives a thoughtful nod. "Maybe, but I didn't see any. So, what's next for you?"

"I'll tell you what I'm not going to do. I'm not going to be the poster boy for animal people's liberation or whatever the hell it is that the elders want. I'm going to keep a low profile. Finish my school year."

"But what if they need you?"

"I'll figure that out if it happens. But I know what being outed means and I'm not going to live in the margins of society. You saw what that did to Elzie."

"Maybe Elzie has other problems."

"I'm going to pretend I didn't hear that."

He nods. "Yeah, that was out of line."

We sit in silence again until finally he stands up.

"Okay," he says.

"Okay what?"

"I see where you're coming from and, for the record, I think you're doing the right thing."

"What about the elders?"

He shrugs. "I've been playing errand boy as a favour to Auntie Min, but this is where it ends. I've done my bit. Now I'm on your team. You need

324

anything, let me know."

"Just like that?"

He grins. "Just like that."

"How can I get hold of you?"

"Give me your phone number."

"I lost my phone."

"Okay. Let's do it the old-fashioned way."

He pulls a stub of a pencil out of his pocket and scrawls something on the back of a receipt.

"Now you've got my number."

He puts it in my hand and then he's gone. Takes a step and he vanishes. Shifted over to the other world. Man, that is such a cool trick.

I have to learn how to do it—right after I figure out how to shift back from my mountain lion shape still wearing clothes.

ACKNOWLEDGMENTS

Special thanks and acknowledgment to those who helped along the way: Lynne Missen, my editor at Penguin Canada, whose keen eye and insightful suggestions made this a much better novel; Andrea Spooner from Little, Brown, whose comments on the first draft also helped me very much; my best pal and Webmaster, Rodger Turner, for unflagging encouragement and support; my agents Russ Galen, Heather Baror and Danny Baror for wise suggestions; my young friend and first reader Charlotte Bonyun, whose unbridled enthusiasm gave me a welcome lift as I finished the book; my sister-in-law Lynn Harris, who helped with final proofreading; and last, but not least, my wife MaryAnn Harris, who helped me edit and fine-tune all along the way. I am grateful to you all.

ABOUT THE AUTHOR

Charles de Lint is a full-time writer and musician who makes his home in Ottawa, Canada. His many awards include the *World Fantasy Award*, the Canadian SF/Fantasy *Aurora Award*, and the *White Pine Award*, among others. Modern Library's *Top 100 Books of the 20th Century* poll (voted on by readers) put eight of de Lint's books among the top 100. With 37 novels and 18 collections of short fiction published to date, de Lint writes for adults, teens and children. Book 2 of The Wildlings series, *Over My Head*, is tentatively scheduled for publication in Spring 2013.

De Lint's most recent adult novel, *The Mystery of Grace* (Tor, 2009), is a fantastical ghost story and a heart-wrenching tale of love, passion and faith. His last young adult novel, *The Painted Boy* (Viking, 2010), tells the story of Jay Li, a Chinese-American boy who inherits his grandmother's mantle as the scion of Yellow Dragon Clan. Dropping out of school, Jay winds up in Santo del Vado Viejo—a gritty Arizona town overrun by violent gangs—where he has to figure out how to awaken, and control, his dragon power.

De Lint's latest collection of short fiction is *The Very Best of Charles de Lint* (Tachyon Publications, 2010).

Visit Charles de Lint's web site at www.charlesdelint.com.

You can also connect with him at http://en.gravatar.com/cdelint which has links to Charles on Facebook, Twitter, etc.

Made in the USA
San Bernardino, CA
30 October 2015